Spe

Sophie knew that if her [...] eyed lover was already he[...] Time to become a woman. Time to begi[...] that truth beating inside her heart, she felt it in her skin, [...] tip of her tongue. She *knew*.

"I'm dead, right?" the stranger said.

"No," Sophie said softly.

"I'm dead, and you're an angel come to take me to heaven. Or send me to hell."

She smiled widely. "No. You're alive, and I am not an angel, a water sprite, or an elf." She didn't add that she *was* a witch. That little bit of information might send the man running, and in spite of his appearance, she hadn't yet decided whether or not she wanted him to run.

"Do you have green eyes?"

The Sun Witch

Linda Winstead Jones

B

BERKLEY SENSATION, NEW YORK

THE BERKLEY PUBLISHING GROUP
Published by the Penguin Group
Penguin Group (USA) Inc.
375 Hudson Street, New York, New York 10014, USA
Penguin Group (Canada), 90 Eglinton Avenue East, Suite 700, Toronto, Ontario M4P 2Y3, Canada
(a division of Pearson Penguin Canada Inc.)
Penguin Books Ltd., 80 Strand, London WC2R 0RL, England
Penguin Group Ireland, 25 St. Stephen's Green, Dublin 2, Ireland (a division of Penguin Books Ltd.)
Penguin Group (Australia), 250 Camberwell Road, Camberwell, Victoria 3124, Australia
(a division of Pearson Australia Group Pty. Ltd.)
Penguin Books India Pvt. Ltd., 11 Community Centre, Panchsheel Park, New Delhi—110 017, India
Penguin Group (NZ), 67 Apollo Drive, Rosedale, North Shore 0632, New Zealand
(a division of Pearson New Zealand Ltd.)
Penguin Books (South Africa) (Pty.) Ltd., 24 Sturdee Avenue, Rosebank, Johannesburg 2196,
South Africa

Penguin Books Ltd., Registered Offices: 80 Strand, London WC2R 0RL, England

This is a work of fiction. Names, characters, places, and incidents either are the product of the author's imagination or are used fictitiously, and any resemblance to actual persons, living or dead, business establishments, events, or locales is entirely coincidental. The publisher does not have any control over and does not assume any responsibility for author or third-party websites or their content.

THE SUN WITCH

A Berkley Sensation Book / published by arrangement with the author

PRINTING HISTORY
Berkley Sensation mass-market edition / December 2004

Copyright © 2004 by Linda Winstead Jones.
Cover art by Bruce Emmett.
Cover design by Lesley Worell.
Interior text design by Stacy Irwin.

ISBN: 978-0-425-19940-4

BERKLEY® SENSATION
Berkley Sensation Books are published by The Berkley Publishing Group,
a division of Penguin Group (USA) Inc.,
375 Hudson Street, New York, New York 10014.
BERKLEY SENSATION and the "B" design are trademarks belonging to Penguin Group (USA) Inc.

PRINTED IN THE UNITED STATES OF AMERICA

15   14   13   12   11   10   9   8   7   6   5

The Fyne Curse

THE COUNTRY OF COLUMBYANA, WHICH STRETCHES FROM the Cardean Ocean on the Eastern Shore to the border of Tryfyn to the west, and from the mountains of the Anwyn to the north to the fertile plains of the Southern Province, which extends to the Gulf of Beldene, survived a great twelve-year war that ultimately left authority in the hands of the Beckyt House. The Beckyts made Arthes, a city in the Western Province, the seat of their government. There they built a great palace, a tower with tapering sides that rose ten levels high. They surrounded themselves with priests and warriors and with those blessed with sorcery.

In the fine palace emperors came and went, sons succeeding fathers. Some ruled with fairness and compassion, while others did not. Even those who abused their power were safe in their tower, because the House's strength had grown to a point where no one would dare to challenge them. Those few who dared to rebel did not live long. Either the priests or the sorcerers or the sentinels who served the emperor put a quick stop to any insurrection.

All the drama of Columbyana did not take place in Arthes.

In the third year of the reign of Emperor Larys, the fifty-seventh year of the reign of the Beckyts, a wizard who'd been spurned by a widowed Fyne witch responded to his heart-break by inflicting this curse:

No witch cursed with the blood of the Fyne House shall know a true and lasting love.

For a hundred years, two hundred years, three hundred years . . . the Fyne women lived on the side of a mountain that came to bear their name. Some of them married, many did not. An unusual number of the men who dared to marry or consort with the Fyne women died before their thirtieth birthdays. Others simply disappeared.

Many of the Fyne witches tried to break the wizard's curse over the years. All of them failed.

Prologue

The 365th Year of the Reign of the Beckyts

ALL NIGHT THE NARROW PATH HAD BEEN DARK, THE MOON-light and starlight dimmed by the thick foliage growing over-head. But for the occasional break in the intertwining limbs that offered a glimpse of the night sky, the men who marched silently along the trail might as well have been traveling through a long dark tunnel. They had to be careful to stick to the dirt footpath. To the left side the forest was thick with ancient trees that rustled with the wind. Animals growled and screeched in the darkness, but they did not bother the travel-ers. To the right the terrain dropped sharply. The deep ravine was so overgrown it was impossible to see until you were upon it.

The springtime chill penetrated their cloaks and trousers, even seeped through their boots. It was best to keep moving, to stay warm by marching ever onward. On occasion a rebel took a misstep and a sword rattled, too loud in the stillness of night.

Sunrise was approaching, and Kane could begin to see a

short way into the thick forest to the north. Fallen limbs were evidence of a storm that had passed a short while earlier. The animals that had made noise all night were now quiet, as if they had retired to sleep away the day. As it was no longer completely dark he could see the shapes of all the men who walked before him, not simply the back of Tresty's balding head. The battered rebels—one short of a dozen—moved silently along the trail that would take them to their leader Arik and the reinforcements. They had been defeated in battle and were weary, but they were not broken.

The emperor's soldiers had taken more than half their number in the last battle, four days gone. Kane Varden was one of eleven tired, hungry men. They had been beaten, and they had been wounded, but they were not ready to surrender. Not now, not ever. Not while the Emperor Sebestyen sat on the throne, hidden away high in his lavish palace while many of his people starved. It wasn't right for one man to have so much, while others had so little. It wasn't right for one man to take what he wanted at the expense of the common man of Columbyana, and like his father before him, that's exactly what Sebestyen had always done. Taken.

Kane's brother Duran, who had the best night vision of them all, led the way. Stopping only for short naps taken in shifts and what food they could catch or pick or steal, their journey would take another six days. Perhaps seven. They would join Arik in the northernmost reaches of the Eastern Province, heal, add to their numbers, and then be off to harass the imperial soldiers once again. Duran was young; barely twenty-two years. But like Kane, his heart belonged to this cause.

One day they would have the numbers to march into the palace itself, and Arik—the late Emperor Nechtyn's bastard son and Sebestyen's half-brother—would take the throne. Kane wanted to be there when that happened. He wanted that more than anything else in this life.

Duran stopped suddenly and raised a stilling hand. The rest of the crew halted as well. Kane laid his hand on the hilt of his sword, as did the men in front of and behind him.

When all was still, Kane heard what had alerted Duran. There was movement in the forest. Movement unlike the whisper of animals they'd heard throughout the night. The crisp rustle of leaves being displaced and the muted snick of metal on metal disturbed the quiet dawn.

Imperial infantrymen burst from the forest with a chilling cry, swords raised as they attacked from three sides. Clad in dark green uniforms that had allowed them to blend into the forest and as road-weary as the rebels, they broke from the shelter of the trees and surrounded Kane and what was left of his unit. The only direction that was clear of soldiers was the south, where the ravine dropped so sharply. In moments the rebels had their backs to that ravine as they faced superior numbers.

The strength of the imperial forces was daunting. How many soldiers poured from the forest? Thirty, at least, with more behind them. The odds weren't good, but it wasn't the first time they'd been outnumbered.

An imperial soldier raised his sword and swung out with a cry as chilling as that of any animal. Kane met the attack, stopping the arc of the sword with his own blade and then dipping down as he struck back with a skilled and fatal blow. When that soldier was down he engaged another. Then another. For a poor farmer's son, he was a damn good swordsman. As was Duran. As were they all. Arik had seen to their training, knowing that there would be moments like this. They did not brandish their swords in a manner that would impress; they practiced killing blows, simple and deadly.

But they were not sorcerers; they had no magic to protect them. They were men. Imperial soldiers fell, but so did the rebels. And the emperor's men kept coming. One fell, and two more took his place. It was as if an endless stream of soldiers poured from the trees.

One cry in the midst of many caught Kane's attention, even though it was no louder or more insistent than the others. It was simply more familiar. He turned his head to see Duran go down. A tall, thin soldier wearing a traditional emerald green uniform stood over Kane's little brother and struck once again. It was a death blow; Kane had seen enough to know.

"No!" He ran, frantically taking on one opponent and then another as he worked his way to Duran and the soldier who had already turned away to fight another rebel. It seemed that every imperial soldier was determined to stop Kane from reaching his brother. His skill with a sword was forgotten in favor of strength and brutality. He slashed and hacked his way through the fight, intent not only on surviving but on reaching his brother's killer. The clang of steel on steel faded, the faces of other soldiers blurred. The point of a clumsily wielded sword caught him across the back, and he spun to plunge his blade into the offending soldier's chest before continuing on.

As he drew closer to his goal Kane focused on the murderous soldier's face. It was gaunt and tanned, the eyes dark and slanted like those of a cat.

All the while, more imperial soldiers came. The rebels were going to lose this battle, and with enemy combatants on three sides and a sharp drop to the other, retreat was impossible. He could surrender and be taken prisoner, or he could die. It was no choice at all.

Kane swung his sword toward the soldier's neck, but the man who'd killed Duran saw the move coming and he jumped back. Not far enough or quickly enough. The tip of Kane's sword caught his cheek. Enraged to be cut, the man turned all his attention to Kane. He commanded his sword with skill, and they fought as the men around them fought. After a moment there was nothing else. No one but the two of them; no sound but their own harsh breathing and the clash of metal on metal. Everything else, the rest of the battle and the grief of Duran's death, faded from Kane's mind.

Kane held his own against the soldier. They fought like men who had been here before. Without conscious thought, without planning each and every move. Each blow was the result of instinct and innate skill and too many years of practice. They were well matched, until their swords met in midair and the blade of Kane's weapon snapped in two. He had a good weapon and such a thing should not have happened, but it did.

He dropped down and rolled to his right to reach for Duran's weapon. His hand shot out, he grasped the hilt and lifted the sword from the ground and stood, all in one smooth motion. But the delay, no matter how short, had given the green-clad soldier an edge. His furious blow caught Kane in the chest; the next one cut his arm. Deep.

Kane realized that he and the soldier who had killed Duran were the only ones who still fought. The once quiet road was littered with the wounded and the dead. A greater number of imperial soldiers than rebels lay dead, but that was little comfort. The battle, such as it was, was over. Kane Varden was to be the last man down.

"Fecking hick insurgent," the soldier said, his voice crisp with the accent of one who had spent his entire life in the capital city of Arthes. With a flick of his sword he ripped the weapon from Kane's hand. When Kane had been disarmed and the tip of the soldier's sword was pointed at his heart, the soldier paused to touch the blood on his cheek. "You marked me, you insolent malcontent. I should mark you ten times before I kill you."

"You killed my brother, you son of a bitch." Kane didn't back away from the tip of the sword. His family was gone; his home had been taken. He had nothing left.

The soldier glanced down at Duran, who lay perfectly still on the ground in a puddle of his own blood. His throat had been cut, and the soldier's slash had ripped his shirt and the flesh beneath.

"This one? He didn't even fight very well. Still, I'll happily put his pretty head on a stick and post it on the wall at Arthes until there's nothing left but a skull. Since you say you are his brother, I'll be sure to display your pathetic head close by."

He poked nonchalantly at Duran's body with the tip of his sword, and Kane lunged. He knocked the sword from the soldier's hand, and they grappled for control of the short knife the soldier drew from a sheath at his waist.

The other imperial soldiers found the hand-to-hand combat amusing. Winded and wounded, they gathered around to watch and cheer and close off any avenue of escape.

Kane fought hard, but he was losing blood and his strength faded fast. The soldier broke away, but the knife they'd fought for was in Kane's hand. If he could only kill the soldier before the others killed him, he could die in peace.

The soldier moved too quickly, spinning around and then lifting one leg and kicking. His imperial boot found Kane's wounded chest, and Kane flew backward. He tried to catch himself, knowing that if he ended up lying on the ground he was finished, knife or no knife. He'd almost managed to do just that, to catch himself . . . and then his foot found air where ground should have been. Momentum took him back another step, and then he was falling . . . tumbling. The air was forced from his lungs when he landed hard on the edge of a boulder. He rebounded, rolled back, and continued to fall. All he could see was a blur of brush and dirt, and then, when he landed on his back with a jarring thud, a brief glimpse of sunrise before everything went black.

IT SEEMED TO SOPHIE THAT EVERYONE OWNED A PART OF the day. A precious few hours when they were more alive. More complete. She and her sisters were no different.

Isadora was a creature of the night. When she sought time alone it was by the light of the moon or in complete darkness. Juliet was at peace when sunset came. She was usually most energetic in the afternoon, and on many a day she could be found sitting on the side of the hill facing the west, smiling contentedly as she watched the sun set.

Sophie, the youngest of the Fyne sisters, loved the morning. She adored the wakening of the day, the soft light of the rising sun, the vibrant sensations of the world awakening. Both her sisters were asleep as she made her way to the pond near their mountaintop home. It was not yet fully light, but summer was fully upon them and the air was mild. The water would be cool, and she'd immerse herself in the pond to watch and feel the day come alive.

Sophie loved her sisters, but some days she felt that they didn't understand her at all. They treated her like a child, even though she was nearing the age of twenty-three. They didn't seem to understand that she didn't want to be like them, that she didn't agree with them on every issue, and she most especially was not in agreement with them where men were concerned.

Since their mother had never dared to love, and their grandmother had enjoyed a marriage of nearly thirty years, it had been easy for the sisters to dismiss the Fyne curse as myth. Perhaps in the past a few of the Fyne women had experienced bad luck when it came to love, but that did not mean that a wizard's curse had survived more than three hundred years.

So Isadora had dared to marry. She had even dared to love. For a while everything had been good and right, but of course good and right were not meant to last. Not for them.

Isadora's husband had died too young and left his wife, the eldest of the Fyne sisters, bitter and heartbroken. Willym had been gone four years, and still Isadora mourned him. She wore black. She rarely smiled. She warned her younger sisters that love was not for them. Not for any of them. They were not meant to have anything so ordinary and beautiful as a husband or a family. Disaster would follow. All they needed was one another; it would have to be enough.

After Willym's death Isadora had searched the cabin for answers. She'd found a box hidden beneath a loose floorboard, and in that box they found proof of the Fyne curse. Letters, notes from their ancestors who had dared to love and then lost, filled the plain box. Young men died before reaching the age of thirty. Older men simply looked at their wives one day and ran, frightened by what they saw. After reading the stories, many of them stained with tears, Juliet—who had the gift of sight—announced that their grandmother had very specifically married a man she knew she would never love, and in return she had lived a life of misery.

So Isadora insisted that there would be no men allowed in the Fyne house. Juliet was not so adamant as Isadora, but she did steer clear of males in general and swore that she would never marry. When Sophie had suggested that her sister take a lover instead, proper Juliet had been horrified. It was her intention that no man would ever touch her. Sophie suspected her sister's vow had little to do with the curse. Juliet could be very skittish where men were concerned.

Unlike her sisters, Sophie adored men. Short, tall, young, old . . . there was something absolutely magnificent about them. They had extraordinary strength, and hairy faces, and interesting large bodies. They were wondrously strange, utterly fascinating, and she loved to hear them laugh when she went to town with Juliet on a rare occasion. They even laughed with strength!

From all accounts Columbyana was filled with many men of different sorts. There were farmers and ranchers in each of the four provinces, brave soldiers—imperial forces and rebels—spread across the empire. If a woman was not afraid of magic, there were shape-shifters, good and bad, and wizards, also good and bad. Sophie had even heard tale of a group of mountain dwellers in the Northern Province who claimed the ancient blood of the Anwyn. They kept to themselves, but every so often they raided the villages at the foot of the moun-

tain and even beyond in search of a mate. Stories of the Anwyn had been used for hundreds of years to frighten young
girls into being home by sunset, so Sophie wasn't sure if the
tales were factual or fantasy. Still, it was intriguing to imagine
that such a primitive man might exist.

To Sophie, the farmers were almost as elusive as the Anwyn. The Fyne sisters saw no men at their home, not since
Willym's death. Women visited on occasion to ask for herbal
remedies or magical assistance, but the males of the community stayed well clear of the Fyne witches. It was Isadora's
fault, Sophie decided. She scared them all away with a sharp
glance or an indecipherable word or a wave of her hand. Some
of the men in town even blamed her for Willym's death, thinking that she'd murdered him in some magical way.

Even worse, Isadora blamed herself because she'd loved
him.

Shandley, the small town in the valley below the mountain
Sophie called home, was the hub of society, religion, and law
in this rural area of farms and ranches. It was far from the capital city of Arthes, far from the revolution. And still, some of
the community's more able-bodied men had gone away to
fight for the Empire, or against it, though no one spoke of the
rebels in anything but hushed tones. Sophie herself admired
the dissidents who fought for what they believed in, even
though they were foolish for taking on a military so large. No
matter what side they chose, war seemed a terrible waste of
energy and money and men. Most especially men.

Sophie didn't want a husband. On that one point, Isadora
might be right. Marriage was not for them. If she took a man
into her bed and her life, wouldn't she eventually take him
into her heart? If that happened, the curse would come into
play. Sophie had seen what burying a loved one could do to a
woman. She didn't want to go through that herself.

The Fyne sisters did not need husbands; they needed only
one another. At the same time, she didn't want to shun the op-

posite sex completely like Juliet did. That wouldn't be right, either. Surely it was a sin to blithely dismiss one half of the population without so much as a second thought.

It had taken months of careful consideration, ponderings best kept to one's self, but Sophie had decided that she would follow in her mother's footsteps. She would love as her body dictated, become an independent woman who took lovers when she so desired, who never regretted a moment of her life and in the end belonged to no man. Someone had to see to it that the Fyne lineage survived. Isadora and Juliet were certainly not doing their part.

One of the reasons the three Fyne sisters were so very dissimilar, in looks and in character, was that they had been fathered by three different men. Lucinda Fyne had told her daughters very little about their fathers, but they each bore the name of the man who had sired them. Isadora Sinnoch Fyne had hair as dark as the midnight she loved and eyes almost as black, and she was quite tall for a woman. She stood eye to eye with many a man, and even looked down on a few. Brown-eyed Juliet Kei Fyne fought unruly red curls and bemoaned her smattering of freckles, and while she was shorter than her older sister, she was still of a nice height. Sophie Maddox Fyne was the youngest and shortest of the three. Her fair hair looked almost white in the right light, and her eyes were a vibrant blue. And while she was shorter than her sisters, she possessed one attribute they lacked. Juliet said that her little sister was "well endowed." The more plainspoken Isadora said Sophie had "big tits." Sophie did not think her breasts were *big,* necessarily, but when compared to her reed-thin sisters the difference was notable.

Lucinda Fyne had told her daughters that in each case she'd dreamed about their fathers for three nights before she met them. None of the men knew that the woman who'd come to them for one night left bearing a child. Lucinda had never married, and she'd never regretted not taking a husband. She had done her duty as the only Fyne of her generation, and given birth to daughters.

There had been Fyne witches on this mountain for more than three hundred years. Sophie knew she and her sisters could not be the last; they shouldn't be the end of their bloodline. If Juliet and Isadora insisted upon living their lives as chaste as the Sisters of Orianan, then it was up to Sophie to see that there were Fyne women on this mountain for another three hundred years.

Her heart beat a little faster as she reached the edge of the pond and quickly pulled her simple nightshift up and over her head. For the past three nights she had dreamt of a man with sad green eyes. She couldn't see much else, but oh, in spite of his sadness the green-eyed man in her dreams made her feel marvelous. She tingled. She trembled. And she woke wanting desperately to reach out and touch him. She couldn't talk to her sisters about what was happening to her. They were so overly protective, they'd probably lock her up until the dreams ceased.

Columbyana was in an uproar, and had been for the past five years, since the rebels had begun to disturb the peace of their land. Sophie didn't worry about imperial soldiers or rebels intruding on her morning ritual. Politics did not concern her or her sisters. Isadora, the most powerful of the three, had cast a spell over the mountain, and that spell kept the war at a distance. There had been no bloodshed here on this ground, and there never would be.

Sophie shook her head as she stepped into the pond. The water was only slightly cool this morning, and she knew it wouldn't be long before it soaked up the heat of the sun and lost the last of its nighttime chill. When she was well away from the bank, she pushed herself toward the center of the pond and let the water wash over her body.

If the war ever ended, would Isadora's spell be lifted? Would men come to Fyne Mountain again? Sophie knew that if her dreams were prophetic, as her mother's had been, her green-eyed lover was already here, spell or no spell. It was time. Time to become a woman. Time to begin her new life. She felt that truth beating inside her heart; she felt it in her skin, on the tip of her tongue. She *knew*.

She swam as the sun rose and bathed her in warm, welcoming light, and she felt as if she had come alive along with the day. Sunlight kissed her face like a welcomed friend. She closed her eyes and drifted in the pond, water refreshing against her bare skin, sun warm on her face. Such a moment was usually relaxing, but deep inside Sophie coiled. It was almost more than she could bear, this anxiety. The waiting. The emptiness.

"A man," she whispered as she floated in the center of the pond. "A lover." Again, she thought of the man she had dreamed of for three nights, and wished she could see more of him. In her dreams there were only the eyes, and the sensation of a mouth against her wrist, and a shimmer beneath her skin that she could not dismiss. "Come to me, my green-eyed man," she said softly.

She swam beneath the water as long as she could, holding her breath and kicking her feet, then broke the surface near the opposite side of the bank with a splash and a deep intake of breath. Her gaze was drawn to the bank, where a fine white horse was tethered in the grove of linara trees. She had not seen the animal from the opposite bank, thanks to the angle and the thickness of the foliage. The trees were in full bloom, their lavender blossoms fragrant and delicate.

Someone was here. Sophie quietly swam closer to the pond's edge until she could see the bundle beneath the flower-laden limbs. As she watched, the bundle moved.

She took a deep breath, her heart pounding. "Hello," she whispered. The shapeless lump beneath the tree moved again. Sophie's chin touched the water, and her loosened, pale hair floated all around her. She really should swim back to the opposite bank, don her shift, and make her way home. Of course, Sophie Fyne rarely did what she should.

"Hello," she called again, louder this time.

The person who was lost in the rough-looking bedroll sat up slowly. Sophie's heart hitched when she realized that it was indeed a man, though he was certainly not the sort of fellow who would make a woman's heart leap with desire. He had a scraggly beard and unkempt long hair, and while both seemed to be a light brown it was impossible to be certain. There was too much dirt in the way. He squinted, blinked hard, and reached for the bottle beside him, taking a long swig before fixing his gaze on her again.

"I'm dead, right?" he said as he set the bottle aside.

"No," Sophie said softly.

"I'm dead, and you're an angel, come to take me to heaven. Or send me to hell," he added in a softer voice.

She smiled widely. "No. You're alive, and I am not an angel, a water sprite, or an elf." She didn't add that she *was* a witch. That little bit of information might send the man running, and, in spite of his appearance, she hadn't yet decided whether or not she wanted him to run.

He sat up a little straighter. He appeared to be tall, was wide in the shoulders, and had nicely long arms. His clothing was well-worn and dirty, but the short leather boots had once been very nice, and the loose trousers tucked into those boots were of fine-quality cloth. As she looked closer she could see that there was a wicked-looking knife sheathed at his waist. On his tattered cloak he wore an embroidered shield of Arik, the rebel leader who claimed to be the rightful Emperor of Columbyana.

"You're a soldier," she said softly.

"I was," he answered in a low voice.

"A rebel," she whispered.

He nodded.

Perhaps he had given up the fight as futile. "Are you going home?"

The soldier shook his head. "There's nothing left to go home to." He gave her a crooked, bitter smile.

"If you're no longer a soldier, and you have no home, then what are you?"

"A thief," he answered without hesitation.

Sophie blinked twice. A soldier, even a rebel, was one thing. But a thief? "What did you steal?"

He lifted the bottle. "This whisky, the horse, and some food."

So, he was hardly a notorious outlaw. He was simply down on his luck, that's all.

"Are you intoxicated?"

He considered the question. "It seems I've slept away my inebriated state, but that will be remedied soon enough."

The man was absolutely filthy, his hair was much too long and tangled, and he was terribly sad. She could feel the sorrow as if it radiated from him in waves. She did not have Juliet's gift, but her senses were very fine-tuned. This man hurt deeply.

"Do you have green eyes?" she asked, and then she held her breath as she waited for an answer.

The man cocked his head to one side. "Yes. Why?"

"I have dreamed of a green-eyed man," she said honestly. Nothing in her dreams had hinted that he might be a rebel and a thief. And yet here they were, alone on a beautiful morning. "Are you . . ." Her heart hitched again. Her throat threatened to close. With a deep breath, she pushed the indecision aside. "Are you gifted in the art of making love?"

A moment of silence followed her question. "Am I . . . what?"

Sophie smiled widely. If she was meant to be with this man, there would be no walking away. Or swimming away. Destiny had brought him here. Fate had sent the dreams to her. "Are you gifted in the art of making love?" she asked again, more slowly this time.

"I don't know," he said. "It's been so long I'm not even sure I remember how." There was a hint of teasing in his low voice, and he grinned. He thought she was teasing him, that she would be so cruel as to taunt him and then swim away.

There was only one way to dispel that notion. Sophie swam closer to the man. Her feet found the bottom of the pond, and she stood slowly. The soldier's smile faded as she walked toward him. His gaze raked over her from head to toe. Slowly. Curiously. She knew very well what kind of picture she presented. Pale, wet hair clung to her skin. Warm morning sun touched her bare back.

"If I asked you to be my first lover, would you consent?" she asked as she came to a halt on the bank of the pond.

"Now I know I'm dead," he said softly. "You can't be real."

"If you don't wish to lie down with me, I won't be offended." She walked to the soldier, knelt by him, and reached out to unfasten his cloak. Already she could read the answer in his eyes. Green eyes, she could now see for herself. Beautiful eyes, too somber for one so young. Too somber for a man who'd lived a hundred years. He had seen too much. He had seen horrible things.

She wanted to wash it all away, and she began by unfastening the buttons down the front of his ill-fitting linen shirt.

As if he'd snapped to his senses, he began to assist in his own disrobing. His gaze swept over her, carefully studying her face, her throat, and her breasts, before whisking downward to ponder her pale thighs and the blond curls at the apex. The sheathed knife at his waist was set aside with some care, but the boots were tossed away with impatience, as were the trousers and the shirt. With her help, he had himself undressed in a matter of moments. When the soldier was as bare as she, Sophie took his hand and stood, and he rose to his feet with her.

Her soldier did have some impressive qualities, Sophie had to admit. He was indeed tall. At least six feet, perhaps more.

Since she barely stood five foot one the difference was startling. Height was not the only difference, of course. Where her skin was pale and soft, unmarked and creamy, his was tough, scarred, and dusted with brown hair. And hard! His chest was hard, his thighs, his arms. And he was already aroused, she noted, though she did try not to stare. Surely that would be considered rude, even amongst the inexperienced.

Evidence of wounds not yet completely healed marred one arm and his chest, but he seemed to pay them no mind at all, as if he felt no pain. There was no softness about him, no hint of gentleness.

He needed her gentleness, she decided, even if only on this one magical morning. His body, his hardness, was the perfect complement to her womanly curves and softness. They would suit one another well, she decided as she took his hand and led him to the pond.

"What are you doing?"

"My first lover should be clean, don't you agree?" she said as they stepped into the water.

"Whatever you say, Angel. Whatever you want."

Sophie smiled brightly as she dipped beneath the water. The soldier followed, his hands reaching for her. She swam away, concentrating for a moment on the rush of water against her flesh, on the morning sun that peeked over the horizon. At the center of the pond she stopped, in a place where she could stand and the water was just deep enough to touch her chin. The soldier's hands found her beneath the water. He touched her waist, then one hand raked up her side and around to her breast. His fingers brushed gently over a nipple, and the jolt that passed through her body was extraordinary. Sophie closed her eyes and sighed.

She had never been touched by a man before, unless the fatherly hugs from Willym counted. They did not, she decided. This was entirely new; entirely startling. She liked it, very much.

Feeling bold, she touched him, too. Tentatively, at first, and then with an unexpected sense of ease, as if this touching were as natural as the sunrise itself. She trailed the tips of her fingers over his hard skin, tracing the muscle. Her eyes drifted open, and she watched the fire in her soldier's eyes grow hotter and deeper.

Sophie plunged beneath the water once again, and this time the soldier followed her. After a short chase he grabbed her, firmly but with an unexpected gentleness, and pulled her body against his. Flesh met flesh. They were hot and cold, hard and soft, and her skin was so sensitive she tingled everywhere he touched her. She felt the swirl of the water all about as if it were alive. Her legs wrapped around her soldier.

He propelled them upward, so that they broke the surface of the water still entangled. His own long hair clung to his face and neck. Rivulets of water ran down his face, down his neck and chest. And amidst it all, those eyes captivated her. A new aspect had been added to the sadness she had first seen there. It was a beautiful sight. Sophie laid her mouth against his neck and tasted the wetness on his skin. Even though he was hard and solid and seemed not to feel pain, a tremor passed through his body. She felt it. She tasted it.

"I'm clean enough," he said as he turned toward the shore.

"Yes," she agreed. "You are."

They swam side by side for a moment, until they reached a shallow area near the pond's edge. There the rebel stood and took her hand, much as she had earlier taken his, but he did not stop there. He laid his mouth on her shoulder and kissed the wet, sensitive flesh. His arms wrapped around her possessively, his hands dipping down to rest on her backside. Those hands were not still, but caressed while his lips teased her shoulder and then her neck. This was better than any dream, Sophie decided, as she followed his example and wrapped her arms around him. The soldier would be a wonderful lover.

With a growl, her rebel swept her up into his arms and carried her out of the pond and to his bedroll. He laid her there, his arms tender, his green eyes watchful.

"Your first lover," he said gruffly as he lay down beside her.

"Yes." He didn't believe her, she could tell, but she didn't care.

"So I should be gentle." He kissed the swell of one breast, and then shifted his head so he could take the nipple deep into his mouth.

"Yes," Sophie said, her heart and the center of her being leaping. Why had no one ever told her how good this moment would be?

"But not too gentle," he added as he moved his mouth from one breast to the other, where he suckled a bit harder. His lips were warm; his tongue quick, and then leisurely, and then quick again.

"No, not too . . ." The words caught in her throat, until she finally stopped trying to speak and allowed him to lavish his attention on her bosom, and then her throat, and then back to her bosom again.

The soldier lifted his head almost reluctantly, dipping back down once to lick quickly at one hardened nipple. Then he took her arm and raised it to his mouth. He kissed the tender skin at her inner wrist, just as he had in her dream. It was marvelous. Beautiful and arousing and tender. He kissed his way up her inner arm, every caress more stimulating than the last. Sophie gasped. It was as if her skin had changed, had become more sensitive to anything and everything. The waft of a warm breeze, the soft caress of a man's lips.

"Can I touch you, soldier?" she whispered.

"I'm yours, Angel," he answered, his drawl soft and somehow different. Judging by the lilt in his voice he was not from the Southern Province. Sophie liked the softness in his voice, the honey in his words. "Touch me," he said, "kiss me, tell me what you want."

The perfect sexual partner, agreeable and talented.

Sophie reached down and flattened her palm against the soldier's flat belly. He twitched. Her fingers danced, itched, and finally closed around his manhood, which was now fully erect. He was hot, silky, so hard she was truly amazed. She kissed his throat while her fingers explored, and he moaned low in his throat.

His hand skimmed down her belly, and she parted her thighs for him. He touched her where no man had ever touched her before, his hands rough and large and curious. His sun-kissed flesh was dark against her milky skin, foreign and yet very right, somehow.

"I can't take much more of this," he confessed, his deep voice a whisper.

"Then it's time," Sophie said. She shifted her body and he shifted his, and after no more than a heartbeat or two the soldier was cradled between her legs. He touched her with the tip of his erection, pushed against and then into her.

Sophie closed her eyes, tipped her head back and savored every passing second as her lover became a part of her. Slowly, tenderly. There was a short, fleeting moment when she thought he would not fit. And then her body opened for him. With a low growl, he pushed himself deep inside her.

She cried out softly, and the soldier lifted his head to stare down at her. Wet hair clung to his cheek and his neck. A drop of water snaked across his shoulder, moving slowly across his skin and then falling to her own damp flesh. "You were telling the truth," he whispered. "About me being your first."

"I always tell the truth," she answered. "Don't stop," she added quickly when he began to withdraw. "Love me, soldier."

He did love her, slowly at first, every stroke a wonder. This coming together was primal, a meeting of bodies, a search for a magnificence that fluttered just out of reach. When she felt herself dancing on the edge of something new and exciting, her rebel began to move faster. He plunged impossibly deeper, and she lifted her hips to meet his thrust.

Her body was on fire. She wanted more, needed more. By the sun and the moon and every star in the sky . . .

Sophie cried out as a wave of release shot through her body. Pleasure so intense it could not be described shimmered through her. The soldier's release came in time with hers, with a shudder and a low cry, with a stiffening of his big body and the hot gift of his seed flowing inside her.

Eyes closed, Sophie reached up and touched his face as the last waves of pleasure drifted through her. She was a woman now. And as she had always suspected, men were marvelous creatures.

The soldier, her rebel, lowered his head to her shoulder, breathing deeply and with difficulty. "Oh, Angel," he whispered.

Sophie trailed her fingers through his damp hair. "I knew you would be an amazing lover. Thank you."

He lifted his head to look down at her. "Thank you?"

She smiled. "You're better than a dream."

He withdrew slowly, reluctantly, and she truly wanted to pull him back. But even though they were no longer joined she could feel him inside her, warm and potent. She would always feel him, she imagined.

He lowered himself to lie beside her on the rough bedroll, and one large, sun-darkened hand rested on the flat of her belly. That hand was so powerful, so different from her own. The fingers were long and there were small scars on the back of that hand. She wondered about each mark, and then reminded herself that it did not matter. She didn't need to know the details of his life.

"Sleep with me, Angel," he whispered as he placed his head on her shoulder once again. "I haven't slept well in so long, I forgot what it's like to dream. Nightmares, yes. Dreams . . . no. Sleep with me, and maybe I can dream again."

Sophie wrapped her arms around him. The act of love itself was done, but she didn't feel that they were finished. She wanted to hold him. She wanted to press her body against his still. "I'll lie with you a little while," she said. "But I can't stay long."

"A little while is better than nothing," he said as his eyes drifted closed.

Sophie nestled her head against his chest. Her body thrummed, her heart hammered. "Soldier?" she whispered.

He answered with a low hum.

"What's your given name?"

"Kane," he answered.

Sophie smiled. "I like that name. It's lovely."

Without opening his eyes, Kane asked, "What's yours?"

Magnificent as their day had been, warm and wonderful as he was at this moment, Sophie knew she didn't need Kane nosing around looking for her at a later date. She had decided not to reject men as entirely as her sisters had done, but that did not mean she was willing to risk loving and losing a man. She would have to be content to go from one lover to the next, as the dreams dictated. She would give her heart to no man. Looking at Kane now, still feeling him inside her, she suspected it would be much too easy to fall in love with a man like this one, and that would never do.

"Angel," she finally answered. "You can call me Angel."

A half smile crossed Kane's face. "I knew it."

Sophie held Kane until he slept. The sun rose in the sky, and the day became bright.

Finally she rose slowly and sat beside him to place her hands over his heart. "A man who takes a witch's virginity and does the task so well deserves a gift." She closed her eyes. "I wish for you a well-healed heart, beautiful dreams, and . . ."

Oh, she wasn't good at this! Not without many hours of preparation. Isadora was magnificent with spells. She always knew what to say and do, and what not to say or do. Sophie usually had to plan her spells very carefully, otherwise they went astray. What did one give a poor rebel who was down on his luck?

"And luck!" she finished with a smile. "I wish you good luck." A breeze ruffled the leaves of the linara tree, and patches of sunlight danced across their bodies. A single lavender petal fell from its place and landed directly upon the soldier's chest, very near her hand. Sophie muttered a few well-chosen words to complete the spell, and then rested beside Kane for a few more minutes. It was probably perfectly natural to feel affection for one's first sexual partner. The warmth in her heart was a lingering reminder of the heat they had generated together. Her reluctance to leave him was surely common for a girl who had just become a woman. She was tempted to wake Kane and ask him to love her again. Just once more.

But no. She would not cling to one man. And besides, their time together had been perfect. One could not improve upon perfection.

Sophie left Kane sleeping soundly. She entered the water quietly, sad to leave him and yet invigorated to have begun anew. Thoughts of her sisters stole her smile for a moment. Isadora would not be pleased, and Juliet would cluck and shake her head like an old hen. While Sophie was tempted to keep the events of this morning to herself, she knew she could never keep a secret of this magnitude from her sisters. Besides, they would know the truth as soon as they saw her face.

In spite of the arguments she knew would come, Sophie remained deliriously happy. This mystical morning marked the dawning of a new phase of her life. She smiled as she swam lazily to the opposite side of the pond. Yes, men were truly wonderful creatures.

I

One year later

KANE DISMOUNTED AND TOSSED THE REINS OF HIS FINE new horse over a low limb. This was it; the place where his life had changed. Here, on this very spot, he had been transformed from a lost soul who had no hope for the future, a man who had every intention of drinking himself to death, to a man determined to put the past behind him and to make something of himself. He had gone to sleep beneath this very linara tree, drunk and hurting and wishing for death, and had awakened to see his Angel in the water. Smiling, asking impossible questions, then walking out of the water more beautiful than any mere woman could ever be. She had loved him, healed him, and changed his life.

With Angel in his arms he'd slept without nightmares. He'd awakened alone.

He'd thought her a dream, for a while. But the next night when he'd stopped for a few hours' sleep he'd found the evidence that she had indeed been very real. A spot of her vir-

gin's blood stained his bedroll. His Angel's blood. He'd
dreamed of her every night since.

He had tried to return to this place when he'd realized that
his Angel was real and not a whisky-induced dream, but
somehow he'd gotten turned around. He'd taken a wrong turn,
then another wrong turn. He'd gotten completely and totally
lost before giving up the search.

Since leaving this mountain he'd been a different man, yes,
and he'd also had the devil's own luck. Not two days after
leaving the hills behind, he'd found a coin on the road. The
gold piece, struck with the image of Emperor Sebestyen as a
regal child, had been sitting there in the dirt catching the
bright rays of the sun. He'd taken that coin and slipped it into
his pocket, and when he reached the next town he walked into
the nearest tavern, intent on drinking it down. But there had
been a friendly card game in progress, and instead of drinking
away his newfound treasure he'd decided to gamble it. He'd
won. He'd won big.

He'd won everything.

For the past year, Kane Varden had gambled his way from
one town to the next. It didn't matter what the game might be.
Whether the pastime of choice were whist or faro or slam, he
always won. He couldn't stay in one place for long. People
tended to distrust a man who couldn't lose. A dozen men or
more had tried to prove that he'd been cheating, but of course
since he had not been cheating there was nothing to prove.
Still, he'd found it was simply best to move on after a few
days in any one place.

Women were drawn to a man with good fortune and a bundle of cash in his pocket, and in the beginning Kane had taken
full advantage of his newfound luck with the ladies of a certain type. But lately—for the past six months or so—he had
been living like one of the emperor's saintly priests. Or, more
rightly, like a faithful married man. In his heart he knew it
wasn't right to dream of Angel while another woman slept in

his bed, and he had come to feel like he was cheating on her when he so much as looked at a pretty woman. He had come to feel like he was obligated to this Angel, and that wouldn't do.

The only way to end that fanciful supposition was to face her one more time. When he realized that the angel he'd conjured in his head was nothing like the real woman he'd shared a moment of happiness with, he'd be able to move on, once and for all. She was a woman like all others.

It had taken him almost a month to find this place. He'd gotten lost again, confused and turned about and downright dizzy. He had finally stumbled upon a narrow path that looked familiar. Luck, again. He'd followed it, riding by the light of the moon until he found the pond and the grove of linara trees that were once again in bloom. Their color and their fragrance called to him.

So here he was once again at dawn, watching the sun come up over this pond. The odds that he would find Angel were slim, he knew that, but this was the place to start.

She couldn't be as beautiful as he remembered; she couldn't be as passionate, as perfect. It simply wasn't possible. Sex was always good, but it was never *that* good. He'd confused memory with his dreams, that was the only explanation. He had manufactured Angel in his mind, and he had to get her out. When he got a good look at the girl, the real girl with all her faults, maybe he'd quit dreaming about her. Maybe he'd be able to get on with his life without feeling like he was haunted by a fair-haired, blue-eyed angel. He'd accepted that the woman herself was real, but the memory he carried couldn't be.

Kane had been a happy man for the past year, and why not? He had everything any man could possibly want. He had not been a happy man when Angel had come to him in the dawn of a year ago. In fact, he had been miserable. He didn't know why he had been so unhappy, and to be honest he didn't care.

It might've had something to do with the war, he supposed, though he no longer remembered much about his life before finding Angel, and in the past year he had steered clear of any and all political situations. His life was easy, blessed. Whatever pain he'd been carrying with him, Angel had washed it away.

The swishing of tall grass on the opposite side of the bank drew his attention there, and immediately he saw a flash of blue among the green. He held his breath until the woman on the narrow path walked beyond the tall grass and into the clearing beside the pond.

He smiled. It was her. His Angel. His smile faded. She was every bit as beautiful as he remembered.

Apparently she'd come here to do her laundry. She carried a very small bundle of clothes in her arms, as if she'd rolled up a stained frock and planned to wash it in the pond. While he watched, entranced, she carefully lowered herself to the ground, sitting on a bed of soft grass with the bundle still in her grasp. Angel lifted her face to the sky and closed her eyes. Loosened hair, impossibly fair and touched with gold, fell around her shoulders and caught the rays of the sun as it tumbled to her waist.

Kane didn't move. He stood in the shadow of the linara tree and watched, his heart beating too hard. This was the woman he dreamed about. She was real.

If he showed himself to her now, would she run? Or would she take off her clothes, dive into the pond, and swim to him with that smile on her face? Would she swim to him, then walk out of the pond with water dripping from her hair and rolling down her body and ask him to lie with her again?

She shifted the bundle of clothes into one arm, and began to unbutton the bodice of her dress. She wore a very plain gown without frills or ribbons; a long, flowing garment of ordinary fabric without shimmer or adornment. The blue suited

her, though it was not as remarkably blue as the eyes he remembered. She deserved better than such a simple frock, and
he had become a man who could afford to give her gifts. He
would buy her a fancy gown before he left this time, he decided. Something befitting a woman of such beauty. He would
buy her other things, too. Jewels and ribbons and satin
shoes—all the things pretty girls liked.

He would take her in a soft place this time, he decided. Not
on the ground, but in a proper bed.

Maybe she was going for a swim, Kane thought as he
watched her slowly unfasten those tiny buttons. Maybe she
would disrobe and step into the water as she had on that morning a year ago. If she did, he wouldn't wait for her to come to
him. He'd follow her example. Undress. Swim to the center of
the pond. Meet her there and make his dreams come true. The
bed could wait, he supposed.

Bodice unbuttoned, Angel folded the blue fabric back,
bared one full, rounded breast, and shifted the bundle in her
arms. She turned her gaze to the bundle and smiled brilliantly.

Kane's heart made a strange move, as if it sought to escape
through his chest, and then his throat. No, that wasn't his
heart, it was his stomach. That wasn't laundry Angel held so
close. It was . . . a baby. His baby? His knees went weak. He
swayed on his feet just a little.

If he revealed himself now, would she run? Yes. He was
quite sure she would run. Instead of moving to the bank where
he could get a better view and Angel could see him, Kane
stepped to the side, his eyes never leaving her and the baby
she held to her breast. Each step was careful, well-calculated,
and luck was with him as he circled the pond without making
any noise.

He would marry her, of course. It was the proper thing to
do. The idea of taking a wife gave him an unpleasant chill. He
had once sworn he would never get married, though he

couldn't remember why. Still, if there was a baby involved he had no choice.

Kane edged his way around the pond. It never occurred to him to leave, to sidle back to his horse and take off. If that baby was his, he had a responsibility.

At last he could see his Angel clearly. The child she held suckled hungrily, mouth closed around a nipple, one little fist resting on the pale swell of a breast.

When he stepped out of the cover of the trees she lifted her head slowly. She was not surprised to see him. He'd been so careful as he approached; had she heard him in spite of his caution?

Would she recognize him? A year ago he'd been dressed in rags, his beard had been months old, his hair had been tangled and wild.

Today he wore a fine suit, and yesterday morning he had been clean shaven. He might have a bit of stubble on his face, but it was nothing like the beard she'd remember. His hair was clean and pulled back in a neat queue. He was a different man. Inside and out, he was not the man who'd camped here a year ago.

"Angel," he said, his voice refusing to rise above a whisper.

Her eyes met his. Yes, she remembered. "Soldier," she said gently.

He stepped closer with caution, afraid he might spook her if he made any sudden moves. There was something unexpectedly moving about that baby feeding at its mother's breast. The sight grabbed his heart and held on, and he couldn't make himself look away.

"Is that"—he stopped, licked his lips, shook off a chill—"mine?"

Angel sighed. "Yes, soldier. This is your daughter, Ariana. Ariana Kane Fyne."

* * *

SOPHIE WASN'T AT ALL SURPRISED TO SEE THE FATHER OF her child at the pond. She'd dreamed of him for the past three nights. As he lowered himself to sit beside her, she sighed. Oh, this complicated everything!

Kane's eyes sparkled with fascination as he watched Ariana feed. Why did he have to be so handsome without all that hair on his face? He looked younger than she'd imagined he was, when she'd first seen him. Years younger. His features were much more comely without the shaggy beard, and the neater hairstyle suited him. His hair was not blond and not brown, but both, as if it had been streaked by the sun or spun with burnished gold. The black suit he wore looked as if it had been made for him, it fit so well, and his tall boots were of the finest leather. The past year had been good to him, as she had known it would be.

Today he wore no knife close at hand, that she could see. If her wishes for him had come true, he had not needed that weapon in the past year.

Almost everything about him was changed, but his eyes remained the same.

"Ariana," he said as he studied the baby. "That's a beautiful name."

"It was my grandmother's name," she said as she shifted the baby to the other breast. Kane watched the entire process without once averting his eyes. Ariana latched onto the nipple of the full breast, and made a low, sweet baby sound of pure satisfaction.

Finally, Kane lifted his head. "I didn't know," he said. "If I'd known, I never would've left."

Sophie gave him a sweet, reassuring smile. "Don't be silly. It was impossible for you to know, and even if you had there was no reason for you to stay."

"No reason?" His brow furrowed. His mouth thinned.

Kane would surely be reasonable about this. With a few well-chosen words, Sophie would ease his mind and send him on his way. "You had already done your part. My goodness, what else could you have done?"

"Married you?"

She laughed. "Don't be silly," she said again.

"Silly?" For some reason, he was getting angry.

Sophie turned her eyes down and ran a finger through the pale downy hair on Ariana's head. "You shouldn't have come back," she whispered. "Your presence here will only complicate matters. While I am glad to see with my own eyes that you are doing well, I suggest that you ride away and forget we ever met."

"I can't forget," Kane said, his voice low for the baby's sake, but his anger unmistakable. "I dream about you every night. A year, Angel. Every night for a year! It's like you come to me in my dreams, like those dreams are more real than my waking hours. And now this. A baby. Our daughter. I can't ride away and leave you to raise my child alone."

"I'm not raising your child alone."

Kane didn't argue. In fact, he didn't say anything at all. He was so quiet Sophie was forced to raise her head to look into his eyes. He was beyond angry, almost enraged.

"You're married to someone else," he whispered. "Another man is raising my child."

She tried to soothe him with a smile. "It's my sisters who are helping me raise Ariana, not another man. By the moon, Kane, I'm never getting married."

She saw the relief in his expressive eyes, and then, a moment later, the fire of determination. "Never?"

"Never," she said emphatically.

"Why?"

Sophie took a deep breath and let it out slowly. She should have taken a hint from her mother and traveled away from home to find her lovers. Then they could not track her down so easily. She already had a soft spot in her heart for Kane, purely because he was Ariana's father, of course. She couldn't possibly allow him to become a permanent fixture in her life. If she fell in love with him, disaster would follow.

Her life must remain unencumbered by the bonds of love. She had to convince Kane and herself of that fact, once and for all. Somehow, she had to make him go away. "I need no man to take care of me. I will have all the lovers I want, when the desire comes to me, and I will—"

"All the lovers you *want*?" Kane interrupted.

"Yes."

He took a deep breath of his own. Then another. "And how many lovers have you had, thus far?" he asked, his voice unnecessarily tight.

Sophie wished she could lie well, but she couldn't. Neither did Juliet, though at least Juliet could tell a small fib without turning purple. Now, if she could spin a tale like Isadora . . . but she couldn't. "Only you," she confessed in a low voice. "So far," she added quickly.

Kane relaxed visibly. "So, in the past year, you haven't met another man you *want*."

"Don't be tiresome," she said softly. "Of course I have not taken another lover in the past year. I knew that first day that I'd conceived, and it didn't seem right to take another man into my body while your child grew there."

"At last, one sensible decision," he muttered.

"And in the three months since she was born, I have devoted myself entirely to Ariana." The mention of her daughter's name warmed her heart. Motherhood was more remarkable and all-consuming than she'd imagined, and every day brought a new wonder.

Sophie tried to tell herself that just because she'd dreamed of Kane for the past three nights, that didn't mean they would be intimate again. It had simply been a warning that he would reappear in her life. Nothing more.

Ariana finished feeding, and Sophie lifted her daughter to her shoulder. She patted the baby's back gently, trying to raise a burp.

"Can I . . . ?" Kane offered his hands as the unfinished question lingered in the air.

"Of course." Sophie very carefully handed Ariana into her father's arms. He seemed almost afraid to take her, as if he felt his hands were too big to properly handle something so delicate. But of course they were not, and in moments he and Ariana were both perfectly at ease. Ariana settled her head against her father's shoulder and continued to sleep.

"Pat her on the back," Sophie instructed as she began to button her dress. "She needs to burp."

Kane did as he was told, patting too gently at first, and then just right. Ariana let out a very unladylike belch, turned her head, and fell into a deep sleep.

"She's beautiful," Kane said as he held his daughter close.

Sophie couldn't stop her wide smile. "She is, isn't she?"

Kane looked past Ariana's head to stare at Sophie. He was not an easy man. He was not one to give up without a fight. "Yes, she is. I hate to think of you going through the past year alone. Did you have any problems?"

"Not really," Sophie said. "I was never sick, and the delivery went as well as could be expected. It was painful, of course, but I was only in labor for three hours, and I only cursed your name once. I didn't mean it," she added quickly. If she had, there might have been all kinds of nasty complications. "And I was never alone. I had my sisters with me."

She really should thank Kane, not only for giving her Ariana, but for helping her to uncover her true gift. During her pregnancy she'd discovered that while Isadora's powers were varied and potent, and Juliet's gifts of sight and healing were unmatched, she had her own talent.

Fertility. With a simple word, a spell or a wish, she could make anything grow. Fields flourished when she blessed them, and Juliet's gardens were especially productive when Sophie uttered a simple spell over them by morning's light. Women who had trouble conceiving would become fruitful with a touch of her hand: Juliet swore it was so.

Sophie looked into Kane's eyes, and like it or not she wanted him to love her again. She wanted the pleasure, the feel of his bare body against hers. But that couldn't happen.

If he touched her again, there would be another child. She knew it, as well as she knew that the sky was blue. Ariana was a blessing, of that she had no doubt. Still, she was not ready to accept another blessing so soon.

Even worse, she knew that if there was another child, Kane would never leave. He would insist upon staying, and he'd likely be annoyingly helpful, and then one day she'd look at him and the physical attraction she felt for him would grow to something more. She couldn't allow that to happen.

Kane very carefully returned Ariana to Sophie. "She's a miracle."

"Yes, she is." Ariana settled in her mother's arms. Sophie lifted her head and studied Kane's face. It was just as lovely as the face in her dreams. "Thank you."

He reached out and touched her cheek with gentle fingers. "Marry me, Angel." His anger was gone; it had been replaced by an unexpected determination.

Sophie shook her head, and tried to remain outwardly calm while her heart leapt and danced and did all sorts of unexpected things. "I can't."

"Why not?"

"I will never marry."

"That's not a reason," he argued.

With marriage came love, and with love came death. Isadora and Willym had tried to deny the curse, and in the end they had all suffered for it. "I barely know you," she explained, "but I do not think we are at all compatible."

"We have a child, that's reason enough—"

"No," she interrupted. "It's not."

Sophie could see the possible future Kane presented too clearly. With her heart dancing the way it did, with her body tingling at his very *presence*, she could very easily say yes. She could marry Kane, and together they would have a dozen children. And they would, she thought with a sigh. A dozen! Maybe more. If he slept in her bed every night, she could not bring herself to refuse him.

In the end, sooner rather than later, she might even come to love him. Her heart hitched. She could still remember what it had been like to go home one afternoon with a basket of berries to find Willym lying on the floor of their little house, dead. He had been like a father to her, the only father she'd ever known, and one day he was simply *gone*. He had a bad heart, Juliet said, and nothing could have prevented his death. They tried to pretend that the Fyne curse had nothing to do with Willym's death, but they all had known the truth as they'd buried a very fine man before his time.

They could not love. Ever.

There would be other children in the years to come, Sophie suspected, but like her mother she would choose carefully. She would go from man to man as her body and her dreams dictated, and she would never make the mistake of falling in love.

"I am an unfettered and adventurous woman," she said defiantly, intent on sending Kane away once and for all. "I don't want to be tied to one man. When the time does come to take another lover, I will choose someone new and exciting. I've already had you. Why would I want to have you again?"

Kane did not like that answer, not at all. His eyes narrowed, his jaw went hard. "A child needs a father."

"I never knew my father," she argued.

"And look at what convoluted ideas you have!"

Ariana stirred and scrunched up her nose.

"Don't wake the baby," Sophie said softly.

"Sorry." Kane turned his gaze to the pond. "We should get married for the baby's sake, whether you like me or not. I don't want my child to grow up a bastard."

"I did," Sophie said softly.

"I want better for my daughter," he said. "I want better for you, too. I can give you so much now. You and the baby. Let me take care of you."

"That's very sweet." Sophie reached out and barely touched Kane's cheek. He had not shaved this morning, and there was a heavy stubble on his face. The skin beneath was warm. It would be nice to just sit here a while, to continue to touch him and let him touch her and . . . she dropped her hand.

He returned his gaze to her. "Marry me."

She shook her head.

Sophie stood slowly, Ariana caught to her breast. "I appreciate your willingness to make such a sacrifice, Kane, I truly do, but it would be best if you returned to your horse and rode as far away from this place as possible." She lifted a hand to indicate the horse he had left tethered on the opposite side of the pond. "Just . . . go away."

He jumped to his feet. "I can't."

Sophie spun on him. Good heavens, he looked like he intended to follow her! It wouldn't do for Kane and Isadora to meet. "Do you want to know the real reason I can't marry you?" she asked sharply.

"Yes."

"I'm not an ordinary woman," she said softly.

Kane grinned. Oh, he had such a wicked, charming smile! "That doesn't surprise me, Angel."

"I'm a witch," she said, chin high, Ariana held close.

His smile disappeared. "Don't be ridiculous."

She didn't want to tell him about the curse. It was complicated and would take time to explain and besides, she didn't want to indicate in any way that she feared she might one day fall in love with him. It would reveal too much. Best to keep it simple.

"You don't have to take my word for it. There's a small town at the foot of the mountain. Stop there as you ride away. Ask the people there what they think of Sophie Fyne." Her chin trembled. "Ask them if I'm a witch."

"Sophie," he said, saying her name for the first time in a soft voice that sent shivers down her spine.

"Ask them," she repeated, knowing what kinds of tales he would hear when he went to Shandley and mentioned her name. "And then escape, while you still can."

With that she turned and ran, Ariana caught up close and safe. Tears fell from her eyes; unexpected, hot tears. She brushed them away, and one tear was flung into the grass. Before she'd taken three more steps, a wildflower sprouted where the tear had soaked into the ground.

2

SHANDLEY WAS LIKE HUNDREDS OF OTHER SMALL TOWNS spread across Columbyana. Everything of importance was located along two cross streets that met at a lively town square, and simple homes were located beyond and behind, growing outward from the center of town like the spindly legs of a many-limbed creature.

The village had everything necessary to make a community run properly: a collection of shops; two taverns, one small and one rather large; a jailhouse; a church; a school. The sheriff of the Southern Province had an office here, but as this was a quiet rural part of the country it was an auxiliary office that was probably manned by a couple of deputies. Maybe three.

Kane always tried to steer clear of the lawmen and soldiers in the towns he visited, though gambling wasn't illegal and he had no interest in politics. There was little rebel activity in the Southern Province, so he wasn't often confronted with the realities of war. Still, the sight of a soldier's green uniform or an official's crimson robe sometimes sent an unpleasant shiver down his spine.

Shandley's largest tavern was near the center of town, and the smaller had been discreetly placed at the south end of one long street. It appeared that both had rooms above to let, for a day or an extended stay. All around, shops flourished. A confectioner's, a dress shop and millinery, a feed and seed store to serve the farmers and ranchers, a shop which, judging by the window display, specialized in swords and other weapons, most more suited to hunting than defense. This was quite the booming small town.

As he rode down one of the main streets on his new gray mare, studying the people and places he passed, Kane was struck by something odd. There were lots of women out and about, shopping or gossiping on the boardwalk. He had never before seen so many expectant women in one place at one time. And they weren't at different stages of pregnancy, from what he could tell. Many of them were about the same size around the middle, a few were a bit smaller or larger, but not greatly so. It was as if a large number of women in town had gotten pregnant at the same time.

Strange.

He didn't immediately dismount and go searching for someone to tell him that Sophie was a witch. *Sophie.* A beautiful name for a beautiful woman. When he dreamed of her tonight, he would call her Angel one moment and Sophie the next.

He had no doubt that he would hear something ridiculous from the people of Shandley. He'd seen the fear on Sophie's face as she'd instructed him to come here and mention her name. What she didn't understand was that nothing could scare him away. Not her stubborn insistence that she would take lovers as it suited her, not a ridiculous story about her being a witch.

Magic was no longer illegal, as it had been during the early years of Emperor Nechtyn's reign and during most of the years of his father before him, but people still tended to distrust what they did not understand. Especially people like these, who lived their lives so simply and easily. They set their sleeping hours by the sun, and knew very little of life beyond Shandley.

Witches were old crones who either lived in caves or plied their trade among the rich and powerful, not beautiful young women who looked like Sophie Fyne. Besides, true witches were rare creatures; he'd never expected to actually meet one. A woman who possessed real magic wouldn't hide away here in this rural community. She'd find her way to a city where she could make a fortune with her talents. In a town he'd passed through a few months' back, he'd heard that a General of the Columbyanan Imperial Army had a witch as counsel . . .

A sudden and severe headache split through Kane's temple and around to the base of his skull. The pain chased away everything else. Every thought, every memory. His brain and his eyes burned, his hands began to shake. The world narrowed and then disappeared, until there was nothing in it but pain and pale shadows, grayness and agony.

Thinking of Sophie never gave him a headache. Kane turned his thoughts to her and immediately the pain disappeared. Relief rushed through him. Ease and happiness.

He hitched his horse in front of the largest tavern in Shandley and stepped into the main room. Not bad for a small town, he thought as he glanced around. The place was clean, the aroma coming from the kitchen was promising, and the matronly, slightly overweight woman who swept a clean plank floor greeted him with a smile.

He returned the smile and stepped to the desk. "I'd like to engage a room. Your nicest suite, if it's available."

That brought a sparkle to the woman's eyes. "Meals included?"

"Of course."

"For how long?"

As long as it takes. "I have no idea."

She propped her broom in a corner and headed for the long bar on one side of the square room. From behind that bar she offered the guest book. Kane joined her and signed his name with a flourish.

"Mr. Varden," the woman said as she glanced down, "I'm Eurneid Driskell. My husband and I own and operate this tavern. Might I ask what brings such a finely dressed and obviously cultured man to Shandley for an extended stay?"

"The woman I intend to make my wife has brought me here."

Mrs. Driskell, who was likely approaching sixty, pursed her lips and batted her lashes. "How charming. What a lucky girl she is. Perhaps I know her?"

"Perhaps. Her name is Sophie Fyne."

Mrs. Driskell's friendly smile vanished; her face paled. "Oh, dear."

Kane leaned casually into the bar. "Do you know her?"

"Yes. Yes, I do."

"Then you will agree with me that no sweeter, kinder, more beautiful woman exists anywhere in Columbyana or beyond."

True, he had no idea if Sophie was sweet and kind or not. He had not known her long enough to be sure. But she was definitely beautiful.

"She is very . . . pretty." The woman pursed her narrow lips.

"Pretty?" Kane lifted his eyebrows. "What an inadequate way to describe an extraordinary woman."

"Mr. Varden," Mrs. Driskell said cautiously, taking one step away from him and the front desk. "You seem like a perfectly agreeable, normal young man. Surely you don't know what you're letting yourself in for. Yes, Sophie Fyne is quite lovely. You're not the first man to look at her and be tempted."

He tried to give the tavern owner a warning glare. It wasn't enough.

"Sophie Fyne is a harlot," Mrs. Driskell continued. "She's an unmarried woman who has a baby, and she will tell no one who the father is. Could be any man in town," the older woman said spitefully. "It's obvious that she's a wanton by the way she looks and moves. When she walks down the street men start to drool as if their brains have ceased to function. All she has to do is smile at a man and he'll give her anything she asks for."

"Really?" Kane asked, his voice low and just short of threatening.

Mrs. Driskell waved an indignant hand. "She plucked one of our innocent men from his home for her own purposes and . . . and . . . well, just consider yourself warned, Mr. Varden." Her mouth became a raisin in disapproval. "Sophie Fyne is a strumpet and a witch. A witch, Mr. Varden! Most days she has the good sense to stay up on that hill with those sisters of hers, and that suits me just fine. We don't want her or her child here. This is a respectable town where decent people live."

Kane sighed. "Thank you so much, Mrs. Driskell, for sharing your opinion with me before I had the misfortune of doing business with you."

She nodded her head. "If I were you, I'd ride away from that cursed mountain as fast as possible. I don't know what she did to you, but—"

"You don't understand," Kane interrupted. "I'm not leaving town, but I will be taking my money elsewhere. You see, Sophie might not be willing to tell a bunch of disagreeable, judgmental busybodies who the father of her child is, but I don't mind at all." He smiled. "You're looking at him."

"Oh." Mrs. Driskell's plump face paled.

"I certainly can't reside in an inn where the proprietor holds my future wife and the mother of my child in such low regard."

"I didn't mean—"

"Of course you did," Kane said as he turned on his boot

heel and headed for the door. There was that smaller tavern at the edge of town. It wasn't as nice as this one, but he'd sleep on the street before he'd give a penny of his money to this hag.

At the doorway, he turned to face the ashen Mrs. Driskell. "A witch?" he asked shaking his head. "Where did you get such a ridiculous idea?"

The older woman nodded. "Oh, it's not a ridiculous idea. All three of the Fyne women are witches, like their mother before them, and their grandmother before her."

Kane stepped onto the boardwalk, leaving the bitter woman to her ramblings. Sophie didn't want him or any other man as husband. She was apparently well taken care of. Yes, she was very pretty, but there were plenty of pretty women in the Southern Province. He did still lust after her, but he certainly did not love her. He loved the woman of his dreams perhaps, but he could not possibly love the real Sophie. As she had said earlier: he didn't even know her.

But the child tied him to her in a way he could not—would not—deny. Other men might've gladly ridden away from such responsibilities, but not Kane Varden.

SOPHIE MANAGED TO AVOID HER SISTERS DURING THE morning hours when they were all busy with the day's chores, but she couldn't escape the closeness of the shared noon meal. Ariana slept, as she usually did this time of day, and as it was Sophie's chore to cook she couldn't very well plead exhaustion and take to her bed. Since she was never sick that wouldn't do as an excuse, in any case.

She made chicken and dumplings, Isadora's favorite, and hoped with all her heart that the meal would distract her usually astute sisters.

The Fyne cabin had stood on this very spot for more than three hundred years, and though from the outside it appeared to be a rough-hewn home, the interior was much finer than one might expect a cabin to be. Over the years the house had been added to, and it now spread far beyond the limits of the simple home it had once been. Each of the sisters had her own spacious bedchamber, and there were two well-furnished parlors as well as a large, well-equipped kitchen.

The kitchen was Sophie's domain, though they all worked here on occasion. Isadora cared for the animals. They had no need for a horse, but kept chickens, a few pigs, and a number of goats. Juliet tended the gardens and the hothouse. They were as self-sufficient as most farms, and needed little from town.

Sophie kept the house. Duties were shared. They helped one another, but they each had their own specific place in this household. Neither of her sisters were as adept with the temperamental wood-burning stove as she had come to be over the years.

Juliet and Isadora came inside within five minutes of one another, and they each went immediately to the kitchen basin to wash up before the noon meal. They were dressed in their work clothes; skirts that had been patched a few times and everyday shirts with the sleeves rolled back. Each of them wore a kerchief to keep long strands of hair away from her face. Isadora's work ensemble was entirely black, though she had mourned for Willym too long. Juliet's skirt was green and her blouse was natural linen. Her kerchief was a dark green, brightened with small yellow flowers.

Sophie remained busy, latticing the top crust of a redberry pie to bake later in the day. She breathed steadily and said very little, hoping her sisters would not realize that her morning had been momentous.

A year ago, on that day when Sophie had met Kane, Juliet had known almost immediately that something had changed. It hadn't even been necessary for her to touch her sister to see what had happened, which was an unusual event. Juliet didn't see everything, not even when she tried, and she had little control over her visions. She had not known that Willym would pass away as he did, and she said her visions of the future where she and her sisters were concerned were impossible to decipher, fuzzy and maddeningly indistinct.

But Juliet had known when she touched her little sister on that day that Sophie was with child. Isadora had been furious when she was told, and it had taken both of the more serene Fyne sisters to keep her from tracking down Kane and exacting her own style of revenge.

If they knew he had returned . . .

"What's the occasion?" Isadora asked as she studied the spread on the kitchen table. "Chicken and dumplings, tarrot beans, your special bread . . . and is that spice cake?" Suddenly she sounded suspicious.

"You two have been working so hard, I thought you deserved a treat," Sophie said brightly. She kept her eyes on the pie crust. "Since the baby's come I've been so busy I feel like I've been neglecting my share of the chores."

Isadora and Juliet had been dismayed when they'd first learned of Sophie's situation, but they loved Ariana dearly and were the most wonderful aunts imaginable. They had been wonderful sisters as well, all but coddling Sophie during the later months of her pregnancy and in the weeks after the baby arrived.

"You've always done more than your share," Juliet said sweetly.

Sophie smiled at the pie. So far, her sisters didn't suspect that anything was amiss. Her plan had worked. She'd distracted her sisters with pie and cake and chicken and dumplings. Her smile didn't last. By now Kane had heard one or two or even more outrageous stories. Someone had confirmed her tale that she was a witch, and he was on his way out of town. She should be pleased, but she wasn't.

To take her mind off Kane, she tried to think of her next paramour. It might be months or even years before she chose to take another man, but when she did he would be different.

Someone not quite so tall, perhaps. Someone not so conventionally handsome. Not a cheerless ex-rebel and thief next time, but a man who would laugh with her. A man who would not dare to mention marriage. A man who would not haunt her and threaten her with what she could not have.

And heaven above, the next time she would make sure her lover did not know where she lived. It caused too many complications.

"Oh, no," Juliet said quietly as she sat at the table.

"What's wrong?" Sophie turned. "Did I forget something?"

Both of her sisters stared at her. Juliet dismayed, Isadora curious.

"He's returned," Juliet said. With a dismissive hand, she brushed back a copper curl that had escaped the kerchief. "He came here looking for you. He saw the baby, he wants to . . . to marry you."

Having a psychic sister had always been incredibly annoying. Sophie never knew what Juliet would see, but decent secrets of any sort were nearly impossible to keep. And she'd been so careful not to touch Juliet today!

But she had touched the fork her sister was using, and the plate, and she had prepared the food. There was no hiding from Juliet, apparently.

Sophie lifted her chin. "Yes, Kane did happen to be at the pond this morning, but there's nothing to be concerned about. I sent him on his way."

"I have a feeling he didn't go far," Juliet insisted.

"Can I kill him now?" Isadora asked calmly.

"No," Juliet and Sophie said at once. Even though Sophie knew her eldest sister would not do another living being harm, she did worry about Kane and Isadora coming face-to-face. No good could come of such a meeting.

"There is nothing to be concerned about," Sophie said as she joined her sisters at the kitchen table. "Perhaps Ariana's father is still in the general area, but he'll be gone soon enough." As soon as he learned she was a witch. As soon as he understood that they had no future together. All they had was a fleeting, lovely moment shared long ago. And a daughter, she conceded silently.

"When do I get to meet this green-eyed man?" Isadora asked as she took a generous helping of chicken and dumplings.

"Never," Sophie said with what she hoped was confidence. "There is no need."

"It wouldn't be so terrible to be married," Juliet offered sweetly.

Isadora snorted. Her view on the subject of marriage was clear.

"Not for myself," Juliet added, "but for Sophie. Marriage without love is certainly possible. It happens all the time, for goodness sake. I have always known that Sophie was destined to have many daughters and a home and maybe even a husband."

"Your vision is unclear," Isadora insisted. "Sophie has a home and she has a daughter. Marriage is out of the question. She is too soft-hearted to maintain any sort of a relationship without love coming into the mix."

"To make matters clear," Juliet said, "I didn't have a *vision* about Sophie's future, I just have a sister's certain intuition that she was meant to have a happy life."

"If Sophie expects happiness, she cannot marry."

Sophie placed both hands on the table, palms down. "As this is my life you two are discussing, don't you think I should have the right to speak?"

"Of course, dear," Juliet answered. "Don't you want children and a husband and a home of your own?"

Sophie smiled. "Isadora is correct when she says I have a home here. I don't intend to leave this cabin, not ever. As for children, I suspect I will have more. Three daughters would be nice."

Juliet nodded.

"And as for men"—Sophie smiled—"they're very interesting. They can be truly fascinating, if you give them enough thought. Men are different. I do like them, but that doesn't mean I'm going to be so foolish as to fall in love."

A mental picture of Kane flitted into her mind, clear and startling. Not as he had been this morning, smiling and cheerful, but as he had been a year ago. He hadn't been so obviously handsome, then. He'd been ragged and rough. Melancholy and desperate.

It would be too easy to fall in love with a man like that one, and that would never do. She knew what would follow. Death for Kane and misery for herself. Sophie shivered. No man would own her, not her soul or her body or her heart. And so she would be safe.

Without warning, Juliet put down her spoon and sighed. "Good heavens, Sophie. What have you done?"

IT DIDN'T TAKE LONG FOR KANE TO FIND A FRIENDLY CARD game in the tavern where he'd settled earlier in the day. His room above stairs was plain and small and the meat and beans he'd been served at the noon hour had been bland and tough. But it would suffice, for now.

The stakes were not high, as card games went, but it was a pleasant enough way to pass the time. He won, of course, and soon found himself without a game. The surly losers went on their way only slightly poorer than before, leaving him alone in the tavern with no one for company but a friendly barkeep named Gudny.

Kane moved from the table where he'd won at cards to the bar, where he ordered a shot of whisky. He had never questioned the past year's good fortune. How could one challenge good luck? The fact that the tide had changed when he'd met his Angel—Sophie—was pure coincidence. Wasn't it?

The previous year had passed in a kind of blissful haze. He had his newfound wealth, a light heart, and dreams of a beautiful woman. He had been able to put his former life—which was even more of a haze than the past year—completely behind him. Sitting in a Shandley tavern and wondering how to proceed, new questions plagued him. Why couldn't he remember where he came from? There were vague memories of a poor and tumultuous childhood, a pretty dark-haired girl who claimed to love him, and then a battle he could barely recall.

He had not asked these questions in the last year because he hadn't wanted to. Asking them now gave him another of those sharp headaches, so he pushed the questions aside. All he had to do was concentrate on Sophie. The tavern proprietor, Mrs. Driskell, was jealous of her, and rightly so. No wonder men drooled when Sophie walked past. She was a sexual creature, as was evident in the way she moved and in the features that made her the beauty she was. Everything about her was curvaceous. Her body, her full lips. Even the slant of her eyes and the curve of her cheek was sensual.

And she was his in every way. Or soon would be.

If his luck held, and he was quite sure it would, she would be his wife in a matter of days. Weeks, perhaps. No, he couldn't possibly wait weeks to make Sophie his wife.

He couldn't wipe the image of his child and Sophie as they had been that morning from his mind, and he didn't want to. It was the kind of sight a man could very well live for. Beautiful, true . . . and his.

Did he love Sophie? No, of course not, though he imagined one day he might. She was incredibly beautiful. Startlingly passionate. And her smile . . .

"Another?" Gudny asked in his hoarse, raspy voice.

"Why not?" Kane pushed his empty shot glass toward the smiling barkeep. One more drink, and then he'd quit. He needed to be clearheaded in order to plan his courtship and conquest of Sophie. He didn't think the conquest would be too terribly difficult. After all, she was the mother of his child, and what woman didn't want a man to take care of her? He was relatively wealthy, with a few thriving businesses that he'd won in the past year. A tavern here, a feed store there, a very nice inn in a small town well west of Shandley. He'd won the enterprises at cards, of course, and even though he'd left them all in the hands of hired men, they continued to make money for him.

No, the task would not be difficult. Sophie would agree to marry him in less than a week, he imagined.

His memory was not good these days, but he did remember her. He remembered the way she had walked out of the pond like an angel, the way her skin had felt against his, her body, her smile . . . He could see it all as if he'd just met her yesterday. It was real, not a drunken dream after all. He could not recall why he had been so lost before she came to him. The headache began again with a single dull throb, and he pushed aside the questions. All that mattered was now. Today.

"Are you acquainted with Sophie Fyne?" he asked the barkeep who was busy wiping down the polished plank counter that separated them.

Gudny's head snapped up. "Why do you ask?"

"She's a friend."

The man stopped wiping. "A friend, you say."

In order to avoid another confrontation he quickly added, "I intend to marry her."

The large man worked his way slowly toward Kane. His eyes flitted this way and that. There wasn't much to study. It was the middle of the day so the tavern was empty, but for Kane. "You seem like a nice enough fella. If she put a spell on you—"

He laughed. "A spell?" More of the witch nonsense, he imagined.

"I'm telling you, mister, those Fyne women are bad business."

"In what way?"

Gudny glanced toward the door, as if to confirm that no one else was here to listen to his tale. "There's three of them, you know. We see Miss Juliet around town now and then, and of the three she's the least . . ." Gudny searched for the right word, pursing his lips and narrowing his eyes as he pondered. "Offensive," he finally finished.

Kane's first impulse was to throw a punch, but his curiosity won over his anger. "Offensive?"

"She helps some of the women hereabouts with medical concerns, and I've never seen her lose her temper or do anything to cause a ruckus, though I did hear a rumor a few years back that she has the sight."

"The sight."

Gudny lowered his voice once again. "She sees things that have yet to happen."

More nonsense.

"Then there's Isadora," Gudny continued. "She's the worst of the bunch. Killed her husband a few years back, put a spell on him, she did, and he dropped dead well before his time. If Isadora gives you the evil eye, mister, you don't have a chance."

"And what of Sophie?"

Again, Gudny looked toward the door. "She's a good-looking woman, and she seems friendly enough. I can't imagine that she'd ever give anyone the evil eye like that sister of hers. But . . ." The big man swallowed hard and his left eye twitched.

"But?" Kane prompted.

"A few months back she comes to town with her sister." Gudny looked directly at Kane once again. "Juliet, not Isadora, thank goodness. The dark one never comes down off that mountain, not since she killed her husband. Anyway, while Juliet was doing her errands as usual, Sophie visited some of the shops in town, said hello to folks, sat in the square and smiled at everyone who passed."

"Well, then she must be a witch," Kane said tersely.

"She did something," Gudny whispered. "I don't know what, exactly, but the gentlemen she passed by closed up shop and hurried home to pay some special attention to their wives, if you know what I mean. After Sophie said hello and nodded to them, women who normally wouldn't give their husbands the time of day got themselves all atwitter and went searching for their menfolk to . . ."

"Pay them some special attention," Kane supplied.

"Exactly."

"I still don't see . . ."

"It's bad enough that in Sophie Fyne's wake men lost their reason and good women behaved like sex-starved animals, but that's not the end of it. The women—they all got themselves in the family way," Gudny explained in a hushed voice. "Even Juno McTanni, who had been told by the doctor that she would never be able to have a child. Even Brenna Finn, who is just barely on the green side of fifty. Even—"

"I get your point." As if by her very presence, Sophie had caused half the town's population to procreate. Ridiculous.

"Even before we learned that all those women were in the family way, we knew something was wrong."

"How's that?"

"The place where Miss Sophie sat, there in the town square. It changed."

"Changed how?" Kane asked, his patience wearing thin.

"All around where she'd been sitting, the flowers that shouldn't have bloomed so early opened. They were brighter and bigger and more sweet-smelling than they should've been, too, as if they were somehow bewitched."

"The flowers were bewitched."

Gudny nodded. "Trust me, mister, you want to stay well clear of the Fyne sisters."

As if they had been summoned by Gudny's warning words, three women appeared. A dark-haired woman with fierce eyes was in the lead. It was she who burst through the door and glared at Kane. For a moment he assumed she was an irate wife looking for her wayward husband. A slender redhead stood directly behind the woman, and behind the redhead . . . Sophie, cradling the baby—*his* baby—in her arms.

"Isadora, don't—" Sophie began.

"By the moon, sister, I can see the spell from here. It floats around him like a lavender cloud. How could you do such a thing?"

The infamous Fyne sisters stepped into the tavern, and Gudny backed away from them all. "A spell," he croaked as he ducked down to squat behind the bar. Out of sight, out of mind. Or so he hoped.

Dismissing the spell nonsense, Kane stepped forward. "You must be Sophie's sisters." He grinned widely, even though none of them seemed at all inclined to return the smile. Sophie had called the angry one Isadora, which meant the redhead must be Juliet. "I'm Kane Varden. I've been looking forward to meeting you."

"We are not here to get acquainted," Isadora said abruptly. "Heaven above, Sophie," she said beneath her breath. "How on earth did you manage this on your own?"

Sophie stepped past the redhead. "I just wished him good fortune. It's not so very different from what you do for—"

"It is *very* different," Isadora interrupted sharply, waving a delicate hand at Kane but keeping her eyes on Sophie. "Was there a linara tree nearby?" She didn't wait for an answer. "There must've been. This is . . . is . . . it's too much," she said in a lowered voice.

Kane's smile faded. "Too much *what*?"

Isadora narrowed her dark eyes. "It's more than good fortune."

Sophie bit her lower lip. "I removed his pain," she confessed in a soft whisper.

Both the other Fyne sisters groaned. Kane remained thoroughly confused.

The dark-haired sister raised a hand, and without warning she pressed two fingertips to Kane's forehead. She said a few words he did not understand—a language unknown to him or utter nonsense, he had no idea which—and then she dropped her hand and stepped back. "Go home," she barked before she turned away and stalked toward the door.

"What have you done?" Sophie asked as she chased her sister. The redhead followed Sophie. Kane was right behind her.

"I took it back," Isadora said as she stepped onto the boardwalk.

"You can't do that!" Sophie insisted.

"I can and I did," Isadora said without slowing her stride.

"But he'll . . ."

Kane stopped in his tracks as a blinding headache sharp as shards of glass sliced through his brain. This was nothing like the other headaches he suffered on occasion. The pain was so great that for a moment he was blinded. Truly, completely blinded. He dropped to his knees.

It was the redheaded sister who reached him first. Juliet, he remembered. A healer. She had the sight, Gudny said. What rubbish. All he could see of her was a blur of red hair and pale skin, as his sight began to return.

"We can't just leave him here."

"Why not?" Isadora asked without pity.

"You go home," Sophie said, her sweet voice almost sharp. "Juliet and I will take care of him."

Perhaps the woman who had touched his forehead and set this anguish into motion did as her sister asked, because Kane saw drab, misty images of Sophie and the redhead. No one else. When the pain began to subside and his vision cleared, he concentrated on Sophie's face. "You're so beautiful," he whispered. "The first time I saw you . . ."

It came back in a rush. The first time he'd seen Sophie he'd been trying, very hard, to drink himself to death. His heart had hurt, the way it hurt now. The faces of friends he had buried, the faces of men he had killed, the home and the family that was gone . . . *gone* . . . would not leave his mind.

He remembered it all now, in a flood of pain that had been buried for the past year. Buried deep and forgotten. How was that possible? How could he have forgotten? The pain once again sliced through his head and his eyes, blinding him, forcing him to remember.

They'd been ambushed. Even though they had eluded the imperial soldiers and taken great care to travel a winding route, somehow the infantrymen had known exactly which road the rebels were taking, and they'd been waiting. His unit had been outnumbered more than ten to one, and they hadn't yet had a chance to recover from the battle that had wounded and disheartened them.

Someone had betrayed them, someone they trusted. And what had come next hadn't been a battle—it had been a slaughter.

Duran.

"Oh, dear," the redhead said softly, just before Kane blacked out and fell face first onto the boardwalk.

3

Kane needed aid from Sophie and Juliet just to walk. Their objective was his second-story room at the tavern where they'd found him. If he passed out again before they got him up the stairs and into bed, what would they do? They couldn't possibly move him on their own, and Sophie knew better than to think that they might get assistance from anyone in Shandley.

As she and Juliet retraced their steps with Kane staggering between them, the women who were out and about backed quickly away. One young mother clutched a small child to her breast as she turned and ran as fast as she could away from the two sisters, Ariana, and their almost helpless patient. By the time they reached the tavern door, the street was deserted.

Sophie simply didn't have the time or the patience to explain that since she wasn't with child her mere presence would have no affect on them today.

The barkeep rose up slowly as they stepped into the tavern, but dropped down quickly when he saw who had opened the door.

"Which room is Mr. Varden's?" Juliet asked.

From behind the bar Gudny answered. "Upstairs, second door on the right."

Juliet carried Ariana and offered an arm of support, and Sophie kept both arms around Kane as she steered him up the stairs. "Why would Isadora do this?" she snapped. "The spell wasn't hurting anyone. It wasn't even a proper spell, just a . . . a . . ."

"A heartfelt wish," Juliet said as they made their way down the second story hallway.

"That's right."

Juliet pushed open the door to Kane's room, and Sophie guided her lover . . . no, her *former* lover . . . to his bed.

"There is no spell more effective than the heartfelt spoken wish of a true and powerful witch."

"I'm not powerful!" Sophie insisted as Kane fell onto his back, bouncing lightly on the bed.

"Of course you are," Juliet said as she handed Ariana over. "Especially when you're pregnant. I suspect the wish you made came after you'd been with him, not before, so that explains the potency of the wish. That and the proximity of the linara tree."

Sophie held her daughter close. What was she to do? Kane was in obvious pain. She might lay her hand on him and make a wish for his well-being, just as she had a year ago. But it wouldn't be the same. She wasn't with child, there was no linara tree . . . and even if she could make the spell work properly, when Isadora found out and undid the wish, would his pain be all the greater?

She watched while Juliet quickly examined Kane without actually touching him, her hands floating close to his face and his chest. Her eyes closed momentarily as she absorbed all that she needed to know. "I can give him an herbal potion to help with the headaches. If he'll take the herbs as I instruct they will alleviate some of the pain and help him to sleep. I'm afraid that's all I can do."

"I made matters worse, didn't I?" Sophie asked softly.

"You didn't know . . ."

"I made it worse, didn't I?" she asked again. "The pain he's feeling now is even greater than it was a year ago."

Juliet paused before opening her eyes and answering softly. "Yes."

Rather than experiencing a year of healing, as he should have, Kane had buried his hurt. No, she had buried it for him, with her wish. Now that the pain was back he'd have to begin the healing anew. What choice did she have but to help him?

"I'm going to stay with Kane until he recovers."

"You can't," Juliet protested primly. "It's going to take days, perhaps weeks for a full recovery. It would be improper for you to stay with him unchaperoned for even an hour." She chewed her lower lip. "In truth, he might never heal completely."

Sophie didn't accept that possibility. If Kane was permanently damaged by the abrupt reversal of the spell, it was her fault. "Well, I can't leave him here alone, and . . ." Her eyes met Juliet's. Her sister had always been more concerned about what was proper than Sophie had been. "I have no reputation to ruin," she added softly. "I can stay here as long as is necessary."

Juliet knew there was no other choice, but she didn't like the situation or Sophie's solution. "Isadora will not be happy when I arrive home without you."

"I'm not afraid of Isadora." Sophie trembled, but just a little. Isadora's anger could be mighty, but she would never hurt a living soul. Well . . . she would definitely not hurt one of her sisters, and it would take a forceful motivation to stir her to cause actual physical harm to anyone . . . wouldn't it?

After seeing the look in Isadora's eyes when she'd confronted Kane, Sophie finally had to admit that perhaps those who feared the eldest Fyne sister had good reason.

Juliet reached into a deep pocket and withdrew a cloth bag that had been tied up tight with a length of red string. "Give him a half teaspoon of this mixed with water or wine every half hour until he's noticeably improved."

Sophie took her sister's offering, not at all surprised that Juliet had the required herbal blend in her pocket. "How long will it take for the medicine to have an effect?"

"A few hours, perhaps. Two days at the most. After that he will need sleep and nutritious food in order to complete the healing process." Juliet gathered together everything Sophie would need. A tin cup stored in Kane's saddlebag, a jug of water that had been left on the nightstand. She helped to administer the first dose, then said good-bye.

A few hours to two days. And how many days after that before he could be truly healed? Sophie pulled the single chair in the room to Kane's bedside and sat, determined to stay with him as long as was necessary.

In sleep, he looked like neither the sad man she had taken as her lover a year ago, nor the smiling gentleman who had proposed marriage to her this morning. There was a harshness about him, an anger that radiated from him even now, when he was oblivious to the world around him.

Sophie didn't understand anger. Her own temper was mild. She never yelled, she never raged, and while she had known moments of sadness in her life, most particularly when her mother had died and then when Willym had passed away, the vast majority of her days had been blessed.

She was capable of love, she knew that well. Worse, she craved a true love to the pit of her soul. It was only that craving for something she could not have that made her life less than perfection.

Kane looked as if he had fought for survival every day of his life. He looked as if he had never known a moment's ease. Well . . . except for this past year. If those days had been the only easy ones in his life, she couldn't be sorry for making her wish. Could she?

KANE OPENED HIS EYES TO FIND SOPHIE HOVERING OVER him. Still. Again. He couldn't be sure which. A single candle burning on the bedside table illuminated one side of her beautiful face for him. From below, the sounds of merriment rose, muted and out of place. Laughter did not belong here, in this place, on this night.

Sophie tried to pour some awful tasting brew down his throat, as she'd done on a regular basis. This time he grabbed her wrist and stopped her before the cup made it to his mouth.

"What are you doing to me?" His voice was raspy, his throat sore.

"It will make you feel better." She smiled at him, but it wasn't a real smile. He had seen a real Sophie smile once, and this wasn't it.

"I don't want you to make me feel better." He didn't think it was possible that anyone or anything could ever make him feel *better*. It would be best if he could forget the past year, but that hadn't happened. He remembered everything. He remembered laughing and smiling and living a life of ease, while his brothers and so many of his friends rested in the ground. God, he hoped they rested in the ground. The soldier who had killed Duran had threatened to put his head on a spike. Was it still there, posted on a wall in the capital city? Had his brother's head been rotting in the rain while he seduced loose women and ate fine meals and slept in soft beds? He had drunk and eaten plenty while the charred remains of his home sat undisturbed and unavenged.

He remembered women. Laughing women who'd been happy to warm his bed, as the woman he had once loved warmed another man's bed.

And he remembered her.

"What did you do to me?"

"Juliet said this would make you—"

"Not now!" He sat up, and his head responded by pounding a thunderous rhythm. "Not now," he said more softly. "When we first met. A year ago. What did you do?"

She looked guilty, at least. "I just wanted you to be happy. After all, you made me happy and I thought it was the least I could do, and you looked so miserable—"

"Sophie," he interrupted. "How did you do it? How did you make me forget?" And he *had* forgotten. He'd forgotten everything unpleasant that had come before meeting Sophie Fyne. The fighting. The death. Going home to nothing.

"It was just . . ." She blushed, bit her lip and looked past him to the dark window. "A wish, that's all. Just a wish."

If that were true then she was truly a witch, as she claimed to be, and the best thing he could do for himself was to get up out of this bed and leave town. He should forget Sophie Fyne and the child she had given birth to.

As if she knew what he was thinking, his daughter—who rested on a pallet on the floor at the foot of the bed—began to coo.

"And the rest?" he continued.

"Good fortune," she said in a lowered voice. "It did not seem like such a large gift at the time, but my sisters think otherwise."

Good luck. Happiness. Such simple things. Things to which he had no right. "Why didn't you just swim away when you were done with me?" he asked angrily.

Her eyes grew wide. Even in the flickering light of that one candle, he could see the startling blue of those eyes. "I couldn't do that," she said softly.

She'd felt sorry for him, and had given him the *gifts* that had colored the past year of his life.

Right now he wanted only one thing from her: the body she

had offered him on their first meeting. The warmth that had truly taken away his pain, for a moment. The feel of flesh on flesh and the sound of her breath in his ear. Nothing else could make him forget; nothing else could clear his mind and make him feel good again . . . for a short while.

"Do you want to make me feel better now?" he whispered, his fingers tightening around her wrist.

"Yes, of course I do. You need to drink this."

He took the offered cup from her and tossed it across the room. The tin cup bounced off the wall with a loud *thunk* and tainted water splashed across the floor. "No. No more witch's brew, Angel. No more of your damned magic. All I need to make me feel better is your body beneath mine." That was what he'd dreamed of for the past year. Not marriage, not babies, not a home. Just sex. He wanted nothing else from her. Not now, not ever.

She had been made for his bed. His memories of their time together were fuzzy and faded, but he did remember the way she'd come to him, as he remembered the soft curves of her body and the way she moaned and moved and smiled when he touched her. He fell back against the pillow and pulled her close so that she was practically lying on top of him.

"I can't," she whispered.

"Why not?" He remembered her words. Sophie wanted lovers, not a husband. Pleasure, not commitment. And right now he needed her to take away the hurt in a way no medicine ever could.

"I just . . . can't."

He shifted his head and pressed his mouth against Sophie's neck, tasting her pulse and the silkiness of her flesh against his lips. He could be a lover, if that's what she wanted. He could lose himself in her body and then walk away in the morning, without commitment, without offers of a lifetime or even a week.

Her body shuddered and she tried to shift away from him,

but he didn't release his hold on her. His mouth stayed steady on her throat, his grip at her wrist did not diminish. Sophie's soft hand fell onto his chest, but quickly moved away as if she were afraid to touch him.

Kane was not afraid. He cupped her breast with his free hand, exploring the soft yield beneath the coarse fabric. Sophie was all woman. She was passion and beauty and pleasure, and he needed her. He needed her to help him forget. His fingers brushed against a nipple. Sophie gasped a little, and the nipple hardened.

"You said I made you happy before," he said, his breath lost against her satiny throat. He trailed the tip of his tongue to a tender spot beneath her ear. "I can make you happy again."

"I . . . I don't want you," she said softly.

It was a lie, and Sophie Fyne did not lie well. He felt her need in every breath she took, in the quiver of her body and the uncontrollable response, which he continued to tease with his fingers. She did want him, but he wasn't going to try to change her mind, not here and now. He had no patience for seduction, no desire to gently coax this woman to lie beneath him.

"I know why you're hurting. You talked in your sleep, some," she explained, trying desperately to change the subject. "You talked about the people you've lost. People you loved."

His grip on her wrist tightened, but she did not get the not-so-subtle hint.

Sophie's face was close to his, her lips full and rosy and slightly parted. "Whenever I find myself missing my mother or my brother-in-law," she said softly, "Juliet tells me stories that make me feel so much better. They give me hope."

"You're not going to sit here and tell me a bedtime story," he said harshly.

She quickly licked her luscious lower lip. "The stories are not fiction, they're true. You must trust what Juliet says. She knows many things that others do not."

"So I hear."

Sophie tilted her head to one side, just slightly. "When I was a little girl and I cried for my mother, Juliet would tell me that there are many other worlds much like this one. In those worlds we live other lives. Lives shaped by the place we live in and the people around us, the decisions we make and all the decisions that have been made before. Some of these worlds have lots of magic, some have none. Some are dark, but many—no, most—are happy places."

Kane shook his head. "Do you really think tall tales are going to make me feel any better?"

"This is not a tall tale," she whispered. "It's true. These worlds are not far away, Juliet says, but very close to us. Closer than we can imagine. They are a dream, a breath, a whisper of magic away, and in at least some of these places our loved ones live on. Close your eyes and imagine—"

"Get out," he ordered, dropping her hand and pushing her away. "And take your ridiculous fantasies with you."

Sophie backed away from him, but she didn't leave the bed. She sat on the edge of the mattress, so close and yet . . . not nearly close enough. "I want to stay with you until you're better," she said.

"I don't think I'm going to get any better."

"I'm sorry. I wish—"

"Maybe you'd better not make any wishes, Angel," he interrupted. "That didn't work out so well the last time."

Sophie bit her lower lip, stared at him for a moment, and then shot off of the bed. She gathered up the child from her pallet and held the baby close to her bosom as if it were a shield. "I suppose you'll be leaving Shandley soon."

"Not much reason to stay."

She shook her head. "No, there's not."

A memory—the sight of freshly spilled blood and the scream that had led Kane to the bottle in the first place—flashed into his mind as if it were a new memory, not an old one. He tried not to flinch. "Go," he ordered.

"You should take more of Juliet's remedy," Sophie said quickly. "I'd be happy to mix up another cupful before I go."

"I've had enough of witches' remedies," he said shortly. "In fact, I've had enough of witches altogether." He didn't care about Sophie, not at all, but he certainly didn't want his daughter to be paraded through a tavern full of drunks. "Take the rear stairway," he instructed.

Sophie backed out of the room, and if his head didn't hurt so much Kane might have felt a twinge of guilt at the pain in her eyes. But he had no time for guilt. Not tonight.

SOPHIE TRIED NOT TO CRY AS SHE RAN DOWN THE SIDE OF the road that would lead her home. Whatever tears she needed to shed had to be gone before she arrived home. Isadora would do her worst if she thought Kane had made her cry.

He had every right to be angry. After everything that had happened, he should never want to see her again, and he didn't. He didn't. And she should be glad. It would definitely be best if Kane rode away and they never saw one another again.

At least she had learned from her mistakes with her first lover. Next time she would go far from home for her tryst, as her mother had, and there would be no gifts. No wishes for healing, no use of her talents at all. Next time . . .

Suddenly she could not even imagine a next time. Did every encounter lead to pain and regret? If so, perhaps one child and one lover would be quite enough.

Remembering the way her body had reacted to Kane's hand on her wrist and his mouth on her neck and his fingers on her bosom, she knew without a doubt that there would be other lovers. One day. But only after she had scrubbed the memory of Kane Varden from her mind.

"Sophie?"

Startled, Sophie turned to face the man who had called her

name. Galvyn Farrell walked toward her with a smile on his face. He was, she confessed, more pleasant to look at than most of the men in Shandley, and he was a well-respected merchant who owned several of the enterprises in town. He had professed an interest in her on more than one occasion. He had even offered to marry her while she'd been pregnant with Ariana, and had repeated the offer once since the baby's birth. She had, of course, vigorously declined.

But as Galvyn was handsome and openly interested in her, why didn't anything about him make her long to touch him? She looked at his face, his thick dark hair, his dark brown eyes, and felt nothing.

Galvyn claimed some kind of family ties to the emperor. He was a distant cousin by marriage, or some such. Whatever the connection, he always used it to his full advantage, mentioning this minister or that general or even the emperor himself, as if to know these people should make him more important.

"You shouldn't be out alone after dark," he said, a touch of concern in his voice. "Please allow me to walk you home."

Sophie shook her head. "No, thank you. It's too far."

"The fair company will make the time pass quickly."

"I don't want to be a bother." She needed time alone before confronting her sisters. Time to fortify herself and manufacture a smile that would fool them both.

"I insist."

Sophie cuddled a sleeping Ariana. "That's very nice of you, but Isadora doesn't like strangers on the mountain, especially after dark."

His easy smile faded, as she had known it would. Like everyone else in town, Galvyn was afraid of Isadora. She suspected that was why his almost frantic attentions were only offered when she went into Shandley—which wasn't often.

"Perhaps I can walk you part of the way."

Sophie conceded, deeming it a fair compromise.

For a while they discussed the weather and local politics—the mayor in particular—and then there was a long, awkward period of silence. The narrow path up the hill toward home was right ahead. Surely that's where Galvyn would make his departure.

"I understand an acquaintance of yours has come to town," he said sharply.

Sophie was so surprised, she practically jumped out of her skin.

"A gentleman," Galvyn said. "I do hope you won't do anything rash, Sophie. You have friends in town, you know. I like to consider myself among them. You don't need to look outside the community for a husband, even if he is . . ." Galvyn looked pointedly at Ariana.

So, Kane had spoken to a few people during his hours in Shandley. How much had he told them? Enough, apparently. "I don't plan to marry anyone. Not now, not ever. I've told you that before."

"Every woman needs a husband," he argued.

"I don't."

"You just don't know what you need," Galvyn said, condescending and superior. "I'll make a fine husband, Sophie."

She shook her head. "Believe me, I will never marry."

"I don't understand," he said, a trace of anger working its way into his voice. "I've offered you everything any woman could possibly want. A home, an attentive husband, an honorable place in this town, a name for your baby—"

"My baby has a name," Sophie interrupted.

Galvyn looked properly contrite. "I didn't mean to sound insolent. Just consider my offer, Sophie. That's all I ask."

"I have to hurry," Sophie said as they reached the turnoff in the path. "Thank you for keeping me company all this way." Before Galvyn could respond she turned and ran onto the trail that would take her to her mountainside home, Ariana clutched to her chest and the sounds of the night echoing in her ears.

KANE STOOD AT HIS WINDOW AND LOOKED DOWN ON A dark, deserted street. Below all was silent. The tavern had closed for the night, and the patrons had gone home or climbed the stairs to their own rented rooms.

His body shook slightly, with deep, subtle tremors that would not stop. He didn't know if it was the returning memories, the remnants of a nightmare, or the witch's potion that made him shake and feel so damn weak, as if his bones could turn to liquid at any moment.

Through the confusion and the pain and the horror, one thought kept returning. He wanted his sword. He needed his knives. He felt naked without his weapons. Vulnerable. What had happened to them? He laughed harshly as he remembered. The sword had been broken by the soldier who'd killed Duran. He'd climbed out of the ravine with the bastard's knife and one other, a small blade he carried in his right boot. Both were gone now. He'd given the weapons away, one at a time, as he'd realized that he no longer needed them. How had he made it through the past year without a way to protect himself? Magical good luck, of course. A blessed man didn't need weapons to defend himself.

Fortunately he had money, plenty of it, and any decent swordmaker would provide replacements.

He could leave Shandley now. In the dead of night, he could saddle his gray mare and head for parts unknown where he could do his best to forget all over again. But where would he go? Home didn't exist. The businesses he'd won in the past year? They're weren't rightfully his. He should return them to the proper owners, every single one of them. His winning, his good luck, wasn't natural. It wasn't right.

None of the past year had been real. Not the serenity, not the good luck, not the comfort in his heart.

That wasn't entirely true. Sophie had been real. He could still see her, walking out of the pond in early morning light, hair slicked back, water running off her bare body as she cast his way a brilliant smile that would light up any man's world. The dreams of the past year . . . were those dreams witches' work? Or were they all his own? He'd probably never know.

The baby was real, he could not deny it. His baby. His daughter, Ariana. Nothing that had happened would change that. No pain, no nightmare, no memory. And no matter how much he wanted to, he couldn't ride away from his child just because the mother had turned his world inside out.

Sophie said she didn't want to marry him. Fine. At the moment marriage was the last thing on his mind. But he couldn't ride away from the baby and not look back. Before he left this place, he had to make sure Ariana would be taken care of. She was the only family he had left.

Ariana's mother was a witch, and so were her aunts. She lived surrounded by unnatural things. Was Ariana safe? Would the Fyne sisters turn his daughter, his only child, into a witch? Was it too late?

As badly as he wanted to run, he couldn't leave this place until he had the answers to those questions. And if the baby wasn't safe? If his daughter was in danger? He'd have no choice but to take her with him when he left.

If it came to that, how would he care for a baby? He had been a farmer once, then a soldier, then a gambler. He was a rebel who had fought for five years in the name of a doomed cause, and somehow he would fight again. None of his pursuits had prepared him to be a father. A man wasn't supposed to raise a child, particularly a girl child, on his own. A little girl would need a mother. She would need the guidance of a woman in the years to come.

At the moment Kane couldn't think about the years to

come. He couldn't bear to think about the past, either. There was only here and now. His child, the only blood-kin he had left in this world, was being raised in a house of witches. The past year of his life was a lie. The woman whose memory had carried him through that year had cast some kind of spell on him—that's why he had not been able to get her out of his head and his heart.

His first instinct was to run, but that wouldn't do. He had to make sure the baby would be cared for, that she'd be safe and loved. It was the least he could do for his own child. And he'd have to get Sophie out of his head once and for all. He'd have to see her for what she really was: a woman like any other; a witch who would make a poor wife; a lie.

As soon as he saw to Ariana's welfare and removed Sophie's presence from his mind, he'd leave Shandley and the Fyne sisters behind him, and he wouldn't look back.

He'd find his way to Arik. That wouldn't be an easy task. The leader of the revolution and the rightful emperor of Columbyana, Arik was heavily guarded at all times and getting close to the man would be dangerous. Especially for a soldier who had been the sole survivor of an ambush and then disappeared for more than a year.

When he'd climbed up out of the ravine and found nothing but blood on the road, he'd instinctively headed for home. He had a woman there, a house, friends, and they called to him with the comfort only home can offer. How many miles had he walked before the daze had cleared and reality had returned to him? The woman was married to another man, the home had been burned years earlier. The friends—they were all either dead or fighting far from home. There was nothing in that little town to call *home*, not anymore.

Wounded inside and out, he had planned to find his way to Arik. What had happened? He'd lost himself in the bottle, for a while. The wound on his arm had gotten infected, and a sympathizer in a small town west of here had nursed him back to health. He'd spent weeks in the back room of a tavern, caught between death and life. One night he'd simply wandered away, without thanks for the woman who had saved him.

And then he'd found *her*. Sophie.

Disappearing for more than a full year after that ambush with no believable explanation for what had happened wouldn't help matters any. Even if he could prove to Arik that he had not betrayed his own unit, how would he possibly explain away the past year?

Somehow he would manage. The revolution was all he had. That was true now more than ever. Emperor Sebestyen had to be removed from the Columbyanan palace, and Arik was a decent option to take his place. Arik claimed to be the rightful heir, the eldest albeit illegitimate son of the man who had been in power before Sebestyen had taken the throne seventeen years ago. Arik and Sebestyen were half-brothers, the only sons of Emperor Nechtyn. Arik was not significantly elder; he had been born six months before Sebestyen. The Emperor Nechtyn and his empress had produced four daughters, along with their one legitimate son. The daughters had been married off to dignitaries or sent to a convent in the Eastern Province, where the Empress Mother had retired after Nechtyn's death. Kane didn't care who replaced Sebestyen, he just wanted the man and all his soldiers dead.

They'd bled dry the village where Kane had grown up, taking more and more taxes every year, demanding more and more of the crops the farmers worked so hard to grow, burning homes when the taxes and the offered crops did not please them. He remembered being hungry growing up, and he remembered being afraid.

Sometimes the soldiers took more than food and money, dragging young girls and married women off in the night. Now and then the women who had been taken returned with daring tales of escape. More often they did not.

It was true that he had not seen such atrocities in every town he'd visited since leaving his home to take up the cause. Many people remained ignorant of the injustices that occurred elsewhere. High taxes were collected from everyone, but the cruelties of Sebestyen's most trusted soldiers were not widespread. When those who resided in more peaceful parts of the country heard the stories, they didn't believe. No one wanted to believe.

The Southern Province seemed to be completely untouched by war and the whims of the emperor's men. It was in the Western Province where Kane had been born and raised, where the capital city of Arthes was located, that the sights of soldiers in the street had been an everyday fear.

They had burned his home. They had taken his sister from her bed when she'd been fifteen and Kane had been twelve. He didn't know if Liane was dead or alive, though in truth he had given up hope of seeing her again years ago. If she was alive she'd be thirty-one years old now. Considering the condition of the girls who had returned to the village mere days after being taken, there was little chance that Liane had survived so long.

And for the past year he had forgotten about her. She had not crossed his mind once; he had not dreamed of her. He had been lost in a world that did not exist. Other things, other people, had not crossed his mind in that time, either. Friends. Stepan and Valdis, brothers gone so long he had almost forgotten their faces. Duran—God, it felt like Duran had been taken from him yesterday, and he had not forgotten that face. He had not forgotten that scream.

Kane closed his eyes and wished for a moment of the oblivion Sophie had given him.

Everyone, everything he had called home, was gone. But in spite of it all he was still a soldier. He remained a rebel. He would return to the fight somehow. He would prove his innocence and take up the sword again, even if it meant he had to storm the palace on his own.

The rebellion and that baby were all he had left. Without them, he might as well be dead.

4

Arthes: The Emperor's Palace

LIANE SMILED FOR THE EMPEROR AS THE SENTINELS WHO had searched her so thoroughly closed the door behind her, leaving her alone with the ruler of Columbyana. She had long ago learned to ignore the queasiness that roiled in the pit of her stomach whenever she looked upon him. There had been a time when she'd feared this man above all others, but now she felt only revulsion and a strange kind of loyalty. Lust, too, played a part in the sensations in the pit of her soul. She'd tried to ignore that aspect of the relationship, but Liane didn't believe in lying to herself. She lied to everyone around her by necessity, she could at least be honest within.

The emperor could have killed her years ago, or worse, banished her to Level Thirteen. But he had not. He had cherished her, in the only way he knew how. He had allowed her freedoms she had never expected when she'd been captured.

The imperial bedchamber on Level One of the palace was the most lavish of all the rooms. Emperor Jahn Sebestyen Alixandyr Beckyt enjoyed his comforts, large and small, and his bedchamber was no exception. The ceilings were twelve feet high and painted like a night sky, dark blue with silver stars and a golden moon so that Sebestyen could lie on his back and pretend that he was brave enough to leave the protection of the palace. The walls were papered in swirling blue and gold and the furnishings in this extravagant bedchamber were fit for a man of royal heritage, with gleaming dark wood and elegantly embroidered blue fabric the color of an evening sky. A sweet scent, the emperor's favorite, filled the air as fragrant oils simmered in ceramic bowls set in all four corners of the room. The only art on the walls was a flattering portrait of the emperor himself, painted just last year.

A large bed draped in bright blue fabric dominated the room, shimmering with artificial light from above. Tall, fat columns rose at each corner of the bed, which was adorned with silky pillows in all shapes and sizes. The emperor, draped in a long-sleeved, floor-length, high-necked crimson robe, reclined upon the bed with his head propped in one hand as he studied her.

Sebestyen, Emperor of Columbyana, was a tall man, slender but not thin, elegant in the right light but certainly not pretty. His face was too angular to be called pretty, though it was striking and masculine and memorable. Yes, he was definitely memorable.

His blue eyes had the ability to see right through a woman, and there had not been a night in the past sixteen years that Liane had not seen or dreamed of or remembered the power of those eyes.

Long, well-shaped bare feet peeked out from beneath the hem of his robe. Beneath the concealing garment he didn't sport bulky muscles like some of his soldiers, but he was well built and was stronger than he looked.

"Is it done?" he asked softly.

"Of course." Liane stepped slowly toward the pale man. Like him, she wore a robe of deep red. The full skirt danced around her legs as she walked to him. The simple robe was a hard-earned symbol of her station in this palace. After years of being a slave and one of many concubines, she had clawed her way into a position of power. A position unheard of for a woman such as herself.

"Did he confess to his crimes against me?"

"Of course not." They never did. Only a fool would confess to conspiring against the emperor. In this case she had not even asked for an admission of guilt. The evidence that had been presented by Minister Sulyen, the emperor's Minister of Defense, had been quite damning. The Minister of Finance had been meeting secretly with representatives from one of the largest clans in Tryfyn, the country to the west of Columbyana. The leader of this particular clan had been anxious to expand into Columbyana for years, but always stopped short of declaring war. Like the rebels who were led by that upstart Arik, the broken clans of Tryfyn were a mere annoyance. The emperor feared a rebellion from within much more than he feared the rebels or the Tryfynians.

Behind the bed upon which Emperor Sebestyen reclined there were heavy curtains that appeared to completely cover a large window, but there was no opening to the outside world there or anywhere else on Level One. They were ten stories off the ground, here in the highest level of the massive and grand Imperial Palace, and yet on this level there was not a single opening to the outside world. The original windows on Level One, as well as a skylight in the main ballroom, had all been filled with mortar and brick long ago.

Shortly after the emperor had taken his throne at the age of thirteen, a seer had told him that when the sun touched his face it would signal the beginning of the end for him. That warm touch would foretell the end of his rule, his happiness, and his life. Sebestyen might've arrogantly dismissed the prediction, but since the wizard Thayne had correctly forecast Emperor Nechtyn's demise only a few months earlier, he took

the warning seriously. It was for that reason that the man on
the bed was so pale. He hadn't seen the sun in seventeen
years, and he left the windowless Level One rarely—and even
then, only well after sundown.

"Did he beg for his life?"

Sebestyen always wanted details, and Liane always gave
them to him. She offered him a mix of fact and fiction, since
her simple methods were not diabolical enough to satisfy the
emperor. She did her job and she was good at it, but she saw
no reason to make her prey suffer simply for the emperor's
entertainment. Her victims had made the mistake of annoying
their leader, either personally or politically, and they had to
pay the price. But she refused to toy with them.

Liane didn't feel guilty about her place in the government
of Columbyana. Death was preferable to Level Thirteen, the
only other option for Emperor Sebestyen's enemies.

She sat on the edge of the bed. "What do you want to know,
my lord?"

"You're to call me Sebestyen when we're alone," he said,
reaching out to touch her face. His fingers were unnaturally
cold for such a warm night. "How many times must I tell you
so? I want to hear you say my name."

"Sebestyen," she said obediently, allowing the syllables to
roll across her tongue as if she could taste them.

He rewarded her with a smile. "I want to know everything.
Every detail. Every word. But first, take off that gown."

She stood and slowly unfastened the garment, which was
all she wore. The fat knotted buttons slipped through her fingers, from the top fastening at her throat to the one just past
her waist. When that was done she shrugged the heavy robe
off and let it fall to the stone floor.

There had been a time when she'd cowered to stand naked
before this man, when she'd shuddered and shivered and
prayed for death at his touch. But no more. Over the years she
had learned that her body was just a tool, like the knives she

wielded at the emperor's order. No man made the woman she had become fearful. She cowered for no one.

Liane was a year older than the emperor, and the eldest of the concubines at his command. But her body was firm, her breasts high, her waist small. There was a hint of honey brown in her skin, so that even when she remained indoors she did not lose all the color from her flesh. As he looked at her, she knew the man liked what his eyes beheld.

One day he would trust her enough to allow her into this room with one of her knives in her hand, and when he made that mistake she would kill him. Not quickly, the way she had earlier assassinated the minister who had betrayed Sebestyen with seditious words, but slowly. Painfully.

But that would not happen tonight.

She crawled onto the bed and reached out to unfasten his robe. Sebestyen had a dusting of dark hair on his chest, and that only made his paleness more striking. Even though his skin had not seen the sun in years, it was healthy and stretched over nicely honed muscles that hinted at his strength. His face was not traditionally beautiful, but his body was everything a woman could ask for. Some nights that fact made her job easier. Other nights, it did not help matters at all.

She traced a muscle on his torso with one finger. "He thought I was an imperial gift," she whispered as her hand slipped lower, delving inside the confines of the robe, "and when I entered his private room through the secret passageway he welcomed me with open arms."

Sebestyen grinned. "He did not even think to search you, did he?"

She shook her head. "Of course not."

"Foolish mistake."

The man who Liane despised took a handful of her hair in his fist and pulled her closer, so that her face was very close to his. Their noses almost touched. He held her so tightly her scalp stung, but she did not cry out. His dominant blue eyes locked onto hers, as if he thought he could hold her by his gaze alone. "Did he run his fat fingers through your hair?"

"Of course not," she said calmly. "That is a privilege reserved for you and you alone, Sebestyen." He always insisted that she wear her hair down, completely unfettered, because he was fascinated by the mixture of gold and brown strands and the way they wove together. No other woman in his palace had such hair. He had commented upon it the first time he'd seen her. She tried very hard not to think of that time.

His own hair was a thick, very dark brown, without a hint of curl. It was slightly longer than shoulder length and usually worn loose, as it was tonight. When he pulled it back into a queue, like so many of the gentlemen did these days, it accentuated the strength of his face and made him look harsher.

"Did you give my traitorous minister a taste of the emperor's favorite concubine before you killed him?"

"Just a taste," she whispered. It was a lie, but it was the lie Sebestyen wanted to hear. She'd killed the poor man quickly, before he'd even had time to shed his crimson robe.

She wished for her knife now, but Sebestyen, for all his words about her being his favorite, did not trust her. He did not trust anyone, which was the only reason he'd lived so long. But one day . . .

"He had wanted you for years," Sebestyen said absently. "On more than one occasion, he asked for permission to have you summoned to his bedchamber."

Liane shuddered. No wonder the minister had smiled so widely when she'd appeared before him. "And you refused him?"

"I do not share you with just anyone, Liane. He did not deserve you. He did not earn you. Not until tonight. I almost hate it that you gave him a moment of joy before you dispatched him."

"It was only a moment," she whispered.

He smiled; for some sick reason it pleased him to think of

her roles in this palace combined into one moment. Sex and death; love and hate.

At Sebestyen's command she removed his robe, slowly sliding the fine fabric off his sinewy arms, working the crimson from beneath his body and tossing it to the floor where it landed beside her own discarded garment.

When they were both naked she touched his body as he liked to be touched. She caressed his skin, gently at first and then not so gently. She raked her fingernails easily down his chest, careful not to mark his skin, then traced the line of dark hair from his navel to his genitals.

She stroked her palms over his muscled thighs, her thumbs teasing the sensitive flesh at his inner thighs until his eyes were hooded with desire and his penis was fully erect. Only then did she wrap her fingers around him and stroke the hard, hot flesh.

He had given her as a favor to many men in the years since she'd been captured, so she knew not all males were like the Emperor Sebestyen, in looks or in temperament. Some were pretty, others ugly but content. Some were stout or terribly thin, while others had bodies that rivaled this one. Some laughed in bed, while others were very serious about the task of making love. They were not all cruel.

And still, she hated them all. Some more than others, but even those few she called friends sometimes roused hatred within her. She'd turned that hate to her advantage, learning to use pleasure to control the men who took her to their beds. Learning to pretend that she wanted to be spread and crushed and helpless beneath them. The old crones and the Masters who kept and trained the concubines who occupied Level Three had taught her well.

Sex was power. Pleasure was a weapon.

"Did he scream?" Sebestyen asked as he yanked her up against him so that her breasts were pressed against his hard chest.

Again he pulled too hard, but Liane did not utter a sound of complaint. She just smiled. "Yes, my lord, he screamed."

"Did you scream, Liane?"

She licked her lips and lied again. "I did."

Sebestyen did not kiss. Not ever. He found it undignified and beneath him. Liane had been kissed before, by the Masters employed to train the emperor's concubines and by men Sebestyen had sent her to as a reward for faithful service or simply to learn if they talked in their sleep. Not the ones he asked her to kill, but the others—the ones she was simply ordered to amuse. Once or twice those kisses had been pleasant, on other occasions they had been repulsive. On some days she longed for a skilled kiss, but not from this man. She was glad she didn't have to endure those lips against hers.

The emperor did not kiss even his own wife. Then again, he rarely touched the empress at all. The Empress Rikka resided in her own quarters on Level Five. Sebestyen had the newest empress brought to him on occasion in an attempt to sire an heir, but thus far he had been unsuccessful. If Rikka didn't find herself with child soon, she'd follow in the footsteps of the others. All the way down to Level Thirteen. It would be a devastating fall.

Sebestyen forced Liane onto her back with a twist and a shove, and she laid her head upon a shimmering blue pillow and made up a story about the assassination. Something sufficiently sordid and violent to please the emperor.

He responded as he always did, caressing her as she told the tale. Listening attentively and touching her. Arousing her.

"Did you tell him, while he was inside you, that I ordered his death?"

"Of course, my lord," she whispered.

"Sebestyen," he commanded. "When we are in my bed I don't want to be emperor. Say it."

"Sebestyen," she said softly.

"Did he have his pleasure before you dispatched him?"

"No. I didn't fancy catching his seed. Only yours, Sebestyen."

"Do you love me, Liane?" he asked, taking one of her wrists in his hand and squeezing tight. Too tight.

She took a deep breath and exhaled. "No."

He grinned widely. "That's why you are my favorite. I have many women on Level Three, all of them younger than you, some of them prettier than you, all of them trained in the ways of carnal pleasure and anxious to please me. If I asked them if they loved me they would say yes without pause. And yet I crave you, Liane. Perhaps because you're more like me than anyone else. You're ruthless and passionate, cold and hot."

She wanted to scream *I am not like you!* But she didn't. To show emotion in Sebestyen's presence would be a mistake. If she showed emotion as the others sometimes did, he would grow tired of her and she'd lose her place on Level One. She wasn't finished here, not yet.

She reached down to grab him once again, to caress him with fingers that had been taught how to touch, how to arouse. "Love is for the weak. Do you think me weak, Sebestyen?"

"Never."

"Good." She licked her lips as she stroked his hard length. "I am not a girl who will fall in love because you have a prick and know how to use it. I am a woman who has become a soldier because you asked it of me, and I fight in your name. I kill in your name. I do as you bid me, here in your bed and elsewhere."

The emperor rolled atop her and spread her legs wide with his knee. His breathing came hard now; his face was flushed.

"You are a soldier, Liane. My soldier. Tonight you have done as I commanded, and as always you were faultless in the execution. What do you ask as your reward?" His voice was gruff, his eyes so deeply hooded they were almost closed.

Liane gave the answer that was expected of her. "Only you, Sebestyen. I want only you."

He filled her roughly and quickly, and she closed her eyes. She hated the Emperor Sebestyen. Despised him to the pit of her soul. But she had learned long ago that she couldn't fool him. Not here in his bed. She had faked her pleasure once, long ago, and he'd known. He'd hit her across the face before sending her back to Level Three, and it had been months before he requested her again. It was then that she had learned how strong he was, in spite of his slender build. It had been many years, but she had not forgotten.

She could not be caught in a lie. Not now, not when she was so close. He did not trust her, but she was as close to him as any minister or general or priest. She was closer than most. When things went bad for him—and that would happen, sooner or later—she would be here. She would be the one he turned to in troubled times. And when he did, she'd be ready.

For now, she turned her mind to other matters. While Sebestyen moved inside and above her, while he touched her as intimately as was possible for a man of his kind, while they gasped for breath and began to sweat and reached for the ultimate in physical pleasure . . .

Liane thought of the woman she might've been if she'd never been captured. She thought of the husband she might've had, the children she might've carried, the simple home in which she might've lived. In her mind, it was that man who joined with her. Not Sebestyen. Instead of a cruel ruler she would be mated to an ordinary man who would never share her, much less give her away on a whim. A farmer, perhaps, or an artisan. A man who truly loved her and would protect her.

And then she didn't think at all, she just felt. His body, hers, their quickened heartbeats and their heated breathing. Her body demanded satisfaction, and the man she hated more than life itself gave it to her.

Liane screamed with pleasure, her legs and arms wrapped around the man above her. She grabbed a handful of his hair and held on while wave after wave of release swept through her body. Her body bucked beneath Sebestyen's. It quivered and clenched. She shuddered and gasped, clutched desperately at the man above and inside her, and came back to reality to find cold eyes staring down at her as Sebestyen continued to ride her.

"Now do you love me?" he whispered hoarsely.

"No," Liane answered breathlessly as he pounded into her.

Sebestyen closed his eyes as he shook above her. She felt his seed infiltrating her. Tainting her. Poisoning her.

When he was finished he withdrew and rolled away. It was Liane's job to clean and dress him, and she did so wordlessly. She collected the ewer of water and the fine linen cloths that had been laid out for his use and placed them on the table nearest the bed. Using her gentlest touch, she bathed him. He reclined on the bed, sated and lazy, while she washed his entire body. She did not know where his mind had gone while she accomplished the chore, but he said nothing and did not fix his eyes upon her. Finally she collected his robe from the floor and helped him put it on. She even knelt before him on the mattress and fastened the braided buttons for him.

She was planning to bathe and dress herself and then go back to her own chamber for a good night's sleep—she'd gotten little sleep last night, after all—but Sebestyen sat up on the bed and reached for her again.

"I wish you could be my empress," he said as he grabbed a handful of her hair and pulled her toward him. He had never before said such a thing, and Liane did not know how to respond. "Rikka is a cheerless girl who finds sex a chore, not a pleasure. She lies beneath me limp and passionate as a pile of rags and says, 'I love you, my imperial highness. I love you so much, my lord and master. Oh, oh, I love you.'" He imitated the poor girl's high-pitched voice.

"She is young and foolish."

"If she does not get me an heir soon she will not have the chance to become old and foolish."

Liane wrapped her body around Sebestyen. Arms around his neck, legs around his waist. She grabbed his hair and held him in place while she looked deep into his cold eyes. "A concubine cannot become empress, as we both well know."

"The laws are mine," he said. "I can break them if I choose."

"And who will dispose of your enemies if I am locked up on Level Five having babies?"

Since three discarded empresses had already been dumped in Level Thirteen, she suspected it was Sebestyen himself who could not produce children. His second wife had become pregnant soon after their marriage, ending the whispers about Sebestyen's ability to produce an heir. But the empress had lost the child early on in the pregnancy, and there had not been another. Liane had often wondered if the girl had already been with child when she'd wed the emperor.

"I can serve you better in my present position," she said.

"I suppose you're right," he conceded.

She almost had him where she wanted him. She was so close. One day she would be able to come and go as she pleased. Level One would be at her disposal. This bedchamber, the emperor's offices, the ballroom where he gave audience to his subjects and servants. No guard would dare to stop or search her. She would have the complete trust of the emperor. "I enjoy my place in this palace, Sebestyen. I will be your lover, your slave, your assassin. I want nothing more."

He grinned widely, pleased with her answer. "Stay for a while, my lovely executioner. Rikka is to join me this evening, but I am not in the mood for sniffling declarations of love and a wife's cold penance."

Liane licked her lips and stroked his length beneath the crimson robe. Already he was growing hard again. "When she comes to you, tell her you don't feel well."

"I will have someone deliver that message for me," he suggested. "It distresses her to see you here, and while I really do not care if Rikka is distressed or not, it is annoying to hear her sniffle and moan."

She wanted to sleep. She wanted to escape the smell of this room and the sight of Sebestyen's cruel smile. But this was an opportunity she could not allow to pass by. What happened between now and the time she killed him did not matter. Nothing concerned her but the end of the game. Not what she had to do to get there, not what might happen to her after.

If he were ever foolish enough to fall asleep while she was in the room with him, she'd bash him over the head with the hideous bust of himself that sat on the opposite side of the room. She'd wrap a length of the cord that decorated his false window around his neck and squeeze until he stopped breathing. She wasn't strong enough to do that now, while he was awake and aware, but if she could catch him sleeping . . .

There would only be one chance, she knew that. If she failed, there would be no second opportunity. He had to trust her. In the end, he had to believe that she was his only ally in Columbyana.

5

SOPHIE SPENT HER MORNING COOKING, AS SHE OFTEN DID
when she was upset. Some days the noon meal was simple. A
stew, or vegetables from the garden, or cheese and her special
bread. When she was agitated the meal was more likely to be
a finely seasoned and perfectly roasted meat, three or four
vegetables—fried or boiled or both—her special bread, and a
choice of two desserts. This morning as she cooked she only
sniffled once or twice, and only two or three tears actually fell.
She allowed herself this luxury because she was alone in the
cabin. Neither Isadora nor Juliet would understand why she
was upset. She wasn't sure she understood herself.

The magnificent noon meal was almost prepared when a
knock sounded on the front door. Sophie wiped her hands on
her apron as she hurried to answer. It was probably someone
who'd come to see Juliet for an herbal medicine or medical
advice she decided as she blinked to make sure her eyes were
dry. No other visitors came to Fyne Mountain. Sophie flung
the door open and, surprisingly, saw Kane standing there.

Kane Varden filled the doorway, tall and broad and seething with anger. He didn't wear a fine suit today, but had clothed himself in a plain black shirt and trousers and those fine leather boots. His long hair was down, not restrained as it had been yesterday.

He had not been armed yesterday, either, but he was certainly armed today. A silver-handled dagger in a new-looking leather sheath hung from his belt, and a short-bladed sword with a slightly curved blade was suspended from the other side in a scabbard that also shone with newness.

"What do you want?" she asked sharply. "You shouldn't be here. Oh, this isn't a good idea, not at all. If Isadora sees you she'll . . . she'll . . ."

"She'll what?" he snapped.

She stepped forward and glanced past Kane to the barn where Isadora worked. "I told you I'm sorry. What else can I say?" A horrid thought occurred to her. "You don't still want to—" She stepped back.

"Marry you?" he finished for her, and then he gave her a grin that was so unlike yesterday's smile, she was momentarily shaken. There was no warmth or good humor in that tilt of the lips. "No, Angel, I'm not here to see you and I most certainly don't want to get married. I'm here to look in on the baby. Ariana is my daughter, after all."

"You want to see the baby?"

Kane nodded his head.

Her mouth went dry. Well, this was an unexpected development. "She's asleep."

"I'll wait."

"If Isadora finds you here—"

"I can handle your sister."

Sophie licked her dry lips. "This isn't a good idea."

"You already said that."

"I'll bring Ariana to town this afternoon as soon as she wakes up." It was a perfectly logical solution.

Though Kane didn't complain, she knew his headaches had not subsided. There was a telling wrinkle to his forehead, and she could actually see the pain in his eyes. She could also see how he fought the pain.

Tired of waiting for an invitation, he stepped into the house. Sophie backed up a few quick steps.

"I want to see where my daughter lives. Where she sleeps." The heels of Kane's boots clipped on the entryway floor, sharp and loud. It had been years since the sound of a man's footsteps had been heard in this house.

Sophie spun around and walked toward the bedroom where Ariana slept in her cradle. "Fine. If you insist you can look in on the baby. Then you have to leave, and you can't come back. Not ever."

"Why not?" He followed her, his steps slower than hers, longer and louder.

"Because Isadora—"

"This has nothing to do with Isadora."

"But she—"

"I'm not afraid of your sister."

Sophie screwed up her nose as she stepped into her bedroom and tiptoed to the cradle. Kane stood right beside her, his green eyes fixed on Ariana.

Everyone was afraid of Isadora. And after what she'd done to Kane, he most definitely should at least be worried. But he wasn't. Maybe he didn't think things could get any worse.

He was wrong.

His entire body relaxed while he looked down at Ariana. The tense muscles in his face eased, and his anger dissipated visibly. He didn't smile, exactly, but at least Kane looked like a man who could smile when the moment was appropriate.

"Is she a good baby?" he whispered.

"Oh, yes." Sophie smiled. "She's started sleeping through the night already."

"Really?"

"And she has a very sweet disposition."

One corner of Kane's mouth twitched. "She must get that from you."

"Perhaps."

He studied Ariana as if she were a work of art or a priceless treasure.

"She has your mouth," Sophie said softly.

"Do you think so?"

"And your chin," she added. "I wasn't sure about that until yesterday, because before . . ." Oh, she should not remind him of what had happened a year ago! "The beard," she said quickly.

Kane just nodded.

They looked down at Ariana for a moment, silent and maybe even content. It was Sophie who broke the silence with a whisper. "You shouldn't have come back."

"I didn't have any choice."

"I wanted you to be happy, and you would have been if only you'd stayed away."

Kane no longer stared at Ariana. He looked at Sophie so hard her knees wobbled. "Why?"

"If you hadn't come back Isadora never would've known about the spell, and you would still have your good fortune and your happiness . . . and . . ."

"That's not what I meant," he interrupted. "Why did you want me to be happy? Why did you care?" Such a question should not sound so fierce, but there was undisguised ire in Kane's soft voice.

"I'm not sure," Sophie whispered.

THREE THINGS HAPPENED AT ONCE. KANE WANTED TO KISS Sophie so much he could almost taste her; the baby woke up; the front door of the cabin opened and closed.

Sophie went pale. "It's Isadora and Juliet," she whispered. "They've come in for the noon meal."

"You go on," Kane said. He wasn't nearly as concerned about the eldest Fyne sister as Sophie. "I'll take care of the baby." He didn't intend to hide here, and even if the thought had crossed his mind, his horse was hitched out front. The sisters would know someone was here.

"You can't take care of the baby," she said.

"Why not?" If he was actually considering taking Ariana with him when he left, he'd have to get accustomed to taking care of her. Not that he'd seen anything thus far to indicate that the child was not being well cared for. The cabin was very nice. Solid outside, well furnished and clean inside. And Sophie obviously loved her daughter. But that didn't mean she'd make a good mother.

"She's hungry," Sophie said simply.

"Oh." It was true, he couldn't very well feed the baby. Not yet. How long before the baby would be weaned? And could he stand to wait around here until then?

Kane reached into the cradle and wrapped his hands around Ariana. She made him feel so big and awkward. So crude and unrefined. So . . . unworthy.

"Hold her for a moment while I get Juliet and Isadora situated. I'll be right back. If she cries, bounce her a little. She likes that."

Sophie dashed from the room. Did she think she could feed her sisters, feed her child, and sneak him out the front door while no one was looking?

Kane held Ariana to his shoulder, where she settled in quite nicely. The baby squirmed a little bit and mewed. It wasn't a cry exactly, but was certainly a prelude to one.

"There now," he said softly.

Immediately she went still and quiet. Was it the sound of his voice? Did she recognize him as her father, or would any man's deep voice soothe Ariana?

"You're so pretty," he said as he bounced her gently, as Sophie had instructed. "And your mama says you're a good baby, too. Can you say papa?"

His answer was a soft "goo" but a moment later Ariana began to cry. He bobbed up and down a little more vigorously, but it didn't do much good.

Kane stepped into the hallway, bouncing a crying Ariana as he walked toward the sounds of three distinct female voices. He wouldn't leave until he knew his child was safe here, and he couldn't take Ariana with him until she was weaned or he made arrangements to hire a wet nurse. If he was going to stick around for a few months, he wasn't going to hide. Not from Isadora, not from anyone.

"You're right," he said as he carried his daughter into the kitchen. "She's hungry."

Two women were seated at the table, and they both stared at him. Isadora's stare was impressive.

"You said the horse belonged to someone from town who wanted to see Juliet, and that this someone went for a walk to pass the time until we returned."

"Kane does need to see Juliet," Sophie said defensively. "He still has headaches." She looked at him, silently pleading him not to ruin her story, even as her face turned an unnatural shade of red. "And he did go for a walk . . . to Ariana's room . . ."

"Which is also your room," Isadora pointed out sourly.

"He came to see the baby and Juliet, not me," Sophie insisted.

"That's true," Kane said.

"The headaches are no better?" Juliet asked.

"They're fading but not gone." He'd tried to ignore the pain; he'd tried to push it deep. At least the headaches didn't blind him today.

"Do you feel like eating?" the redhead asked. "We have more than enough. Sophie outdid herself in the kitchen today."

Isadora shot her sister a censuring look, but it was too late. Kane, only partially out of spite, accepted the offer and took the fourth chair at the kitchen table. There was indeed more than enough food for three, and it all looked good. Was it possible that Sophie was not only beautiful and passionate and sweet, but was a good cook as well?

Sophie was by far the most beautiful of the Fyne sisters, but the other two were certainly striking women. Isadora was all angles, and she would never be called pretty. But she was attractive, and there was something almost regal about her. Juliet was pretty. She tried to appear staid and prim, but her unruly red hair and the sparkle in her warm brown eyes undid that design.

But it was Sophie who caught his eye and held it. Sophie who was so beautiful she should inspire paintings and grand novels and the undying affections of every man she met. Why was he her first lover? Why had there been no others?

Erasing Sophie Fyne from his mind was going to be much more difficult than seeing to Ariana's well-being. Perhaps if he could discover her flaws, he could forget about her more easily. Surely she had flaws. Lots of them. Beautiful women always did. They lied, they stepped on the feelings of those who were less beautiful, their vanity could be grating. They were unfaithful.

"I'll eat later," Sophie said as she took Ariana from his arms. Immediately the baby stopped crying and began to root around for her own noon meal. As Sophie turned away from the table she was already unbuttoning her dress. Kane watched her walk away, until she rounded the corner and disappeared from view.

When Sophie was gone, Kane studied her sisters; Isadora and then Juliet. One was angry, the other skeptical.

"You don't belong here." Isadora spoke in a lowered voice.

"Now, sister," Juliet said. "Mr. Varden is a guest, and he's

Ariana's father. The least we can do is feed him before he leaves."

He wasn't sure if she meant before he left the cabin or before he left Shandley altogether. Not that it mattered.

"What makes you think I'm leaving?"

No matter what happened with Ariana, Kane knew he needed to discover who had betrayed his unit more than a year ago by leading them into the ambush. Only then could he safely return to his place in the revolution. He was far away from the fighting and had been for the past year and two months. In all that time he hadn't run into anyone who recognized his name or his face—friend or foe.

It was Sophie's gift of good fortune that had protected him, he knew. Now that his good luck was gone he would have to be more careful. Judging by the expression on her face, he would do well to be very careful around Isadora Fyne.

All of a sudden her face softened. She almost smiled. If anything, Kane was more wary than ever. "I have a proposition for you, Mr. Varden," she said in a deceptively sweet voice.

"I know what you want from me," he said. "You want me gone. What do you think you have to offer in return?"

"Did you enjoy your good luck in the past year?" She kept her voice soft, no doubt so Sophie couldn't hear. "I took it away, and I can give it back. I can give you all you had and more. The pain—the headaches and the memories—I can take them away, too." She waved her hand. "Just like that, Mr. Varden."

He had no intention of taking the offer, but he asked one question anyway. "Would I remember Ariana and Sophie?"

"Of course not," she replied, thinking that she'd already won.

He wasn't that easily taken care of.

"No, thanks." Kane stood without taking a single bite, and

followed in Sophie's footsteps. One low, caustic word drifted to his ears as he walked away from her sisters.

Trouble.

KANE COULD BE VERY QUIET, WHEN HE CHOSE TO BE. SOPHIE didn't hear him coming down the hallway, not until it was too late. She shifted the blanket on her shoulder so that it covered her breasts and Ariana's head.

"What are you doing here? You haven't had time to eat."

"I came to this house to see Ariana, not to eat an awkward meal with your sisters."

Sophie dipped her head so she wouldn't have to look at him. In all her imaginings, it had never occurred to her that Kane might be interested in his daughter. She had never known her own father, and neither had Isadora or Juliet. Were they decent men who would have wanted to know their children? Until now she had never even considered the possibility.

"It's not proper for you to be here."

"I thought you didn't care about proper," he said as he walked into her room. He didn't hesitate, but reached out without shame to move the blanket that offered her some privacy. "Besides, I've seen this before."

Kane sat on the edge of her bed, since Sophie and Ariana occupied the only chair in the room. He made himself comfortable there, as if he belonged in this room. The sun that poured through her window caught the golden streaks in his hair and made them glimmer.

It was actually very pleasant to sit in her chair and look at him. There were so many nice things to admire. Strong hands, muscled forearms, those long legs and broad shoulders, all so decidedly male and deliciously potent. That strength was tempered with expressive green eyes, and extraordinary hair, and the most lovely pair of lips . . .

Kane was, she knew, the finest example of manhood she

would ever see. Determined, strong, scarred and sinewy . . . and still beautiful. How was that possible? How could a man be so very male and still be pretty?

"I never thought I'd have children," he said.

"Why not?"

He gave her a bitter smile. "When I met you last year, I didn't have anything to offer a woman or a child. I thought my life was over."

"Over?" she whispered.

"My family is gone, all dead. The farm where I grew up was taken over by the emperor's men years ago. They gave the land to the sheriff and burned the little house that wasn't nearly good enough for him." A muscle in his jaw twitched. "The woman who was supposed to become my wife got tired of waiting. I'd been gone a long time before she gave up on me. Maybe she figured after three years I wasn't ever coming home. Whatever the reason, she married someone else. Just as well."

There was more, she knew it instinctively, but Kane had said all he intended to say. "I'm sorry."

"Don't be," he said sharply. The way he furrowed his brow, she knew the headache was bothering him more than it had before. "I don't need your pity."

"What I feel isn't pity, it's sympathy. There is a difference, you know. You've known much heartache, and for that I *am* sorry."

The tension on his face did not ease. "Everyone dies eventually. We all lose the people we love."

Sophie opened her mouth to respond but Kane stopped her with a quick, "And please, don't try to soothe my pain with ridiculous tales of other worlds."

"I hope they're not ridiculous," she said. She really did like to think that her mother and Willym both lived on—somewhere other than the land of the dead.

"As for the land, I was never a good farmer," Kane said, ignoring her declaration. "My heart was not in it. And the other . . . well, women are fickle. I just learned that lesson later in life than most men."

"All women are not fickle," Sophie said defensively.

He did not look convinced. "Look at you. You say you'll take other lovers, when the time comes or the mood strikes you. No one man is good enough for you. No one man could ever be enough for you."

"Yes, but I've always been honest about the plans for my life."

"Angel, that's not a *plan*," he said sharply. "It's a convoluted whim."

She looked down at Ariana so she wouldn't have to see Kane's face. How could she explain to him that the life's plan he considered distasteful and shocking was her only option? The family curse made a normal life impossible for her. There could be no husband, not for her. The idea of living all her years without being touched, without being held—it made her cringe and shrivel, deep inside. She needed to be held, the way the earth needed the sun.

"I wouldn't make a good wife," she said softly. "Not for you, not for anyone."

The room was so quiet, she looked up to make sure Kane was still sitting on the bed.

"Why would you say that?" he asked.

"I can't deny who I am. *What* I am."

"A witch."

Sophie nodded.

"If you're a true witch, if you can do magic, why are you hiding on this forsaken mountain? Why aren't you sitting in a palace somewhere, dressed in silk and draped in jewels and being waited on hand and foot by those who adore or fear you?"

There was so much anger in his voice and in his eyes. Those green eyes that had haunted her dreams, then and now.

"This is my home. I wouldn't be happy anywhere else."

"Have you ever been anywhere else?"

"No."

"Then how do you know you wouldn't be just as happy?"

His attempt at logic did not sway her. "I have no especially useful talents. I can't read minds or manipulate objects, and my abilities with traditional spells are, well, less than impressive. One out of ten might work as it should. I make things grow, that's all. And even if I did have a more imposing talent, I wouldn't want to be some man's puppet or weapon. Here I am my own woman, and . . ." And Isadora's spell kept unwanted men away. Usually. "You should not have come back here. We would all be much happier if you had never returned."

"Then I never would've seen Ariana. I wouldn't even have known she existed."

Her heart thudded, her mouth went dry. "It's hardly a fair trade. You're still having headaches, and there won't be any more good luck coming your way." She hoped there wasn't a glut of bad luck to balance the scales she'd thrown out of whack. It was too soon to tell. "And you remember—"

"Yesterday I lost something I shouldn't have had in the first place," he interrupted. "Does it hurt? Hell yes, it does. Do I wish I didn't remember some of the things that happened to me in the past? You bet. Ask me if I'd go back, if I had the choice. Ask me if I'd trade finding you again and seeing the baby for a return to the mindless bliss of my past year."

Sophie swallowed. Kane couldn't do this to her. He couldn't sit here and make her like him all over again. He couldn't actually tell her that he'd rather be in physical and mental pain than lose Ariana, a child he hadn't even known of until yesterday. He had no idea how dangerous this could be.

"Ask me," he said again.

Sophie shook her head.

"Fine, I'll tell you anyway. Ariana's real and she's mine."

"Ariana's not yours. She's . . ." Sophie started to say *mine*, but realized that was wrong. "Ours," she finished softly.

Kane shook his head. "When I saw the two of you yesterday, there was no question in my mind. We'd get married, we'd have more babies, we'd . . ." He wisely did not finish.

"You don't still think—" Sophie said.

"No," Kane answered quickly and without trepidation. "Even if I didn't remember everything from before, I certainly don't want a wife whose intent is to take lovers as she sees fit."

Sophie felt a blush rise to her cheeks. "It never occurred to me to be your wife."

"I understand that."

It surely wasn't wise to talk about the morning they'd met. Keeping Kane at a distance would be so much easier if she didn't remember, so vividly, what his body had felt like against and inside hers. But having him here, sharing a moment with their child—she couldn't make herself pretend that what had happened didn't mean anything to her.

"I didn't know with certainty, when I went to you that morning, that we would make a child, but later, it seemed as if I had always known."

"I didn't even believe that you were real for a day or more."

She switched Ariana to the other breast, and Kane watched closely. Talking about their first meeting seemed to make him uncomfortable. It certainly didn't help her to relax.

"How long are you going to stay in Shandley?" she asked.

He lifted his head, and when their eyes met Sophie's heart leapt. She could not allow a man, any man, to have this kind of effect on her!

"I haven't decided," he answered. "I need to rejoin the rebels, but there's some work to do before I can reclaim my place."

"What kind of work?"

After a short pause he said, "I don't think I should tell you."

She tried not to be hurt that he didn't trust her. After all, why should he confide in her? They were strangers still. Lovers, parents, and strangers. "In any case, you really shouldn't stay long."

"Worried about what people will say?"

Sophie smiled. "I ceased to care what people said about me when I was eleven years old. When your mother, grandmother, and two older sisters are impressive witches, people don't exactly say kind things about you."

"What about you?" he asked. "Aren't you an impressive witch, too?"

She shook her head. "No. I do have some newly discovered abilities, but I am nowhere near as capable as my sisters." She didn't tell him that those powers had been increased a hundredfold while Ariana had been growing inside her.

"Why do you stay here?" he asked, his voice lowered so no one else in the house could overhear. "You're so beautiful, any man in the world would be happy to have you as his wife. You could leave this place, find yourself a wealthy man, make your own family—"

"And deny who I am?" She didn't tell Kane that the very idea of leaving Fyne Mountain terrified her. "No. I'm satisfied here. I have a home and my child and—"

"*Our* child," he corrected her.

"Our child," she said reluctantly. "And I have my sisters. I don't want or need anything else to make my life complete."

He didn't argue with her, but she could see very clearly that he didn't believe her. Unfortunately, she didn't truly believe herself.

One question had been nagging at her for the past couple of days. The answer was not important, since she had no intention of falling in love, and still . . . she had to know.

"How old are you?" she asked, her eyes not on Kane but on Ariana.

"Twenty-eight."

Her heart hitched a little. When she began to like Kane too much, she'd have to remind herself that if she made the mistake of loving him, he wouldn't live another two years.

6

OVER A GAME OF WHIST IN THE TAVERN BELOW HIS RENTED room, Kane confirmed that his lucky streak was indeed finished. Last night he'd lost everything he'd won a few days earlier—and then some. Worse, he was almost certain that the deputy who'd been drinking at the bar had eyed him suspiciously as he'd climbed the stairs, shortly before midnight. For a year no one had recognized him, but his magical luck was over and he'd have to be more careful from here on out.

No more gambling, at least for a while. He had to make the cash he had left last. It had to last until he departed the Southern Province and headed north to find Arik. From what he heard in the tavern, that's where the bulk of the fighting was these days, in the city of Falsha near the Northern Palace where Emperor Sebestyen's eldest sister and her husband lived.

Since his luck had been so terrible last night, he was surprised when he answered a knock at his door to find not the curious deputy or a gambler from the past out for his blood, but Sophie Fyne, dressed in a pale green gown that hugged her curves to show her fine figure to its best advantage. It was not high-necked, like some of her everyday frocks; the collar dipped softly, draping in spring green folds around her bosom. She did not have the baby with her this morning. He didn't know whether to be disappointed or intrigued.

"Come in." He stepped back to give her room to enter and she did, but not without a suspicious glance to his bare chest.

"You're not dressed."

"You've seen me in less," he said as she closed the door behind her. For a woman who claimed to be free-spirited and interested only in physical pleasure, she certainly did blush deeply.

"We need to talk," she said, sitting on the edge of a chair.

"Where's Ariana?" he asked.

"With Juliet. I thought perhaps we should have a few minutes alone."

He raised his eyebrows.

"To *talk,*" she insisted.

Kane sat on the side of the bed facing her, hands on knees, stomach churning. "Talk away."

Sophie straightened her spine and threaded the fingers of her hands together. She clasped those hands so tightly the knuckles went white. "The next time you want to see Ariana—"

"I was thinking about this afternoon," he interrupted.

Sophie's eyes widened. "So soon? You just saw her yesterday. She hasn't changed or learned anything new. I thought perhaps you'd like to see her once or twice a week and we could make arrangements so that Isadora could be elsewhere or else Ariana and I could come to see you, rather than you making the trip to the cabin."

He had to smile at her protests. She was so intense and determined. "How would you like to see your child once or twice a week?"

"That's different. I'm her mother."

"I'm her father."

"But until a few days ago you didn't even know she existed!"

"That only means I have lots of catching up to do."

"But—"

"Besides," he interrupted her again. "I can't stay here indefinitely. I'll be moving on soon, and I don't know when I'll be back. Once or twice a week is entirely unacceptable."

She had no argument for that. "I did not think you would care at all," she said softly.

"I do."

"I can see that." Her gaze dropped, and she fixed her eyes on his bare chest. "Does it hurt, still?" she asked softly.

He glanced down to see that she stared at the scar he so rarely thought about. How had he ignored that telling mark so completely for the past year?

Magic.

"No."

"What happened?"

The pale and puckered flesh so close to his heart was not the only scar on his body, but it was the worst. He didn't want to tell Sophie the details; he knew without doubt that she was not made for tales of war and bloodshed, but for the consolation that came after.

The only spoils of war he'd ever wanted were a safe home, a happy family, and a woman like this one to hold it all together. He'd given up on those dreams long ago.

"It's a boring story, Angel. Not fit for your pretty ears."

"I'm tougher than I look," she insisted, haughtily lifting her chin.

"I don't doubt it." She didn't look tough at all. She looked fragile, feminine. She was everything he had ever wanted and never expected to have. She'd kept him going through hard times long before he'd ever met her, this dream woman. This Angel. How could he look at her and not think about the day they'd met?

"I don't remember kissing you," he said, and she jumped in her seat. "Did I?"

She averted her eyes. "Well, not on the, uh, mouth," she answered.

He lifted his eyebrows slightly. How much of that encounter had he forgotten? "Where did I . . ."

Sophie stood briskly, and the fine fabric of her gown danced around her. "I didn't come here to talk about that. If you want to see Ariana we need to make arrangements. I can't have you showing up at the cabin without warning. If Isadora is in a bad mood—"

"I'm not afraid of Isadora."

"You should be."

Kane stood slowly, taking a deep breath and letting his muscles uncoil. Yes, he did want to see his daughter frequently, while he still could. But right now he was more concerned with getting Sophie in his bed again. Just once. One time when he was clearheaded and could remember every detail.

"What if I want to see you?"

She shook her head. "I will be there when you come to see Ariana or when I bring her to you, but—"

"That's not enough."

She backed away from him until her spine was pressed against the door, and he kept moving until he was directly in front of her. This close it was impossible not to be affected.

"It will have to be enough," she whispered.

He dipped his head to bring his face close to hers. "Admit it, Sophie. You still want me. We were good together and next time—"

"There won't be a next time."

He ignored her. "Next time we'll be even better than before. I won't be hungover and wounded, you won't be a virgin. We can make love all night on a nice, soft bed."

She licked her lips. "All night? That's not necessary, or even possible. Is it?"

"For someone who claims to be a woman who's interested in nothing but sex from a man, you seem to know very little about the possibilities."

"I know everything I need to know," Sophie insisted. She put on a pretty good show, but there was more than a touch of uncertainty in her voice.

"Do you?" he whispered. "Are you sure?" With an insistent finger hooked beneath an impossibly creamy chin, he tipped her face up. Blue eyes sparkled, pale cheeks flushed pink, and lush lips trembled just before he touched them with his own.

At first Sophie kissed like a woman who had never been kissed before. Tentative. Uncertain. She held her breath and did not move. And then her lips parted slowly and surely. Her tongue answered his. She made an interesting little noise deep in her throat.

No, on that day they'd first met he had not kissed her. Magic or no magic, he would've remembered something as fine and stirring as this. The woman kissed with her body and her soul. She drew him in with every breath, with every taste. She tasted like sunshine.

He ended the kiss because he knew if he didn't he would take her here, against the door.

Her eyes had gone dreamy; her lush lips looked well kissed. It was a sight to grab any man's baser instincts and hold on. Hard.

"Your cabin, this afternoon," he said, his voice gruffer than he'd intended. "I don't care if your sister is there or not."

"I can bring Ariana to town—"

"No." He was still worried about that deputy who had checked him over in the tavern last night. Better to keep his family away from potential trouble.

His family.

Kane's heart lurched. Like it not, that's what Sophie and Ariana were. His family. His blood. All he had left in this world.

DO YOU? ARE YOU SURE?

Sophie hurried down the road, her step quick. She didn't quite run, but she moved at what was definitely more than a leisurely walk. She was anxious to see her daughter, she reasoned, that's why she walked so quickly toward home.

Her mind was not on her daughter at the moment, but instead was firmly set on the child's father. What kind of possibilities had Kane been talking about? And what was that nonsense about making love all night? The first and only time they'd had sex, the deed had been over quite successfully in a matter of minutes. The blood rushed through her veins too hot, and her heart beat too fast. All she could think about were Kane's words, and the way the very sight of him affected her, and the way he kissed . . .

She felt very much as she had a year ago, when she'd first met Kane Varden. On fire. Incomplete. Wanting. Oh, why had he come back? Why could she still feel his lips on hers? Still taste him, still feel that odd weakness in her knees . . .

"What a surprise to see you in town again so soon."

Sophie stopped and took a deep breath before she turned to face Galvyn Farrell. She'd almost reached the edge of town and safety; the main thoroughfare of Shandley stretched behind the man who'd stopped her, bustling as a healthy town should. The people who walked and shopped and played there paid her no mind, except to cast the occasional quick and suspicious glance her way.

She knew they would pay her much more mind if she were walking toward them instead of away.

"You look particularly lovely today," Galvyn said, his gaze raking over her.

Sophie had chosen her gown with Kane in mind, though she had not admitted as much to herself as she'd taken it from her wardrobe. She wanted him to think she was pretty and desirable and worthy of affection and admiration. She had not dressed nicely for Galvyn Farrell.

She was going to have to get past this silly infatuation with the father of her child. Had her mother mooned over a man, ever? Of course not. Had she been so foolish as to fall in love? Never.

"Mr. Farrell," she said, trying to make her heart be still. "How very nice to see you again."

He gave her a surprised and charming smile. "You must call me Galvyn, Sophie. We are friends, after all. Aren't we?"

"Of course."

He looked her up and down as if he appreciated what he saw. Sophie pushed aside the initial impulse to be insulted.

"There's going to be a town dance tomorrow night," he said.

"I didn't know."

"I was afraid word hadn't reached everyone on the outskirts of town. I do hope you'll be there."

For a moment, Sophie didn't know what to say. No one had ever invited her or her sisters to participate in any of the town socials.

"There will be music and dancing," Galvyn said. "I was hoping if I asked soon enough you'd save a dance for me."

Sophie shook her head. She knew what kind of reception she'd get from everyone else in town, if she were so foolish. "That's very sweet, but I can't."

"Please," he said softly. "I so have my heart set on a dance with you."

Sophie looked at Galvyn in an entirely unbiased way. It was true she had never liked him much, but perhaps she'd been hasty. He had some unpleasant qualities, but he had good qualities, too. A handsome face, well-groomed hair, a healthy-looking body. If she were to stand Galvyn and Kane side by side, would she really find her daughter's father so much more appealing? If the beat of her heart and the low roil in her belly were telling her that it was time to take another lover, would Galvyn not do as well as Kane—or any other man? If she approached her newfound life with complete abandon, what did it matter whether or not she liked him?

Somehow she knew that falling in love would never be a danger with this man.

"Perhaps I will stop by, for a short time," she finally agreed.

"And you will dance with me?"

"Yes." Sophie tried to forget about Kane's kiss. She was a grown woman, much too strong to have her will tested in such a simple way.

"I know you have not been involved in the town's social activities in the past, but it's time to remedy that oversight, Sophie. At the summer dance, those ladies of a marriageable age who are looking for a husband wear white frocks to let the townsfolk know they're ready for that important step. If you were to wear white . . ."

"I don't own a white dress," she said quickly. "And even if I did I would not wear it."

"I have a few ready-made white dresses in my store, one in particular that I think would be lovely on you. I can have it delivered this afternoon."

"No one delivers to the cabin," she argued. "It's too far."

"If I ask, it will be done."

Sophie shook her head quickly. She most certainly did not want to advertise the desire for a husband when she had none!

Galvyn took a step closer to her. "The gown will be my gift to you. All I ask in way of thanks is that perhaps after the dance you'll allow me the honor of walking you home."

Her heart lurched unpleasantly. Surely her mother had never been intimate with a man she didn't even *like*. Besides, Galvyn had mentioned marriage on more than one occasion. It wouldn't do to encourage him in any way. "Actually, I'm not sure that I'll be able to attend."

In spite of her protest, he seemed very pleased with himself. "I understand Sheriff Kynyn might stop by tomorrow evening. He's an old friend, you know."

"I believe I've heard you mention that before."

"He'd love to meet you. There's not a woman in the capital city who can rival your beauty, Sophie."

She averted her eyes. "I'm sure that's not true."

"I'm just as sure that it is." Galvyn glanced over his shoulder. His shop was located at this end of town; she'd walked right past it on her way home. Galvyn also owned the livery and a sweet shop and a couple of other businesses, though he did not run those himself. He had purchased them from merchants who found themselves down on their luck, and now paid those former owners a pittance to see to the operation of the businesses, while he took the profits.

"I must get back to the shop," he said. "When I saw you pass I wanted to ask you about tomorrow night."

Relieved that the encounter was almost done, Sophie said, "I'm sure you have more important things to do, and I really must get home."

"Tomorrow night, then," he said as he backed away. "I'll have that gown delivered this afternoon, just in case you change your mind."

Sophie forced a smile as she shook her head. "Please, don't. Your kind invitation is gift enough."

It was ridiculous to be so skittish where Galvyn Farrell was concerned. What better way to erase one man from the mind than to embrace another?

Surely her mother had been with more than three men in her lifetime. Not every encounter had left her with child, and it would be that way with Sophie. With some men, the rendezvous would be entirely about pleasure.

Sophie wrinkled her nose. When she tried to imagine taking such a step, she felt nothing. No excitement, no yearning. And yet, loveless encounters were all she could ever have, where romance was concerned.

She had to consider the possibilities that would come with such encounters. Would the herbs Juliet gave to those women in town who wanted to prevent babies work for Sophie? She didn't think so. She was different from other women in more ways than one.

Did it matter overmuch? There were four years between Isadora and Juliet, two between the middle Fyne sister and Sophie. But there was no reason for her to follow her mother's example exactly. Her children might be closer together in age than she and her sisters were, but think of what fun they'd have growing up together!

Sophie's step slowed as she approached the path that turned and twisted up the side of Fyne Mountain. She could only fool herself to a certain degree. She wasn't ready for another child. She kicked at the dirt at her feet. And hadn't she just promised herself that she would not take another lover who knew where to find her? Galvyn had already expressed an interest in marrying her, for goodness' sake. Taking him as a lover would be foolish beyond belief.

She had never dreamed of those dark brown eyes.

To be honest, she wasn't ready to sleep with another man. Not yet. But maybe if Kane believed she would take that step he'd quit kissing her until her clothes felt heavy and scratchy, and he'd stop looking at her as if he knew something she did not. And he wouldn't talk about making love all night and . . . possibilities.

Do you? Are you sure?

*   *   *

SOMEHOW SOPHIE HAD GOTTEN RID OF HER SISTERS. KANE didn't ask how. He didn't care. Today the three of them—his woman and his child and himself—were alone, sitting in the parlor this time instead of the more intimate bedchamber.

"Ariana sleeps a lot," he said as he rocked the slumbering baby.

"She's three months old," Sophie said softly. "Of course she sleeps a lot."

For as long as he could remember, this was what he'd wanted. A cabin far away from war, a woman, a child.

But the cabin wasn't his. Neither was the woman. The child was his, though. Beautiful and heartwarming proof that no matter how bleak and hopeless his circumstances had become, life continued on.

He already knew he couldn't take her from Sophie. The Fyne sisters were witches, and there was magic in this cabin. But Ariana was well loved. Besides, it would destroy Sophie to lose her child. He wouldn't do that to her.

"I've been invited to the town social tomorrow night," Sophie said, her voice too quick to be casual. "A local gentleman asked me to attend, so that we might dance."

"What man is this?"

She blushed. "A very important local merchant. He's good friends with the sheriff."

"And is this merchant to be your next lover?"

Sophie hesitated, but not for very long. "Perhaps."

He could not bear to think of Sophie with another man. His reaction made no sense, since there were no bonds between them but for Ariana. But then, what did make sense these days?

"Would you do me a favor?" he asked gently.

"If I can."

"Don't take up with another man until after I'm gone. I don't want to watch you dance with someone else, much less think of . . ." He stopped. No, he could not bear it. "I won't ask you to wait very long. I'll be leaving soon." He rocked in time with his own steady heartbeat.

"Where will you go?" Sophie asked softly. He'd expected happiness at the news that he wouldn't be around much longer to harass her and annoy her sisters, but she sounded almost disappointed.

"I need to find the leader of the rebels. Arik."

"You've been gone more than a year. Won't they wonder where you've been?"

Kane laughed lightly. "Oh, yes. They'll wonder."

He glanced up to watch the woman who sat just a few feet away, her hands in her lap and her eyes on the baby who slept in his arms. How could he be so sure he'd miss Sophie Fyne with all his heart, when in truth he barely knew her?

"Before you go, I want you to talk to Juliet," Sophie said, her voice too quick. "Let her hold your hand for just a few moments, and she can tell you where future dangers might be lurking for you along the road. And perhaps Isadora can cast a protective spell over you. If we ask nicely and I make her something special to eat and we assure her that you're really leaving, maybe we can convince her. I'm not sure how effective the spell will be once you venture away from Fyne Mountain, but it would be worth a try."

"Why?"

She raised her eyes to look squarely at him. "I know little of war, but I do understand its dangers. If you know where peril awaits you can avoid it. And a simple protective spell might bring back a touch of the good luck you've enjoyed for the past year. If all goes well, someday you might return here. To see Ariana, of course," she added quickly. "I never knew my father. Since you've found us and there's nothing to be done for that, then you might as well be a part of her life."

She would not admit as much, not out loud, but she wanted him to survive. He wished he could tell her that was likely. "I don't think your sisters will do anything to protect me."

"They will if I—"

"I don't want you to beg for me, Sophie. I've survived this long without magic. Maybe I can survive a while longer on my own."

She did not look convinced. "At least ask Juliet for a warning or two about your immediate future."

The sight, Gudny had called it. If Juliet Fyne was indeed psychic, why did she live here on a mountainside far away from everyone and everything of importance? Magic was revered in the big cities, not feared as it was among simpler folk like the ones who disparaged the Fyne sisters at every opportunity. She could make a fortune if she aligned herself with the right people. Perhaps her talents were weak. Perhaps she wasn't psychic at all.

"I'm more interested in the past than in the future," he said absently. If he could discover who had betrayed his unit, then gather the evidence to prove that he was innocent, he'd soon be in Arik's good graces.

"Juliet says the past is much easier to see than the future," Sophie said. "Some parts of what is to come are potentially open to change, whereas the past is set in stone. Done and done, she says. But what good will looking into the past do you?"

It might be worth a try. Wouldn't hurt. "There are a few things I need to know before I rejoin the rebels."

Her face went very pale. Was she worried? Why, when she proclaimed to care nothing at all for him? "When I first saw you, you wore a cloak adorned with the rebel emblem."

"I lost it, shortly after leaving this place."

Of course he had lost it. Anyone who saw that design would know he was a rebel, and that would've put a quick end to his streak of good fortune.

"Why do you want to rejoin them?" she asked, almost impatiently. "Most of the fighting seems to be in the Northern and the Western Provinces, so I have heard very little about the revolution, and to be honest I know nothing at all about warfare. But I know your forces are too small to defeat the emperor's army. It is a lost cause, Kane. Are you willing to sacrifice your life for a fight that cannot be won?"

A year ago, the answer had been a resounding yes. Holding Ariana, he had to hesitate before answering. "Yes."

"That's . . . that's silly."

"Silly?"

"You cannot win," she said sternly. "It would be foolish to sacrifice your life because the illegitimate son of the old emperor thinks he should be on the throne rather than his legitimate half-brother. What difference does it make to your life who sits in the royal palace?"

"You have no idea," he said softly.

"Then tell me," Sophie whispered. "Make me understand."

He had never shared the dark moments of his life with anyone. In the past few years, he and Duran had stopped talking about Valdis and Stepan. They never mentioned Liane and the possibility that she might still be alive. It had been such a long time. Would they even know her if they saw her?

Not *they,* not anymore. Duran was gone, too. Duran, who fought harder than any of them. Duran, who had cried when they'd buried Valdis after the battle of Lyliantha and then fought all the harder the next day.

Duran, who had lost his head to the blade of an imperial infantryman who wished to put it on display.

"Do you really want to know?" he asked.

Sophie nodded her fair head.

"Promise me that you won't take up with another man until after I leave here, and I'll tell you everything."

She agreed quickly, before he had even finished his sentence. He stared into her intense blue eyes as he began to speak.

7

SOPHIE STARED WITH HORROR AT THE MONSTROUS WHITE gown that was spread across her bed. If this is what Galvyn Farrell thought of her, she was glad she'd promised Kane she wouldn't go to the dance.

Juliet reached out and touched a wide ruffle as if there might be snakes hidden within the folds of stiff, heavy fabric. "It is very . . . fancy," she finished suspiciously.

"Some women might find it an attractive garment," Sophie suggested, trying to be charitable. No one she knew would find it attractive, of course, but then she didn't know many women or what they liked. Isadora would roar with laughter at the very thought of her little sister wearing this much-adorned, full skirted, high-necked, lace-bedecked curiosity.

She was glad Kane had departed before Galvyn's errand boy had arrived with the gift. Well, the errand boy had not arrived, precisely. He'd tossed the package containing the gown at the Fyne doorstep, knocked loudly, and run. She didn't want to explain to Kane that Galvyn had actually suggested that they marry. She didn't want anything, not even a small annoyance, to come between them in the small amount of time they had left.

"I'll return it tomorrow, when I go to town to see Kane."

Juliet sighed. "Isadora is not pleased that Ariana's father has been coming around. I know it's best that you meet him elsewhere, but I hate for you to go into Shandley so often. Especially if Galvyn Farrell is sending you gifts and inviting you to town socials."

"What choice do I have?" Sophie asked.

"Send him away," Juliet suggested. "The sooner the better."

She would agree with her sister, if she didn't now know more about Kane than she wanted to. It was no one's fault but her own. She'd asked. More than that, she'd truly wanted to know.

He'd had so little happiness in his life, she could not be sorry that she'd given him a year of good luck. She could not be sorry that she'd found him beneath the linara tree and seduced him. And she most certainly could not hurry him along on his journey, not if it meant a return to a joyless life.

"If Kane asked you some questions about the past, would you be able to help him?"

"What kinds of questions?"

Sophie didn't want to share the entire tale with Juliet. Kane didn't give much of himself to others, she knew that. Until she knew without question that Juliet would be able to help, she would not spread the tale of his life as if it were gossip. "Questions about the actions of others, actions that deeply affected his life."

"Perhaps. I never know what I'm going to see. You know that."

"Yes, I know." There was something else she needed to know. Asking was not so easy. "Could you give me something to prevent conception, should I decide to lie with him again?"

Again Juliet sighed, but she was not surprised. "I don't

think so. We could try, but I suspect you will need something extraordinary."

"I found myself with child the first time I lay down with a man. Is that unusual? Does it mean that every time I—"

"I don't know," Juliet interrupted, her lips puckering just slightly.

"Will you give it some thought?" Sophie asked. She had a distinct feeling that before Kane left town they'd be together again. Every time she looked at him, her body reacted in some telling way.

"Do you love him?" Juliet asked.

She should have been prepared for that question, but she was not. The proper response would be an unequivocal "no," but that's not the answer that sprang to her lips. "I like Kane very much, but as you well know, loving him is not an option."

Juliet put an arm around Sophie's shoulders. "I'm sorry. It isn't fair."

"Not to any of us," Sophie said stoically.

"I like my life as it is," Juliet said. "I truly want no man to be a part of it. Isadora misses Willym terribly, I know that well, but at least she knew true love once. But you . . . Sophie, there are moments when I feel so certain that you were put on this earth to love and be loved."

It was a dream, one she could never realize. "I do like Kane more than I should." Sophie slipped out of her sister's embrace, before Juliet could sense the uncertainty in her heart and mind. "And I've been having the dreams again." Lovely, long, real, disturbing dreams. "Please be assured that what I have with him now won't lead to marriage. Kane just . . . He needs me." She didn't want to worry about what would happen to him when he left the Southern Province, but she knew where he was going and what kind of life he was returning to.

"I'm drawn to him much as I was a year ago, but it's too soon for me to have another child. Don't you have anything that will help?"

"Nothing I could offer with confidence."

"I have something that will work."

Sophie and Juliet both turned their heads to watch Isadora enter the room. The eldest Fyne sister glanced at the cradle where Ariana slept, then at the bed where the white gown was laid out. Her grin was wide. "If you wear this dress I doubt you'll have to worry about birth control of any kind. It's hideous. What were you thinking?"

As Sophie told her sister that the dress was a gift from Galvyn Farrell, and also explained the significance of wearing white to the summer social, Isadora's smile died.

"Willym never trusted him," she said softly when Sophie was finished.

Sophie took her sister's hand and squeezed tight, but after a moment Isadora gently pulled her hand away. She had never been one for displays of affection, but that did not mean she didn't love her sisters dearly.

"Do you really know of a potion to keep me from conceiving, if I do decide to lie with Kane again?"

Isadora sighed. "Yes, I do," she said reluctantly.

"What is it?" Sophie had to tilt her head back slightly to look her sister in the eye. Isadora's dark eyes and her own blue ones were as different as night and day. In truth, she had very little in common with her elder sister.

"A bit of magic together with a bit of herbs mixed in the proper proportions," Isadora said.

"And you will help me?"

Again, that sigh. "I do not approve of Kane Varden, you know that. Getting involved with a man like that one is bound to bring trouble to this house. But you are a grown woman capable of making your own decisions and I won't stand in your way if he is what you want."

"He is," Sophie whispered.

"When?"

Sophie thought of the way her body responded when she

looked at Kane, the dreams she'd been having of late, and the way she woke in the night feeling empty and aching and on the edge of a scream.

"Tomorrow," she said. "Tomorrow night."

WHILE HER SISTERS AND HER NIECE SLEPT, ISADORA walked away from the cabin she called home. She had dressed for bed hours ago. Her feet were bare, her linen shift so thin the cool night breeze cut through to her skin. The further away from the house and her family she got, the easier and fuller her heart felt. Expectation was a wonderful and terrible thing.

There was not a cloud in the sky tonight, and the half-moon shone brightly to light her way. Over rocky ground and through a thick patch of trees she traveled, until she arrived at the clearing where she passed so many restless nights.

Maybe tonight he would be here, but she could not be sure. He came less and less often. In the past year, how many nights had she sat on a rock waiting for him to come? Waiting, and waiting, and waiting. It didn't matter the season or the weather. She would endure anything to see Willym again, even for a few moments.

She sat on a flat rock, lifted her arms, and looked up at the moon as she whispered her husband's name. The darkness remained quiet and free of spirits, so she began to recite the spell that had brought him to her on other nights. She whispered soft words, strange incantations in the ancient language her mother had taught her, and she controlled the energy she created with the sway of her hands. It was almost like a dance, the way she used her hands to direct the flow of her power. She asked that her husband be returned to her, and when that didn't work she demanded that he appear before her.

In the beginning, when she had been so wretched with grief that she'd wanted to die, the spell had worked without fail. But as the months and years passed, it was as if he were fighting her. The spell didn't work every time.

It did not work tonight, and she sat on the rock with tears streaming down her face and her heart pounding too fast.

"I never should've loved you. You never should've left me," she said as she swiped angrily at her tears. "We were supposed to be together forever." Two years was well short of forever. The short years of her marriage seemed like the twinkling of an eye, they had passed too quickly.

The five years since his death had passed with excruciating leisure.

Isadora reclined on the flat rock and stared at the moon and the stars. "If I had known my love would kill you, I would have sent you away the first time you came calling. Senseless man," she whispered. "Most men know better than to court a witch, but not you. You were . . . fearless when it came to love."

Willym had not cared for her use of witchcraft, and she had indulged him by using her talents infrequently. Her husband had loved her as a woman, not as a witch, and for those two precious years . . .

"Sophie doesn't understand why I dislike her Kane Varden so much," she said, her voice directed to the sky, since Willym chose not to appear tonight. "She doesn't know how much it will hurt if she falls in love with him and he is taken from her, the way you were taken from me. How do I explain that to her without breaking down and crying?" She had to be strong, for her sisters and for herself. She wouldn't sob and beg like an old woman. "How do I explain without feeling that awful, deep pain all over again?" She crossed her arms across her chest. "I would do anything to keep her from experiencing the hurt I felt when you left me."

"Don't cry, Izzy." The wind whispered in her husband's voice.

Isadora sat up quickly, her eyes scanning the clearing. At first she saw nothing, and then he was there. He stood fifteen feet away, smiling and dressed as he had been on that final day, in a white shirt and tan work pants and those worn boots she'd hated and he'd adored. He was solid for a moment, and then he started to fade away.

"No!" She leapt from the rock and ran toward him, her steps long and quick. "Don't go!"

But Willym faded before she reached him, as he always did, and all she had left of him was that whisper on the wind that teased her ears once again.

"Don't cry, Izzy."

MUTED STRAINS OF MUSIC REACHED SOPHIE'S EARS AS SHE hurried toward town. The social was to take place in Elmyr Cadman's warehouse at the other end of town, so hopefully no one would see her walking into Shandley for the second time today.

On her first visit, she'd returned the white dress to a surprised and unhappy Galvyn Farrell, and then she and Ariana had spent some time with Kane. They'd met at his rented room above the tavern, and then when the confines of the room became too much they went for a long walk. Away from town, not through it. They'd found a pretty, quiet spot where a bubbling brook ran across sparkling rock, and wildflowers and thick grass grew on the bank. They'd sat there for hours. They'd talked a while, and she'd laughed at the way Kane played with his daughter.

He loved his child, of that she had no doubt.

Tonight Sophie was alone. Juliet and Isadora were watching Ariana, who was down for the night.

Sophie fingered the vial in her pocket, and her heart hitched. The potion was not for her, as she'd expected, but for

Kane. Isadora said he was to drink it, and once that was done they had to wait for at least a quarter of an hour before uniting their bodies.

Kane didn't know she was going to him tonight. What if he wasn't there? What if he didn't want her?

She dismissed her reservations. He might not be in his room, but he did want her. It was in his eyes, in the way he touched her, in the way his body shifted when he saw her. Yes, he wanted this night as much as she did.

All night, he'd said. *Possibilities.*

She'd dressed for the occasion in something much more fitting than Galvyn Farrell's ridiculously ornate gown. Her gown was of the palest blue and hung in soft layers to midcalf. The hem was uneven, angular and irregular and layered, and it floated around her legs when she walked. The neckline of the frock plunged deeply. The sleeves were as layered and irregular as the skirt. Her hair was down tonight, and her fine slippers matched the gown perfectly.

She went to the rear door, rather than walking through the tavern where a few who did not care for the revelry sat and drank. The music from the social was muffled but still audible, as she climbed the rear stairwell. Strings and flutes played in perfect harmony, with no mistakes that Sophie could discern. Then again, she knew little about music. There was none on Fyne Mountain, and she had never ventured down the hill for a social in the past. The tunes were surprisingly nice. Since it was a warm night perhaps Kane would have his window open and they could listen to the music while they made love. All night.

Kane answered her knock so quickly, she wondered if he'd known she was coming to him tonight. His eyes widened slightly at the sight of her.

He wore all black; shirt and trousers and boots, and she could tell that he had not shaved since morning. His jaw was rough with an evening's stubble. She reached out and ran her palm across that rough beard. "You look surprised. Surely you knew I would come to you tonight."

He took her wrist in his hand and guided her into his room, closing the door behind her. His window was indeed open, and strains of gentle music wafted into the room on the night breeze.

"I dreamed about this last night," he said gruffly. "There was music," he said. "You were wearing blue in the dream, too."

Sophie reached out and pressed her hand to Kane's chest, not pushing him away but simply touching. His heat seeped through the shirt and into her hand, and this close the very scent of him made her insides quake. She let her hand slip around his body, and she fell into him. Her cheek rested on his chest, her arms encircled him.

All she could give was her body, all she could take was the physical pleasure Kane promised when he looked at her, when he touched her. It would be enough, because there was no other way.

His hands raked up and down her back, comforting and arousing at the same time. Suddenly, she felt an unexpected shyness well up inside her. She wanted this night to be perfect.

Kane tilted her head gently back, and when he laid his mouth on hers she felt the heat and the pleasure of it all through her body. To her toes, to the top of her head, she felt his kiss. There was no haste in the kiss. It was leisurely. It was wonderful.

He took his mouth from hers, dipped his head, and latched those lips to her throat. Her body shook in response. Just a kiss, and already her knees were weak.

"I have never known a woman like you," he said, his voice almost lost against her throat. "I never even knew such a woman existed."

"Am I so very different from other women?"

He slowly raised his head and looked her in the eye. "Don't you know, Angel?"

Instead of answering, she cupped his face in her hands and kissed him again. He pulled her body against his, so close she felt his erection pressing against her flesh. She imagined what it would feel like when he pushed inside her, and her center clenched in response.

He danced her toward the bed, never taking his mouth from hers, and one hand reached up to cup her breast and gently tease the nipple. They would fall on the bed, clothes would be discarded, and then in a moment they would be truly together. Sophie took her mouth from his and delved into her deep pocket, withdrawing the vial Isadora had given her. "I want you to take this," she said breathlessly. "Then we'll have to wait a quarter of an hour before joining."

"Why?" Kane asked as he took the vial from her.

"To prevent another child," she whispered.

Kane studied the vial for a moment, then uncapped it and drank the shimmering green concoction in one long gulp. With no more questions about the contents, with no apparent reservations. He trusted her.

He placed the empty vial on his bedside table and drew back the covers to reveal white sheets beneath. "A quarter of an hour, you say."

She nodded and glanced at the clock on the mantel.

"I'm not going to waste even one of those fifteen minutes, Angel." He unfastened the buttons at her shoulders, then untied the silky cord at her waist. The blue gown fell to the floor, leaving her bare. She kicked off her shoes and reached out to unfasten Kane's shirt.

"Did you really dream about me?" she asked as the buttons slipped through her fingers.

"So many times I can't even count them all."

"Perhaps there was a witch among your ancestors," she said. "Prophetic dreams are quite common . . ." She squealed when he lifted her off her feet and deposited her onto the bed.

"Kane!" She laughed as he landed beside her. "It hasn't

been anywhere near a quarter of an hour. Maybe you'd like to tell me about your dream to pass the time."

He took off his boots and tossed them aside so they thudded to the floor, then he sprawled out beside her wearing only his trousers. "There are better ways to pass those minutes than to talk."

Kissing. Much more kissing. She rolled onto her side and he rolled to his, and their mouths came together. Bare chest to bare chest, on a soft, comfortable mattress, they kissed. Today she was not surprised by the power of the kiss, and whatever shyness she had felt when she'd walked into this room was now gone. When Kane speared his tongue into her mouth, she copied his move. When he sucked against her bottom lip, she did the same. Soon her body was wrapped around his and his hand rested on her backside as he held her in place.

She glanced at the clock. No, not yet a quarter of an hour.

"How long can you stay?" Kane asked.

"I need to be home before sunrise."

He grinned and kissed her again, then he lowered his head to her throat and sucked on the sensitive skin there. "Then there's no need to hurry," he whispered against her neck. "Angel, I'm going to make you cry tonight."

"Why would you do such a thing?"

Kane lifted his head and looked down at her. "Trust me, it's a good cry." He traced her jawline with his thumb, and it seemed her skin was more sensitive than it had ever been before. She tingled everywhere, she could feel the rush of her own blood through her veins. Kane's hand raked down her throat, over her breasts, down to her belly and below, to spread her thighs. With that hand he stroked her inner thighs, one and then the other, just barely allowing his fingers to brush against her where she wanted him so badly.

"Close your eyes," he whispered, and she did. "Relax." Again she followed his direction, as best she could. The mattress dipped as he moved away from her side. She licked her lips and shifted her aching body slightly as Kane touched her with arousing, gentle fingers.

He put his mouth on her, his tongue flickering over her in a way she had never imagined possible. Sensations more intense and pleasurable than she had ever dreamed of began to grow, to dance through her body like ribbons of sunshine. Her body rocked, her hips lifted, and Sophie was no longer in control. She was ruled by the needs of her body and the man who continued to feast upon her.

Only their bodies existed, along with the night breeze, and a hint of music. Everything else ceased; all cares, all plans, all needs other than the one Kane fulfilled.

She did cry, as he had said she would. With need and desire, with amazement, she cried. And then Kane's touch changed and she shattered, and the cry changed. She called out his name and her body leaped. She made sounds she had never heard before, strange moans and cries of awe and delight and contentment as an intense pleasure fluttered through and tugged at her body.

And still the world did not return. Nothing existed outside this bed. Not for tonight.

Kane crawled over her like a cat, his smile wicked and endearing. "And that, my love, was just the beginning."

She wrapped her arms around his neck and glanced at the mantel clock. "Three more minutes."

"What can we do with those three precious minutes?" he asked, his voice husky.

Sophie untangled her arms and reached down to unfasten his trousers. Surely twelve minutes was close enough to a quarter of an hour! She wanted Kane inside her . . . and she wanted to make *him* cry.

Her hands fumbled, her breath came hard. So did his, and yet he allowed her to work the buttons of his trousers alone. He did not help, he did not hurry her as she worked his trousers down and off. Soon he was as wonderfully bare as she. Sophie wrapped her legs around Kane's hips and guided him toward her.

"Sophie," he whispered her name and closed his eyes. "Something's wrong."

No, nothing was wrong. Nothing could possibly be wrong on a night like this one.

Kane shuddered and then collapsed atop her, inert.

"Kane. Kane!" Sophie rolled him into his back, a difficult task since he was unconscious. She hovered over him, checking his heartbeat and his breathing and finding them normal.

Isadora had done this, Sophie had no doubt. All her words about her little sister making her own decisions had been lies. Deceitful, manipulative lies. Again she laid her hand over his heart. It continued to beat, healthy. Strong. She lowered her head so she could hear his breathing in her ear. Steady. Deep.

How long would he sleep? If this was Isadora's idea of a joke, Kane could be out for a few minutes or for the entire night. Surely she wouldn't have filled that vial with a fatal poison! No, she wouldn't do that.

Sophie was tempted to get dressed and run home as fast as she could to confront her sister, but she didn't. She laid down beside Kane, resting her head on his shoulder.

"I'm sorry," she whispered. "I should have known she'd try something like this." But it had never even occurred to her that Isadora's intentions were anything other than sisterly. Sophie did not see deceit in others because it was so foreign to her.

She kissed Kane's shoulder and sighed. "Maybe you'll wake up in a few minutes or in an hour or two, and we can begin again. You mentioned possibilities, and now you have shown me. I want more, Kane Varden. I want everything from you." Everything but love, which would ruin her life. And his.

GALVYN STOOD BENEATH THE BOARDINGHOUSE WINDOW and stared up. Anger was not a sufficient word for what he felt at this moment. His hands clenched and unclenched. He wanted to hit something. No, someone. He wanted to hit and hit again until his rage subsided.

When he'd glanced down the street and seen Sophie rounding the tavern, he'd thought for a minute that he must be mistaken. After all, she'd told him she would not be able to attend the dance tonight.

But that hair, loose and gleaming in the moonlight, was unmistakable. He'd crept to the tavern, stood beneath Kane Varden's window, and listened. He could not hear the words they spoke, but he had heard enough. He had heard more than enough.

She'd lied to him. She'd smiled and thanked him for his gift, which she'd refused to keep in spite of his pleading that she do just that, and told him she could not attend the dance. And then she'd come *here*. To *him*.

Sophie was his. He had done so much for her, and she did not appreciate any of his efforts! Like other men in town, he'd always admired her beauty. Not enough to risk the social stigma of consorting with a witch, of course, but she had provided more than one erotic fantasy through the years.

Galvyn had always known he would marry a woman with political connections. He had ambitions well beyond owning most of a small, rural village. When he'd discovered Sophie's secret he'd known she was the one. She was his way out of Shandley once and for all.

He'd gone to great lengths to ensure that he would one day have her as his wife. He sought her out whenever she was in town, and when he spoke to her he was the finest of gentlemen. He'd begun to defend Sophie to numerous townspeople, making her out to be the innocent victim of those older Fyne sisters. That way when he made his move they would not be surprised. He was to be Sophie's savior, her friend . . . her hero.

If that didn't work, and it looked as if it would not, he'd have to find another way.

And he would. She didn't know it yet, but Sophie Fyne was his pathway to power and prominence and riches well beyond anything he could find here in Shandley. She would take him to the capital city, to the palace itself, and there he would finally have a position worthy of himself.

He was tired of waiting.

8

SOPHIE RAN UP THE HILL TOWARD HOME, NO LESS FURIOUS with her sister than she had been when she'd realized that Kane had been drugged. Dawn was coming in less than an hour, and Kane still slept. He slept deeply, so still and quiet she had spent much of the night making sure he was still alive. Ariana would soon be awake and hungry, so Sophie had been unable to remain in town with the unconscious man any longer.

But as soon as she collected and fed her daughter, they would both join Kane in his room above the tavern.

She didn't know that she'd ever return to the cabin where she'd lived all her life. It no longer felt like home to her. Isadora had deceived her, and no matter how good her intentions might've been, the fact remained that there had been a very real betrayal. Juliet had not been involved—at least Sophie didn't think so—but she must've known Isadora's potion wasn't a harmless method of birth control. She should have said something. Sisters were not supposed to betray one another, not for any reason.

The parlor and kitchen were dark, so Sophie lit a lantern. The cabin was eerily quiet. No one stirred. No one snored. No mattresses creaked. Sophie did not try to be quiet as she carried the lantern to her bedroom and peeked inside. Hungry for the sight of her daughter after such a long night, she needed to see Ariana before she confronted Isadora. And she *would* confront Isadora. Yes, her sister was six years older, much more powerful, half a foot taller and infinitely more stubborn, but that did not mean that Sophie should not or could not stand up for herself when necessary.

She had never stood up to Isadora before. Not like this.

The cradle was empty, but Sophie was not unduly alarmed. Perhaps Ariana had awakened early, even though she had been sleeping through the night for a month now, and was resting in bed with one of her aunts. Juliet, most likely. It wouldn't be the first time Sophie had found those two sleeping together, cuddled into a snug, warm ball. Juliet really should get over her fear of men and have a few babies of her own.

Juliet's bed was empty, too, though it had been slept in. The coverlet was rumpled, and one pillow had been tossed to the floor.

That left only Isadora's room, which was at the end of the hallway. Sophie headed in that direction determined to give her elder sister a piece of her mind and collect her daughter. If all three of them had crowded into Isadora's bed, then Ariana had not behaved as usual. Maybe the baby had kept them up all night. Sophie could not be sorry.

But Isadora's bed had not been slept in at all. The coverlet was crisp, all the pillows neatly in place.

Sophie's heart thudded too hard. Something was wrong. "Juliet!" she called as she turned about and returned to the middle bedroom. "Isadora! Where are you?"

She stopped once again at the doorway to Juliet's room, and this time she heard a faint noise. A soft, broken moan.

Sophie ran into the room and rounded the bed to find Juliet lying facedown on the floor. As Sophie dropped to her knees and placed the lantern on the floor, she saw that there was a bloody gash on Juliet's head.

Isadora had not answered her call. Sophie calmed herself with the knowledge that her eldest sister had the baby and was taking good care of her, wherever they might be. That was the only imagining she could allow herself.

Juliet moaned again and Sophie touched her sister's face. She was afraid to try to move her. Juliet was the healer; Sophie didn't know what to do.

"What happened?" Sophie whispered. "Please wake up."

The sound of her voice seemed to rouse the wounded woman. Juliet tried to lift her head, then gasped in pain and pressed her forehead to the floor.

"You're home," Juliet whispered. "I thought you would never get here."

"Yes, I'm home," Sophie said gently. "Where are Isadora and Ariana? How did you hurt your head?"

Serene, practical Juliet started to sob. "They took her," she cried into the floor. "I tried to stop them, I did, but one of the men hit me over the head with something and everything went black."

"They took Isadora?"

"The baby," Juliet whispered. "They took the baby."

Juliet continued to talk, but Sophie did not hear a word. A roar filled her ears, and she could hear and feel the pounding of her own heart. Juliet was not herself. The head wound had her talking nonsense. She had to be wrong.

Sophie left her sister lying on the floor and ran from room to room calling Ariana's name. She searched everywhere, even though with every step she realized more clearly that

Juliet had not been wrong. Someone had taken her baby. Someone had taken Ariana away.

Sophie was searching the parlor when the front door opened slowly and Isadora crept in. The eldest Fyne sister wore nothing but her nightshift and her hair was caught in an untidy braid, and she tiptoed on bare feet like a woman who was trying not to get caught.

"Where have you been?" Sophie cried.

Startled, Isadora spun to face her sister. After a moment's surprise, she said, "I went for a walk." Her defiant chin was held high.

"All night?"

Isadora managed to be intimidating even in her night-clothes. "Ah yes, I suppose you have a bone to pick with me. Was your evening with Mr. Varden disappointing?" She actually smiled.

Sophie shook her head. "Someone has taken Ariana and hurt Juliet. Where were you? You should have been here!" Isadora could've stopped the intruders. She could've saved Ariana and Juliet with a wave of her hand. "Where were you?"

Isadora's smile disappeared quickly. "If this is your idea of a joke . . ."

Juliet stumbled into the room, one hand against the wall for support, the other pressed to her sticky head wound.

"It was Galvyn Farrell and some brutish man I have never seen before," she said weakly. "Sophie, Galvyn gave me a message for you."

Isadora hurried to Juliet and assisted her to the rocking chair. "If you want to see Ariana again, you must go to the palace in Arthes and present yourself to the Minister of Defense. There you are to ask permission to take Galvyn Farrell as your husband."

"Why would I ask permission from the Minister of—" Sophie began.

Juliet lifted a silencing hand. "You're to wear the white dress he gave you," she continued. "He put it in your wardrobe."

Sophie's head spun. "I don't understand. This doesn't make sense!" She ran toward the door. "I can change Galvyn's mind, I can make him see reason. Maybe I can catch him if I hurry."

"Stop!" Isadora and Juliet ordered, their voices in unison.

Sophie turned to face her sisters, their faces blurred through her tears. "I can't stop. He took my baby."

"And you will get her back," Juliet said. "But not like this. Come here." She lifted her hand.

Sophie returned to the parlor and knelt before her sister. She took Juliet's blood-sticky hand in her own, and Juliet held on with surprising strength.

"Ariana will be fine. He is afraid to hurt her, though I'm not sure why. Something to do with power, but"—she shook her head—"you musn't travel alone."

"I don't see what choice I have. Isadora needs to stay here and take care of you," Sophie insisted. "I'll be fine."

Juliet shook her head. "The baby's father will escort you. He's a soldier, Sophie. He knows how to travel and how to stay safe on the road, and you need him with you."

"I can't—"

"You won't survive the trip without him," Juliet insisted. "Do not try to catch up with Galvyn, because you will not. You won't see Ariana again until you reach the palace." Juliet did not release her grip on Sophie's hand. "Tell Kane the answer to his question is sorcery. General Corann, one of the emperor's highest soldiers, took a seer as his mistress. For several months she gave him counsel. It was she who told him where to place his soldiers on that day. The rebels know of the seer and her part in that and other ambushes. They've . . . killed her, just a few days . . . a few weeks past. Kane's fear that they will think him responsible is a groundless one.

They'll be surprised to see him, though," she added. "They believe him to be dead, like all the others."

Kane would have an answer to the question he had never asked Juliet.

"We must leave *now*," Sophie insisted, "and Kane is . . . is . . ." She glared up at Isadora. "I will never forgive you."

"Are you pregnant?" Isadora asked sharply.

"Of course not!"

"Then the potion worked as it should."

Sophie raked both hands through her hair, reaching for order and reason and the ability to continue without falling apart. "I'm not coming back here," she said as she stood and headed for her bedroom to pack the dreadful white dress and whatever else she might need.

"You and Kane will leave directly from town," Isadora called after her as she began to attend to Juliet's wound. "That's good."

Sophie didn't answer, not until she'd changed into a traveling outfit and gathered her things. She wore loose trousers tucked into tall boots and a man-style shirt, and her hair was pulled up and back and twisted into a loose knot. She walked into the parlor with a bag in her hand.

"You didn't understand me correctly," she said calmly. "I'm never coming back here. This is no longer my home, and you are not my sister."

Isadora glared, but in those dark, angry eyes Sophie saw something else. A fear that almost matched her own. "Just because I put your beau to sleep for a few hours—"

"If I had been here I might've stopped Galvyn!" Sophie shouted. "My baby would be in my arms and Juliet would not be hurt. And I would have been here if not for your petty determination to get your own way!"

Isadora had the decency to go pale. "Even if I had not interfered with your plans for the evening, you might not have been here, Sophie. Don't be rash."

"Rash? How dare you—"

"You were not meant to be here," Juliet said weakly. "Don't blame Isadora. Everything that has happened, it was meant to be."

Sophie shook her head. She needed someone to blame, someone she could yell at now, and Isadora had interfered for the last time.

"I can't believe it was fate that took my daughter from me," she whispered. Tears dripped down her face, even though she tried to stop them. She needed to be strong. For Ariana.

"Shhhh," Juliet said when Sophie began to cry. "It is also fated that you will get her back. Trust me, darling."

"You'll need herbs to stop your milk from coming in until you reach Ariana," Isadora said sensibly. "Even if you take the shortest road and travel across the barren heart, the trip to Arthes will take more than two weeks."

"Two weeks!"

"Three," Juliet whispered.

Sophie closed her eyes. Three weeks was a lifetime, much too long to be away from her child. "What about Kane? When will he wake up?"

"I'll give you an antidote," Isadora said as she reached for the cabinet where the medicines were stored. "Two drops on his tongue and he'll wake feeling bright and alert. There will be no aftereffects from last night's potion."

"He'll feel fine," Sophie said bitterly, "until I tell him that his daughter has been kidnapped and I don't know why."

"Power," Juliet whispered. "You must hold onto that, Sophie. Galvyn won't hurt Ariana. He needs her to be well and happy. She'll be well taken care of."

Juliet pressed both hands to her eyes. A simple vision often gave her a headache, and this one had been going on for some time.

Armed with the antidote to the potion Isadora had fashioned for Kane, an herbal mixture to keep her breasts from growing heavy with milk, enough food for three days, water, and the blasted white dress, Sophie headed down Fyne Mountain at a run.

She didn't know what she'd do once she had Ariana in her arms again, but she knew she wasn't coming back here. Fyne Mountain was no longer her home.

ISADORA MADE SURE THE BANDAGE ON JULIET'S HEAD WAS secure and that the bleeding had stopped.

"I should have stayed home last night," she muttered as she gently washed dried blood from her sister's temple. "I could have stopped them."

"Yes, you could have," Juliet said weakly. "I suspect that's why you weren't here."

"Fate again."

"Yes."

She hated Juliet's easy acceptance of everything that happened, calling it fate or destiny. To accept everything with such serenity was unnatural . . . and it would also mean admitting that she and Will had never been meant to have more than those precious two years.

Isadora helped Juliet to her feet. Now was not the time to argue. "We're going to change that gown and wash off the rest of the blood, and then you're going to get some sleep."

"How can I sleep?" Juliet asked.

"You must heal; you must get stronger," Isadora insisted. "You need rest."

They made slow progress down the hallway. Isadora couldn't help but glance into Sophie's room as they passed. The cradle was empty, clothes Sophie had rejected as she'd gone through her things had been scattered about the room. The gown she'd worn to town tonight had been tossed onto the floor, beauty and allure forgotten in favor of more important things.

"I should've been here," she said again.

"Where were you?" Juliet asked. "I know you often walk at night, but you don't usually stay out so late."

"I fell asleep." Two nights in a row she'd gone looking for Willym's spirit, and two nights in a row she'd seen him. Briefly. Indistinctly. But for that split second when he looked so real, she felt good again. Whole and happy and full of hope.

But of course Will was dead, and there was no hope. Not for her.

"I shouldn't have deceived Sophie with that potion. I didn't intend to hurt Varden," Isadora said hotly. "I just wanted her to have one more night to rethink her position."

"How do you rethink love?" Juliet asked as she sat on the edge of the bed.

Love. Her heart clenched. "Is it that serious?"

"I'm afraid so. Sophie doesn't realize the full depth of her feelings yet, but the love is already there."

For the Fyne women, with love came pain and death.

But those two years with Willym had been so wonderful. She would give anything to have him back . . . but she would not give back those two years.

Isadora sighed. "Perhaps I did make a mistake. I only wanted what was best for Sophie. She's the baby, and it's my job to look out for her. I've been like her mother since she was fourteen, and I just don't want her to suffer."

"I know you did your best for both of us."

"Sophie will be back, won't she?" she asked as she helped to remove Juliet's nightshirt. For some reason, Isadora's heart hitched as she asked the question. She didn't have Juliet's gift, but it was as if she already knew the answer.

"Our baby sister will never see this house again," Juliet whispered, tears in her eyes. "Never."

* * *

FROM HIS SADDLE ATOP THE FINEST HORSE IN HIS STABLE, Galvyn glared at the squalling baby. If he didn't need the brat . . . if he wasn't afraid to harm a hair on her soft little head . . .

Bors, a deputy sheriff who wasn't above a little bribery, theft, or kidnapping here and there, rode alongside on his own horse, and he carried the child in a sling across his chest. The ear-splitting noise didn't seem to bother him at all. Then again, the big man had six or seven kids at home.

"Can't you make it be quiet?"

"The babe's hungry," Bors said sensibly. "As soon as we collect the wet nurse she'll be fine. We'll reach the farm in an hour or so."

"Wouldn't feeding it from a wineskin make more sense?"

Bors looked pointedly at Galvyn. "When we hit that long stretch of road where there are no towns for miles, where will we get the milk?"

Galvyn shrugged. They could take the more well-traveled road that cut south for many miles before turning north and west again. Along that road there would be many towns and villages, farms and ranches. But it would also extend the journey from two weeks to a full month or more. Best to travel across the barren land that would keep their journey short.

The ugly deputy returned his attention to the baby he'd snatched from its cradle after hitting Juliet over the head.

Galvyn watched the road, his mind on the events of the early morning hours. Maybe Juliet was dead. Bors had certainly hit her hard enough to accomplish that deed. He wished Isadora had been there, as well as the redhead. If both elder sisters were dead, there would be no one to care for Sophie. No one but him.

She was everything he'd ever wanted in a wife. Beauty, of

course. Sweetness, which would surely turn to compliance once they were wed. Her body was luscious, hinting that as a wife she would be exciting where wifely matters were concerned.

But it was the political connections of which she was unaware that sealed the deal for him. He would have the perfect wife and a place in the emperor's palace.

The big man who carried Sophie's baby said, "The wet nurse will also keep the baby clean and soothe her when she needs sleep. Are those chores you would like for yourself?"

"No," Galvyn said tersely.

The trip to Arthes would be a long one with the baby, Bors, and a wet nurse in the traveling party. But what waited at the end of the journey would make all the suffering worthwhile.

KANE SLOWLY OPENED HIS EYES. WHAT HAD HAPPENED? One minute it had been nighttime and he'd been making love to Sophie, and the next it was morning and she leaned over him with tears in her eyes.

When had she gotten dressed and restyled her hair? What had happened to the night?

He dismissed all his questions when she took his face in her hands and repeated herself. "Are you listening to me? Galvyn Farrell has kidnapped Ariana!"

He sat up, feeling strangely invigorated. Physically, at least. "Why would he do such a thing? What does he want?"

"He wants me," Sophie said softly. "He's taken Ariana to the palace in the capital city, and he's left specific instructions on what I'm to do when I get there."

"When did he leave?" Kane leapt from the bed and reached for his clothes. "We can catch him . . ."

Sophie laid a hand on his arm. "We can't," she said softly. "Juliet says we will not catch him on the road, that it will take us three weeks to get there, and—"

"Two," he said. "Maybe a couple days more."

She shook her head. "No. Kane, you must listen to me. I need you to escort me to the palace in Arthes, but once we're there I will do what I must to save Ariana. Alone."

"You expect me to take you to the Imperial Palace and just leave you there?" He sat on the edge of the bed to pull on his boots.

"You can return to the rebels. I know that's what you want. They never thought you a traitor, Kane, though they do think you're dead," she said passionlessly.

"Juliet again," he said tersely.

"Yes. She said your position was given away by a seer who once served as General Corann's counsel and mistress. The seer is dead now."

"And what are you going to do while I return to the revolution?" he asked.

"I'm going to go to the Minister of Defense and ask for permission to take Galvyn Farrell as husband."

He shook his head. He felt alert, considering that he'd lost the night, but none of this was making sense. "Why would you ask the Minister of Defense for permission to marry?"

"I don't know," she said softly.

He stood, took her face in his hands, and bent down to give her a quick kiss. "We'll go to Arthes, and I promise to have you there in less than three weeks. You can speak to the Minister of Defense if you'd like, but as soon as Galvyn Farrell shows his face I'm going to kill him. And then you and I are going to take Ariana and get out of that cursed place. Together, Sophie."

She closed her eyes in what seemed to be relief. No matter what she said, she didn't want to do this alone. "I want my baby, Kane."

"I know you do, Angel." He strapped his knife and sword to his belt and slipped yet another into a sheath inside his right boot. From the corner of the room he collected a bow and a quiver of arrows. He was a better swordsman than archer, but when it came to weapons he had found that it was always best to be prepared for any and every need.

"I'll do anything to get her back." Sophie's eyes were wide, and while she was scared she was also determined.

"You won't have to marry a lowlife kidnapper in order to hold your daughter again, I promise you."

She shook her head. "How is Galvyn connected with the Minister of Defense? I've never even heard of the man, and with a title like Minister of Defense I doubt he's in charge of any sort of matrimony."

"I never actually met Minister Sulyen, but I understand he's one tough bastard. He's had to be to survive the last two emperors. Sebestyen's father had a nasty habit of doing away with those who disagreed with him, and his son has inherited that penchant."

"Minister Sulyen," Sophie said as she watched Kane gather his things for the long trip ahead.

He knew how to pack quickly, how to clean every hint of himself out of a room in a matter of minutes. He'd purchase a new horse before they left town; the trip was too long for them to share a mount. His mind was already on the trip ahead. Which road to take, when and where to stop so the horses could rest.

"Do you think perhaps Sulyen is a relation to the Farrells? Galvyn was always talking about his connections to powerful people and even to the emperor himself."

"Could be," Kane said, "though from what I hear Maddox Sulyen isn't exactly a family man."

He faced Sophie, ready to leave Shandley behind. A moment ago she had been scared but determined. In a heartbeat, she went deathly pale and her hands began to shake. "*Maddox* Sulyen?"

"Yes."

"Oh." Her pretty blue eyes rolled up and she fainted into his arms.

THE BATH ON LEVEL THREE WAS LIANE'S FAVORITE PLACE TO relax, especially when she'd ordered everyone else from the room and had the massive and hushed chamber to herself. She floated alone in the main bath, a marble pool larger than the first room she'd slept in here at the palace. She'd shared that room with five other frightened girls, all of them captives, like herself. She was the only one who had survived more than a year.

Bowls of soft flame floated in the pool with her, casting soft, flickering light into the water and onto the walls and even faintly to the ceiling far above. Flowers floated around her, too, fragrant and lovely. Liane allowed her fingers to caress one velvety, white petal as it floated past.

She did not think of the other girls very often, though they had been her friends in those first terrible months. It seemed as if that time had happened to another person, not her. She no longer gave herself the luxury of fear or tears, and that frightened child who had been taken from her home because she caught the eye of an imperial soldier had been dead a long time. When she looked back it seemed that she and all the others had been such lamebrained children. Such fools.

All of them had been so sure their families would rescue them from this hell. Even Liane. Even though she'd known that her father was a farmer who would never know how to fight the imperial soldiers, and her brothers were all children themselves, and her mother could not have fought for her even if she had not been ill, she had somehow expected . . .

She closed her eyes and made herself dismiss all thoughts of those days. The Liane she had become didn't expect anything from anyone.

"May I join you?"

Liane jerked up, coming out of the water with a surprised splash. Her feet quickly found the bottom of the pool. She did not stand in the waist-deep water, but crouched there with the water touching her chin. Heavens, she had allowed herself to become so lost in the past she had not even realized another had entered the room! She relaxed when she saw who had joined her.

"Minister Sulyen," she said, her voice not giving away so much as a hint of her surprise. "How lovely to see you, as always."

He grinned and began to unbutton his crimson robe. "Why so formal this evening, Liane?"

She glanced beyond him to the doorway. None of his guards waited there, and he had closed the door. And locked it? She could not be sure. "Are we alone?"

He nodded as he shrugged off his garment and stepped into the pool. She had seen him naked before, and he had seen her, but it had been years since they'd been intimate. He had become her friend, early in her time on Level Three. He was the reason she'd been the one of all those frightened girls to survive.

"You have your own room for bathing, Maddox," she said as she swam toward him.

"Yes, but there are no beautiful women in my bath."

She returned his smile. Maddox Sulyen had become Minister of Defense at the young age of thirty-two, twenty years ago. He'd survived not only seventeen years of Sebestyen's reign, but the last three volatile years of the previous emperor's regime. The first few years of Sebestyen's rule had been tumultuous. He'd been thirteen years of age, not yet a man and yet not a child who required an adviser to make all decisions. The priests had done their best to control him, in those days, but their dominion had never been complete. Sebestyen had always been stubborn and independent, not easily influenced by the whims and desires of others.

A few ministers and generals who'd thought themselves capable of manipulating a thirteen-year-old ruler had found themselves dead or banished to Level Thirteen, in those early years. Maddox had been much too clever to fall into that trap.

He was a handsome man, not particularly tall but fit and always well groomed. His hair remained a fair blond, with no sign of gray or thinning, and his remarkable blue eyes sparkled like those of a much younger man. He had always been demanding in his sexual needs, and his delight in women had not diminished over the years.

"How are you?" he asked in a lowered voice, when she was close. In the palace, it paid to be cautious.

"Fine," she answered just as softly. "And you?"

"I have survived." Maddox reached out and touched her face, the way a friend might. "These days that is a feat all its own."

She nodded, understanding. "Why are you here? The truth, Maddox."

He smiled again, that warm grin that had captured hearts all across Columbyana. Fine lines around his eyes crinkled, making him look cheerful and harmless. Minister Sulyen was most definitely not harmless. "I'm traveling to the Northern Province to meet with my generals."

"When?"

"In the morning. I plan to leave before daylight."

"Why can your generals not come here?"

"Because the fighting is there, at the moment, and they do not wish to leave their troops."

The war seemed more of an annoyance than a danger, from behind palace walls. But Liane was very well aware that real dangers did exist. "The rebels are not so fierce that they command the presence of not only four generals but the Minister of Defense himself," she argued.

"They have become more fierce and more organized in the past seven months."

Liane shook her head. "Kill Arik and there will be no revolution."

He grinned at her again. "If you're such an expert on warfare, perhaps I should make you a general."

"Don't patronize me, Maddox. Arik is the driving force behind this annoyance. Kill him and the rebels have nothing to fight for."

"If we could find him, we would." He brushed a strand of wet hair out of her face. His touch was gentle, but not sexual. "I'm afraid the rebels have become much more than an annoyance, Liane. A month ago they defeated an army of superior forces. They captured and killed General Corann's counsel—a clairvoyant, if you can believe it—and now they have taken the Northern Palace."

She came up out of the water, standing tall. "What? Does the emperor know this?"

Maddox grabbed her arm and pulled her back down. "No," he whispered. "Sebestyen knows only what I tell him, and if I inform him that Arik has taken the Northern Palace he'll have my head. Or worse. By the time I return, the palace will be in imperial hands once again, so there's no reason to tell the emperor anything at all."

If she told Sebestyen of this betrayal—and withholding such information was indeed a serious betrayal—Maddox would be killed or sent to Level Thirteen, and as the one who'd uncovered the information she'd be one step closer to becoming Sebestyen's sole ally. And one step closer to killing the bastard.

"Then I will wish you good luck," she said softly. "This is all very interesting, but that still doesn't explain why you're here."

"A woman, of course," he said. "I'd like to be well laid before I leave on my long journey."

"Are you thinking of anyone in particular?"

His blue eyes sparkled for a moment and he winked at her, but she knew he was teasing. They were friends, not lovers. That time had passed long ago. "You choose for me, Liane."

"Someone tireless, then," she said with a smile.

He kissed her on the forehead, in an unexpected gesture of friendship. "Send two."

She laughed as Maddox swam toward the pool steps. "If you ever decide to retire your post I will get you a position here as a Level Three Master."

"Ah, my true calling," he said as he climbed the steps, wet muscles rippling in the firelight.

Minister Sulyen had been a fierce general and was a well-respected Minister of Defense. He understood warfare, intellectually and emotionally, his generals adored him, and he knew how to handle Sebestyen.

At the top of the steps he turned to watch her as he reached for a fat towel and began to dry himself. He was already hard, and impressively so. Yes, even at his age he'd make a fine Level Three Master.

Maddox had never married. He had never told her why

he'd remained unmarried when any woman he asked would be glad to be his wife. And she didn't mind that he did not reveal all his secrets. Perhaps he remained unwed because he could not be faithful to any one woman. When it came to pleasure, he enjoyed a variety of women too much to be bound to any one. Then again, maybe he had once had a great love and she'd been taken from him or wed to another. That was unlikely. She'd never met anyone who behaved less heartbroken than Maddox Sulyen.

Liane swam toward the steps herself. She would choose two women for Maddox and then she'd retire for the night. She'd visited Sebestyen earlier in the evening, and she'd already been dismissed.

"Are you sure you're all right?" he asked softly.

"Of course." Liane reached not for Maddox but for her own towel. She gently dried her skin. "I have everything any woman could possibly want. Servants, clothes, fine food, a luxurious bedchamber." She gestured to the pool behind her. "This and more, and all for doing nothing more than any wife is expected to do for her husband."

Maddox surprised her by leaning over to kiss her on the cheek. Then he whispered in her ear. "He is not sane, Liane. Perhaps he never was, but he's getting worse. You're so close to him you must see it. Be careful."

She held her breath. If not telling Sebestyen about the capture of the Northern Palace wasn't treason, this certainly was.

"Make it three," he said as he stepped away.

"Three?"

"Three women, none of them new."

While he was past the age where it was possible for him to reach fulfillment three times in such a short period of time, he would see that all three ladies were well satisfied. Maddox had always received as much pleasure from the sexual delight of his partners, as well as his own.

"I know just the trio of ladies to send you off."

He was dressed and out of the room before she had the chance to don her red robe. She took her time, brushing out her wet hair, pinning it back, smoothing the wrinkles out of her garment.

She went directly to the Level Three residence hall and chose three girls for Maddox. One tall, one short, one buxom. They were all enthusiastic and they all adored Maddox and were happy to be chosen for him. He would begin his journey well-satisfied, just as he desired.

From there Liane went to her private quarters. She was the only one of the emperor's concubines who had her own bed-chamber. She'd earned it, just as she had earned everything else she called her own.

The room was decorated in silver and blue, like Sebestyen's bedchamber, and was embellished with a mini-mum of feminine frippery. Her luxuries were a soft mattress, a full-length mirror, the dresser where her oils and lotions sat, an upholstered chair with a matching hassock. She had a heavy coverlet for winter, a thinner one for summer. The floor was of stone, of course, but a number of luxurious rugs were laid out so that her bare feet need never step upon a cold floor. Her clothes filled not one but two massive wardrobes. One of those wardrobes had been reserved for crimson robes in vary-ing fabrics and styles.

If she wished a servant to help her prepare for the night, she could have one with a single word. But tonight, as on most nights, she preferred to be alone.

Sleep did not come easily, as she had hoped it would. Her mind spun with plans and secrets, memories and possibilities. She tossed in her bed, sleeping in short snatches that were never long enough, and rose before the sun.

Her window had been left open to let in the night air, and Liane went to that window and looked down at the city below.

She had not left the palace in so long, the city was foreign to her. She had survived here; she wasn't so sure she would be able to survive down there.

She took a deep breath and held it. On Level One there was no fresh air. Fans worked constantly to bring air up to the emperor's Level, but it was not the same as the air she breathed as she leaned out the window. On some warm nights she had convinced the emperor to come to her, so that the heat was not so stifling as they pressed their bodies together. Not this summer, though. It had been more than a year since he'd come to her quarters.

On the nights when he had been here he'd glanced several times toward the window as if the sun would appear in the night sky to fulfill the wizard's prophesy. It hadn't mattered that she'd made sure the window was completely covered with the dark drapes that were now pulled back to allow the air to rush in.

Was it only a matter of time before Sebestyen ordered every window in the palace bricked in? If he did, the place would be all but uninhabitable, even with the lights and the fans that were powered by the machine on Level Eleven. No—that wouldn't happen. Maddox was wrong; the emperor was not insane. He was cruel and cold, but his actions were not those of a madman.

She stood there, allowing her mind to wander and enjoying the fresh air, until she saw Maddox leave with his entourage. They rode the strongest, fastest horses; he had the finest men as his guard. She watched as he worked his way through the city, valiant and unhurried.

Maddox Sulyen was the only person in this world she called her friend. If not for him, she would have been dead long ago. He'd taught her how to survive, how to become the woman she needed to be in order to remain here on the upper levels. The Level Three Masters had taught her about pleasure, her own and that of the men she entertained. But Maddox had taught her to separate a young girl's idea of love from sex. He had been the one to teach her that her body was a weapon like any other, and if she learned to use it properly she would survive.

Maddox had taught her how to make herself indispensable. She had become all that Level Three stood for. She was decadence, she was pleasure. And she never, ever confused sex with love.

Some days she wished the soldiers had killed her instead of bringing her here, but not today. Today she had a purpose. She had a goal that was so important, nothing could get in her way. Nothing could stop her.

"I have no choice," she whispered as she watched Maddox ride away.

The day passed like many others. Liane had a position of importance on Level Three. The crones managed things nicely, and a number of servants—young girls in training, in most cases—waited upon the concubines whose only duty was to please and entertain. But Liane was expected to be present in order to give guidance and direction when necessary. The other girls either envied or feared her, and she did not have friends among them. But she did her best to make sure they understood those truths that had saved her.

In the afternoon, she took a long nap. Sebestyen was expecting her tonight, and it wouldn't do to arrive on his doorstep with a yawn and circles under her eyes. Yes, she did need to speak with him, but as Maddox was already gone there was no need for urgency. Tonight would be soon enough.

She didn't allow herself to consider that she was giving Maddox a chance to move far enough away from Arthes so that Sebestyen would not give chase.

Liane took her time getting ready for Sebestyen, choosing to wear not one of her red robes but a dark green diaphanous gown. Why pretend that she was going to his chamber for any reason but sex? With the green fabric draping her body, she adorned her neck with gold chains of varying lengths, and put fine gold loops in her ears and a circlet of gold on her hair.

There was no rush, not tonight. Sebestyen was to entertain his wife this evening, in hopes of impregnating her. Rikka had been empress for two years, and still was not with child. Sebestyen's patience wore thin more quickly these days. His first wife had lasted almost four years, the second three, the third not quite that long. Rikka's time would soon be up, if she didn't find a reason for the emperor to keep her alive.

Rikka would not remain in her husband's bedchamber any longer than necessary, and Sebestyen expected Liane to be waiting when he was ready for her.

When Liane was finished with her preparations, she drank the elixir that had been placed at her bedside. All the sexually active women on Level Three took this same elixir daily, to keep from filling the palace with bastards. As badly as Sebestyen wanted an heir, he just as desperately wanted that heir to be legitimate. After all, he had denied Arik's heritage on the grounds that his mother had come from Level Three and he was therefore unfit to serve his country in any way.

His own child could not be the offspring of a whore.

Liane had been taking the elixir for so many years she was quite sure she'd never be able to have a child. Her monthly flow was so light and sporadic that at times she went for months with no cycle at all. She'd never bear a child, and even though she did not care for children and she did not dream of being a mother, that was simply another reason to hate Sebestyen.

She studied her reflection for a few moments, looking for flaws in her appearance. Her lips were much too colorless tonight, so she darkened them with rouge. She brushed her hair once again, knowing Sebestyen would expect it to be perfect for him.

The lift carried her to Level One. Before coming here she'd had no idea such a contraption existed. There were many wonders in the emperor's palace. Lights that came not from flame but from glass rods powered by a noisy machine on Level Eleven. The lift which made it possible to travel all the way from Level Ten to Level One, powered by the same contraption. The fans that made Level One habitable were also artificially powered.

She stepped off the lift to face three familiar sentinels. Two young, one rather old, all of them dressed in sharp emerald green uniforms and well armed. Liane smiled at them and spread her arms wide. The translucent gown left no doubt that she was unarmed.

Taneli, one of the younger sentinels who had risen to a position of power, insisted on checking her over carefully, spinning her around and patting at her in places where it was quite clear she hid nothing.

"Do you really think it's necessary to search me?" she asked with a smile.

"Emperor Sebestyen orders it," Taneli said. "We even search the empress when she visits." He nodded to the closed door.

"She's still in there?" Liane asked.

He nodded.

Liane listened carefully, but all was quiet behind the closed door.

She turned a bright smile to the young sentinel. "Do you examine the empress as thoroughly as you examine me before allowing her entrance?"

His eyes remained firmly planted on her breasts. "Um, of course."

"Why do I not believe that?" She took a step closer to the young soldier. He turned red in the face. "You probably give her a cursory pat here and there, but never on her tits. And I can't imagine that you ask the empress to spread her legs so you can thrust your clumsy hands between them."

He turned redder, and his left eye twitched. "Well, she is the empress."

Liane took a deep breath. In the past sixteen years, she'd outlasted three empresses. "I'm not impressed," she said softly, before spinning around and throwing open the doors to Sebestyen's bedchamber.

She had hoped to catch them in the act, but all was finished, apparently. The empress was buttoning her robe and a naked Sebestyen reclined on the bed with a bored expression on his face.

That expression brightened when Liane smiled at him.

"I got tired of waiting," she said, ignoring the Empress Rikka and walking toward Sebestyen.

"You never were one for patience." Sebestyen offered her his hand. "I'm glad you're here. Duty is done. Now it's time to indulge myself in one of my few true pleasures."

Liane tried to pretend she didn't see the glare Rikka shot her way. In fact, she did her best to ignore the girl. Did Rikka really love Sebestyen? If so, she was a fool.

Robe in place, Rikka walked quickly toward the door, her head high and her spine straight. But once there, she stopped and turned to face the bed. Liane sat beside Sebestyen and reached out to touch his bare chest. His eyes swept over Liane's scantily clad body and the physical response was exactly as she had hoped it would be.

"Once again you have taken my breath away," he whispered. He cupped one breast in a cool hand and teased the nipple that was clearly visible through the sheer green and Liane placed her head on his shoulder and her lips on his neck.

"I deserve your respect," Rikka said in a soft voice.

With a sigh, Sebestyen looked at his wife. "What did you say?"

"I said—"

"Can't you see we're busy?" Liane said impatiently, raising her head to glare at the empress. She did not like this foolish girl, but if Rikka started standing up for herself and demanding things from Sebestyen, she'd soon find herself in Level

Thirteen with whatever remained of her predecessors. Sebestyen would again begin the search for a new and suitable bride from the important families of Columbyana. It was always such a tiresome search, and it affected his mood in an adverse way. She didn't need that complication, not now. Not when she was so close to getting everything she wanted.

The empress ran from the room, and one of the sentinels closed the door behind her.

Liane reclined on the bed beside Sebestyen and placed her mouth close to his ear. "I'm glad she's gone," she whispered.

"So am I." Sebestyen threaded his fingers through her hair and held on tight. "If she isn't pregnant within a month, I'm going to get rid of her. I'm going to—"

Liane laid her fingers over Sebestyen's mouth. "I don't want to talk about her, and I don't want you to talk about her. She is insignificant, and you are a young, virile man who has many years left in which to produce an heir."

He drew her hair back and kissed her throat. "You are right, of course. You are always right. Heaven above, you are so beautiful tonight."

She sighed and smiled, but before Sebestyen could go further she took his face in her hands and looked him in the eye. "I have something very important to tell you." The words she needed to say caught in her throat. She had killed traitors, she had spied upon men who believed she cared for them, she had used men for pleasure and allowed them to use her. What did one more infraction matter?

10

THREE DAYS INTO THE JOURNEY, SOPHIE STARTED TO CRY. Without warning, the tears had come. Soft tears, then sobs, then soft tears again. They were relentless, miserable tears. Kane was a soldier, he knew the sword and the knife. He knew how to live off the land; how to sneak up on an enemy without being heard; how to kill silently. He didn't have any idea how to comfort a woman who wanted her child so badly she ached.

She cried for the better part of a week, but whenever Kane suggested they stop on her account she balked. They stopped to purchase supplies in the towns they passed through, they stopped to allow the horses to rest, and they stopped to sleep a few hours here and there.

But they did not stop for even five minutes because Sophie's heart was broken.

Her womanly cycle had slowed them down a bit, though she tried not to let it. Still, for a few days there had been frequent stops for female functions Kane wanted to know nothing about. Sophie seemed angry at her body for slowing them down, as if it had betrayed her.

At first glance, Sophie Fyne was a pretty girl who would spend her life being cared for by someone else. Her sisters now, a caring husband or an attentive lover—since she insisted she had no intention of marrying—later in her life. But beneath the blue eyes, the pretty face, and the luscious body— beneath the tears—she had a backbone of steel and the determination of a soldier. She was as much a warrior as he had ever been.

Kane tried to convince himself that this illusion that he loved Sophie was brought about by pity and empathy and sexual frustration. As soon as she had her baby in her arms and he spent one night in her bed, this aching need to care for her and comfort her and keep her forever would pass. It had to.

Sophie believed that Minister Sulyen was her father, though Kane was not yet convinced. Her evidence was slim; a shared name and Galvyn Farrell's insistence that she present herself to Sulyen upon arrival in the city. She said she'd know the truth when she saw Sulyen face-to-face. Apparently her mother had told her on more than one occasion that she had her father's eyes.

If Sophie was indeed Minister Sulyen's daughter, it explained Farrell's newfound obsession with Sophie. Marriage to the daughter of a minister so highly placed and respected would certainly be a step up for the ambitious merchant.

Sophie deserved better than to be wed in the name of ambition.

"It's almost time to stop for the night," Kane declared. Sophie had gotten ahead of him on the road, as she sometimes did. She'd often prod the mare she rode onward, her eyes on the horizon as if she expected to see the Imperial Palace appear before them at any moment.

"Not yet," she said without looking back. "We can go a little farther before full darkness falls."

At this rate it would take them at least another week to reach the capital city, but certainly not the full three weeks Juliet had predicted. Even though he wasn't ready to believe every word that the witch said, he had been alert in days past, looking for trouble that might cause a delay. So far the journey had been uneventful. Perhaps Juliet had simply been wrong.

"There's a good camping spot just ahead," he explained. "Food for the horses, a small cave as shelter for us." He looked up at the gray sky. "It will be dark in less than an hour, and it's going to rain tonight."

Sophie looked up, too, as if the sky had betrayed her. "The weather will slow us down, won't it?"

"Maybe."

"Will it delay us for a full week?"

"I don't think so." Even if the rain was worse than the gray skies indicated, it surely wouldn't delay them more than a day or two.

Sophie didn't say a word about missing Ariana, but he could see the pain on her face. It was a pain he would gladly suffer for her if he could.

His own physical pain lessened every day. The headaches still came and went, but they were not as intense as they had been in those early days, and they did not last as long. The pain he suffered now was much like Sophie's. Over the past several days an ache had settled into his chest, and it sat there like a crushing boulder. He barely knew his child, so how could it be that losing her hurt so much? He tried to push the pain aside and concentrate on caring for Sophie, on easing her pain. It was easier than facing his own unexpected heartbreak.

Galvyn Farrell would die, he'd see to that. It was the only thought that got him through one day after another.

When they reached their campsite, Sophie excused herself to go wash her face in the pond while Kane unsaddled the horses. She would cry there, he knew. In the past few days she'd been trying not to cry while he watched, but when she came back from a few moments alone her eyes were always red and her face was puffier than it had been before.

He'd wanted to stop her, before she went to the pond to wash up and cry in private. He'd wanted to hold Sophie and tell her everything would be all right, and comfort her with a simple touch. Not a kiss, not a sexual touch. He just wanted to hold her and take away her pain, and that was an entirely new need for him. He wasn't sure he liked it. In all his life he'd never felt so helpless.

In the end he hadn't stopped Sophie, but had let her go to the pond to cry as she wished.

While she cried, he filled his head with thoughts of revenge. No, *justice*. Kane didn't want to kill Farrell simply for taking Ariana, though that would have certainly been reason enough. He wanted to make the man suffer because he'd made Sophie suffer.

Maybe she wouldn't be his woman forever. There were too many obstacles between them to even think about forever. But she was his woman now, and that meant he had every right to protect her from men like Farrell.

He'd just finished unsaddling the second horse when he heard the cry. It was short and sharp, as if Sophie had started to scream and then been interrupted. Kane ran toward the pond. Maybe she'd seen a snake, or been startled by some other encounter with wildlife. They hadn't passed another traveler in more than two days, and there were no towns nearby. There was no reason for anyone else to be here. Still, that cry had been alarming. All was silent.

"Sophie?" he called.

The silence was more disturbing than the abrupt scream had been, and he began to run faster. "Sophie!" He cut through the tall grass, reached the edge of the pond, and glanced down. A soft ripple chased across the once still waters. Kane turned around, his sharp eyes scanning in all directions. Sophie could not have simply disappeared, witch or not.

His heart began to pound hard and his breath would not come as it should. He had been in battle, he had lost loved ones, he had faced death. But he had never faced anything as frightening as finding himself suddenly and inexplicably alone by this pond, as the last ripple on the water died.

"Sophie!"

SOPHIE OPENED HER EYES TO CONFUSION. IT WAS DARK, AND she could not move. Her hands were bound behind her back, and her ankles were lashed together. She was lying flat against hard, cold stone, and she realized as consciousness returned that it was completely dark because a length of soft cloth covered her eyes.

She remembered splashing cool water on her face, then turning around to find herself confronted by a wide, bare chest. She'd screamed, but something sweet-smelling had appeared beneath her nose, carried there by a very large and definitely male hand. And then . . . nothing.

Sophie whimpered. This wasn't right. She needed to reach her daughter *now*. Every minute that passed without Ariana was one minute too long.

A deep, soft voice said, "I thought you would never awake."

Sophie turned her face toward the voice. She should be afraid, but she had no time or patience for fear at the moment. "Who are you? What have you done? Kane will not allow you to harm me, so you might as well just let me go right now. Maybe then I can convince him not to hurt you when he finds us." She tried to sound confident. When he finds us. Not if. Never if.

Sophie gasped when the man hauled her into a sitting position and placed his face near her neck to take a good long sniff. She could not see him, but she could certainly feel his presence and his breath. "Stop that!"

"Perhaps you are not the one," her abductor said, disappointment dripping like honey from his deep, velvety voice. "When I smelled you coming, I thought you were the one, but I might be wrong."

"You *smelled* me coming?"

"For the past two days."

True, bathing had not been high on her list of priorities since leaving home, but really . . . she was insulted.

"I'm going to take off your blindfold now," her abductor said. "Don't be afraid."

Sophie nodded as he reached around her to untie the silky fabric. Somehow she had to keep her wits about her and convince this man to release her at once. Kane must be frantic. How much time had passed since she'd been taken? She had no idea if it had been minutes or hours since she'd splashed cool water over her face to hide her tears.

Sunlight hurt her eyes and answered that question. Hours. It had been close to dark when she'd stopped by the pond. Kane had predicted rain for the evening, and so far he'd always been right in that respect. There was no rain or clouds now, just blue skies and sun. She blinked once, twice, then fixed her squinted eyes on the man who had taken her. Everything had happened so quickly, all she'd really seen as he'd grabbed her was his chest and a large hand. Now that she could see him fully, she realized he was even bigger than she'd imagined. When he stood, he'd be more than six and a half feet tall, surely, and he was wide in the shoulders. Wellmuscled, too, a fact which was easy to discern since all he wore was a . . . a short kilt of some kind. It appeared to be made of a tanned animal hide. His face was angular and even, and he was, oddly enough, clean-shaven.

Perhaps he was not clean-shaven at all. There was no hair

on his broad, muscled chest, so perhaps none grew there, or on his jaw. He certainly didn't look like a man who'd spent the morning before a mirror, taking care with his appearance.

While angular and stoic, the face was a handsome one, with full lips and a finely shaped nose. He sported no hair on his face or his chest, but the hair on his head was as long as hers, and almost as pale. There was more gold in his hair than in hers, though, and it fell in unkempt, tangled strands over his shoulders. A few tangles covered one half of his face.

His eyes were a deep, startling gold, and they seemed to look right through her. There was no fear in those gold eyes, no worry that Kane, or anyone else, might find them here. "I cannot release you until I know with certainty that you are not the one."

Her heart hitched. "Of course you can release me. I won't tell anyone what happened. To be honest, I don't have the time. I must reach the capital city as soon as possible." Did the wild man have sympathy in his big heart? If he did, then he would not keep her from her child. "I have a baby," she explained.

"I know." He sniffed the air around her. "I can smell the milk in you, and the fear."

Her lower lip trembled. "She was kidnapped more than a week ago, and I'm going to reclaim her."

"The man who travels with you, who is he?"

"The baby's father," she explained, "he's coming for me. If you let me go I can meet him and lead him away from you."

"I am not afraid to face this man."

Sophie glanced at her abductor's large hands, his bulging muscles. No, he would not be afraid of much, she imagined.

If fear wouldn't motivate him, perhaps friendship would. "What's your name?"

"Ryn."

"I'm Sophie. Would you please untie my hands and feet? I doubt I could outrun you even if I tried."

Ryn saw the truth of that and began to untie the ropes at her ankles. He hadn't used a rough rope, but something almost silken in texture. Taking her had not been a mistake, but a well-planned misdeed. What had he meant when he'd said that he had to make sure she was not *the one?*

"What did you use to make me faint?" she asked as he turned her about and began to untie the bonds at her wrists.

"Why do you want to know?" His voice was decidedly cultured, for such a wild-looking creature.

"If I remember correctly it was a leaf you held beneath my nose right before I passed out. I'm interested in plants and their many uses." Still sitting, she turned to face Ryn. She rubbed her wrists and studied his utterly masculine face. Could she scare him with the truth? "You see, I'm a witch."

"I know." He stood, grasping her wrist in his large hand and hauling her to her feet. "I smell the craft on you."

Sophie tried to jerk her hand away but was unsuccessful. "Would you cease your observations about how I stink! I've been traveling, and there hasn't exactly been time to stop for sweetly scented baths along the way."

A half smile crooked his mouth. "I did not say you stink, I said you smell. There is a difference, you know."

"The plant," she said tersely. "What was it?"

A small bag made from the skin of an animal hung from his waist, and he opened it with one hand and dipped long fingers inside to grasp a leaf. It was small, oddly shaped, shiny and deep green. "I have heard that the tanni tree grows only in the mountains to the north. Perhaps that is why you have not heard of it. When the leaf is broken and the scent inhaled, it causes a brief period of unconsciousness."

"Brief? I was out all night!"

"It works in different ways with different people."

She studied the innocent-looking leaf, leaning toward Ryn's hand. She even reached out and gently touched the rough edge. Without warning, she snatched the leaf from Ryn, broke it between two fingers, and reached up to hold it beneath his nose.

He smiled at her before taking the broken leaf from her and tossing it aside. "The tanni leaf has no affect on Anwyn."

KANE LED THE HORSES WHILE HE STUDIED THE TRACKS. He was hours behind Sophie and the man who had taken her, and he hadn't been able to track at all during the night hours. Hours in which they'd moved away from him.

For a long time, there had been only one pair of footprints. Bare, large footprints widely spaced from the edge of the pond toward the hills to the north. A light rain during the night had slowed him down, but it had not stopped him and it had not completely obliterated the tracks.

Sophie and the kidnapper had rested on a rock outcropping before moving on; there were two sets of footprints from that point on. He had found no sign of violence, but that did nothing to ease his mind. The tracks would have been impossible to follow to anyone who hadn't spent more than two years scouting for the rebels.

A few weeks ago he hadn't remembered Sophie as anything other than a dream, and he hadn't known about Ariana at all. And now he felt like he would be worthless and useless without them. He'd lost everything else . . . he couldn't lose them, too.

He glanced up at the cloudless sky. The rain had moved through quickly, last night. He and Sophie should be well on their way down the road to the capital city. Instead he was heading off into the wilderness . . . away from the palace and his daughter.

In the distance mountains loomed, blue and gray and hard. They seemed to climb forever—even from so far away. A man could hide for years in a place like that. A woman could be lost forever.

Throughout the day the ground had grown rockier, harder to track. The thought that he might lose the tracks altogether almost made him panic. If he completely lost the trail, what should he do? Continue his search into the mountains, or go to Arthes to rescue his daughter? Surely God wouldn't make him choose.

Just when he was about to lose hope, he saw it: a spot of color where there should be none. He ran in that direction, smiling when he saw the scrap of fabric. When he'd last seen Sophie she'd been wearing a yellow blouse tucked into tan trousers. The torn fabric might've worried him, if it hadn't been tied into a neat little bow.

He looked down, and there at his feet was a marking in the dirt. A furrow, perhaps made with the heel of a boot.

An arrow, drawn in the dirt. It pointed north.

"That's my girl," he said softly as he jumped into the saddle of his horse and followed.

"PLEASE," SOPHIE PLEADED, NOT FOR THE FIRST TIME. "YOU must let me go."

"I haven't yet decided what to do with you."

Those matter-of-fact words sent a chill up her spine. "There's no need for you to do anything but release me," she said.

Ryn led her by the silken ropes that once again bound her wrists. He'd forgiven her failed attempt with the tanni leaf, but he still carried a grudge because she'd pulled his hair and then tried to run.

Foolish move.

She'd never been anywhere but Shandley and Fyne Mountain, and the landscape here was very different from home. To the north, an imposing mountain range awaited them. To the west, the plains were flat and harsh and seemed to go on forever.

She had heard of the barren heart of Columbyana, that harsh stretch of land so unfriendly to farms and ranches that no settlement had lasted here more than a few years. In the past hundred years no one had tried to make the heart of the country habitable. The land was hard, that was true. It was harsh and unwelcoming, but also magnificent in a way she had not expected.

Sophie stared at Ryn's tangled hair. What kind of magic would set her free? A heartfelt wish, a traditional spell . . . she wasn't sure. She should have studied with Isadora more often and more diligently. She wasn't familiar with a spell that would help her in such a circumstance.

If Juliet had not been able to stop Galvyn, what chance did Sophie have? They had never studied a magic that might be used against violence, because they'd never thought the need would arise.

"Your scent teases me still, as if you are the one, and it's time."

"Time for what?" she asked sharply.

"You ask too many questions."

"Perhaps you should have kidnapped someone else!"

Ryn ignored her, this time.

Tears stung her eyes. When Juliet had warned her it would not be safe to travel alone, she should have been more specific. When she'd said the journey would take three weeks, not two, she should have reached deeper to find out why. A warning about large, stubborn Anwyn would've been helpful.

Juliet would've given such a warning, if she had seen. Sophie knew that. But still . . .

"You cry too much," Ryn said dispassionately, without so much as looking at her to know that she was once again near tears.

"I do not need personal criticism from a . . . a . . . from the creature who kidnapped me."

Ryn had a gift for ignoring her. "You wear your feelings too close to the skin. It's as if they flutter just beneath the flesh, rather than finding a seat deep inside as they should."

"Spoken like a man who obviously doesn't know what a feeling is," Sophie muttered.

"They weaken you," he continued. "There is strength in your passions, and you shed them through drops of water from your eyes. One day you must learn to hold onto that strength and expel it in a more useful manner. I will help you," he added softly.

"I don't want or need your help," Sophie replied, anger drying her eyes.

Ryn ignored her, and they walked unerringly forward. Did the man's long legs never ache? Did he not need food or water or rest? He moved with such ease, the muscles in his legs and in his bare back rippling beneath the sun-bronzed skin, the long hair lifted only slightly when the wind stirred.

She did not understand why he had kidnapped her, but the way he talked of helping her to harness her emotions . . . obviously he had no intention of releasing her. What if Kane never found her?

"I need a moment of privacy," she said demurely.

He stopped, turned slowly, and glared at her. "Again?"

"I'm nervous," she said defensively. "It's all your fault."

She'd requested a moment of privacy for personal matters five times since they'd begun traveling. Perhaps there was a hint of civility within the man because he had not yet denied her request. He had begun to grumble, though.

He eyed her suspiciously, but finally released her and pointed to a small outcropping of rocks. "Hurry."

Sophie headed in that direction. Sharp words followed her. "If you try to run I will be very angry!"

She could not imagine making someone Ryn's size very angry. So far he had only been annoyed, perhaps a bit confused. Behind the shelter of the rocks Sophie untucked her blouse and ripped off a thin strip, as she had five times previously on this long day. Making the initial tear had been tough. She'd pierced the fabric with a sharp rock, and then she'd torn the fabric and ripped off a thin, longish scrap. Since then it had been easier, as the tail end of her shirt was already in tatters.

The ground was growing more desolate, so there was no limb to tie the fabric to. She made a small bow and placed it on a small rock that she prayed Kane would see. She and Ryn had been heading unerringly for a mountain in the near distance, and she used the heel of her boot to draw an arrow that pointed in that direction.

She smiled, rounded the rock, and almost ran into Ryn's massive bare chest. Her chin reached just slightly above his belly button.

"I expect you to respect my privacy," she said, as soon as her heart started beating somewhat normally again.

Ryn made a noise that sounded suspiciously like a growl, then rounded the rock.

"Wait!" Sophie called.

Too late. Ryn found the yellow bow and the arrow in the dirt.

For a long moment he was very quiet. He did not look at her at all, just studied the bow and the sign in the dirt. "How many times?" he asked quietly.

"I don't know what you . . ."

Ryn reached out, his hands quick for a large man, and untucked her blouse. He studied the hem, where she'd ripped away the scraps that might very well lead Kane to her.

Surprisingly, Ryn replaced the bow where he'd found it. Then he destroyed the arrow she'd drawn in the dirt.

"Make another," he commanded. "That way." He pointed west.

Sophie shook her head. "No." If Kane headed across the desolate plains, he'd never find her!

Ryn looked her in the eye and glared, as if he thought that glare might change her mind. She shook her head, and her stomach lurched unpleasantly. Her mouth went dry. It was one thing to stand one's ground, but another altogether when doing so meant facing down a man who was arguably twice her size and definitely more than twice as strong.

He waited for her to relent. She didn't. When Ryn realized that he wasn't going to sway her with that glare, he dipped down and grabbed her ankle, then forcibly removed her boot. He used the heel to make an arrow of his own. It pointed west. He stood slowly and looked toward the plains. And he smiled.

With the other booted foot, Sophie kicked him in the shin. "You bastard! Let me go this instant! I'll make you sorry. Kane will make you sorry. He'll find me anyway, no matter what kind of tricks you pull."

Ryn leaned down to place his face close to hers. The smile was gone. "I could kill him, you know, simply for touching you. It is allowed."

Sophie suddenly felt dizzy. No, Kane wasn't supposed to get hurt. "That makes no sense," she tried to sound calm, but her voice trembled. "How can it be allowed?"

"It's time to go," Ryn said calmly.

Sophie planted her feet; one booted, one sporting nothing but a dirty stocking. "No."

He lifted her and tossed her over his shoulder as if she weighed no more than one of his tanni leaves. "By tonight I will know if you are the one or not. If you are the one, we will be married long before your former lover ever finds us."

"Married? I'm never getting married. And if I do, it won't be to a half-dressed savage who kidnaps women."

"If you are the one, we will be married," Ryn said calmly.

"The one," Sophie scoffed. "The one *what?*"

"My mate," he said.

"I am not . . . that's ridiculous . . . what a preposterous . . ."

"Anwyn recognize their mates by smell."

Smell, again. "Well, there's something wrong with your nose, sir."

"I know," he said softly. "You are true, and yet not true. Tonight I will know with certainty if you are my mate or not."

"Not," she said succinctly, even as her heart kicked.

"You must learn to accept me, Sophie, if it is right that you do so."

She looked back at the rock where the false signal waited for Kane. Why couldn't she do something? Why couldn't she set herself free? What good was magic if she couldn't even escape from one big hulk of a monster? She was an absolute failure as a witch. All she could do was . . .

Sophie lifted her head and studied the barren, rocky ground as if with new eyes. Was it possible? She concentrated on a dry patch of dirt and whispered a few words.

Nothing happened.

She tried again, even gesturing with one hand, this time, and concentrating so hard everything else in her line of vision blurred. Nothing.

After a few more minutes of jostling, she sighed. "Put me down. I'm getting a headache hanging this way."

"Give me your word that you won't run."

"You'd just catch me," she grumbled.

He gently deposited her on her feet, and she pushed the tangled hairs away from her face. She could try to reason with him one more time. "I won't marry you no matter what," she insisted, "and even if you force me into some primitive sort of marriage, I won't stay with you."

"Of course you will stay," he said calmly. "Anwyn mate for life."

"I'm not Anwyn!" she argued. "Why must you kidnap women for wives? Can't you marry one of your own kind?"

He grinned at her. "Anwyn make only one girl child every fifty years or so. But it does not matter. We recognize our mates—"

"By smell," Sophie finished. "I know. I hate to be the one to tell you, but I think your nose is broken, Ryn. I am *not* your mate."

"I will know tonight," he said ominously.

"How? What happens tonight?"

"Full moon."

Just when she thought he might allow her to continue on unbound, he grabbed her wrists and quickly trussed them together.

II

HE ALMOST MISSED IT. THE SCRAP OF FABRIC WAS NOT TIED to a branch but sat on an outcropping of rocks. The flash of yellow caught Kane's attention and he dismounted.

It would be dark in a few hours, and Sophie would begin her second night as a hostage. That realization caused a moment of panic he could not afford. He should have caught up with her and the abductor by now, since they were on foot and he was on horseback, but he'd passed through some rough terrain that he could have traveled over more quickly by foot, and he was not only riding his own horse but also leading the black gelding he'd purchased for Sophie as they'd left Shandley.

The arrow in the dirt pointed west, and for a moment he turned his attention in that direction.

The arrow was very much like the other signs Sophie had left for him, but something wasn't right; he felt as much as saw the difference. Instead of hurrying in that direction in order to find the woman he'd lost, he dropped down on his haunches to study the furrow. The depth wasn't the same as the others—it was deeper—and it wasn't quite as straight. He lifted his head and stared toward the plains before him, squinting and becoming very still, opening not only his eyes and his mind, but his heart. There was nothing out there. Nothing.

His gut told him Sophie had not made this particular arrow, which meant two things. She was in trouble, and the man who had taken her knew Kane was following.

He looked in the opposite direction, searching for a sign . . . and he found one. The land was barren and had been for miles, but a small cluster of lavender wildflowers had cropped up in an odd pattern. He walked toward them. It was almost as if the flowers formed . . . an arrow.

Kane followed the direction of the wildflower arrow. A few feet away he found footprints. A single set, once again, but deeper, like those he'd discovered leading away from the pond.

The bastard was carrying her.

LIANE TOOK THE LIFT TO LEVEL SEVEN, WHERE THE WITCH who prepared the potions for Level Three—potions to prevent babies and elixirs to enhance pleasure—resided, along with others of her kind. Emperor Nechtyn's father had once banned magic altogether, but his son had relaxed the prohibition during his command. The benefits had outweighed the risks.

She did not care for Level Seven. It was dark, much like Level One, and there was always an odd smell in the air. The stench of simmering concoctions and dried herbs was musky and mysterious, and it reminded her of the days when she had not been so privileged as she was today. Her first dose of the concoction meant to keep her childless had been forced down her throat, and her first whiff of the foul potion had made her gag and cry.

These days she didn't so much as flinch as she swallowed it down.

Liane quickly sought out Gadhra, the old woman who supplied the Level Three potions. The sooner this was done and she could return to her own Level, the happier she'd be.

Gadhra had a series of rooms, which indicated her importance in the palace. There was a bedchamber, which Liane had no desire to see, a large room where she met with visitors and trained apprentices, and a kitchen of sorts, where the witch did her work. It was that kitchen that made this Level reek. Liane covered her nose as she entered the kitchen. She'd have to bathe before going to Sebestyen. Perhaps twice.

A woman of power should dress better, Liane thought as Gadhra greeted her. Even though the witch was less than five feet tall, beyond ancient, and as homely as any man or woman she'd ever seen, you'd think she would clothe herself in something other than rags.

And her clothes truly were no better than rags. It was impossible to tell if the old woman wore a dress, a blouse and skirt, or a wrap of some sort. Whatever it might be, the garment was loose and ragged and dirty.

Straight to business. "The emperor is not feeling well. He needs something to brighten his mood."

Gadhra lifted one eyebrow. "Sebestyen does not take my potions. Ever. He is afraid I might forget my loyalty and poison him, or that someone else might slip an ingredient not of my making into the liquid before he partakes. He has not changed his mind on that subject, of that I'm quite sure."

"Fine," Liane snapped. "I need something to lift *my* spirits."

The old witch smiled and shook her head. "I have not lived so long by being foolish. I can, of course, give you an elixir which will lift your spirits, but if you try to convince the boy to take it he will know you're trying to deceive him and he will be very angry."

"The Emperor Sebestyen is not a boy," Liane said in her coldest voice.

The witch seemed not at all surprised or concerned by

Liane's anger. "He will always be a boy to me, just as you will always be a girl."

Liane did not tell the old woman that she had not felt like a girl since the age of fifteen. "Just give me something."

Since the moment she'd told Sebestyen about Maddox, he'd been angry or depressed or both. Maddox had been at his right hand, in the days when he'd been too young to rule entirely without counsel, and the news that his most trusted ally would lie to him . . . he was taking it harder than she'd expected. These days Sebestyen was given to long periods of silence, and when his temper did rise to the surface and explode it was mighty and unpredictable. She could not control him when he was this way. Something to soothe his nerves, that's all she needed.

"Should I have it delivered or will you wait?"

"I'll wait," Liane answered.

Gadhra quickly assembled the potion Liane had requested. She hummed as she worked, as if she enjoyed her job. She tossed a splash of this and a dash of that into a small silver bowl. She stirred the mixture with a wooden spoon, then studied it for a moment before adding one more pinch of a dried herb from her shelf. When she was finished, she poured the thin amber liquid into a small bottle, capped it, and all but skipped back to Liane.

"Here you are," the witch said as she handed the bottle over.

Liane took it, ready to make her escape. She would have asked for the potion to be delivered to her on Level Three, but the fewer people who knew about her association with Gadhra the better.

As Liane turned, Gadhra said, "The boy will not take it from your hand. He does not trust you."

She spun on the old woman. "He does trust me."

Gadhra shook her head. Wild gray wisps of hair went in all directions. "No, but perhaps one day he will. I think perhaps . . . yes."

Liane took a step toward the witch. "Do you see something of the future?"

"Seeing what is to come is not my gift." She shrugged her shoulders. "I make potions and I teach. That is all."

Disgusted, Liane turned to leave. As she began to close the door she heard the old woman say, "But some nights, I have the most vivid dreams . . ."

RYN QUICKENED HIS PACE AS SUNSET APPROACHED, HEADing unerringly for a small hill that was a preface to a landscape of small hills that seemed to stretch forever before them. Mountains, much more stark and majestic than what she called mountains at home, loomed in the distance. There was something quite frightening about those mountains.

Sophie glanced up as they turned onto a narrow path and began to climb. For the past several hours the land they marched across had not been entirely desolate. Gnarled trees and scrubby brush grew here and there, and in the distance there were signs of green forests that marked the end of the barren heart. The hill Ryn climbed so easily showed signs of being quite green, in places. "Is this your home?"

"No. Hurry."

"I'm no closer to collecting my daughter. In fact, you're leading me away from the road I need to take! And I'm tired," Sophie protested. "My feet hurt, my shoulders ache, and I'm hungry."

It was the first time she could remember being hungry since she'd discovered that Galvyn Farrell had taken Ariana. Kane had encouraged her to eat, now and then; he'd even forced her to eat one night when she'd been particularly downhearted. But she had not noted hunger until this moment.

"We will eat after," Ryn said brusquely.

Sophie slowed her step. *After?*

"Hurry!"

Ryn gave her bonds a tug and she ran after him to keep from falling on her face. If she fell, would he just drag her along? Likely, considering his haste. He turned onto an even narrower path that wound up the hill, much like the path that had taken Sophie home so many times. But this was not Fyne Mountain, and there was no cabin, and no sisters, awaiting her at the end of a long trail.

They did not go to the top of the hill, but cut off the trail about halfway up the slope. Ryn seemed to know exactly where he was going. He dipped under branches and parted thick underbrush for her, his step quick and certain. And that step was rushed. He no longer told her to hurry, but she felt the haste in every move he made.

Nothing worried her quite as much as the assured way he said they'd eat *after*. Ryn was under the mistaken notion that she was his mate, and she knew very well what that meant.

Making love to an Anwyn would be interesting, the sort of thing any truly free woman of unbridled passion might find acceptable. Ryn did not know where she lived, and so he could not become a problem in the future. And it wasn't as if he weren't an attractive man, in his own decidedly primitive way.

But she did not want him to touch her. Her daughter was in danger, Ryn had given her no choice in the matter . . . and then there was Kane. She had not changed her mind about what she wanted and did not want in her life, but at the moment Kane was hers. And she was his. She knew it wouldn't last, couldn't last, but for now she was committed to him in a way she had not expected.

They came upon a wide cave opening, and Ryn all but shoved her inside.

"No, Ryn, please," she said as he entered behind her. The last of the daylight was almost gone, and all was black inside the darkness of the cave. She made herself look up and into Ryn's face, only to find that his eyes glowed golden in the darkness.

She gasped.

"Don't be afraid," he said. His voice, which she had noted on several occasions was quite beautiful, was deeper than before. Huskier. His breathing changed, became quicker, louder. "I won't hurt you." This promise was followed by a noise that sounded suspiciously like a growl. "Sit."

She was so startled by what was happening that she did exactly as he ordered. With her back to the cold stone wall of the cave, she watched as gold eyes that glowed so distinctly drifted down to join her. Those eyes were all she could see, and they hovered directly before hers.

Ryn took a long, deep breath, then leaned into her. He smelled her, much as he had this morning, sniffing at her neck and her face and down the length of her arm. And then he did something she had not expected.

He raked his tongue across her throat. Slowly. With leisure and . . . something else. Something she could not describe, it was so foreign to her. Teeth nipped along skin he had just recently tasted. Those teeth did not hurt Sophie, but they certainly did startle her. She began to tremble, and it wasn't a pleasant tremble, like the one she'd experienced when Kane had kissed her.

"Ryn, please . . ." Sophie tried for calm, but her voice had a decided edge of panic. He continued to nibble on her neck, so she reached up to push him away. Her hand landed on his chest.

A very hairy chest. Until this moment his chest had been smooth and muscled, without so much as a dusting of hair. But there was hair beneath her hand. It was thick, and silky, and definitely *not* human.

She was trapped here in this cave, with her back against the stone wall and a . . . a . . . she didn't know what he was . . . before her. She raised her hand to touch Ryn's face, wondering what changes she would feel there. But somehow he knew what she was doing and he stopped her with a quick and strong hand at her wrist. A hand and not a hand. It too was hairy, and what could only be claws bit into her flesh as he held her hand away from his face.

"You are not the one," he growled.

She was hardly in a position to say *I told you so.*

"But you are close," he whispered. "So close." Ryn licked her throat again, slowly trailing the tip of his tongue from one side to the other, ending the exploration with a nip at the curve of her shoulder. "Remember," he said, his voice so gruff it was now unrecognizable. "Don't cry."

And then he was gone.

A FULL MOON IN A CLOUDLESS SKY ALLOWED KANE TO CONtinue on long into the night. At the present time he rode Sophie's horse and led his own, and would continue to switch animals throughout the night and into tomorrow.

For the first time, he asked himself the question he'd been avoiding since he'd discovered that Sophie was gone. *What if I don't find her?* or worse, *What if I don't find her in time?*

The very thought of coming across Sophie's lifeless body on the rocky ground made him shudder like a child who had never before faced danger. It was an unimaginable thought, one he could not bear to contemplate. He had lost loved ones in the past, he had buried friends. But he had never before been so scared.

Sophie was life itself, and the idea that someone might take that life from her was unthinkable. She should live to be an old woman, to get laugh lines around her eyes and gray hairs among the gold. She should have other children, and grandchildren. Sophie loved children; she should live to a ripe old age surrounded by them. But if she died . . .

He didn't see how he could go on without Sophie, but how

could he abandon Ariana to Galvyn Farrell? He couldn't. Sophie's ghost would haunt him forever if he didn't finish the quest they'd begun.

There had been a time when he'd considered taking Ariana from Sophie himself, but that had been before he'd truly known her. Before he'd realized what kind of person she was. Witch or not, she was a remarkable woman who loved her child. It was unthinkable that he might end up raising his daughter alone because her mother was gone.

He hadn't found a single sign since leaving the boulders where he'd seen the false arrow in the dirt and the strange tuft of wildflowers. Perhaps the arrow in the dirt hadn't been meant to mislead him after all, and he was heading in the wrong direction. Maybe the wildflowers had been nothing more than wildflowers growing in a strange pattern. Long before complete darkness had fallen, he'd lost the ability to track Sophie and her abductor. The ground had become rockier, and there were streams where his prey might cross without leaving a trail. Since there was always the possibility that they might double back to cover their tracks, he questioned every turn, every decision.

A while back he'd come across a narrow rocky path that looked as if it had been recently disturbed, and that path had led him to this place. The trail he was on led toward green hills in the near distance and gray mountains beyond. A man might hide there for years and never be found.

He'd lost her. The truth hit him sharp and deep, as if it were a weapon. Kane continued forward, the horse he rode and the one he led moving at a slow pace. It would take a miracle for him to find her now. A miracle . . . or magic. Sophie possessed magic, but he did not. He had only himself to rely on. His skills, his wits. And they had failed him, just as they'd failed him when Duran and the others had been killed.

The unexpected sound that drew his attention away from the road was so soft, he brought the horse to a halt and strained to hear it again. For a moment all was silent, and then the noise, faint and sweet, reached his ears once more.

It was a voice. A woman's voice. He hadn't seen another living thing all day, except for a few birds, bugs, and ratlike creatures. He closed his eyes and listened, placing the voice and identifying it.

She was just ahead, and it was Sophie.

Kane dismounted and led the horses to the side of the road, where he quickly hitched them to the low-lying limb of a gnarled tree. Sophie didn't sound frightened, which was a relief, but Kane didn't expect the man who had kidnapped her would be happy to be caught. He drew his sword and kept to the side of the road, his steps silent. It sounded as if Sophie were coming toward him, not moving away, but she was too far away from him to see her. The road twisted and turned, and ancient trees in full leaf obscured his view of the road and the people ahead.

He was so relieved to hear her voice he almost smiled. It was all he could do to keep from running to meet her on the road. But that would be foolish and reckless. He was many things, but he wasn't reckless.

She was close. He heard only her voice. Either she was talking to herself or her captor listened without responding.

"Juliet was right," Sophie said. He could hear her footsteps on the road, too, steady and sure. "This delay will surely cost us days of travel. Days without my baby. That just isn't right."

And then he heard the sound that had first caught his attention. She began to sing. It was a child's song, perhaps something she sang to Ariana on occasion. Her voice was sweet, without anger or fear, and her footsteps were in harmony with the gentle tune about birds and butterflies and sunshine.

When she was almost upon him, Kane stepped into the shadows to stand hidden amongst the trees. The hilt of the sword fit comfortably in his right hand. His left rested ready and able over the knife that was sheathed at his waist. Just in case. He couldn't move until he saw Sophie and the man who had taken her. The bastard might be right beside Sophie, or behind her, just waiting for Kane to show himself. He would wait here for them to pass, and then he'd attack from the rear.

Sophie came walking around the corner, her stride even and in time with the song she sang, her hair silver in the moonlight. She appeared to be unhurt and was in fact in good spirits, or so it appeared. Kane waited for a stealthy and silent captor to appear behind her, but Sophie passed him and continued down the road, and no one else materialized.

Kane stepped into the road and called her name, and Sophie turned quickly to face him. For a moment she was silent, stunned that he had stepped out of the forest without warning. But after a moment she ran toward him, and when she reached him she threw her arms around his neck and held on so tight he could barely breathe. He put his arm around her, too, and lifted her off her feet.

"I knew you would find me," she said softly. "I knew it! I wished on the moon for you to find me, and you did. You did."

"I thought you were lost," Kane admitted as he held her tight.

"I was kidnapped!" she said, her voice light and quick. "By an Anwyn, of all things. I thought they were nothing more than legend, but they're real, Kane. They're real! And he was . . . he . . ."

"Did he hurt you?" Kane asked softly.

Sophie shook her head. "No, he thought I was his mate, but of course I'm not, and . . . I can't explain it, not now. I just want to hold you for a while. Can I do that? Can I just hold you?"

It was what he wanted, too, to hold on. To cradle Sophie in his arms and assure himself again and again that she was here and safe and he wouldn't have to continue to imagine what this world would be like without her in it. "We'll find a place close by to camp for the night. The horses are not too far down the path. In the morning, we'll head back to the main road and continue on to Arthes."

She nodded and pulled slightly away from him, but she kept her arms around him. He stepped away only long enough to sheath his sword, and then he pulled her close again.

"I never doubted that you would find me," she said as they walked down the path. Her arm around his waist, his over her shoulder.

"Neither did I." It was a small lie. He had only begun to doubt in the last few hours. Terrible hours. Hopeless hours. The moon lit their way, and suddenly he was aware of the beauty of this place. The trees, the night sky, even the dirt trail; it was all beautiful, because Sophie was here and safe. What kind of a dimwit was he? He had no home, no life, no money except that which he'd come by thanks to Sophie's magic. He had absolutely nothing to offer a woman. But then again—he couldn't imagine his life without this woman in it.

"Sophie," he said, as they rounded a bend in the road and the horses came into view, "I think I love you."

She sighed. Not the response he'd hoped for, exactly. What had he hoped for? A smile? A declaration of her own?

"Love is a dangerous thing," she said softly. "And besides, you haven't known me long enough to know whether or not you could truly love me. I might not be at all the person you believe me to be. Perhaps I have only shown you the pieces of myself that I wish for you to see. It takes years for a man and woman to understand one another well enough to know if true love is possible. Then again, when you say *love* you might be thinking entirely of physical passion, which of course we know is glorious and exciting but not the same as a lasting and romantic love."

"You've given this subject a lot of thought," Kane mumbled.

"Of course I have." Again, Sophie sighed. "I think I love you, too."

* * *

LIANE BATHED BEFORE GOING TO SEBESTYEN. SHE CHANGED her clothes and scented her skin with lotion and oils, and still the stench of Level Seven teased and burned her nose.

As she prepared herself for the evening, she glanced often to the vial that sat on her dresser. It looked innocuous sitting there amongst the creams and lotions, as if it belonged. It sat, plain and benign, next to her hairbrush. So why did its presence eat at her?

She could simply tell Sebestyen what was in the bottle and ask him to take it.

But he wouldn't.

She could coax him, but considering his mood she didn't think he'd coax easily, and the attempt could damage her position.

If the stuff didn't smell like shit she'd rub it all over her body and hope that in the course of the evening Sebestyen would lick enough of it off to do him some good.

But it did smell like shit, and if he ever suspected that she would dare to trick him, she probably wouldn't live long enough to see Level Thirteen.

If she thought Gadhra would give her poison, she'd rub that all over her body and let Sebestyen lick that away until death claimed him. But the old witch would never do such a thing. She had a fondness for the emperor, even though he detested her work and had refused to see her personally for the past ten years or so.

He hated magic, but he feared it more.

Gadhra hinted that one day Sebestyen would trust her. Could she put any faith in an old woman's dreams?

He had not been himself since she'd told him about Maddox. His greatest fear, rebellion from within, was on his doorstep, and he knew it. He was living his nightmare, and it was eating him alive. He wasn't going to take this potion from her hands, and she didn't dare try to trick him. Not even for his own physical and mental welfare.

Liane grabbed the bottle and carried it to the window. Before she could change her mind she tossed it far into the night. She listened, and in a moment it landed far below with a distant, muted chime of broken glass.

THEY MADE CAMP IN THE FOREST NOT FAR FROM WHERE Kane had left the horses, and they both slept for a couple of hours. They slept together, hanging on to one another as if they'd be separated again if they weren't connected. Sophie slept with her head on Kane's chest and her arm draped around him; he held onto her and imprisoned her legs between his own.

She and Kane had not spoken of love again once they'd begun to set up camp, but the mere mention of the word had remained, as if it echoed silently around them. They had spoken the words, and those words would be with them for the rest of the journey, and beyond. The possibilities were more frightening than the massive Anwyn who changed with the full moon and nipped at her throat as if he might find it tasty.

She couldn't tell him that her love for him would lead to his death. Not now. If she could take the love back and save him she would, but it was too strong to deny and there was nothing she could do to change what she felt.

She doubted that falling out of love would save Kane. Only breaking the curse would accomplish that, and how many Fyne witches had tried to do just that? Breaking a three-hundred-year-old curse was impossible.

Maybe, just maybe . . . nothing was impossible.

Sophie slowly sat up. It was still dark, but she'd slept soundly for a couple of hours. She was ready to move on.

They had wasted so much time. The forest away from the road remained completely dark, but to the east there was a touch of gray in the sky.

Something flashing in the darkness of the forest caught her eye. That dancing light was small, and intense, and gold. She watched as the light came closer, and it wasn't long before she realized it wasn't one bit of light but two that claimed her attention.

Eyes. Ryn's eyes?

A large golden wolf stepped into the clearing where Sophie and Kane had slept. The animal was larger than any wolf she had ever seen, but that wasn't saying much. She had only seen one such animal in her life, on the mountain she called home, and it had been much smaller than this creature. His flaxen hair was longer than the wolf she'd seen.

There was nothing average about this beast.

If she had not touched Ryn in the darkness of the cave, if she had not felt the claws, she would never believe what she saw before her. She was not afraid.

"Don't move," Kane whispered. She heard the whisper of metal on metal as Kane drew his sword. Ryn heard it, too, and the wolf growled, but did not make a move, not forward or back.

"He won't hurt us," she said.

"You can't know—"

"I do know," she said. "Trust me."

Reluctantly, Kane lowered his weapon. But he did not sheath the sword. It remained in his hand, ready.

The wolf walked toward them, steps slow and graceful. Muscles moved smoothly beneath the blond fur, and the eyes remained focused on Sophie's face. She smiled, and the golden eyes sparkled. Sophie knew she was in the presence of a magnificent creature, something grand and mystical and beyond beautiful.

"Sophie," Kane whispered. "I want you to get behind me."

"You can't kill him."

He sat up very slowly. "It won't be easy, but it can be done."

Ryn turned his gaze to Kane and growled again.

"A blade to the throat might do the trick."

Again she heard the whisper of steel against leather, as Kane drew a knife from somewhere on his person. He wore so many she could not be sure which one he had drawn, but she did know he held a sword in one hand and a knife in the other.

Ryn stopped in his tracks.

"See? Now you've scared him."

"He can't understand what I'm saying, and I doubt seriously that anything would scare this monster."

"He's not a monster, he's just . . . different." Kane had no idea how very *different* this animal was. She offered her hand, palm up, and again Ryn stepped forward.

"Sophie!" Completely ignoring her wishes, Kane lifted his sword so that it hovered between her and Ryn.

Long before reaching Sophie's offered hand and the protective blade, the wolf turned his golden gaze to the east, where the sky grew gradually lighter. He seemed transfixed for a moment, and then in a flash he turned and ran, disappearing into the forest.

When the wolf was well gone, Kane resheathed his weapons and wrapped both arms around her, and with his mouth against her neck he sighed in obvious relief. "I know you are a trusting woman," he said gently, "But Sophie, you should never offer your hand to a wolf. The creature might've bitten you, or worse."

She felt quite sure that Ryn wouldn't hurt her, but how could she tell Kane that the creature in the forest and the man who had kidnapped her were one and the same? The explanation would take much too long, and she was anxious to get back on the road. Ariana needed her.

"Perhaps there is a beast in the heart of every man," she said.

"But that doesn't mean there's gentleness in the heart of every beast . . . or man," Kane countered.

Soon there was enough light for her to see the clearing well. Sophie rose to her feet and stretched out sore muscles. She was not used to riding all day, walking all day, or sleeping on the ground. Still, nothing and no one would make her slow down for even a minute. The journey was difficult, but what awaited at the end of the journey was worth any sacrifice.

Kane rose too, stretching out his long limbs. He was oddly fetching in the morning, with his hair mussed and his beard coming in and his eyes sleepy.

"Last night you didn't want to talk about the man who abducted you," he said.

"I was very tired." And so glad to see Kane she'd wanted nothing more than to hold him.

"If not for Ariana, I would track him down today and kill him, but we can't spare the time."

"No, we can't."

Kane took a moment to check all his weapons. Knives, sword, bow and arrow in place. "But I have to know if he's going to be a problem. Will he try to take you again?"

Sophie shook her head. "No. You see, the abduction was a mistake. Ryn won't be a problem, poor thing."

"How can you call your kidnapper a *poor thing?*"

He was angry and confused, and she could certainly understand why. "We don't have time for lengthy explanations. Our daughter needs us, Kane."

His face was tense, his neck corded as if he carried that tension all through his body. "It was very smart of you to make the arrow from wildflowers. You did do that, didn't you? Near the rocks with the false sign?"

"I thought it didn't work!" The soil was hard and flowers must've grown after the patch of ground was out of her sight. "If I had known, I would have left more signs along the way."

"I wish you had," he said softly. "For a while I thought . . ."

"You thought what?" she prompted when he fell silent.

"Nothing."

Not nothing, she imagined, but nothing he wanted to share. She would not push him on the matter. Not now. "Let me ride with you for a while," she suggested, "and while we make our way to Ariana I will tell you an incredible story."

"The two of us on the same horse?" he asked skeptically.

"Just for a while. It will make the telling a little easier."

And besides, she still felt the need to hold Kane. To rest her head on his shoulder and touch his hair and wrap her arms around him as if he alone could keep her safe and warm.

She would tell him about Ryn, but she wasn't sure he'd believe her. The man she had begun to love was stubborn in that way. He had a tendency to believe only that which he could see and explain. He was a rational man. But because he was so beautiful and noble, she could forgive him that one flaw.

12

LIANE WATCHED SEBESTYEN PACE IN THE MASSIVE GRAND ballroom, which seemed even more enormous than usual, since only the two of them presently occupied it. She never should've told him about Maddox's betrayal. Learning that the minister who had been with him from the beginning would lie to him had made Sebestyen furious. It had also made him more paranoid than ever.

But what was done was done.

She refused to consider that passing on the news of Maddox's treachery had been a mistake on her part. Betraying her only real friend in the palace to Sebestyen was a decision she could not undo. She would have to make the best of this new situation. She and the emperor were alone in the ballroom, where he lorded over grand parties and listened to the pleas of those who wanted something from him and met with those in power who served directly beneath him. Ministers from Level Four; priests from Level Two. He had asked for her this afternoon, as he had on so many afternoons of late. He had requested that she be here with him, in this trying time. Not his wife, not a minister or a priest. Her.

She walked toward him, her own crimson robe flowing behind her. It was more lightweight than his. He would get overheated in that garment that was better suited for winter than summer. She would tell him so, very soon. The advice would sound as if she cared about his comfort and health.

"Sebestyen, darling, sit," she said gently. It had been days since she'd told him of Maddox's lies of omission, and still he fretted.

It was a good thing she had not told Sebestyen that Maddox thought him insane.

"I don't want to sit." He continued to pace.

"I'll have some wine and bread sent up. You didn't eat enough of your luncheon."

"I shouldn't eat at all," he insisted. "Someone is trying to poison me, I know it."

"I will taste the wine and the bread myself," she promised. Loyal sentinels manned the kitchens and guarded against any possibility of poisoning, so the risk to herself was a small one. She reached Sebestyen and laid her hand on his arm. When she touched him he stopped pacing. "Let me take care of you, Sebestyen," she said softly.

He looked down at her, and she could see the desperation in his eyes. The loss. The anger. "Why?" he asked. "It is not your duty to take care of me. I have attendants to see to such mundane matters."

Attendants he didn't trust, men and women he called on only when absolutely necessary. "Have I not proven myself to you, my lord? Have I not given you everything a man could ask from a woman?"

"You have," he agreed in a lowered voice.

He relaxed visibly and allowed Liane to lead him to the dais at the back of the room. A gaudy throne, where the emperor often sat when he met with his subordinates, overlooked a deserted floor where on rare occasions people danced, and on other occasions Sebestyen's subjects stood to ask for favors or mercy. There had been little dancing in the room in the past several years, and even less mercy.

All four of his wedding ceremonies had taken place in this room, the first when he'd been a mere fifteen. Liane had not seen any one of them.

She held his hand as he sat, and then she leaned over and kissed his forehead as she might a child's. With a smile, she gently ordered him to stay in his chair.

When Sebestyen was settled, Liane hurried to the doorway and threw open one of the massive double doors. She gave Taneli her list of demands, and the young sentinel listened intently. A lightweight robe, a ewer of water and a washcloth, a comb from the emperor's chamber, wine and bread. Taneli didn't like her and he certainly didn't trust her, but he did not complain about the requests. Others in the palace were beginning to notice that the courtesan Liane was most favored these days.

As she finished making her demands, a man carrying a baby appeared with an official escort. She had seen him several times in the past few days. He was continually requesting an imperial audience. His timing could not have been worse.

He locked his eyes to hers and said, "Please, madam. I must see the emperor."

Liane ignored the man and started to close the door in his face when his words stopped her. "At least tell me when Minister Sulyen will return."

She leaned against the door and glared at the man. He was passably handsome, but too short and small to be striking, too ordinary to rouse her attentions. Why would a man like this one be asking about Maddox? "What is Minister Sulyen to you?"

The man lifted the child so that Liane could see a beautiful little face and a tuft of pale hair. "This is his grandchild."

Liane's heart climbed into her throat. That infant was Maddox's grandchild? Impossible. "Minister Sulyen has no family," she said calmly.

"No legitimate family," the man responded. "My name is Galvyn Farrell. I come from a small town in the Southern Province. Shandley. I doubt you've heard of it, it's very small. Just a short while ago I discovered that Sophie Fyne, a young lady who lives nearby, is Minister Sulyen's illegitimate child. This is her daughter. I plan to make Sophie my wife." Farrell spoke quickly, as if he were afraid Liane would close the door in his face if he took a breath. "Sophie is on her way here to present herself to her father and ask his permission for the marriage to take place. Since the minister is not currently in the palace, she will most likely be brought here. It's important that the emperor agree to her request. I'd like the marriage to take place right away."

Liane glanced down at the innocent face of Maddox's granddaughter. "Go home," she said softly. "Don't come back."

She tried to close the door, but the man caught it with one booted foot. Behind him, a sentinel raised his sword. Liane held the soldier off with a wave of her hand. She could handle this little man, if it came to that, and bloodshed on the doorstep would only upset Sebestyen.

"My mother is cousin to the emperor's mother's aunt by marriage," Farrell said quickly.

Liane gave Farrell a narrow-eyed glare. Columbyana was overrun with distant cousins of one sort of another.

The man did not give up easily. "I'm quite sure that Minister Sulyen would like to know he has a daughter and a granddaughter!"

Liane closed her eyes when she heard the footsteps behind her. Why had Sebestyen not stayed on his throne as she had requested?

"Sulyen's daughter?" Sebestyen said, a touch of brightness in his voice.

"And granddaughter," Farrell said briskly.

There was a moment of heavy silence. Farrell did not dare to ramble in the emperor's presence, and Sebestyen was quiet as well. Liane was about to forcibly remove the annoying man with the baby when Sebestyen spoke.

"I want them," he said softly. It was the first time in days she'd heard life in his voice.

"One moment," she said to Farrell. She gave the man a gentle shove that sent him a step backward, then she closed the door and turned to Sebestyen. His eyes sparkled, and a touch of color returned to his cheeks. Dammit, she was supposed to be the one to instill him with renewed life, not news of an illegitimate child that filled his heart with thoughts of revenge. And he would want revenge. If Maddox wasn't here to feel his emperor's rage and suffer his vengeance, then what better substitute than the minister's own flesh and blood?

She placed a stilling hand on his chest. His heart beat fast and hard. "The daughter is not yet here, and in any case, retaliation would be best executed after Maddox's return, don't you think?"

"When will she get here, this daughter?"

"I don't know."

Sebestyen smiled and touched her cheek with tenderness. "I will leave it to you, Liane. Put that man and the baby where they can be guarded at all times. I don't want them slipping through my fingers."

She sighed, annoyed at the complication. "They won't."

"And when the daughter arrives, I want her brought to me immediately."

"Of course."

Liane led an excited Sebestyen—who was already making his plans for revenge—back to his throne, before returning to Farrell and instructing a sentinel to take their new guests to one of the suites on Level Five. Farrell was pleased; he had no idea what being housed on Level Five near the empress meant.

Farrell and the baby were taken away, and it was only minutes before everything Liane had asked for arrived. When she and Sebestyen were alone again, she undressed him, bathed him, and then redressed him in the robe that was better suited to summer weather. She stood behind him and combed his hair, taking care not to tug at the tangles, while he discussed the ways in which he might avenge himself on Minister Sulyen's unsuspecting daughter.

"But you must be patient," Liane said. She wasn't worried about another woman in Sebestyen's bed, and she definitely didn't worry that a woman might steal his heart. He had none. Neither did she, which made them the perfect match. A match made in hell. "You can make the girl a concubine, you can chain her to your bed, you can degrade her in a thousand ways, but if Maddox isn't here to see it then you've wasted a golden opportunity. You must be patient, darling."

He sighed and relaxed. "I like it when you call me darling."

She tasted the wine and the bread, and when it was clear neither was poisoned she shared them with Sebestyen. Since Sebestyen truly believed that someone in the palace would like to poison him, he saw the gesture as a grand one.

Sebestyen's spirits were much improved by his newfound plans of vengeance. He actually smiled for the first time in days. While they ate he cupped her breasts and teased her with his long fingers, then he hauled her onto his lap with such force that she spilled her wine. He had not been an attentive lover of late, but as she sat on his lap he promised that would change shortly.

Tonight. He had other plans for the afternoon. Exciting plans he did not share with her. It was a surprise, he said as he left her on the dais to walk to the door and deliver an order of his own to the sentinels.

That done, Sebestyen sat on his throne and once again pulled Liane onto his lap. He unfastened a few buttons and pushed her robe to one side, so he could kiss her throat and suckle at her breast. Her body responded, as it always did, and soon she had her fingers threaded through his hair. Head back, she pulled him closer. He drew the nipple deeper into his warm, wet mouth.

She did not hate him when he touched her this way; she couldn't. It was as if he became another man, for a while. As if he put away everything ugly in these moments. Yes, it was pleasure, not love. It was entirely physical, not of the heart or the spirit. But it was a special pleasure she had never known with any other man.

Sebestyen lifted her robe and teased her with his fingers, but he would not allow her to touch him. He wanted only to watch her find pleasure, he said, as he stroked the damp folds and the nub at her entrance. He wanted to make her scream and shake in his hands.

And he did.

There were moments when she imagined Sebestyen was the common man she would never take as husband, an ordinary lover who had not given her to other men when it suited him.

If they had met in another time and place, and he wasn't emperor and she wasn't a concubine, would she hate him still? Would she dream of killing him?

She was lying in his arms, shaking still, when the doors opened and two sentinels led the Empress Rikka into the room. Liane tried to leave Sebestyen's lap, but he would not allow it. He wrapped both arms around her and made sure her robe remained as it was, so that her legs were bared and one breast was exposed. While his wife watched he laid his mouth on Liane's neck and kissed her almost tenderly.

Rikka turned and tried to stalk away, but at a signal from Sebestyen, Taneli stopped her. Taneli, who always searched her so insolently. The other sentinel, Ferghus, stood behind Taneli, trying very hard not to reveal that the unfolding scene shocked him.

He had not been long in the palace.

When Rikka tried to walk away from her husband, Taneli lifted her straight off her feet and carried her to the dais. Her feet kicked furiously, heels landing on the sentinel's legs. He didn't flinch, much less slow down.

Rikka was a small woman, too young and naïve for the job of satisfying Sebestyen in any way. She was also an odd combination of meek and hotheaded. Most days she was downright docile, but on occasion her temper flared. It was a miracle she had lasted this long.

"How dare you bring me here to watch you play with your whore?" Rikka asked, regal but for her pink cheeks.

Sebestyen smiled and offered one hand, palm up, to the second sentinel. Ferghus laid a vial in the emperor's hand. The glass vial was less than half an inch in diameter and about three inches long, and it had a small hole in one end and a plunger in the other. It was filled with a grainy brown powder that had a perfectly harmless appearance.

Panwyr.

Liane choked back a horrified protest. It was too late for Rikka. Nothing she could say would change Sebestyen's mind, and begging for the empress would only make her appear weak in his eyes.

"You've been rather a disappointment to me, Rikka," Sebestyen said.

"You haven't exactly lived up to my expectations, either," the empress countered.

Normally such a statement would send Sebestyen into a rage. But not today. He just smiled. This was an argument Rikka would not win, and he knew it. Liane felt sorry for the stupid girl.

Sebestyen relaxed his grip on Liane, giving the bared breast a gentle, friendly squeeze before guiding her from his lap. Rikka gave her husband's concubine and confidant a hateful glare, but Liane ignored it.

"My lord," Liane said softly as she righted her robe, "perhaps this isn't the time for such a—"

"I have a plan," Sebestyen interrupted. "A grand one. But there is a problem that must be taken care of before I can proceed."

Rikka was the problem.

Sebestyen departed his throne and the dais, leaving Liane behind. His defiant wife stood before him; the two sentinels remained behind her, not to guard her from harm but to make sure she didn't run.

Perhaps she realized this was her last chance, because as Sebestyen reached Rikka the girl stared up at her husband and said softly, as if the words were for him alone, "I have only tried to love you, my lord. Why won't you allow me to do so as a wife should?"

Sebestyen took Rikka's chin in his hand, tipped her face up, and smiled down at her. He said not a word of response as he quickly shoved the glass vial up her nose. Startled, she tried to withdraw, but Sebestyen wrapped one arm around his wife and held her fast as he pushed the plunger in the vial, sending the Panwyr up her nose and into her system.

The change was immediate. Rikka relaxed; her body and her face. Her once coiled fingers unwound, and her lips softened. Her eyes dilated until they were almost completely black. And she smiled. Liane's heart constricted. The empress looked so young when she smiled.

"That feels very good," she whispered. "What is this gift you have given me, my lord? I can feel it all through my body. Like . . . like . . . oh, that's very nice."

"Panwyr has a variety of effects, depending upon the individual," Sebestyen explained. "Some feel imbued with a strength such as they have never known, some experience an overwhelming sadness and then euphoria. Others experience a sexual pleasure, something you would never allow yourself to enjoy." He looked into her eyes. "This is what you were missing when you insisted on lying beneath me like a lifeless hunk of meat."

Rikka threw her head back and took a deep breath, and a shudder worked through her petite body. "It's fantastic, my lord. It's . . ." She wobbled on her feet. Only Sebestyen's grip kept her standing. "My knees have gone all soft." Again, she giggled.

Liane laid a hand on Sebestyen's arm. "My lord, let the sentinels take her now." With any luck, they would decide to have their way with her before tossing her in Level Thirteen. She didn't know Ferghus well, but Taneli was certainly capable of such a vile act. That would give Liane time to excuse herself from the ballroom and take custody of Rikka herself. She didn't like the giggling, whining, hateful girl, but she was just a child, and did not deserve Level Thirteen.

"I believe I'll escort my wife to her new quarters myself," Sebestyen said with a grin.

"New quarters?" Rikka asked. "How very sweet of you. I'm getting quite bored with the old ones." She stared beyond Sebestyen to the bare wall behind the dais, and her eyes widened. "Oh, look at the pretty colors! Will there be such pretty colors in my new quarters?"

"Yes," Sebestyen said brightly as he led the way to the double doors.

Liane remained on the dais, feeling slightly ill. Her own knees felt weak.

At the door, Sebestyen turned to her. "Come with us, darling," he said.

Liane shook her head. "I can't. I . . ." She licked her lips.

He'd called her darling. To her knowledge, Sebestyen had never called anyone darling before this moment.

She left the dais and walked toward the door, the sentinels, the drugged empress, and Sebestyen. Liane kept her spine straight and pushed down the queasiness that threatened.

"You never call me darling," Rikka said, pouting prettily. "Never, not once. Not one . . . oh, is that a butterfly?" She pointed to the opposite side of the ballroom. "A hundred butterflies. Aren't they pretty, my lord? Aren't they lovely?"

Liane ignored Rikka's ramblings. Sebestyen was getting rid of the empress, and he had called her darling. She couldn't allow herself to imagine what that might mean.

They took the private lift down to Level Ten. Rikka giggled and talked the entire time, her chatter louder than the hum of the lift. She even turned her attention to Liane once and stuck out her tongue, then laughed at her own childishness. She tried to grab Ferghus's privates, much to Sebestyen's amusement, but the sentinel managed to step out of her reach and she did not try again. Before they'd reached Level Ten she'd managed to unbutton her crimson robe to her waist, complaining of the heat. Taneli had a difficult time keeping his eyes off the small swell of her breasts.

They exited the lift at Level Ten, and went directly through a doorway to the right. Steep stairs led them down to Level Eleven, which hummed noisily as always. Then they descended the steep, curving stairway to the level below. On Level Twelve, they walked along a lengthy corridor that seemed, for a moment, to be deserted. But near the end of the corridor four well-armed guards waited.

A couple of the guards were surprised to see the emperor and empress. The others were not. One guard, a man with a nasty scar across his cheek, actually grinned as if this moment had been arranged for his own amusement.

Sebestyen ordered Taneli and Ferghus to wait at the stairwell.

"Where is this place?" Rikka asked. "Are my new quarters here? Oh, it's so pretty. There are so many nice colors."

There were no colors to speak of on Level Twelve. There were cold gray walls and floors and ceilings and the green of the officer's uniforms. Nothing more.

But Rikka saw more. She turned to her husband and smiled. Her robe was loose and hanging half off her small body, her cheeks were flushed, her eyes were dilated. What did she see? Rikka lifted a delicate hand to Sebestyen's face.

"You think I'm lying when I say I love you, but I'm not. I do love you. I loved you from that first time I saw you, when I was walking down the aisle with my father on my arm and you were waiting for me there with that fat priest." Again, she giggled. "I thought you were the most handsome man in the world, and I was so sure that we would have such a lovely life together." Her smile faded. "What happened?"

Sebestyen nodded to the man with the scar, and he knelt down to slip a key into a padlock on the floor. The sentry unlocked the padlock and set it aside, and then he and two other guards lifted a massive trapdoor. The door was so heavy it was an effort for the three men to move it. One person alone would never be able to lift the door.

The stench that rose from Level Thirteen was horrid; the noises were worse.

"What's this?" Rikka stood on the edge of the opening and peered into the darkness.

Weak voices and excruciating moans rose from the opening in the floor. And from somewhere in the depths of Level Thirteen, Liane heard something she had not expected. A baby's cry mingled with the plaintive laments of the addicts who had been banished to this hellish hole in the ground.

For some, Sebestyen considered death too good an end. Those who had been sent to Level Thirteen were meant to suffer. And they did. They were first given a dose of the powerful drug, Panwyr. That one dose would not kill them, but it assured they would be addicted. Then they were thrown into Level Thirteen, where it was dark and the inhabitants fought for their survival or died.

Every day the guards threw down rancid food and small containers of Panwyr.

But not enough for everyone.

Rikka looked up and back at her husband. She still had no idea what was coming. Again, Liane heard a very faint baby's cry. The others either did not hear or else they were accustomed to the sound. Her mouth went dry and her heart pounded too hard. Surely the child had been born down there. Not even Sebestyen would toss a child into Level Thirteen.

Would he?

While Rikka looked into Sebestyen's eyes, innocent and dazed, he gave her a gentle shove that made her teeter on the edge of the pit. No longer did she smile and giggle. She was finally alarmed. She clutched at Sebestyen's robe, but he pushed her hand away and after a moment's struggle she fell.

Liane closed her eyes as she heard Rikka hit the ground below and scream.

"I fell," she shouted on the end of a scream. "I think I sprained my ankle, my lord." There was a gasp, a shout, and then a horrified, "Get away from me you . . ."

Sebestyen nodded to the guards and they replaced the trapdoor, cutting off life and hope and Rikka's scream.

Liane didn't watch the scarred sentry replace the padlock, but she heard the metal clicking as it was put back into place, as the key turned once again.

"There now." Sebestyen took Liane's arm and lead her away from the only entrance to Level Thirteen, where Ferghus and Taneli waited. "All done."

"You should have let me kill her," Liane said, trying her best to keep her voice calm. A quick death would have been kinder. Quicker. Rikka would not last long down there.

In the back of her mind, she heard the baby's cry. Most of

the inhabitants of Level Thirteen were men, but there were the discarded empresses and a few other females who had been banished there. Some poor woman had given birth down there, in that filth, surrounded by half-starved addicts. She would have been a half-starved addict herself, so how had a child survived?

Liane stiffened her spine. Perhaps she hadn't heard a child at all. It had been a prisoner's high-pitched cry, perhaps, or her own imagination.

No one said a word as they made their way back to the lift on Level Ten, and up to Level One. The sentinels were solemn, while Sebestyen had an almost dreamy expression on his face, as the lift rose slow and steady.

Instead of returning to the ballroom, they were escorted to Sebestyen's private chambers. The emperor ordered a large supper to be delivered in an hour and a half, then closed the doors on the sentinels.

Liane kept her chin high. Killing Rikka had excited Sebestyen, she could tell by the sparkle in his eye and the crook to his smile.

She hoped he had killed Rikka. She hoped the girl was dead already, had died while the drug was still strong within her and she hadn't realized what was happening.

Liane took a deep breath and pushed all her sympathy and horror aside. She couldn't allow anything, not even this, to interfere with her plans. She'd killed, she'd betrayed her only friend in this world . . . she couldn't let sympathy stop her now.

So she smiled. "You mentioned a grand plan."

Sebestyen threaded his fingers through her hair and held on tight. "Yes, I did, *darling*." He smiled. "Even in her drugged state Rikka was livid to hear me use such an endearment for you."

Liane's heart sank. Only for Rikka's benefit had he called her by such an endearment. She should've known.

Rikka's final words echoed in her head. She could understand how a young, impressionable girl might look at Sebestyen and fall in love. There had been times when Liane had fancied herself a little bit in love with him. Long ago, between fear and hate.

No more, though. She knew him too well. He was not ordinary and never would be. There was nothing of the man she sometimes imagined him to be in that cold, slender body.

Love and hate were both passions. She was, she had to admit, passionate about Sebestyen.

"I would like to hear about your plan." Maybe he wanted to marry her, as he had suggested in the past. If he suggested it at this moment, maybe she would say yes. What better way to gain his trust?

"Maddox's daughter has a child, so we know she's not barren," Sebestyen said. His fingers moved in her hair with an unexpected gentleness. "I'll marry her before he returns. What better match than the emperor and the daughter of my most trusted minister?"

Liane did not allow her smile to fail. "What better match, indeed."

"She'll give me an heir, Liane, and when that's done I'll dispose of her."

"The same way you disposed of Rikka?"

"Perhaps."

"This is your grand plan?"

"I will welcome Maddox home, when he comes," Sebestyen said. "He will not know that I learned of his unfaithful words. Not right way, at least. In the months to come he will learn to love his daughter and granddaughter, I'll see to that. We will be a happy family."

"For a while," Liane whispered.

"For a while. I want Sulyen to love his daughter well, before he watches her die. I want him to feel the pain I felt when I learned that he had lied to me."

Liane did not allow her unexpected disappointment to

show on her face or in her voice. "What if Maddox's daughter is a horse-faced hag?"

"Then I will plow her in the dark and pretend it's you who lies beneath me." His smile and the lilt in his voice made it seem he was teasing, but she suspected he was telling the truth.

"She's supposed to marry that little man Farrell."

"Farrell will soon join Rikka in Level Thirteen, leaving Maddox's daughter without a fiancé."

"And the baby? Maddox's granddaughter?"

"The baby will live as long as it suits me, but I imagine the brat will be disposed of with its mother."

Sebestyen wanted no children but his own in this palace. It was the reason his sisters had been wed to powerful men who lived far away from Arthes. It was the reason the sister who had refused to marry had become a Sister of the Orianan Order and banished to a convent on the other side of Columbyana, as far away from the capital city as possible without pushing her into the sea.

The sweet-faced baby Farrell had brought to the ballroom door would not outlive her usefulness, not if Sebestyen had his way.

Liane remembered too clearly the cry she'd heard, the baby's cry echoing from the bowels of Level Thirteen, but she pushed the memory away. She pushed it so deep she could almost convince herself the cry had never been real. To imagine a child down there . . . it was too much. She could not bear it.

Sebestyen sighed and his breath touched her neck, and Liane relaxed. He might take another wife—he might take a dozen more—but no one would ever take her place.

"Sometimes I think everyone in this world would betray me, given the chance," he said as he held her close.

"Everyone but me," Liane whispered.

Sebestyen hesitated, then responded, "Everyone but you."

13

AFTER SEVERAL MORE DAYS OF TRAVEL, SOPHIE AND KANE crested a lush green rise and the city of Arthes finally came into view. She saw the top stories of the palace first, gray stone against a brilliant blue morning sky. When she could see the entire city laid out before her, Sophie reined in her horse and stared in wonder. Arthes was huge, unlike anything she had ever seen before. From the tall building at the center it spread outward like a living thing. She could almost see it seething, as if the city itself breathed.

She stared at the Imperial Palace, her eyes raking upward. It was not a pretty building. It was too plain, too unadorned to be pretty. The bottom levels were a bit larger than those at the top. The change in size was gradual, gently sloping so that the palace looked like a smooth, granite mountain that rose up out of the center of the city. The palace was impressive in its sheer massiveness. It was also a bit frightening. The walls were thick, and it was so tall.

"Our baby is in there, Kane."

"Yes, she is."

It had been three weeks to the day since she'd left her sisters behind. She still didn't know if she'd ever return to Fyne Mountain. The heat of anger was no longer upon her, but she had not forgiven her sisters, either. Right now she just wanted to find a safe place for her and her baby and the man she loved.

Kane guided his horse beside hers and smiled at her. "Ariana is fine," he said in a reassuring voice. "We'll collect her, I'll kill Farrell, and then we'll get out of the city and never look back." He squinted as he stared at the palace. The smile didn't last but she didn't mind. It had not been a genuine smile. Kane was as tense as she. More so, if that was possible. "It's not a good place," he said. "Not a proper place for a lady like you, and certainly not fitting for my daughter."

Kane saw only danger ahead, but Sophie still had hope that they might make quick work of collecting Ariana. "I would like to see Minister Sulyen for a few minutes, if that's possible. He might remember my mother. He might want to know he has a daughter."

Kane's jaw clenched. "That's not a good idea."

He was interested only in getting in and out of the city as quickly as possible. She shared that interest with him, but she also wanted a moment, just a moment, with the man who had sired her.

"It never occurred to me that my father would care to know he has a daughter, not until I met you. In all my life, I never considered it unfair to keep the knowledge of my existence from my father, but of late I have changed my mind." She looked at Kane. He was a much more comforting sight than the big city, and the idea of letting him go when this was done ate at her heart. Not the way losing Ariana had, but still, it was painful and unexpected. A gust of wind caught a length of sun-streaked hair and lifted it off his shoulder.

He looked at her, and in that instant she had the feeling that she'd never be alone again. Not because she had Ariana, not because she had her sisters. But because she had this love for Kane building and growing inside her.

Loving him was everything she had always been so certain she did not want and could not have, so why did it feel so wonderful, even now? Their future was uncertain in many ways, and still nothing could dim the brilliance of love.

"We'll make arrangements for you to see Minister Sulyen, if we can," he said softly, "but you'll have to make your visit a brief one."

"Thank you."

"Whatever you do, don't mention my name."

She nodded and they spurred the horses onward.

KANE HAD BEEN IN THE CITY ONCE BEFORE, YEARS AGO. It was as dirty and noisy and unpleasant as he remembered. People were crowded into small houses, they teemed around the markets and taverns, they laughed too loudly in the streets.

He had found a trustworthy stable master and paid the man well to look after the horses until he and Sophie finished their business. She wanted to storm the palace and claim her child, but he had suggested a more subtle plan of rescue.

A tavern near the palace's north entrance looked promising. He hated to take Sophie into such a place, but he hated worse the thought of leaving her behind. Dressed in manly clothes and battered boots, her unwashed hair pulled back, her face dirty, she was still beautiful, and men stared. No, he could not let her out of his sight.

There were other women in the tavern, some who worked here, others who were patrons. But all eyes drifted to Sophie, anyway. It was clear to everyone that she did not belong here the way the others did.

One table in the corner was occupied by laughing soldiers. Kane did his best to keep his face turned away from the emperor's men. The odds that one of them would recognize him were low, but it wasn't impossible that he might've faced one or more of them at some time in the five years he'd fought with Arik. He'd get the information he came here for, then get out and find a safe place to stay until they rescued Ariana.

He ordered whisky for himself and ale for Sophie, and paid the barkeep with a gold coin. He still had money from his lucky year as a gambler. Lots of it. Fortunately he had won that money in the Southern and Eastern Provinces, and he saw no familiar faces in the crowded tavern. That sort of encounter might be almost as dangerous as a run-in with the soldiers.

Most of the patrons soon returned to their own activities, and while he and Sophie sipped at their drinks they were no longer the center of attention. He kept one arm around her in a way that warned the others present that she was not for sale or rent. Even though she had never been in a place as rough as this one, she recognized the dangers and she stayed close. Very close. The length of her body was pressed along his and she kept her eyes on the ale she sipped.

Kane nodded at the barkeep and the man leaned toward them, his eyes straying to Sophie in an all-too-interested way. "Another round?"

"No." Kane put a coin on the counter and pushed it toward the barkeep. The man found the gold more interesting than Sophie. His eyes lit up. "I need information."

The man grinned as he covered the coin with his meaty hand. "You've come to the right place, friend. What kind of enlightenment can I offer you?"

"Palace enlightenment."

The barkeep's smile died quickly. "You can always ask the sentinels," he nodded to the crowded table in the corner, where imperial soldiers drank and laughed. They were talking about women at the moment, and fortunately they cared nothing for the type of woman one might find in a tavern like this one.

"And if I wish to avoid speaking to the sentinels?" Kane asked softly.

The man hesitated, and for a moment Kane thought he was going to return the coin and call for the soldiers; plotting against the emperor or any of his soldiers was potentially fatal. But in the end greed won out over fear. "What do you want to know?"

"A man has recently arrived in Arthes. It's likely he went straight to the palace in search of Minister Sulyen."

"Minister Sulyen is not in residence at the moment. He's traveled to the Northern Province."

Sophie sighed, and Kane squeezed her arm lightly. She was disappointed, but he was not sorry they wouldn't have to seek the man out for the conversation Sophie had in mind.

"I am most interested in the man who came here in search of him. The man's name is Galvyn Farrell, and he traveled here with a baby."

"Oh, yes," the barkeep said softly. "The man with the baby. I did hear that he was still living in the palace, a *guest* of the emperor. Is he a friend of yours?"

"No."

The man nodded, and then he looked at Sophie again. He didn't leer this time, but studied her thoughtfully. "I hear he's staying on Level Five, which he and the baby have to themselves since the unfortunate empress passed away just a few days ago."

"Is the baby well?" Sophie asked in a hushed voice.

Kane didn't trust the barkeep with too much information, so he asked a question of his own. "What happened to the empress?"

"I hear she had a fit of some sort and died just like that." He snapped his fingers and Sophie twitched. "Emperor Sebestyen has mighty bad luck with his wives."

Kane doubted *luck* had anything to do with the number of wives Sebestyen had buried, but he kept that opinion to himself.

"How does one get to Level Five unseen?"

Sophie was practically bouncing up and down on her toes, she was so excited to be this close. Kane had learned not to get excited about being close. He wouldn't celebrate until Sophie and Ariana were safely away from the palace and Galvyn Farrell was dead.

"One moment," the barkeep snatched up his gold coin and walked to the end of the bar. He busied himself there for a moment, rearranging glasses and wiping down a spill on the bar, then he leaned over and spoke to the man sitting at the very end.

Kane listed slightly forward to get a better look at the patron the barkeep spoke to. The man was large and had a homely but jovial face. He was dressed as a civilian, but that didn't mean a thing to Kane. He laid his hand over the knife at his side, just in case.

The barkeep returned as casually as he had left, stopping along the way to handle a couple of mindless chores. When he reached Kane he stopped to wipe up a nonexistent spill.

"If you gave us up, I'll kill you," Kane whispered.

The barkeep didn't look worried. "Bors has connections in the palace, and he has no love for the emperor. He will take you to Level Five, but you'll have to give him one of those gold coins."

Kane nodded.

"He'll meet you out back as soon as he's finished his drink, and he'll expect you to be waiting for him. Bors has no patience, so I suggest you two run along quickly." He gave instructions that would take them out the front door and through a side alley. Bors would use the rear entrance, but it wouldn't do for the sentinels to see Kane and his lady leave by that same exit.

"I don't like it," Kane said as they followed the barkeep's instructions, stepping onto the street and allowing the door to close behind them. Night had fallen. There were too many dark corners in this city, too many desperate people lurking in those dark corners. Compared to this, Shandley was paradise. By day the city bustled with prosperous shops and colorful vendors and the activities of the middle class. But the complexion of the city had changed since sunset. It was likely Sophie had no idea how dark and dangerous the city could be, and if he had his way she never would. He couldn't keep her close enough.

She was excited. "I can understand why a man might not care for the emperor and his ways. He's going to take us to Ariana, Kane, I can feel it!" She smiled brightly, and he stopped in the alleyway, taking her arm and making her face him.

"Be careful," he whispered.

"You, too."

"If this Bors turns out not to be who he claims to be, I will distract him while you run. Go to the man who's caring for the horses. He seemed like a trustworthy sort, and I believe he would guide you to a safe place. I have several coins hidden in a secret compartment in my saddlebag, the one with the engraving on the flap."

Her smile finally faded. "You would ask me to run and leave you in danger?"

"One of us has to get to Ariana," he reasoned.

Sophie nodded her head, and then she reached up to lay her hand on his face.

There was nothing left to say, so he kissed her. For three weeks, they had raced to get here. There had been so little time to think of what might come after. If there *was* an after.

And he wanted this kiss now, in case he never had another chance. Even if all went well, he needed this kiss.

Sophie was so soft, so gentle. She kissed with her heart and her soul, and she drew him in. With a kiss and a sigh and the way she laid her hand on him, she took him to a place he'd never thought to be. There was pure goodness here, in this kiss and most of all in *her*.

He ended the kiss and brushed his thumb across a spot of dirt on her cheek. "Don't hesitate," he reminded her again. "If I order it, you run."

She nodded and took his hand, and they continued down the dark alley, fingers intertwined, hearts beating in time.

A moment after they reached the stone courtyard behind the tavern, the door opened. Light spilled onto wet stones for a moment, and then Bors closed the door and their only light came from a few dingy windows along the way.

The big man turned to Kane and offered his hand. Kane placed a coin there and Bors smiled. "Are you sure you want to go into the palace? Level Five can be a dangerous place." His eyes cut to Sophie. "Especially for a lady."

"We have no choice," Kane said.

He nodded. There was little light here in the courtyard, but in the moment Bors had been bathed in light from the tavern, Kane had taken a good long look at the man who had promised to assist them. His face was craggy, his beard heavy, his eyes narrow. Perhaps he did have reason to hate the emperor and was willing to aid those who wished to sneak into the palace.

A drunk began to sing at the top of his lungs, his discordant voice drifting down the alley that led to the courtyard. The distinct sound of urine splashing against the tavern wall explained the man's detour.

Bors studied Sophie carefully. "You look like Minister Sulyen, very much so."

"I do?"

"Yes. No one will ever doubt that you are indeed his daughter."

Kane drew his sword and pointed the tip at Bors's heart. "I never said anything about her being Sulyen's daughter."

Bors smiled, not at all threatened by Kane's weapon. "Put it down, boy. You don't have a chance." And then he looked over Kane's shoulder and nodded.

The soldiers who had been drinking in the tavern spread out and surrounded them. Strains of the drunken ditty, sung by one young man who was still righting his trousers, grew louder, and the rest of the soldiers joined in. His song had been planned to cover the sounds of men walking in the alley, and it had worked. They had been caught completely off guard.

Kane began to circle, trying to create an opening for Sophie to make her escape. But there were too many soldiers in a space that was too narrow, and they were all armed. He and Sophie were surrounded by eight drunken, armed soldiers.

"Kill him," Bors said, "but don't hurt the girl. She's a mother, after all. Besides, the emperor has offered a very nice reward for her." He took Sophie's arm and gripped it tight, and the others moved in on Kane. He drew a knife, and faced the soldiers with a blade in each hand. The odds weren't good, but the emperor's men had been drinking for hours and thought this would be easy, since the numbers were in their favor.

Kane swung his sword at the closest sentinel. If only he had just a touch of Sophie's good luck left in him . . .

SHE WANTED TO CLOSE HER EYES, BUT COULD NOT. THERE were too many of them! Kane didn't have a chance. For a moment he held his own, surprising the soldiers. He knocked two of them to the ground, then another, drawing blood each time. One soldier took a step toward Sophie, and Kane spun around and threw the knife as if he had known the moment danger moved near her. The knife landed in the advancing soldier's thigh, and he dropped to the ground with a yell.

There were too many armed men fighting in close quarters, and still Kane held his own. He spun as he fought, dipping down and slashing out with his sword, keeping track of each and every soldier in a way that told her he had done this before. Many times. At one point, when he dipped down he drew a knife from his boot, so that once again he fought with two blades. The soldiers, surprised by the way he fought, began to fall back. And then, with a burst of anger that one man could make them retreat, they moved in once again.

Kane's movements were quick, well-timed, and precise as he fought them off. Sophie was a bit surprised. She'd had no idea he could move this way, with speed and precision and strength. For a moment she thought that maybe, just maybe, they had a chance against the soldiers.

And then, while he engaged one sentinel who seemed more skilled with a sword than the others, a man Kane had knocked to the ground rose behind him. The sentinel had lost his own sword, but surprised Kane with a punch to the lower back that sent him to his knees.

The soldier Kane had been fighting raised his sword and held it over the kneeling man who had held them off for much longer than they'd expected. One swing, and it would be over.

"Stop!" Sophie commanded, yanking her arm from Bors's grasp. Her heart beat so hard she could hear it, feel it, but she made sure no one else knew how scared she was at this moment. She looked at the soldiers, one and then the other. "Do you know who I am? Do you have even an inkling? I am the daughter of Minister Maddox Sulyen." She stepped into a soft beam of light that cut across the alley, so they could see her face well, and she made absolutely sure she did not show her fear.

"If you harm this man, I will have your heads. If you do not treat us as honored guests of Columbyana's most respected minister should be treated, you will spend the remainder of your pathetic military careers cleaning out stables." Bors kept behind her and silent, and six of the soldiers stepped away from Kane. One still lay on the ground, wounded. And one brave sentinel, the one who was moments away from taking Kane's head, lowered his sword and touched the tip to Kane's neck.

Sophie glared at him. "Would you like to continue to wield a sword? Would you handle a shovel of manure with such confidence?"

"He hasn't yet surrendered," the soldier insisted.

"Will you escort us unharmed to the palace?" Sophie asked.

"Sophie . . ." Kane protested.

"If . . . he drops . . . his weapons," the soldier said tersely.

"I'm sorry," she said softly, her eyes on Kane's face. "I won't run from you or from Ariana. This isn't the way we planned to get into the palace, but it'll have to do." He would fight and die here, she knew it, and she did not want him to die. "I don't want to go in there alone," she whispered.

Kane dropped his knife and sword with a curse, and the stubborn soldier raised his blade from Kane's neck. Sophie reached for him, but Bors grabbed her arm again and dragged her back before their hands could touch.

She should have known that Kane would not go willingly. As he rose he elbowed an unsuspecting soldier in the gut and hit another across the jaw, sending them both reeling. He was about to take on another, when the soldier who had played the melodious drunk broke a bottle of whisky over Kane's head.

Kane slumped to the ground, whisky in his hair and on his face and dribbling over his shirt.

Sophie tried to move forward, but this time Bors held her fast. She didn't even dare call out Kane's name. She had not forgotten that warning.

"I warned you," she said in a low voice.

"The Minister of Defense does allow his soldiers to disarm those who attack them," one sentinel said testily.

Bors yanked Sophie back so that she stood at his side. "Take the prisoner to Level Twelve and hold him there until you hear from me. I'll take this one to the emperor." He sounded very much like a soldier, even though he did not wear a uniform. And the sentinels listened to him obediently.

Two soldiers lifted Kane from the ground and dragged him away. Two others assisted the man who had been stabbed. The sentinel who had held a blade to Kane's throat stepped forward. "Don't forget about our share of the reward, Bors."

"I won't forget."

"Don't you forget that the man you're escorting is a guest of the Minister of Defense, not a prisoner," Sophie said hotly.

"Don't worry, little girl." The sentinel patted Sophie on the head, the patronizing oaf. "He's safe, for now. He's safe until your papa comes home and tells me to take his head." The man grinned widely. "If you'd like I'll deliver that head to you personally."

14

SEBESTYEN'S MOOD WAS MUCH IMPROVED SINCE HE'D COME
up with his plan for revenge, but in the past few weeks—
months, perhaps—he had not given enough of his time and attention to the affairs of Columbyana. Liane had found herself
prodding him to see to the simplest matters, to meet with his
ministers and keep the priests happy. His duties as the leader
of this country had often been left to others, most especially
to the ministers he had so carefully chosen to serve him, but
there were certain matters that commanded his attention.

To Liane, this chore was another step in making sure
Sebestyen trusted her completely. She guided him, as if she
were a minister herself. When they were alone she advised
and supported and coddled him.

And still, she was searched before she saw him. Every
morning when she joined him after sleeping in her own chamber. Every night, when she went to him for more personal
matters. No matter what the reason for her visit, the sentinels
showed her no more respect than they had in the past. It didn't

matter that she had made herself important to their leader in many ways. To them she was a whore and would always be a whore. Even if Sebestyen did decide to make her his empress, the sentinels would continue to look at her as if she were no better than a prostitute who worked the taverns on the streets below.

One day she would make them all pay. Every single one of them.

Sebestyen lounged on his bed and Liane sat beside him. At the moment his mind was on matters of state, so they were both fully dressed. Sex would come later, when Sebestyen had tired of more mundane concerns. He was worried, he was distracted, but later he would look to her as a way to forget.

Liane enjoyed this time with Sebestyen, more than she liked to admit. She had become his ear. He wanted her opinion, he trusted her instincts. She considered herself worthy of this position. She had slept with many of the ministers over the years, and they had all talked to her. And she had listened intently, learning the nuances of politics, absorbing every word the ministers whose only aim was to inflate their importance in her eyes had said. Many of those ministers were gone or dead. But she remained. In a very real way, she was more important than any of them had ever been.

She stroked Sebestyen's head gently while he discussed the possibilities of war or truce with the clans of Tryfyn. He was scheduled to meet with an ambassador from one of the more important clans in a few days—the very same clan the late Minster of Finance had been accused of conspiring with—and he could not decide if he should have Liane kill the man, or impress him with the wealth and hospitality of Columbyana.

"You could make him an ally, for now," Liane said. "I have heard that on occasion the rebels find shelter in Tryfyn."

"Then perhaps you should kill him."

Liane shook her head. Sebestyen was often rash. He didn't

always think ahead, as he should. "You don't want the Tryfynians and the rebels working together. Make Tryfyn our ally, ask for their help in defeating the rebels, and when Arik is no longer a problem you can take Tryfyn on, if you're still of a mind to."

He almost smiled. "It would be a great legacy, to expand the borders of Columbyana during my reign."

"Yes, it would," she whispered.

"They're a rich country," he mused. "Their natural resources are abundant. Silver, gold, copper. And yet they fight amongst themselves constantly. Conquering them would be good for Columbyana. When I get that bastard Arik off my back I'll do just that."

"But for now," Liane said, "you will make the Tryfynian ambassador an ally."

"Yes," he said softly. "That would be best, for now."

Liane stretched out beside Sebestyen and rested her head on his chest. There it was, the beat of his heart. He placed a hand in her hair and held on, almost tenderly.

The ruler of Columbyana could be cruel, she knew that better than anyone. He could be unreasonable, and petulant, and yes, perhaps he danced on the edge of sanity, on occasion. But there were moments when she saw Sebestyen's good qualities. Maybe it was necessary that she find those qualities, in order to do what had to be done. Although he occasionally tired of the details and he was constantly afraid of treachery, in his own way he did want to be a worthy emperor. The people of this country, people he so rarely saw, were important to him. He wanted to be loved by them, and in a very basic way he considered them his children.

He had established a Ministry of the Arts a few years ago, revitalizing a concern that had been neglected under his father's rule. There was a new museum in Arthes, and she heard that it had been filled with paintings and sculptures which were a pleasure to behold. She had never been inside the mu-

seum, and likely never would, but still, it was a good thing
Sebestyen had done. He'd also reinstated the festivals his
grandfather had outlawed during his later years. The people in
the city danced and sang and laughed during those festivals,
which came with every new season. Liane had often watched
from above, wondering what it would be like to be down there
amidst the revelry.

Sebestyen had a great interest in machines that Liane did
not fully understand, like the one that powered the lift and the
artificial lights and the fans in the palace. At the moment, he
kept those advances and the men who conceived them to himself, but she could imagine that one day he would share the
wonders with the rest of his country.

He had even quietly ended his father's practice of kidnapping women for Level Three, though that change had come
much too late for Liane.

Now and then he talked about the future and what it might
hold, and he'd expressed an interest in leaving this country a
better place than he had found it. That would be his legacy.
After his death, he would be remembered well.

He could be cruel—he *was* cruel—but Sebestyen was not
completely without kindness. He presented her with flowers
and perfumes and jewels when she pleased him. Of late, he
had presented her with a gift of some sort almost every day,
and when she was delighted he was delighted. It was almost as
if he no longer found joy for himself, but he saw it and tasted
it through her.

The idea that Sebestyen would actually marry Sulyen's
daughter was ludicrous. She was doubtless a country bumpkin
like Farrell, and once he saw her he'd change his mind about
actually making her his wife. He could just as easily make the
girl a concubine and allow her to service the ministers and
priests her father served alongside. Would that not serve as
sufficient vengeance?

She still hated him, but Liane knew she and Sebestyen

were a good match, in a soul-deep way. If he asked her to be his empress, she would say yes. Together they could rule for years, and they would rule well. She could be the woman behind the throne, the voice of reason when Sebestyen knew none. Together, they could rule the world.

There were moments, brief, hazy moments, when she questioned her resolve to kill him. She questioned that resolve most often when her body responded to his. There were days—nights—when all he had to do was touch her and that response began. It had begun now, with a thrum and an ache.

She wrapped an arm around him and held on tight. Tighter than was necessary, perhaps. Their bodies were so close she could not help but feel his own response. He grew hard and warm. He fisted his hand in her hair.

Talk of war was over, at least for tonight. She laid her lips on his throat and allowed them to rest there. Softly. He tasted of salt and soap, and the scent of him was entirely male. Entirely Sebestyen.

On some nights he took her quickly, without the touching and holding, without the closeness that was so rare for both of them. But tonight he was in no rush. His hands explored and aroused, his lips teased her throat. Tonight he did not order her to undress, but began the process himself. He unfastened the top three buttons of her robe and spread the fabric away from her heated skin.

If he asked her to be his empress now she would say yes without hesitation.

If he asked her if she loved him . . .

The knock at the door made Liane jump. It was late, much too late for anyone with a smidgen of common sense to disturb the emperor. Sebestyen sighed as he rolled away from her, leaving her lying on the bed alone and wondering when he would return. Quickly, she hoped.

No, she did not hope. She could not hope. All this time, she had wanted nothing more than to make Sebestyen need her. She had never expected that she might come to need him, as well.

Sebestyen opened one of the double doors and allowed Taneli to enter the room. The soldier cast a quick glance to Liane, then whispered into Sebestyen's ear. Liane sat up and glared at the sentinel. How dare he! There was no need for secrets in her presence, and Taneli knew it well.

She heard Sebestyen's response. "Bring her in." He turned to her and grinned. She had not seen such a smile since long before he'd rid himself of Rikka. He walked to the bed and offered Liane his hand. "She's here."

Liane took Sebestyen's hand and stood. Her heart sank, but she was very careful not to let that reaction show. "Maddox's daughter? So soon?"

"Yes. She and an escort were trying to bribe their way into the palace in order to rescue the child."

"An escort?"

Sebestyen shrugged. "He is on Level Twelve at the moment. I'll decide what to do with him later"—his smile widened slightly—"after I take my new bride. I can't think of anything else, at the moment."

Liane grinned, but it was an effort. A moment ago he had been lying beside her, and she knew without doubt that she had commanded his full attention. She had even thought that perhaps he would ask her to be his empress. Now he spoke to her of his new bride.

"How unlike you to get so excited about a woman you have not even seen," Liane said as she fastened the buttons of her robe. "You're usually much more discriminating, Sebestyen."

"Are you jealous?" he asked, his eyebrows raising slightly.

"Don't be ridiculous," she said sharply. "There have been other women in your bed for as long as I've known you. Why should I become jealous now?"

"Because things have changed," he whispered.

"One thing has not changed," she answered just as softly.

"Neither of us is capable of love, and without love there can't be jealousy."

He kissed her on the forehead as the doors to his chamber opened again.

Liane's heart sank when the woman was dragged into the room on the arm of a large man dressed in civilian clothing. She was not horse-faced, and she was most definitely Maddox's child. That pale hair and the blazing blue eyes were gifts from her father.

She was beautiful.

Sebestyen was pleased. He walked away from Liane and toward the girl and her escort. "I understand you claim to be the daughter of Minister Sulyen."

"Yes," the girl answered in a soft, trembling voice.

Sebestyen shooed away the large man who had ushered the young woman into the bedchamber, and promised that they would discuss the offered reward at a later date. The man was not pleased by that response, but he didn't dare to argue. He left reluctantly.

"My . . . my name is Sophie Fyne," the girl said. "It's true that Minister Sulyen is my father, but I have never met him and that's not why I'm here."

"Why are you here?" Sebestyen ran an interested finger across the girl's cheek.

Sophie Fyne was no fool . . . and no girl, Liane decided. She was a woman, and she knew very well what the gleam in the emperor's eyes and that wandering finger meant. "My baby has been kidnapped by a man who sought your protection," she said. Yes, her voice still trembled, but she did not cower.

"Farrell," Sebestyen said.

Sophie's eyes brightened. "Yes. All I want is my baby. And . . . and I'd like my friend released."

"Your friend?" Sebestyen asked. "I assume you are referring to the man who was with you this evening. Does your friend have a name?"

Sophie swallowed and her eyes cut away from the emperor. "Ryn," she said quickly.

It was a lie, Liane knew immediately. But a name was of no consequence. The prisoner would be dead within a couple of days. He might already be dead, for all she knew.

"Please, my lord," Sophie said gently. She nervously worked her delicate hands. "I know you are a kind and generous man. I am not asking for anything more than my child and my friend. We will leave this place tonight. I expect nothing from you or from my father. Nothing."

"I have a better idea," Sebestyen said gaily. "You see, I am in desperate need of a new empress and a mother for my heir, and since your father is my most trusted minister, you would make a fine candidate for the position."

Sophie's blue eyes widened. Her nervous hands became very still. "My lord, I'm flattered, but I can't possibly . . ."

Sebestyen leaned closer to the girl. "I did not ask for your opinion or your approval, Sophie Fyne."

Sophie went pale.

Sebestyen glanced back at Liane. "Round up a priest. There's no reason to delay."

"But . . . but . . ." Sophie sputtered. A touch of color rose in her cheeks.

Liane walked toward Sebestyen. "Tonight?"

"Why wait?" he responded.

Liane studied Sophie with critical eyes. Yes, this woman could be a threat to all the plans she had made. She wasn't like the others. She wouldn't be meek or throw temper tantrums or look at the floor whenever her husband was near. She had the beauty and the courage to capture and perhaps even hold Sebestyen's attention.

She could be a serious problem.

Liane grabbed a length of dirty blond hair and tugged. "You are emperor, my lord. You deserve an empress who is worthy of you. This creature is unbathed and dressed like a peasant, and I seriously doubt she would have any clue as to how to satisfy a husband."

"She has a child."

"Just because she knows how to spread her legs doesn't mean she is acquainted with true pleasure."

Again, the girl's cheeks blossomed with color.

"Your previous wives all came from upstanding families. A proper training period would have been deemed inappropriate in those cases, but this girl is yours to do with as you please."

"I don't care—" Sebestyen began.

"The others all disappointed you. Let me prepare this one properly, my lord." Liane laid a stilling hand on his arm. "When Sophie's father returns, he will be pleased to find a proper empress at your side. Will he not?"

Sebestyen's eyes met hers. "A proper empress."

"A proper, happy, and devoted empress. Isn't that what you want?" She remembered his plan too well. A scared girl who'd been forced into marriage and raped upon arrival would hardly provide Sebestyen with the happy family he wanted to present to Maddox and then take away.

Besides, she needed time to think things through. To plan. She could not allow a mere girl to disturb her place in this palace.

Sebestyen looked more intrigued than impatient; that had to be a good sign. "How long will it take you to transform this country girl into a proper empress?"

Liane took a deep breath. No, she was not jealous, but she wasn't yet ready to share Sebestyen with this woman. "A week."

He laughed at her. "You have three days. No, two and a half. I believe an afternoon wedding would be most appropriate. The Tryfynian ambassador will be here, and we can impress him with the magnificence of a royal wedding and the feast that will follow. Make the arrangements."

Liane took Sophie's arm. The girl had been listening, and was terrified. But she was not panicked.

"If I'm going to agree to this . . . this marriage," Sophie said breathlessly, "might I make a few requests?"

"You may make all the requests you'd like," Sebestyen said. "That doesn't mean I'll grant them."

Sophie lifted her chin. Another girl in a similar situation might faint, or cry, or shake with fear. Sophie Fyne did none of that. Yes, she was most definitely Maddox's daughter.

"I want to see my baby. Tonight."

Sebestyen shrugged. "That can be arranged."

"And before the wedding takes place, I want my daughter and the friend who was taken prisoner tonight to be released. I want you to let them go home."

"That sounds reasonable," Sebestyen said with a gentle smile.

Sophie relaxed. After a moment she even smiled. Liane knew Sebestyen had no intention of allowing Maddox's grandchild to escape, and she doubted very much that he'd allow her *friend* to leave the palace. But Sophie didn't have to know that. Not until after the ceremony.

Liane looked up at Sebestyen. "Two and half days is not enough," she said. "I need a week to prepare her."

Sebestyen's impatience returned. "I cannot wait a week!"

"You can," she whispered. "I'll be back as soon as I get this one settled. We will make the week pass quickly."

Sebestyen looked at Sophie, and Liane could see the admiration in his eyes. Even dirty, and smelling of mud and sweat, and dressed like a man, the creature who was to be Sebestyen's next empress was a very beautiful woman. It would be easy to hate her.

"No," Sebestyen said absently. "There's no need for you to come back tonight." He glared down at her. "Two and a half days, Liane, that's all the time you have."

Sophie's remarkably blue eyes widened. "Liane?" she repeated softly. And then she recovered her wits. "What a pretty name. I don't believe I've ever heard it before. It's quite lovely."

Heaven above, the girl was a terrible liar. She might've heard the name anywhere in the city . . . perhaps even in the Southern Province. Anyone who visited the palace might speak of the woman who was Sebestyen's most favored concubine. No one outside this room knew that Liane was an assassin, but why else would the mere mention of her name startle the girl?

When they left Sebestyen's chambers, two sentinels escorted the women to Level Five, and the other two stayed behind to guard the emperor's door. Sophie didn't say a word, and neither did Liane. The strange girl stared in wonder at the lift, as it quickly carried them from Level One to Five.

Liane had once found such things wondrous, but no more. Heaven above, this woman could be trouble.

It would be easy to kill Sophie Fyne. The girl had no weapons, and would not see the blade coming. She would not expect violence from another woman. Liane was not without sympathy; she knew how to make death quick and painless. Well, almost painless.

But she had not yet fallen to that depth. She wasn't yet ready to murder an innocent girl who only wanted her child and her freedom. It was unlikely Sophie would have either for any length of time. Besides, Sebestyen would be livid if she did away with the girl before he was finished with her.

In the hallways of Level Five, Liane was directed to the chamber where the baby was being cared for. When Sophie realized where they were going, her face brightened. "Have you seen Ariana?" she asked brightly. "Is she well?"

The sentinels remained directly behind them, as if they expected trouble from Sophie, but Liane ignored their presence. She was accustomed to finding green-uniformed soldiers at every turn, but the way Sophie sometimes cut her eyes at them made it clear that she was not.

"Mr. Farrell arrived with a wet nurse in his company, and she has remained to care for the baby."

"Ariana is well fed and happy?"

"I haven't actually monitored the details of the child's stay," Liane muttered. She didn't care for children. Messy, stupid, self-centered creatures, she had never understood the attraction. If she'd ever possessed a maternal instinct, Sebestyen had killed it long ago.

All had been silent as they walked down the long hallway, but suddenly a child's cry, soft and plaintive, rose from the silence. Sophie stopped in her tracks and held her breath. Liane stopped, too. That cry—it sounded very much like the wail she had heard emanating from Level Thirteen. Her heart clenched and her stomach dropped, but she pushed the unexpected response down.

"Come along," she ordered.

Sophie began to run as if she knew exactly where she was going. Blond hair dingy with road dust, so much like Maddox's after a long trip, danced down her back. She stopped before a door. The correct door, though how she knew that Liane did not understand. She hesitated, only a moment, and then threw the door open.

The cry grew louder, and a chill danced down Liane's spine.

She stood in the open doorway and watched as Sophie lifted her child from a cradle that had been placed beside a narrow bed in this servant's chamber. The nurse had been sitting nearby, and she rose to her feet as she looked from the crying woman who held the baby to her breast and the courtesan and sentinels who watched the touching reunion with callous eyes.

Sophie Fyne held her child tightly, but with tenderness. Her entire body shook, and she whispered soft words none but the two of them could hear. Words of relief and thanks and love, no doubt.

"Go," Liane said to the nurse. "You won't be needed until morning. Tonight you may sleep in your own room."

The nurse nodded and slipped past Liane gratefully. Farrell had his own quarters on this Level, but he never left them without an armed escort. She wondered if he had yet come to the conclusion that he was not a guest but a prisoner.

He would not remain on Level Five long. Now that Sophie Fyne was here, he would be taken to Level Twelve, or perhaps even Level Thirteen. Liane felt no sympathy for the man who had taken a child from its mother.

Sophie had been beautiful before, but as she held her child Liane felt what could only be the emotion Sebestyen had accused her of earlier. Jealousy. There was so much love in Sophie's eyes, so much pure joy. And there was love on the baby's face, as well. Could a baby know love? It should be impossible. They only had needs. To be fed, to be cleaned, to sleep. But it seemed that Ariana recognized her mother. And loved her.

"I will collect you in the morning," Liane said sharply. "We have much work to do."

Sophie nodded absently, her eyes on the baby.

Liane closed the door and ordered the sentinels to stand guard through the night.

Sebestyen would never forgive her if she lost his bride.

15

THEY'D TAKEN HIS KNIVES, HIS SWORD, AND HIS BOOTS, AND then they'd chained him in the corner of this small room with stone walls and a cold stone floor. The chains were loose enough to allow him a small amount of movement. But not much. He couldn't sit, he could only stand in a crouched position that already had his shoulders aching.

Kane yanked at the chains that tethered his hands to the wall of his cell. They rattled, but didn't come loose. They were solidly set into the wall, just as the heavy door was solidly set. There were no windows, no light at all. A small bit of light crept through the crack under the door, and his eyes had adjusted to the darkness a while back.

He was trapped here. Without weapons, without luck. Without hope. So much for rescuing his daughter. So much for keeping Sophie safe.

While the cell was solid and dark and small, it was not entirely silent. Guards walked up and down the hallway, their boots clipping against the floor. The door and the walls were too thick for Kane to make out what they were saying, but he could hear their voices and their laughter. Stifled screams and muted mutterings drifted up from below, and occasionally he heard a scrape on the other side of the stones at his feet.

He didn't know what might be down there, but he suspected it was not something so benign as rats. What could only be a scream reached his ears. No, that was not a rodent of any sort. Sounded more like . . . a woman.

He closed his eyes and prayed. It had been a long time since he'd talked to God. A very long time. But in a place where women screamed, where babies were kidnapped and young girls were forced to serve as whores, and where people who disagreed with the emperor simply disappeared . . . prayers were definitely called for.

Kane didn't ask anything for himself. He asked for Ariana and Sophie to be safe. He asked for them to be taken away from this place.

He wanted revenge, he wanted justice. But he wanted to claim those things himself, so he didn't ask God to strike down those who had ripped his family away.

The door to his cell flew open, and for a moment Kane was blinded by the glow from the bright lantern the soldier carried. It was all he could see for a moment. Bright light, then the green of a uniform, then a length of dark hair.

And then the soldier said, "Fecking hick rebel. When I saw them drag you in, I thought I recognized that pretty face."

That voice . . .

As the lantern moved downward, Kane finally got a good look at the soldier's thin face and the scar that marred one cheek. The smiling sentinel in Kane's cell was the man who'd killed Duran.

SOPHIE HAD VERY RELUCTANTLY LEFT ARIANA IN THE CARE of the nurse, when Liane had come for her early in the morning. Liane was dressed in a very official-looking crimson robe, and in stark contrast Sophie—who had slept in her underthings with Ariana tucked at her side—was dressed in the same old clothing she'd been wearing for days; men's clothes that should be burned when this adventure was over.

Liane took Sophie's wrist in a tight grip and led her away from the baby. Was it possible this was Kane's sister? The name was not an entirely uncommon one, but Kane's Liane had been brought to this place, long ago. She did have the same unusual hair color—gold and brown woven together— and green eyes, though the shade was not exactly the same.

But that's where the resemblance ended. Kane was kind and good and noble. This woman was calculating and manipulative and possibly evil. That was certainly an evil gleam in her eyes as she dragged Sophie up a narrow winding staircase, into another Level of the palace, and down a wide hallway. One sentinel had remained behind to guard Ariana's door; the other followed the two women closely, as they stepped into a large, dank room. It was morning, so where was the sun? All the light in this echoing chamber was artificial. Strange lamps set in the walls glowed yellow; soft flames burned here and there, even in bowls that floated upon the surface of a large, still pool of water.

"Take off those disgusting clothes," Liane ordered as she released her grip on Sophie's wrist.

"But there are . . ." Sophie glanced around the room. More than half a dozen girls were in different stages of dress and undress. They bathed in the pool, they laughed, they fixed their hair. In addition to the soldier who had followed them to this room, three men guarded the doorways. Not soldiers dressed in green, but younger men in loose fitting skimpy blue tunics that displayed muscled arms and long legs.

"If you are cursed with modesty," Liane said sharply, "I suggest you repair that trait quickly. Your husband will have none of it, I assure you."

"I am not cursed with modesty," Sophie replied. "But neither am I accustomed to displaying myself without restraint."

"I suggest you become accustomed," Liane said with a
half-grin.

Definitely evil, Sophie decided.

When she did not make a move to remove her clothes,
Liane lifted her hand. One of the half-naked men in blue
headed their way.

"This woman is soon to be your new empress, Brus," Liane
said. Her eyes remained fixed on Sophie's face, as if she were
searching for . . . fear? Compliance, perhaps.

Brus, a handsome young man with his dark hair slicked
back and caught in a knotted ribbon that matched his tunic,
bowed crisply.

"Brus is a master-in-training," Liane explained. "One of
his jobs, during the training period, is to assist the ladies in
undressing, if they so wish."

Sophie had no idea what a master-in-training was, but she
certainly understood the rest. "I am perfectly capable of undressing myself."

"Prove it," Liane snapped.

Sophie began to unbutton the shirt she wore, and Liane
lifted her hand to order the young man to depart. He did, without uttering a word. Brus returned to the others, who were
likely also masters-in-training. Whatever that might be.

Sophie turned her back and quickly disrobed. She stepped
into the pool, descending down wide marble steps until she
was immersed in the pool. The water was neither too cool nor
too warm, but perfect. It was also nicely scented, with just a
touch of fragrant oils.

She would prefer her own pond and the warmth of the morning sun, but she had to admit, the bath felt very, very good.

A bath such as this was a luxury, and she closed her eyes
for a moment and enjoyed the sensation of water on her skin.
Then she dipped beneath the water, soaking her face and her

hair and then rising up slowly. If the sun shone down on her face, and Ariana was sleeping nearby, and Kane was with her, all would be perfect.

But nothing was perfect.

Three new women entered the room. They weren't dressed in red like Liane, but wore robes in varying shades of blue that were made of thin material that hugged their bodies when they walked. At the side of the pool they dropped those robes casually, and then they walked down the steps to join Sophie in the water.

"These ladies will bathe you properly," Liane instructed. She watched Sophie and the other girls with cold eyes.

"I am perfectly capable of bathing myself," Sophie insisted.

"If you are to be wed to the emperor, then you must learn to behave like an empress. He does not want an unwashed peasant as his wife."

"Then perhaps he should marry someone else," Sophie snapped.

Liane smiled, but there was no humor in it. "I will tell the emperor of your reluctance. He will be distressed to learn that you have already forgotten that the only reason your daughter and your escort are welcomed guests in the palace is because you will soon be his wife and he wishes to please you."

"No," Sophie said sharply. "There is no need to speak to the emperor." She lifted her arms slowly and stood there, ready to accept whatever indignities Liane offered.

The girls who joined Sophie in the pool fetched washcloths and scented soaps. They were young—all of them younger than Sophie, one of them surely no more than fourteen years old. They bathed their new charge gently, washed her hair and rinsed it clean. It was an odd feeling, to stand calmly while others took charge of such simple and personal chores.

For Ariana and Kane, Sophie kept reminding herself.

When that was done the girls walked with Sophie from the pool. They climbed the wide steps together, and when the cool air hit her bare skin she shivered. Brus and his friends watched, interested but not leering.

Near the steps a stack of towels sat. The girls who had bathed Sophie dried her thoroughly, then they rubbed a sweetly scented lotion on her skin until it felt like silk. She sat, and one of the girls very gently combed her hair while another rubbed lotion on her feet. Another collected a gown from a small stack of clothes in a far corner. When her hair had been combed and her feet had been rubbed with the balm, Sophie stood and allowed the girls to dress her, as meekly as she had allowed them to bathe her.

The white gown was made of such fine material, it felt airy against her skin, almost as if she were wearing nothing at all. The material was so thin, in proper light she'd most likely look as if she were wearing nothing.

But Sophie did not complain. Her cooperation kept Kane and Ariana safe, for now. She could not forget that.

She faced a triumphant Liane with her chin high and steady. "Now what?"

Liane smiled. "Now it's time for you to meet the Masters of Level Three."

HE WAS BACK, THE BASTARD. KANE LIFTED HIS HEAD TO look the soldier in the eye. Twice more since his initial visit the man had come into the cell to torture Kane. For some reason he could not kill the captive who had given him a nasty scar on his cheek, but he didn't have any qualms about hitting. Repeatedly.

And talking. The soldier did not shut up as he hit and kicked at his prisoner in chains. He talked about how the rebels on the road had died. He talked about the heads he'd taken and the way the rebels had cried and screamed in defeat. He talked about severed heads posted around the city, hanging there until they rotted.

The soldier talked about how Kane had run away from it all. It might've been made to look like a fall, but they both knew that he was a coward who'd fled from the battle he knew he couldn't win, leaving his friends and his brother to rot. The scarred soldier then contradicted himself, saying if he had known it was possible to survive such a fall, he would have climbed into that ravine and taken Kane's head.

In between taunts and torture, the sentinel asked questions. What was his name? Where was Arik? Why had he come to Arthes? What seditious plans could he share in exchange for a cessation of blows?

Kane didn't know if it was night or day, as the guard walked in once again. Apparently the sentinel hadn't found his fists and booted feet to be entertaining enough; he carried a stick and a short knife with him this time.

"Hello, you fecking rebel. Ready to give me a name? I was told your name is Ryn. It seems your lady friend cares nothing for your secrets. Is that your given name or a family name? Ryn *what? What* Ryn? When you're dead I might want to look up the family and pay my respects, but how can I do that with no more than Ryn to go by?"

Kane didn't respond. Ryn? Sophie must've given them that bit of false information, remembering the warning not to mention his name.

"Your brother would've given me a name, by now," the soldier said as he walked closer. "That cowardly poor excuse for a soldier—he had no business calling himself a rebel. He was a flea, easily stepped upon and squashed. As you will be, as soon as I have permission to step on you once and for all."

Kane looked the sentinel in the eye. "I will step on you before I leave this place. What's your name? I'd like to know what to call you, when I post your head outside the palace."

The soldier lashed out with the thick stick, hitting Kane across the legs. The blow stung, and what was coming would no doubt be worse. But Kane didn't cry out.

The soldier balanced the stick in one hand, the knife in the other. "I have no reason to keep my name a secret. It's Nairn. Iaso Nairn. Slayer of rebels and for the past seven months keeper of the gate to Level Thirteen." He leaned in close. "Your brother died too quickly. I suppose it's a good thing I've been ordered not to kill you just yet. Your death will take a very long time, rebel."

Kane flinched as Nairn cut his shirt away. "Yours will be quick," he whispered as the soldier raised the stick again.

Nairn answered with a swipe of the knife tip across Kane's cheek.

"Not so fecking pretty now, are you rebel?"

SOPHIE SAT IN A VERY COMFORTABLE CHAIR IN A ROOM JUST down the hall from the bathing pool. At least there was no crowd around, this time. The sentinel who had been guarding her was posted outside the door. Inside the nicely furnished but gaudy room there was only Sophie and Liane, this red chair, a large bed covered in red and pink and littered with pillows of all sizes and a long table covered with feathers and oils and things she could not identify.

There was a window, and the sun actually shone into the room. Sophie stared at that window for a long time, trying to draw the sun to her. She was so tired of the dark.

She did not dare to look at the chains that hung in one corner, or the whips that dangled nearby.

"You look almost presentable," Liane said as she paced before Sophie's chair. "And you no longer stink. The emperor will be pleased."

Liane was not pleased; Sophie saw that much.

She might not be educated or worldly, but she knew why Liane hated her. She was obviously jealous, though to suggest such a thing would not be wise.

"I do not want to be empress," Sophie said gently. "I only

want my daughter and"—she almost said Kane's name, but she caught herself—"my friend."

"In this palace, no one cares what you want. In all of Columbyana, no one cares what *you* want."

"You seem to have a very close relationship with the emperor. Perhaps you can convince him that I would make a poor empress and he should search elsewhere." Sophie lifted her eyes expectantly. It simply made no sense for her to wed the emperor.

"Once Emperor Sebestyen decides he wants something, he doesn't let anyone dissuade him."

"But you—"

"I exist for his pleasure, not as adviser on matters that extend beyond the bed," Liane snapped. "As you soon will, too. If you are accustomed to living in a place where others care what you think and what you feel, I suggest you come to terms with the fact that your life will not be that way here. You are here as a brood cow, to carry and deliver the emperor's son."

"It's very unlikely that I will ever have—"

"Cease your whining and accept your lot." Liane cut her off.

There would be no assistance from this woman, even though she obviously disliked the idea of Sophie marrying the emperor. And she did not even care to hear that it was impossible for a Fyne witch to deliver a son.

"When will my father return?" He might be her only chance to get out of this situation.

"Weeks," Liane answered. "Perhaps months. By the time you see your father you will be empress."

Sophie licked her lips. Somehow she had to find a way to escape. There was only one window to this room, and it was much too high off the ground to be a means of escape. Again she looked in that direction, hoping to draw strength from the sunshine. But all the strength she had to rely on was within herself.

"Why are we here?" Sophie asked, meeting Liane's glare.

"The emperor will be a demanding husband. He will expect a bride who knows how to do more than lie on her back and spread her legs."

Sophie's mouth went dry.

"But your husband-to-be is much too impatient to be a teacher of any sort. He will expect you to come to your marriage bed trained in the ways of sexual pleasure."

"Trained?" Sophie asked weakly.

"His most recent wife was not, and he found her naïveté quite annoying. To be honest, all four of the emperor's brides were disappointing in bed. It is my job to see that you do not offer the same annoyance. Since you don't have a moneyed and well-blooded family to protest, I can train you as if you were a concubine. In that way you can be the perfect bride for Emperor Sebestyen." Liane's eyes hardened. "You will be well-connected through Minister Sulyen, and well-trained by me."

"I do not wish to be well-trained or well-connected," Sophie whispered.

"No one cares about your wishes."

An unfamiliar anger fluttered inside Sophie. "Why would any man care about the sexual pleasure of a brood cow?"

Liane did not react at all to that question, much less answer. "Drink this." She offered a small crystal glass. No more than a tablespoon of a shimmering ruby drink sat in the bottom of that glass.

"What is it?"

"It won't hurt you."

"But—"

"Drink it."

"I'd like to know what's in this before I—"

"Drink it or your escort will pay for your stubbornness."

Sophie closed her eyes and upended the glass. A sweet, thick liquid dribbled down her throat. Almost immediately she felt a strange heat spreading in her stomach like warm fingers.

Liane went to the door and opened it, and three men walked in.

"These are the Level Three Masters," Liane said as she closed the door behind them.

Suddenly, *master-in-training* made sense. "Oh." The heat from her stomach spread to her limbs.

Liane was bolstered by Sophie's reticent reaction. She almost smiled.

The three men were dressed. Barely. Chests and flat bellies and long legs were revealed, while a mere scrap of fine blue fabric stretched across firm hips. Men in the Southern Province rarely wore kilts. They were farmers and shopkeepers, and preferred more traditional clothing. These Masters, like Ryn, wore practically nothing at all.

Why was it that she felt more threatened by these silent men than she had when Ryn had turned into a monster beneath her very hands?

"Catus is a skilled lover," Liane said calmly. "I promise you, there's not a more talented pair of hands in all of Columbyana." A black-haired man with plenty of dark hair on his chest stepped forward. He was handsome, as they all were, but he was also brutishly large. Muscles made his arms and thighs bunch, and while he was not tall, his body was as hard as rock and massive. There were even rippled muscles across his torso. When introduced, he bowed much as Brus had done.

Liane stepped to the man in the middle. He was fair-haired and much prettier in the face than Catus, and he had very little hair on his trim torso. Put him in a gown and he could almost pass for a woman.

Almost. He was already aroused; the little skirt he wore did nothing to disguise his erection. He had muscles of his own, but nothing like Catus. He looked gentle, next to the larger man. "Waryn, why don't you show the emperor's bride your area of expertise."

The pretty man stuck out his tongue and rolled it. It was, without a doubt, the longest tongue she had ever seen.

"Trust me," Liane said softly. "He knows how to use it." She patted him fondly on the butt before moving to the next man. His fair hair was oddly short, barely covering his ears. It curled there and over the nape of his neck. He was not as large as Catus or as pretty as Waryn, but he was taller than the other two and he had a masculine air that was almost magnetic.

"Vito has been a Master for many years. While they are all gifted lovers, he remains a favorite." She boldly lifted his kilt to display the reason he was so favored. Vito was aroused like the others, but he was much larger.

Much.

Sophie closed her eyes. Her head spun. What had been in that glass? She felt out of control, a little dizzy . . . and her limbs were so warm.

Three talented, handsome men were here to pleasure her. To teach her to pleasure them. This was everything she'd decided she wanted a year ago, wasn't it? The freedom to pleasure and be pleasured without the complications of love. Exploration and lust and the company of whatever man she might desire. No bonds, no commitments, no involvement of the heart.

Sophie opened her eyes quickly. "I can't possibly sleep with any of these men. What if I become pregnant? The emperor wants an heir, I heard him say as much. He won't take a chance—"

"There is no chance," Liane interrupted. "Everyone on Level Three is incapable of reproducing. The Masters and the concubines all consume daily medications to prevent conception."

"Oh. Still . . ." How could she explain to Liane that she was not like other women, that it was likely she would become pregnant, no matter what measures had been taken to prevent it?

"Your training will not begin with actual intercourse, in any case," Liane said with a wave of her delicate hand. "There are so many other things to learn. Of course, if you beg sweetly and desperately enough I'm sure one or more of them will be willing to accommodate you. You will, after all, soon be empress, and they will desire your favor."

Sophie licked her lips. "I won't . . ." A wave of sensation shot through her body, as if Kane had laid his mouth on her neck, as if he had kissed her. "What's happening to me?"

Liane explained, in that cold voice of hers. "The elixir you drank will help you relax, it will get rid of those nasty inhibitions you seem to carry around with you. Who knows? You might very well find this session quite enjoyable."

Sophie tried to smile at the men who were lined up behind Liane. It didn't work. It was as if her face had frozen in place. "They haven't said a word. Perhaps we should all get acquainted before we—"

"Level Three Masters do not speak," Liane explained. "When it comes to matters of the body, there is no need for words."

"They can't speak or they just . . . don't?"

"Well, we haven't cut out their tongues, obviously," Liane responded.

Liane stepped aside, and all three of the men dropped their kilts and walked toward Sophie.

Her head swam, but just a little. Whatever Liane had given her, it wasn't strong. Just . . . warm.

The Masters were all fine specimens of manhood. Handsome, virile, attentive. Their eyes did not leave her, and yes, there was passion in those eyes. All six of them. This was everything she'd thought she wanted, a year ago. No, even a few weeks ago, she had still entertained thoughts of taking lovers as she so desired, in order to maintain the Fyne House and so that she would not have to live her life without a man to, at least on occasion, hold her.

But that had been before she'd fallen in love with Kane. She had fought it, and there was still the curse to consider and conquer, but the love had come. Slowly, surely, and strongly, it had come. No matter what sort of potion Liane gave her, she didn't want any man but Kane. By the stars, how was she going to get out of this?

Catus, he of the fabulous hands, took her hand in his and gently pulled her to her feet. He and Vito removed her diaphanous gown, turning her this way and that until she was dizzy. In a moment the gown was on the floor and she stood before them completely naked.

No man but Kane had ever seen her this way, and she felt as if she were betraying him just by standing here.

But to resist could mean death for him and for Ariana. How could she fight when she had so much at stake? Her own desires meant nothing, compared to the lives of those she loved.

Catus did have gentle hands, an odd contrast to his large and utterly masculine body. He touched her as he led her to the bed. He caressed her neck, her back, her arms. Every touch was tender and, whether she liked it or not, physically arousing.

"The most sensitive area of a man's prick is the head," Liane said in a businesslike voice. "Vito, show her."

At the bedside, Vito took Sophie's hand and guided her fingertip along the head of his erection. She barely touched him, and yet it was clear he was affected by the gentle caress of her fingers. He was warm and smooth and hard. Her hand trembled, but his was rock steady as he guided it down the shaft and back up again.

Waryn lifted Sophie, luring her gently away from Vito's attentions. He spun her around and placed her on the bed. She was still breathless when he leaned over her, dipping down slowly, tilting his head as if he were going to kiss her on the mouth, then changing direction and giving his attention to her throat, her ear, the sensitive skin beneath her ear. The tip of his tongue flickered against her skin.

She rested naked on the softest, silkiest bed she'd ever laid upon, and three finely built and handsome men gave her their full attention. Their *full* attention. She should be ecstatic; she should be floating off the bed in sheer delight. What woman did not dream of such a sensual experience?

And yet, she did not feel the warmth of the potion in her heart; only in her traitorous body.

Sophie closed her eyes so she would not have to see what was happening to her. Her heart pounded so hard, and she still had not regained her breath. If she refused to participate, would Kane and Ariana pay the price? If she had no choice, she could pretend it was Kane touching her. She could pretend . . .

Tears stung her eyes, and she pushed them back. Ryn had told her she lost strength through her weeping, and she needed all her strength at this moment.

A man lay down beside her on the big bed, pressing his bare body to hers while his hands very gently caressed her breasts and his mouth feathered tiny kisses here and there. Another Master speared his fingers through her hair and lifted it so he could have access to her neck. Still another spread her legs gently.

The first tear slipped out of her eyes and fell to the pillow.

"Don't be a child about this," Liane said sharply. "Do you know how many women would kill to have the full attention of these three men?" The Masters did not stop. They caressed her skin. They kissed her. They licked and nipped and prodded.

"Sex is a participatory sport," Liane instructed. "They are touching you. Touch them."

Sophie lifted a trembling hand and found a face. A hard, unfamiliar face.

"Open your eyes, damn it!" Liane ordered.

She did, and she found herself staring into a pair of dark,

deep eyes too close to her own. There were now only two Masters on the bed with her. Vito was on the other side of the room, standing before the table with the oils and the feathers and the other . . . things. He returned to the bed with a bottle of oil and one long, blue feather.

He dribbled oil on her breast, and Catus stopped the path of the warm oil with one gentle hand. He massaged the oil into her breasts, into the valley between, down her torso. His hand dipped beneath her belly button, but went no further.

Vito took her wrist in his hand and lifted her arm, and then he brushed the feather against her skin from hand to shoulder and down again. It felt good; it made her insides quake and feel hollow. She nearly jumped out of her skin when he grabbed her ankle, lifted her leg, and brushed the feather against her inner thigh.

The elixir Liane had forced Sophie to drink did more than relax her. It was an arousing elixir, a love potion, perhaps. But Sophie was stronger than most, and she had no intention of being controlled by anything so common as a love potion! No, an arousal potion, she thought as her insides quivered. There was no love in this. No love at all.

"If you will stop fighting, you'll find this most enjoyable," Liane said from her post beside the bed.

"I can't."

"Of course you can!"

Vito returned Sophie's leg to the bed and placed the feather in her hand. Her hand trapped beneath his, he guided that feather over his own body. He looked her in the eye as the feather brushed over his erection, and he smiled. Catus rubbed his hand over her inner thigh. There was still a touch of oil on his palm, and it felt different. It felt good. Waryn flicked his tongue across one nipple and then another, and like it or not her body responded.

"How can I feel this way when I'm in love with someone else?"

"The reaction of the body when it's properly stimulated has nothing to do with love," Liane said without compassion.

"That's what I always thought, that's what I wanted to believe, but . . ." More tears came, tears which would only annoy Liane. Tears that would sap the strength she needed. But she couldn't stop them. She wanted Kane, no one else. This was a disaster of major proportions.

Catus took her hands and helped her into a sitting position. Then he sat on the bed behind her, cradling her in his arms while he kissed the back of her neck and teased her breasts with long fingers. Waryn gently spread her thighs and caressed the tender skin there. Vito took her hand in his and led it to his own hard body.

She did not sob, but a few silent tears streamed down Sophie's face. Was this what she'd thought she wanted? Pleasure. The freedom to love as her body dictated. Here in this room was everything she'd thought she wanted, but she wasn't free and unfettered. She wasn't independent and unconventional.

She was bound to Kane Varden and always would be. The curse would kill him, if they didn't find a way to break it, but they had *time*. They had time to live and love and try to find a way.

Fighting now could get him killed. They wouldn't harm the baby, she couldn't believe they would be so cruel, but Kane . . . he would be made to pay.

She did her best to relax, but her legs trembled. "I'm sorry, Kane," she whispered as the man between her legs laid his mouth on her inner thigh. "I'm so sorry."

16

Liane took a step closer to the bed, where Sebestyen's bride was being trained.

The potion she'd collected from Gadhra this morning had not been necessary for this session. Perhaps it wasn't wise at all. But she'd wanted to see this girl squirm. She'd wanted to see Sophie Fyne degraded. No one could be as beautiful and good and loving and disturbingly *perfect* as this woman appeared to be.

That was what Liane wanted, right? This girl would be no shy bride on her wedding night. She'd be well-educated in the art of sex, she'd be no better than any other concubine.

So why had one word made Liane's blood run cold?

"What did you say?" she whispered.

"I'm sorry," Sophie said again.

Liane grabbed Vito by the hair and forcibly pulled him away from the girl. He stumbled back awkwardly. "You're sorry *who*?"

"Kane," Sophie whispered. "I love him, isn't that terrible?

I wasn't supposed to fall in love with him, but I did. And as if that isn't bad enough, now look at me . . ."

Liane shooed the Masters away, and reluctantly they left Sophie's side.

"That's enough for now," Liane said.

The Masters didn't argue, but Vito did raise an insolent eyebrow.

"I'll send for you if I need you."

They quickly dressed and left, closing the door behind them, and Liane sat on the bed beside Sophie. She covered the naked and trembling girl with a pink silk bedspread. "This Kane you speak of, what is his family name?"

Sophie shook her head and grasped the coverlet to her breast. "I can't say. I can't. I shouldn't have said even his given name. I promised I wouldn't."

The way Sophie had jumped when she'd heard the name Liane . . . was it possible? "Is his family name Varden?"

Sophie's eyes flew open. "I didn't say that, did I? At first I thought maybe you were his sister, but . . . that can't be. You're not like him. He's fine and honorable and good . . ." She swallowed hard. "They'll hurt him if I raise a fuss. That's what you said. I have to marry the emperor so they'll let him go."

Sophie actually believed that Sebestyen would release his prisoner if she did as he asked. Where had she been living all these years, to be so naïve?

"Kane is your friend?" Liane asked, horrified. "He's the one the soldiers are holding on Level Twelve?"

"Yes," Sophie whispered. "Don't let them hurt him. Please. Let him go and I'll do anything. I'll even marry the emperor if I have to."

Liane brushed a strand of hair away from Sophie's face.

"The baby, is she . . . Kane's daughter?"

"Yes," Sophie whispered.

Liane closed her eyes. What was she to do now? Everything had been going her way in the past few weeks. Everything! Sebestyen relied upon her more every day. She had his ear; she had his body. She'd betrayed Maddox to get to this place. How could she risk it all in the name of a boy she hadn't seen in sixteen years?

But risk she would. Sebestyen had taken the possibility of simple happiness away from her. Home, family, children—they were impossible. She wouldn't allow him to take her little brother.

KANE LIFTED HIS HEAD AND STARED AT THE SOLDIER NAIRN through a red haze. Blood stung his eyes and marred his vision, pain shot through his body from head to toe. His cheek hurt, where Nairn had marked him. His head pounded, there above the eye. Blood poured from the wound, blinding him.

It was a nightmare that would never end. The soldier who'd killed Duran hit and slashed and kicked and talked. He talked and talked until the sound of his voice was as painful as the blows and the cuts.

Where was Sophie? Was she locked in a dark cage like this one?

No, her father was a minister, an important man. She'd be safe here. Who would dare to hurt someone so beautiful and kind? What kind of a monster would raise a hand to someone like her, a woman who would never hurt another living soul?

No matter what he couldn't say her name, not even right before he died. He couldn't let Nairn know what Sophie meant to him. They had been traveling together, that's all. The soldiers didn't need to know anything more.

So when her name came to his lips he bit it back. He swallowed it. He tasted it.

Kane was vaguely aware that his clothes were in shreds, and there was blood pooling in other places on his body, not just on his face. Nairn swung his stout stick once again. Pain radiated through Kane until it was no longer specific, but wafted through his entire body. Was the left leg broken? Was something beneath the skin, on the left side of his body, also broken?

The soldier swung again, and the stick landed on the leg that hurt so badly. Kane's vision began to go and he was glad. Unconsciousness would be a relief.

But it didn't come. He held on because he knew with unconsciousness would come death. He wasn't ready for death, not until he knew Sophie was being cared for.

Even Nairn was surprised when the door to Kane's cell opened and a woman walked in. Kane blinked, but still couldn't see well. It wasn't Sophie. That's all that mattered. He didn't want her to be in this awful place; he didn't want her to see him like this, chained to the wall and bleeding. The woman who entered was dressed in an official red robe, and her hair was not fair like Sophie's.

"What are you doing to this man?" she asked sharply.

Nairn lowered the stick he'd been using this go-round. "He's a prisoner."

"A prisoner you were ordered not to harm."

"No, I was ordered not to kill him," Nairn argued. "He's not dead. Yet."

The woman walked closer to Kane, her blurred movements slow and graceful. She removed a scarf from around her neck, wet it in Nairn's drinking water, and wiped the blood from Kane's face. Her hand on his cheek was so gentle. "This is bad, but it can be fixed. There will be a scar, I fear."

There was something familiar about that voice. The woman who wiped the blood off his face and out of his eyes sounded very much like his mother. His mother had been gone so long, he was amazed he remembered her voice at all. Maybe it was a hallucination. Maybe he was already dead.

"The fecking rebel marked me in battle," Nairn protested indignantly. "It is my right to mark him in return."

Kane blinked as the woman bandaged his bleeding head with her scarf. He could see her a little bit better now. He really was hallucinating. The woman looked like his mother. Before she got old and broken by hard work. Before the loss of her daughter made her age twenty years overnight. The truth hit him hard, making his heart hitch.

"Liane," he whispered.

She smiled and nodded.

Nairn became concerned. He hefted his stick in one hand and took a step toward Liane and the prisoner. "I was not informed that the prisoner was of interest to Emperor Sebestyen. I was told we'd most likely be allowed to do away with him in a day or two. If I was misinformed then you have my deepest apologies."

Liane lifted her hand, and Nairn stopped in the center of the cell. He came no closer. "I'd be happy to escort the prisoner to more appropriate quarters if his position in the palace has improved."

"Don't listen to Nairn," Kane whispered. "He's lying."

"Why would I lie?" the soldier snapped. "I live to serve Emperor Sebestyen. Please allow me to see the prisoner to better quarters, if that is the emperor's wish."

Another minute with Nairn, and he'd be dead. Kane knew that. "Don't listen to him. He wants to kill me the way he killed Duran."

Liane's eyes filled with tears, quickly and briefly. And then they were dry. "No. Not Duran. He's the baby. You're mistaken."

Kane shook his head. "I wish I was mistaken, but I saw him die. This bastard sliced him open and posted his head on a *stick* and—"

He didn't know where the knife came from, but Liane moved quickly and suddenly there was a short but deadly-looking blade in her hand. She drew, spun, and before Nairn knew what was happening she'd slit the soldier's throat.

Nairn barely had time to lift a surprised hand before he dropped to the floor.

Liane snatched the keys from his belt and began to unlock the chains that tethered Kane to the wall. "I'm going to get you out of here," she said.

Kane shook his head. "I can't leave without Sophie and the baby. Help me find them and then the four of us can escape together."

"No," Liane snapped. "I've done all I can do. I've jeopardized enough. I'm going to walk you to a side exit. No one will question us. I want you to get out of the city as quickly as possible, and don't come back."

Kane shook his head. "I'm not leaving Sophie."

Liane pushed him against the wall. He was so weak, he thudded against the stone wall and lost his breath.

"Don't you understand?" Liane snapped. "Your Sophie is going to be empress, two days from now. It's been decided and there's nothing you can do about that. It's too late for her. But it's not too late for you. Forget Sophie. You can find another woman, someone like her perhaps. Make more babies, build a house, plant in the spring."

"I can't forget Sophie."

"Why not?" Liane snapped. "You forgot me."

Kane lifted a weak hand to Liane's cheek. Constant pain radiated through his body, but by focusing on her face he remained strong. After all these years, she was here before him. Changed and yet . . . not so very changed.

"I never forgot you. None of us *ever* forgot you."

Her expression did not soften one bit. "I couldn't tell it from here."

He raked his thumb along her cheek. It was worse than he'd imagined. All this time, had she thought her family didn't care? That they hadn't tried? "The day you were taken, Father went to the local sheriff and demanded action. He demanded your return. He was killed right there at the sheriff's office."

Liane flinched.

"Mother was never the same, after you left. She buried Father and tried to keep the farm running. When Stepan insisted on going to the palace itself to rescue you she tried to stop him—but not very hard. She hoped and prayed that her eldest son could find her only daughter and bring her home."

"Don't tell me this," she whispered.

"He made it to the city, but when he reached the palace and demanded your release, the soldiers killed him. They brought him home and tossed him on the doorstep like a bag of garbage. I wanted to march to the palace and revenge Stepan and you, but Mother wouldn't allow it."

"You were twelve years old," Liane whispered. "You wouldn't have had a chance."

"I wanted to try to save you. We all wanted to try. Mother used to say a prayer every night—"

Liane closed her eyes tight. "No more."

After all these years, she was right here before him. A different person. A woman, not a girl. He did not know the woman she had become, but she was his blood. And all this time she'd thought her family didn't care. That was as ugly as her kidnapping and all that had followed.

"Did you really think that you'd been forgotten?"

"Yes."

"We never forgot you," Kane said. "We've fought for you since the day you were taken. Mother died in shame and sorrow, and they burned the house and gave away the land. Six years ago, when the rebels banded together under Arik's direction, Duran and Valdis and I all joined."

"No!" Her eyes flew open. "My brothers are not rebels!"

"Brother, not brothers," he said in a harsh voice. "It's just me, now. Valdis didn't last a year."

Those tears shone in her eyes again, but the eyes were hard. So hard. "All the more reason for you to get out of here *now*."

"Not without my woman and my daughter. I'd rather be dead than leave them here."

Liane cocked her head to one side and gave him the strangest look, as if she had no idea what that kind of love was all about.

THE QUARTERS THAT HAD BEEN ASSIGNED TO GALVYN WERE very nice, if a touch feminine for his tastes. Servants were available at all hours of the day; they came at the tinkling of a little silver bell that sat on his bedside table, ready to serve his every need. He was well aware of the guard posted at his door, and he knew what that meant. For the moment, he was a prisoner as well as a guest, but that would soon change. When Sophie and he were married, everything would change.

He made the best of his stay, prisoner or not. The bed was soft and warm. The food was the best he'd ever tasted, the wine sweet and rich. Beautiful women bathed and dressed him, and even though they did not say so, he knew that if he wanted any one of them in his bed they would be on their backs in the blink of an eye.

But he showed no interest in them. The women who served him were pretty, especially the redhead, but he doubted they'd be discreet. It simply would not do for word to reach Minister Sulyen that his daughter's fiancé sought pleasure elsewhere.

He had not seen Sophie's baby since being assigned to these quarters, and that suited him well. Of course, one day he and Sophie would have children of their own, and when that came to pass the little brat would have to meet with a tragic accident. His children would not share their mother's love and attention with a bastard. The brat was being cared for, of that he was certain. The emperor would be sure to take good care of his Minister of Defense's grandchild.

Bors had taken up residence in the city for the time being.

Soon he'd return to his post in the Southern Province, but not until this new and highly placed connection in the palace was in order. He wanted to be sheriff of the province he called home, and a friend in the palace would help spur that dream along.

Bors was not a patient man.

Yes, the new quarters were very nice, but Galvyn was getting anxious. He'd been in Arthes a week. No, more than a week. Eight days. Where was Sophie? She should've been right behind him; she should have been here by now. Maybe she was having trouble entering the palace, since Minister Sulyen was still away. But surely the emperor had told his sentries to expect her. Maybe she'd taken the longer southern route, though he had expected her to choose the most direct road to her daughter, no matter how harsh.

Maybe she wasn't coming at all. Maybe she'd rather sacrifice her own child than become his bride. The idea roused a knot of hatred in Galvyn's gut. If she didn't show up soon he'd go back to Shandley and collect her himself, and he would not be as gentle with her as he'd been with her child.

Surely Minister Sulyen would understand that at times a woman must be forcefully told what's best for her. Even if that woman happened to be his daughter.

One way or another, Sophie's lover would die. Maybe he'd do the deed himself. Then again, when he had an army of men at his disposal, he could relegate unpleasant chores. He'd like to see Kane Varden try to take on an entire army. More, he'd like to see Varden lose.

When the door to his quarters opened in the middle of the afternoon—after luncheon and long before dinnertime—Galvyn jumped out of his chair. Finally! Sophie was here, and he would be summoned to the emperor. Would they be wed right away? Or would the emperor make them wait until Sulyen returned?

He didn't want to wait. If Emperor Sebestyen learned that

Sophie was a witch as well as a beautiful, well-bred woman, he might very well decide that marriage to a distant cousin and successful merchant wasn't good enough for her.

The sooner they were wed, the better.

Sure enough, it was two green-clad guards who entered his quarters, not the usual meek women who served him.

"It's about time," he snapped as he joined them.

The guards looked at one another; one of them almost smiled. "You're anxious to get to your new quarters, then," the amused sentinel said.

"New quarters? I'm not being summoned to the emperor?"

"Not at this time. But Emperor Sebestyen seems to think these new accommodations will be more to your liking."

Galvyn glanced back at the feminine room. How thoughtful of the emperor. "Should I collect my things now or . . ."

One of the sentinels took Galvyn's arm. "We'll have your belongings delivered later in the day."

People in power did not tote their own things from place to place. There were servants for such duties. "Of course."

The sentinels flanked him, and that one continued to hold his arm. They walked not to another room on this Level, but to the end of the hallway and the stairway there.

"We're moving to another Level?" Galvyn asked.

"Yes." The sentinels walked faster than Galvyn was accustomed to and he had to hurry to keep up, since they still held onto him as if they thought he might fall.

"Can't we use the lift?"

One of the soldiers laughed. "The lift is reserved for the emperor and his most honored guests and companions."

"I am an honored guest," Galvyn argued.

The soldiers did not respond, and the three of them continued to move downward. The stone staircase twisted and turned, it spiraled downward steeply. When Galvyn looked all the way down the center of the stairwell he became dizzy. They did not stop at Level Six or even Level Seven, but kept moving down. At one point the noise was so loud he covered one ear with his free hand, but then the noise subsided, and at last they reached their destination.

The stairway went no lower.

One sentinel pushed the door open, and the three of them stepped into a long, bare hallway. Unlike Level Five, there were no carpets on the floor, no flowers in alcoves, no pretty servants. Only a long, plain hallway with many wooden doors and a couple of rough-looking soldiers.

He balked. "There's been a mistake . . ."

"No mistake." The soldier dragged him halfway down the hallway and one of the soldiers in the corridor unlocked a heavy wooden door. It was flung open with a screaming creak, and Galvyn glanced inside.

Stone walls, stone floors, no bed, no chair, no window. There were only two things besides cold stone in this cell: chains hanging from the wall and a chamber pot. The chamber pot was half full, and it filled the cell with a stench. Galvyn gagged and put his hand over his nose as he was shoved into the room.

"This is a mistake," he said again. "I am the emperor's cousin. I am to be married to Minister Sulyen's daughter!"

The heavy wooden door closed on his protests, and a frightened Galvyn retched onto the floor of his new quarters.

LIANE KICKED THE SOLDIER ON THE FLOOR AS SHE WALKED past. Nairn. Kane had called him by that name. She would have done more than kick Nairn, but he was dead and she needed her strength to support Kane.

Her brother was in bad shape. He had lost a lot of blood, and he couldn't put more than the slightest bit of weight on his left leg. His face was swollen and so was his body, and what was left of his clothes would have to be burned. There was no way they could be saved.

Another blow very well might've killed him. If he didn't get care right away, he could still die.

If everything Kane said was true, they were the only ones left. The rest of the family was gone. Dead. All because when she'd been fifteen she'd caught the eye of a soldier who thought she might please the new, young emperor.

"Let me lead you outside," she whispered. "You'll get out of the city and find a doctor. I'll do what I can for Sophie and the baby. I'll make their lives here as pleasant as possible."

Kane shook his head. "No. I'm not leaving here without them."

She didn't know if it would be possible to save Sophie from Sebestyen. She wasn't even sure she knew how to try. "Don't be ridiculous," she snapped. "Would you truly give up your life for a woman?"

"Yes," Kane said without hesitation. "I would."

Liane faced the closed door to Kane's cell. Both sentinels on duty had seen her enter the room. They still stood in the hallway. From the sounds of commotion on Level Twelve, a new prisoner was arriving. New sentinels, too. A cell door slammed on the man's protests, and a couple of the guards laughed at his distress.

Liane stared at the wooden door. She couldn't sneak out of the cell, she couldn't disguise Kane or ignore Nairn's body. If there were only two guards, she could kill them both and then make her escape.

But there were more than two sentinels, now. Four, at the very least.

She couldn't fight her way out of here, but she could bluff her way out. She'd been bluffing her way out of tough situations all her life.

She opened the cell door and stepped into the hallway, supporting Kane as best she could. The sight of the emperor's favored woman and a wounded prisoner arm in arm shocked the sentinels—four of them, she noted—but they recovered quickly.

"Nairn is dead," Liane said simply. "He dared to touch me, and no man touches me without the emperor's approval. He should've known that."

The sentinels stopped where they stood, keeping their distance. "What about him?" one young soldier asked, nodding to Kane.

"He's to be a Level Three master-in-training," she explained. "After he's healed, of course. Nairn damaged him." She glared at each sentinel in turn. "Did any of you have a hand in damaging this prisoner?"

They all shook their heads quickly. "We didn't touch him," one sentinel said. "Nairn said the prisoner Ryn was his."

Yes, Sophie had given that name when Sebestyen had asked for one. Ryn. Had she known the name Varden would rouse suspicion? A shiver walked down her spine. Did Sebestyen even know her family name? Did he care?

"I don't believe we're allowed to release prisoners into your custody," the eldest of the guards said suspiciously.

Liane smiled. "Do you not know what goes on within these walls, soldier? I not only have Emperor Sebestyen's ear, I have his hand and loyalty and support. A command from me is the same as a command from the emperor. If you doubt it, ask him yourself." Her smile widened. "But I do have to warn you, he is not in the best of moods today."

"Do you require assistance?" A younger sentinel who hung to the back asked.

Kane would be difficult to move on her own, she knew that. But she didn't want any one of these men to lay their hands on him.

"No. I'll manage."

She and Kane did manage to walk down the hallway, though his limp was severe and he was unsteady and wheezing. The sentinels parted, giving them wide berth. No one would question why she claimed a prisoner for Level Three. They would all assume that he had some talent, some extraordinary attribute that made him suitable for the position.

And not one of them would dare to confront Sebestyen, about this or anything else.

17

LIANE LED KANE TO ANOTHER CELL, THIS ONE MADE OF metal instead of stone. He walked warily through the doors of the box-like contraption and dropped into one corner as if he had no bones, no muscle left. His leg screamed, his body wanted nothing more than to shut down completely. The doors closed silently, Liane pushed a lever near the doors of the new cell, and it began to move. Up. His stomach did not move in time with the mechanism, but seemed to lag behind.

"You're taking me to Sophie," he said weakly.

"Yes," Liane answered. "Against my best judgment, yes."

He relaxed, resting his head in the corner of the box as it moved. Up and up, as if he were being lifted on a cloud. He'd been so close to death. He'd felt it, creeping upon him. And now here he was. Liane was alive. Sophie would be with him soon . . .

The contraption stopped, and Liane offered her arm. Kane took it and painfully rose to his feet.

This Level was not at all like the one he'd been taken to

upon arrival at the palace. There were plush rugs on the stone floor, colorful paintings on the walls, tapestries, flowers . . . and there were beautiful women everywhere. Some of them were half-dressed, others wore frocks he could see through. He blinked, to make sure it wasn't his imagination. It was definitely possible that he was actually dead.

There were a few men, too, but not many. Men dressed in blue stepped out of rooms along the hallway to watch as Liane led him along. One or two of them offered to help, but Liane would not accept their assistance. So they all just looked on.

They finally reached a door where Liane stopped. A large, older woman stood there, arms crossed over her massive chest.

"Has anyone come here looking for her?"

"No," the woman said simply. "And no one's been in or out of the room, as you instructed."

Liane sent the woman away with a wave of her hand, and opened the door on a large room decorated in pink and red.

Sophie lay on the bed, naked and half covered with a pink sheet. Her wrists had been bound with silk scarves, and she was lashed to the bedposts.

Kane found a burst of strength and broke away from Liane. "Who did this?" he asked gruffly. "I'll kill him, I swear . . ."

Sophie started to smile at him, and then as she noted the state of his face and the blood on his tattered clothes, the smile died and tears leaped to her eyes. She tugged on the scarves, trying to free herself.

"Who did this?" Kane asked again, and Sophie's gaze cut to Liane.

Liane swept past Kane and began to untie the scarves. "I had no choice. She was . . . well, let's just say it wasn't safe to leave her unattended when I left her here."

"She's naked!" Kane said.

"I didn't have time to dress her," Liane said sharply. "I was in a bit of a hurry to get to you."

Kane sat on the side of the bed as Liane removed the second scarf from Sophie's wrists. When she was free, Sophie threw her arms around his neck. Gently, and yet—hard—as if she couldn't hold him tightly enough. As he wrapped his arms around her, he knew just how she felt.

No, he wasn't dead. He was alive, and Sophie was very real.

For a long while they just held on to one another. Liane stepped away from the bed, silent and almost shy.

Kane thrust his fingers in Sophie's hair. "Have you seen Ariana?"

Sophie nodded quickly. "She's fine. She's grown so much, as you can imagine. Three weeks," she whispered. "I never thought I'd go an entire three weeks without seeing her."

"I know." He comforted her with his hands and with soft kisses on her cheek.

Liane pulled a chair to the side of the bed and sat. "We need to talk," she said in a formal voice.

Sophie wrapped herself in a pink sheet and sat beside Kane. Their arms were entwined, their thighs touched. She rested her head on his shoulder.

"In two days . . ." Liane took a deep breath, an indication that she was not as calm as she appeared to be. "No, it's actually less than two days, now. Closer to one and a half. When that time is up Sophie and the emperor will be married."

"No, they will not," Kane replied.

Liane laid her eyes on him. "Some things are beyond my control. You, I can see safely out of the palace. Her"—she nodded to Sophie—"she stays."

"If you can get me out of here, you can get her and the baby out, too."

"He'll kill me," Liane said simply, without fire or fear. "I am responsible for getting Sophie ready for her role as empress. If I lose her, Sebestyen will blame me, and he will kill me. Or worse."

"Come with us," Kane said as he tightened his arm around Sophie.

Liane shook her head. "I can't go. I have . . . things to do here."

"But—"

"This is my home," she interrupted. "I've lived in this palace longer than I've lived out of it."

It was true. For so many years he'd wondered if she was alive, if he could save her, if everything would one day be the way it had once been.

She was alive, but not the girl he remembered. He couldn't save her; it was too late for that. And nothing would ever be the way it had once been.

"I'm not leaving her here," he insisted.

Liane glanced toward the window. "Fine. Stay. Sophie won't be the first empress to take a lover. His second wife was quite fond of one of the masters-in-training. Unfortunately they were caught in the act. The empress was dropped into Level Thirteen and the master-in-training was . . . well, you don't want to know what Sebesteyen did to him. We'll be more careful than they were," Liane said sensibly. A smile crossed her face. "It's actually perfect. Sebestyen is desperate for an heir, and I suspect he is incapable of producing one on his own. The next emperor will be your child, Kane. You can have Sophie to yourself almost all hours of the day and night. Sebestyen only requires a few hours a day from his wives. Sometimes only a few minutes. Once she's with child, he'll likely not need to see her at all, so you'll have her completely to yourself."

Kane stood to loom over his sister. "Sophie is not going to marry Sebestyen."

She gazed up at him. "Yes, she is."

"I will not share her with another man!"

"You can't stop it."

"I can," Sophie said softly.

"What?" Liane snapped.

Sophie held her head high. Her spine stiffened. "I think I can stop the wedding."

SOPHIE WRAPPED HERSELF IN THE SILK SHEET AS SHE STOOD and gave Liane a list of the supplies she needed. Linara leaves and blooms, preferably fresh. Water and bandages for Kane. Clothes that were not sheer. Soup, again for Kane. Her baby, brought to her for feeding and for comfort.

When that was done, she wanted to be left alone. With her baby; with Kane. She looked at him and smiled, and stroked his unmarked cheek gently.

Liane reacted to that request. "The potion should have worn off by now," she said.

"It has," Sophie said. "For the most part."

"He is in no condition to—" Liane began.

"I'll take care of him," Sophie interrupted.

Liane left the room, and Sophie insisted that Kane lie down on the bed. She touched his face, her fingers barely brushing again the damaged skin. He had come very near death; she could feel it.

It was everything she'd feared, when she'd resisted falling in love. Yes, she might lose Kane, one day. She might lose Ariana, she would one day lose her own life, either in old age or by accident or in battle or in any one of a thousand ways.

But not loving—not living—that was no alternative at all.

"I love you," she whispered.

Kane took her hand and squeezed it. "I love you, too."

She unbuttoned his ragged, bloody shirt and removed it gently, wincing at the damage that had been done to him. Could she fix this when she was not carrying a child inside her? Did she have enough power within her to heal the man she loved? In time?

Liane returned with everything Sophie had requested.

Everything but Ariana. Sophie once again asked for her daughter. Her breasts were heavy and it was past time to feed her child. Liane did not want to leave the room when Sophie asked it of her.

And then Sophie commanded, with every ounce of strength she possessed. Reluctantly, Liane left the room. Sophie knew that Liane was still afraid when she heard the lock turn.

She finished undressing Kane, then she bathed him and dressed his wounds. He fell asleep while she ministered to him, and that was just as well. It would be difficult to explain what she was doing. Especially since she didn't know if it would work or not. She flinched at every cut, every bruise. Those marks of violence hurt her as if they were on her own skin.

Liane brought Ariana to the room, along with a bassinet. While Kane lay upon the bed, covered in that awful pink sheet, Sophie fed Ariana, rocked her to sleep, and laid her in the bassinet.

It was time.

Light came through the window differently, now. It was softer, hinting that soon afternoon would be over and evening would come. This was best done by the light of day. She wasn't sure how she knew that, but she knew.

Sophie laid the linara leaves and blooms around the bed and across Kane's body, and then she placed her hands over his heart.

"I wish for you, with all my heart, a prompt healing of this body."

She waited for the bruises and cuts to disappear, but they didn't. Her hands began to tremble. Was the healing of his body so much more difficult than the good luck and healing of the mind she had offered him last time? Did she have to be with child in order to be the powerful witch Juliet claimed she had always been?

"Heal now," she said in a softer voice. Nothing happened. "Please."

Kane slept on, and the wounds remained. Disheartened, Sophie laid down beside him and wrapped her arms around his battered body.

"I wish I had studied more, the way Isadora suggested, so that I might be a more powerful witch today. If I were more powerful I could fix everything with a wave of my hand." But of course, life was not so easy. Perhaps it wasn't meant to be.

She had tried to understand her gift, and perhaps that was beginning to happen. When she'd gone to Shandley and all those women had gotten pregnant—it hadn't been a day filled with unharnessed lust that left those women with child. Husbands and wives had come together on that day; lovers had sought one another out. It hadn't been random lust that brought them together, but *love*.

She had been in the presence of the affected women and men, even if only for a moment or two. On that day, her mind had been on the baby growing inside her and, yes, she'd been thinking of the rebel she had found lying beneath the linara tree. Juliet had said her gift had something to do with out-of-control emotions, and Sophie was just now beginning to understand what that meant.

Her love had spread beyond her body to affect those around her. If she were with child and the emotion she felt was something other than love, would that spread to those in her vicinity in the same way? Would she emit a cloud of emotion that would touch those around her?

She could not recall being truly angry at any time during her pregnancy. What would happen if it was anger that rushed through her instead of love? How would those around her be affected?

"Heal, Kane," she whispered as she laid down beside him and snuggled against his cool body. He needed her warmth. "Heal for me." She closed her eyes and drifted off to sleep.

* * *

KANE WOKE TO FIND THAT EVENING HAD FALLEN. HE SLEPT naked in a soft bed, beneath silky sheets, with an equally naked Sophie curled up beside him.

He lifted his arm, and noted that there was no pain. He and Sophie slept in darkness, so he could not see the bruises on his arm. But they'd certainly been there when he went to sleep.

His face didn't hurt, either. Maybe Sophie had given him some witch's potion that took away the pain. He lifted his fingers to his face and felt the place on his cheek where the wound should be.

All he felt was the thin ridge of a scar.

Had he slept for months, losing time the way he had after meeting Sophie by the pond? Was Sophie empress?

He shook her gently. "Wake up, Sophie."

She moaned and wrapped her arm around him. "Do I have to wake up? I was having the most wonderful dream."

"Are you married to him?" Kane asked.

Sophie raised up slowly and looked down at him. It seemed as natural as breathing that they were lying there together.

"I'm not married to anyone. What are you . . ." A touch of moonlight shone through the window, enough so that he could see her smile. She laid her hand on his face. "It worked."

"What worked?"

"The heartfelt wish of a true and powerful witch," she whispered.

"You wished for this?"

Sophie nodded. "I wasn't sure that the spell would work, but it did. It just didn't work right away, like the wildflowers."

He touched her face, traced the cheek with his fingers. "So, I've fallen in love with a witch whose every wish comes true?"

"Not every wish," she whispered.

She was thinking of escape, he knew. Wishes and healing

were her strengths. Escape was his. "I'll get us out of here, I promise you."

"I know you will," she whispered tentatively.

He threaded his fingers through hers and held on tight.

"There's something I must tell you," she said, her voice sweet and low, and obviously uncertain. "I don't want to, but . . . it wouldn't be fair of me not to. I only hope you don't hate me when I'm done."

"Nothing could ever make me hate you."

She took a deep breath, as if instilling herself with courage. "I tried so hard not to love you."

"I know."

"I didn't want to love you."

He reached up and touched her face, and felt a single tear on her soft cheek. "Are you so upset that you won't live that decadent and unencumbered life you planned?"

"There was a reason for that plan, Kane. There's a curse; a curse upon the men the Fyne women love. It's the reason Willym died too young, and the reason my mother never stayed with one man for too long."

"I don't believe in curses."

"I didn't want to," she whispered. "Neither did Isadora. We convinced ourselves that the curse was a myth, because it isn't right that an entire family should be forced to live three hundred years without a true and lasting love."

"What's the nature of this curse?"

Sophie touched his hair, gently. "You'll die," she whispered. "The records indicate that you won't live to see thirty years." She straightened slightly, and her voice grew stronger. "We can separate, and I can try very hard not to love you, and then maybe . . ."

He drew her down so that she was lying across him. "No. I won't leave you, and I won't allow you to leave me. If I know nothing else in this world, I know that I would rather have a year with you than fifty years without you."

"Those are pretty words, Kane, but do you really and truly mean them?"

"Yes." The feel of her skin on his was so right and beautiful, after days of pain and separation. He wouldn't give it up, not for anything.

"I might be able to break the curse," she said, with a touch more of life in her voice. "I am discovering new powers every day, and once I learn how to harness that strength maybe I'll find a way to undo what a scorned wizard did ages ago. If a wish will heal you, then maybe . . . just maybe . . ."

"One problem at a time," he said. "First we get out of here, then we'll see what we can do about this curse of yours."

She nodded, and placed the palm of her hand over his heart. "I have one more wish, Kane, but I can't make it come true on my own. No spell can give me what I need to-night."

He would die for her, fight for her. He would give her his heart and his body and his very soul, if she'd have them. "What's your wish?"

She listed toward him, her hair hiding her face as it fell across her cheek and down to his chest. "Your child, inside me. Now."

LIANE SAT ON THE EDGE OF SEBESTYEN'S BED AND WATCHED him pace. He was restless, more restless than she had ever seen him. She only knew one way to calm him down: She began to unbutton her robe.

He realized immediately what she was doing, and with a lifted hand and a sharp word, he ordered her to stop.

It was her worst fear. Worse even than never having the opportunity to kill him. Worse even than being drugged and thrown into Level Thirteen.

He no longer wanted her.

"I spoke to Father Merryl today," Sebestyen explained. "He advises that my best hope of siring a child quickly is to abstain for a few days before the wedding night."

Father Merryl despised Liane and her place in Sebestyen's life. No doubt he saw this as a way to drive them apart. It was working. "Perhaps we should postpone the wedding," she suggested.

"No." His answer was gruff, but certain.

Liane refastened her robe and leaned back on the bed. She still had hopes that Sebestyen might change his mind. He did need her, and he always wanted her. Father Merryl had never been able to keep Sebestyen from her, though no doubt he had tried.

"The girl. Sophie. What are you going to do to her?"

"Get her pregnant, let her give me a son, and then . . . I haven't decided what will come next. I probably should just kill her, I suppose, but then it will be over." He sighed, as if the end of his vengeance would be painful. "Should I just humiliate her again and again? In front of Sulyen, of course, so the humiliation will be his as well as hers."

"He is the one you wish to destroy," Liane said.

"Maybe I should order her to provide entertainment for the next council meeting. In the old days I used to have one or two of the girls and one or two of the Level Three Masters put on an erotic show at the end of the day. Everyone seemed to enjoy it, especially Maddox. Would he enjoy the show so much if his daughter was a participant?"

"You don't have to marry Sophie in order to debase her in that way."

"True. And there are one or two priests remaining who have some scruples about such matters. They might turn a blind eye if the woman on display is a concubine, but if it's the empress, they'd surely raise a fuss over the matter. I suppose I should just stick with the original plan to get her with child and then kill her after the baby's born."

Sophie had at least a few months before she had to worry about her husband trying to eliminate her. Liane suspected Sebestyen would always take pleasure in humiliating Sophie, whether Maddox was around to watch or not. It would be best if the new empress did not become pregnant right away. She'd warn Kane tomorrow that he and his woman must take care. The sooner Sophie gave Sebestyen a child, the sooner she'd be expendable.

"Is she taking to her lessons well?" Sebestyen asked. He moved closer, his movements smooth and quiet as he walked to the bed and looked down at Liane with amusement in his eyes.

"Very well. You'll be pleased, I imagine." Many men, perhaps most, would certainly not want their wives and lovers trained in the ways of sex by such talented men. But Sebestyen was confident, and with good reason. He was as skilled as the masters, in his own way.

"I'm sure she cleaned up nicely. She was quite pretty even when she was dirty and dressed like a beggar. Will she make a properly beautiful empress?"

"Yes. The two of you will make a lovely couple," Liane said harshly.

Sebestyen smiled. "You're jealous of her."

Liane sat up straight. "No, Sebestyen, I am not jealous. I am in need of a man's attentions, and you have shown me none for days."

Sebestyen sat beside Liane and placed his arm around her shoulders. The mattress dipped, and she fought to keep from rolling against him. "There are men available to you on Level Three, are there not?" he asked casually.

She thought of the way Kane had refused to share the woman he loved; she thought of the way he had looked at Sophie when she'd led him into the room where she waited.

What she had with Sebestyen was exciting, at times. It was pleasure and power and the joy of her planned revenge. But it was empty, compared to what her brother had.

Sebestyen lifted her robe and skimmed his hand along her thigh. "Then again, if you don't want another man to pleasure you I can always make you quiver without wasting the bodily fluids I'll need on my wedding day."

That was how he thought of her; a meaningless place to deposit his precious bodily fluids. A barren repository. She had wanted so much for him to truly need her, but she'd been fooling herself.

Liane clamped down on Sebestyen's wrist and pulled his hand away from her body. She tossed that hand aside and straightened the skirt of her robe. And then she held her breath. Men had been killed for less.

But he didn't looked inclined to kill her. Not yet, anyway. "You're right of course," she said calmly. "There are men on Level Three, all of them capable of fulfilling my needs quite well. Would you like to watch? That used to be one of your favorite pastimes, but it's been a long while since I fucked another man in your bed. Should I ask Vito to join us here? Perhaps you'd prefer to make the trip to Level Three tonight. I have a very comfortable chair in my bedroom."

His eyes changed in an instant. They went darker, the lids dropped. She couldn't tell if he was aroused or violently angry.

Aroused, most likely.

"Not tonight," Sebestyen said as he stood. "Perhaps another time. You go ahead, though. Obviously there's no reason for you to remain here."

"And tomorrow night?" Liane rose and brushed a wrinkle from her robe.

"I doubt I'll have need of you tomorrow, either."

If she told him, here and now, that his bride was in bed with another man nursing his wounds and planning to cuckold her new husband, there would be no more wedding to worry about, no beautiful woman to come between Liane and her emperor. None of the other empresses had been a threat to her. Not like this one would be.

But she didn't want to see Sophie dead any more than she wanted to see Kane hurt. They belonged together, and she would see that it happened. Somehow. She would do one good thing in her life. No matter what it cost her.

KANE WAS WONDERFULLY HEALED, HIS SKIN UNMARKED BUT for the small scar on his cheek. His strength had returned while he slept. The leg was healed, the bruises almost entirely gone. He made love to her fast and hard, and it was more beautiful than the first time she'd joined with him, more passionate and right. There was an unexpected strength in their lovemaking, as if it were spiritual and earthy at the same time. She exploded beneath him, he shuddered above and inside her. And then he held her in his arms and slept again.

She could not sleep as he did, but she did doze on and off. A short while later, she felt his child quicken in her body. It was what she needed, and what she wanted.

Ariana woke, and Sophie fed her. The baby had once slept through the nights, but they'd been apart and everything had changed. While Sophie fed her daughter, she talked softly about the sister Ariana would have in a few short months. Kane would surely like to have a son, but that was impossible. The Fyne women produced daughters, they birthed witches. It had been that way for hundreds of years.

A few hours passed, and Kane woke her with a wandering hand. This time he made love to her slowly. The child she needed was done; this coming together was for them and them alone. It was for love and pleasure, for all they'd missed and all they had to come.

She climaxed three times. Once when he touched her; twice while he was inside her. Each orgasm was more powerful than the last, and when Kane came with her, that last time, she was so exhausted she fell asleep while his large body was crushing hers, and he was still tucked inside her body.

When she woke he was lying beside her and had his hands in her hair. The sun was coming up; Ariana would be awake soon, and she would need to be fed again.

"What are we going to do?" Kane whispered.

If they escaped, Liane would be killed. Neither of them doubted that. If they stayed, the secrecy of their relationship and the fact that she would be married to another man would eventually tear them apart. They likely wouldn't last until the child she carried was born.

"I'm going to call the wedding off," Sophie said, "and the Emperor Sebestyen is going to gladly let me go."

"It's a nice plan, Angel, but I don't think he's going to release you that easily." Kane raked his hand through her hair. "I wouldn't. I won't."

"He will." She turned to face him. By morning's light she could see the scar. She ran her fingers over the ridge that marred his cheek, and before her eyes the scar diminished. It did not disappear, but the scar was now no more than a thin, pale line that would always remind them of a time when they'd almost lost each other.

And the day wasn't over yet.

"Make love to me again," she whispered, cocking her leg and draping it over Kane's hip.

He smiled. "You're going to have to marry me this time, you know."

"I know." She laid her mouth on his and kissed him deeply. And then he was inside her, fast and hard.

When she clenched around Kane and his climax came in time with hers, Sophie allowed one tear to fall.

JULIET WOKE WITH A START, COMING UP OFF THE BED WITH her heart in her throat. The sun was barely over the horizon; it was Sophie's time of the day.

She jumped from the bed and ran into Sophie's room, not

sure why she needed to be among her sister's things at this moment. The room was just as Sophie had left it. The dress she'd been wearing that morning, when she'd come home and found her daughter gone, was still laying across the bed. Isadora wouldn't even allow Juliet to clean the room, insisting that Sophie would take care of it when she returned.

Isadora refused to believe Juliet when she said Sophie would not step foot in this cabin again. It was rare that Juliet had visions about her sisters, and she never had visions about herself. But this one fact she knew without a doubt.

Juliet sat on the bed and grabbed the dress, clutching it to her chest with one hand and rubbing the soft sleeve over her cheek with the other. In an instant she saw her youngest sister as clearly as if she sat before her. Sophie and Ariana and Kane Varden were together, and they were happy. There were forces that wanted to change that simple fact. Powerful, dark forces.

Sophie was sunshine itself; she should not have to face darkness.

Juliet clutched the dress tighter, wrinkling it in her fists. She'd always tried to protect her sister, as Isadora had. Maybe they'd protected her too staunchly, and for too long. The youngest Fyne sister had learned some tough truths in recent weeks.

Juliet's eyes rolled up and her heart rate increased. A shaft of knowledge knifed through her body. Sophie was stronger than she had been when she'd left Fyne Mountain. Stronger in heart as well as in body and mind. She was determined; she was discovering the strength of her true power.

All these years, they'd thought Sophie was the least powerful of the three sisters, but that wasn't true. She had more power than Juliet and Isadora combined, and she had harnessed that power after all these years. She was mighty; she was powerful.

And she was in trouble.

18

Sophie walked the halls of Level Three, while Kane and Ariana slept in the room the three of them had shared last night. She wore the new gown Liane had procured for her—a simple, but not transparent, yellow frock with a snug fitting bodice and a flowing skirt that just barely swept the floor.

Residents of this Level stared at her as she passed. They did not speak to her. By now they all surely knew that before the end of the day tomorrow she was to be their empress. Some of them were afraid of her, others were simply curious. In different circumstances she might've stopped to speak, to smile and assure them that they should not be afraid of her. She wanted to tell them all that their curiosity was wasted since she most certainly was not going to be empress. But she walked silently and alone. If she couldn't do this, she might very well become empress.

And perhaps there was reason for fear.

She entered the large room where the baths were located. No matter what the hour of the day, it always seemed to be night in this room. There were no windows, and the lighting was odd. Those bowls of flames and the strange rods set in the walls cast a yellow glow everywhere.

Four women and one man stood in the pool. The man was Brus, whom she remembered too well. The five laughed softly and bathed one another, washing each other's hair and splashing like children. When they realized that they were not alone, they all turned to Sophie and went silent.

Sophie went inside herself and examined her emotions. Hate was too volatile to control, and until Galvyn had taken her daughter she hadn't known that emotion at all. She pushed it deep. Love brimmed within her, but she didn't know if she could control that, either. She already knew what a disaster that emotion could cause. Fear, lust, joy, grief; she had known them all.

She watched the five beautiful people in the pool, all of them young and pretty and apparently without a care in the world. Even Brus. In fact, it was possible he was prettier than the women.

They all led privileged lives, here in this palace. Decadent, yes, but also favored, in many ways. Had they ever known sadness?

Sophie thought about the day her mother had died. She'd felt so lost, so betrayed and bereaved. Willym's death, years later, had affected her in much the same way. A tear trickled down her cheek. The loss of a loved one was a terrible thing, and it was a trial everyone would have to deal with in their lifetime. Knowing that didn't make the pain any less sharp.

She remembered looking down into Ariana's cradle and realizing that her daughter was gone. The grief she'd experienced at that moment had been much the same as the realization of death. She had never felt so helpless.

And she thought about her sisters. She had loved them so much; she still did. But they had betrayed her, and even if they were reunited and she forgave them, nothing would ever be the same. That was sad, too, that she would never again love her sisters in the same way she once had.

The sadness built up inside her. She held it there, within, until it was so strong it affected the beat of her heart and the warmth of her skin.

And then she released it. For a few moments it was as if she could actually see the sadness radiating off her skin. It was a strange shade of green, and shimmered like the surface of the water as it spread outward. Sophie stepped closer to the edge of the pool, and the shimmering green moved with her. It touched the bathers, and they shuddered.

They seemed unaware of the green shimmer, and after a moment Sophie could no longer see it, either. But it was still there. One of the girls began to cry right away, tears streaming down her face.

Brus placed his hand on her shoulder and asked, "What's wrong, Petra?"

He whispered. The masters-in-training were not permitted to speak, according to Liane, but apparently in the company of friends the rules were changed. Or ignored.

Petra turned to Brus and buried her head against his shoulder. "I don't know. I haven't thought of my father for years, but suddenly I remembered the day he brought me here. He was so sick . . ."

The other three women began to cry, too, each in their own way. One sobbed, another sniffled, the other stood there while silent tears ran down her cheeks. Petra continued to seek comfort in Brus's arms.

But Brus was feeling pain of his own. Sophie could see the grief in his eyes, even though there were no tears.

Now it was time for the true test. Sophie pulled the emotion back into herself. She tried to see the green shimmer, as she concentrated on sucking it back within her body. At first she did not succeed, but eventually it happened. The sadness that had affected the others receded. It returned to Sophie. For a few long minutes it floated around her like a cloud, and then it ebbed into her body.

The people in the pool did not immediately stop crying. The memories the wave of sadness had brought to them were very real, and it would take time for them to recede. But the tears did slow, somewhat. And Brus looked up at Sophie with an unspoken accusation in his eyes.

He wondered what she had done, but he did not dare to ask.

Sophie turned and walked away from the pool, her stride sure and purposeful. It wasn't much, but it was a start. Her power, such as it was, could be controlled.

She retained the thoughts of her mother and her sisters and Willym in her mind as she walked down the hallway, but she kept her emotions harnessed. She passed by women who continued to talk to one another in soft voices, laughing and gossiping, unaffected by Sophie's sadness. It wasn't easy to hold the emotions in, but she imagined with practice it would get easier.

At the end of the hall, a window looked down on the city. The morning sun was shining brightly now, and she went to that window to offer her face to the sun. That sunshine gave her strength. It always had, she just hadn't understood. There was so much she had never understood.

Sophie laid her hands over her belly, and her sadness faded away. A smile crossed her face. She had always known her time with Kane would be filled with long sleepless nights and babies. At one time, she'd imagined that to be the worst of fates, but now . . . now she knew that's what was meant to be. Somehow they would find a way to end the curse. She wouldn't allow the possible pains of tomorrow ruin today.

She was not like her mother or her grandmother or any of the Fyne women who had come before; she was her own woman. A mother, a woman who would love only one man until the end of her days, a powerful witch.

Powerful enough?

* * *

Liane awoke after a mere three hours' sleep, snug in her own bed. She was a little bit surprised to find herself still alive and still on Level Three. Last night she'd purposely prodded Sebestyen, she'd purposely angered him. That was never wise.

Maybe he was waiting until after the wedding ceremony before tossing her into Level Thirteen. Maybe he wanted to make his bride watch, or participate.

Liane had not gone to one of the Masters, or a master-in-training, after leaving the emperor's bedchamber last night. She'd certainly thought about it, not because her body demanded release, but because she wanted to prove to herself that any man could fill her bed and her body as well as the emperor she longed to kill.

She rose and dressed in a crimson robe, and in a fit of pique twisted her hair back and up and secured it tightly. Not that Sebestyen would see her today, but knowing he preferred her hair down made her determined to cinch the long strands severely. There was no color to her face this morning, as if her argument with Sebestyen had leeched the bloom from her skin. The lack of color made her look older, so she darkened the rims of her eyes and applied rouge to her cheeks and lips. If he did see her, he would be sorry he hadn't laid with her last night.

When Sebestyen got tired of Sophie and asked for his favorite concubine, she'd send someone else in her place.

If he sent for her. If she wasn't fighting for her life far beneath the surface of the earth.

Liane jumped when an unexpected knock sounded on her door. Had Sebestyen sent for her already? If so, then he intended to dispose of her before the wedding, not after. The wedding wasn't scheduled to take place until early tomorrow afternoon. A number of priests and those ministers residing in the palace would be in attendance, as well as the Tryfynian ambassador who was scheduled to arrive later today. Sebestyen had not sent for his mother or any of his sisters, since a wedding was not exactly an uncommon event for Columbyana's emperor.

Sure enough, it was Taneli, one of Sebestyen's personal guards, who stood at the door. He'd most likely get great enjoyment out of watching her fall.

"Emperor Sebestyen has requested that his bride's child be brought to him. The nurse on Level Five informed me that you fetched it yesterday."

Liane pushed down her panic. Why would Sebestyen ask for Ariana? Surely he wouldn't harm the baby. She remembered the cry from Level Thirteen. Perhaps the haunting sound hadn't been her imagination after all.

"Why?" she asked sharply.

The sentinel's ruddy face hardened. "The emperor didn't tell me why, he just told me to collect the baby."

Of course.

She could refuse to hand Ariana over to Taneli, but what good would that do? Sebestyen would have the palace searched, Ariana and Kane would be found, Kane would fight . . . and Kane would die. He was already half dead, thanks to the beating Nairn had given him.

"I will take the baby to the emperor myself," she said, leaving her room and closing the door behind her.

"I'll escort you."

Liane walked down the hall with the damned sentinel at her heels. Sebestyen likely did not wish to see her, and she certainly didn't wish to see him. But she would not hand her niece over to Taneli. She'd take the child to Sebestyen herself.

When she reached the room where her brother and his family had spent the night, she hesitated. "Wait here."

Taneli balked, but she gave him her best glare and he took a step back. He even leaned against the wall beside the door, as if settling himself in for a long and impatient wait. Liane entered the room, and the sight on the bed almost stopped her heart.

Kane lay there on his side with a sleeping Ariana tucked against his chest. Sophie was nowhere to be seen.

The way her brother held his child was enough to move her heart, but that wasn't what made her react so strongly. Kane's bruises and cuts were gone. All that remained was a thin white scar across his cheek.

"This isn't possible," Liane whispered. "You're . . . healed."

Kane lifted his head and smiled. "One of the benefits of falling in love with a witch."

Liane stepped closer to the bed. "Sophie is a witch?" she asked in a properly lowered voice.

Kane nodded and returned his gaze to the sleeping child. His smile was so unlike anything she herself had experienced in the past sixteen years that she was envious. Envious of her own brother and his happiness.

"Sebestyen has asked for Ariana to be brought to him."

Kane's smile faded. "No. He can't have my daughter."

"I'll take care of her," Liane said.

"No!"

She stepped closer to the bed. "If you want to see the child and Sophie dead, be stubborn," she said softly. "Insist on having your way, face the sentinels all on your own, raise an uproar. Sebestyen will kill Sophie and Ariana and he'll make you watch, and then he'll kill you."

Kane's face hardened; his eyes were like fire. He placed one large hand over the baby, and she squirmed in her sleep.

"I promise you, I'll take care of Ariana." She touched his cheek, where—impossibly—only a thin scar marred his young face. He was just three years younger than she, but at the moment she felt absolutely ancient, and in her eyes Kane was still a child.

She remembered Sebestyen's words from last night—all of them. Some of them she would never forget.

"It's important that Sophie not get herself with child just yet. She will be safe until—"

"It's too late," Kane interrupted.

Liane shook her head. "Even if you did lie with her, you can't know—"

"It's too late," he said again. "She's going to have another baby, and I'll be damned if I'll let it come into this world bearing the name Beckyt."

Liane reached down and gently took the child from Kane's arms. "If you fight this, you'll all end up dead."

He leaped from the bed, amazingly agile for one who had just yesterday been beaten so badly he could barely breathe, much less move. "Wait for Sophie to return before you take the baby. If she comes back and Ariana's gone—"

"I can't wait. In fact, I need to hurry. There's a sentinel waiting in the hallway."

Neither of them had a weapon; Taneli was well armed.

Liane turned away from her brother. "I won't let anything happen to her. I promise."

"But . . ."

As Liane reached the door, she spun on him. "I haven't made a promise in sixteen years. I don't make them lightly, and nothing could make me break this one."

He sat heavily on the side of the bed and nodded, running his fingers through his hair in sheer frustration. Liane left him there, slipping through the door and closing it quickly.

Taneli pushed himself away from the wall. "You took your time in fetching that babe."

"Do you think it's easy to coax a child from her mother's arms?"

He shrugged his shoulders. "I wouldn't know."

Liane led the way down the hall, hoping and then praying that they didn't run into Sophie along the way. Taneli would wonder who had been in that room with Ariana, and why Liane had lied about taking her from her mother.

But luck was with her, and they entered the lift without seeing Sophie.

Sophie would be furious when she returned to her room and Ariana wasn't there with Kane, but there was nothing to be done for it.

Liane's mind spun as the lift took her up. Sophie was already with child, according to Kane. Was it possible? How could she know without fail? She was a witch, and a powerful one judging by the way Kane's wounds had mended overnight. How would Sebestyen react to this news? Would he take full advantage of the power at his fingertips, or would he dispose of Sophie without waiting for Maddox's return?

He had feared magic since the wizard's prophesy, and would have outlawed it just as his grandfather had done if not for the benefits to himself. The witches on Level Seven made sure there were no babies born on Level Three, and a witch had concocted the first batch of Panwyr. Some of the generals had witches or wizards or seers in their employ, advisers when it came time to plan for battle against the rebels.

Sebestyen didn't mind such happenings, as long as they did not touch him directly. Should she tell him that his bride was a witch? Would he be pleased or afraid?

When they reached the ballroom where Sebestyen waited, two sentinels opened the double doors wide. Ferghus looked at her strangely as she approached, Ariana snug in her arms, but neither of the sentinels tried to stop her. They did not search her.

Sebestyen waited on his throne, and while he did not smile at her, he did rise and step down from the dais.

"I did not expect to see you in the role of caretaker, especially after such an ardent and amorous night."

Liane ignored the bait, and did not tell him that she'd slept alone. "Why do you want this child?" she asked.

"It occurred to me that my bride might try to demur in front of the priests at our marriage ceremony or, heaven forbid, sneak out of the palace altogether. If the child is in my custody, she will surely cooperate."

"Are you so determined to have her?"

He cocked one eyebrow, shrugged one shoulder. "I want her, and I always get what I want."

"You want her for revenge."

"Yes."

Holding the baby snug in her arms, Liane walked toward Sebestyen. The baby made her feel stronger, more confident, more complete. She looked Sebestyen in the eye. "Let her go," she said softly. "Sophie and the baby, send them home where they belong. When Maddox comes back to the palace, talk to him. Ask him why he felt he couldn't trust you with the news that the Northern Palace had fallen. Listen to what he has to say, and then make peace."

"When did you become a diplomat, Liane?" Sebestyen asked. His eyes were emotionless, a paler, colder blue than she remembered.

"He has always served you well, my lord. Surely there is a reason why he kept the news from you."

Sebestyen reached up and removed one pin from her hair. Then another, then another. She stood there without moving, without protest, while the strands of hair fell down, past her shoulders and down her back. When that was done, Sebestyen clasped his hand behind his back.

"You always liked Minister Sulyen," he said absently.

"Yes. He's . . . he's a friend."

"And yet you came to me with his betrayal."

Liane's heart jumped. "I felt I had no choice."

"And now you beg sympathy for his family. I find that rather odd."

Ariana squirmed in her arms, thinking of waking, mewing, and reaching for her next meal. She wondered if Sebestyen would allow her to call for the wet nurse. The thought of the baby going hungry distressed her.

"Yes," Liane said quietly. "I beg sympathy for Maddox's family."

Sebestyen looked down at her, and a touch of amusement made his eyes sparkle. The corners of his lips twitched.

"This is rather enlightening. In the past you have only begged for me. In the interest of repaying you for years of loyal service, I will seriously consider not disposing of Sophie Fyne and her brat when I'm done with them. On one condition."

"What's that?"

He gave in to the smile that had been teasing a moment earlier. "I want you to personally execute Maddox Sulyen."

SHE HADN'T HAD A CHANCE TO RETURN TO HER ROOM, AFter walking the hallways and testing her newfound control. The experiment in the bath had not been enough; she'd tested herself several times, being careful not to cause any sort of a ruckus. Just when she was thinking of returning to Kane and Ariana, an older woman found her near the bath and exclaimed that it was time to prepare for the day. As future empress, apparently there were standards to be met.

Because she was too tired to fight, Sophie complied. Harnessing and releasing her energy and then retrieving it again was physically and mentally exhausting. It might be a good idea to regain some of that strength before she returned to Kane.

There were several ways in which she could use her newfound power in order to escape. With Kane and Ariana, she could very well walk out of the palace, swaying those along the way who might otherwise stop them. But there was always Liane to consider. If she continued to refuse to join them in their escape, they'd be putting her life at risk by leaving the palace.

Then again, she could use her powers directly on the emperor himself, convincing him to call off the ridiculous wedding. She wasn't sure exactly how she'd do that, but it should be possible to sway him.

Sophie was bathed, her hair was styled atop her head, and she was dressed in a gown of blue. The same young girls who had bathed her assisted, along with two older women. All the while Sophie contemplated the words she would say when she saw the emperor again, and she was very careful to rein in her emotions.

One thought calmed her, in spite of the circumstances. She and Kane and their baby would walk out of this palace, unharmed and together. One way or another.

She refused the rouge that was offered, and the woman who had dressed her hair backed away quickly. Was there a new force in her voice because she had found herself, or did the woman fear her because she thought Sophie would soon be empress? For whatever reason, they were all a little afraid of her.

One of the crones insisted on escorting Sophie back to her room. She suggested more suitable quarters for the emperor's bride, perhaps a suite on Level Five. Sophie declined, telling the old woman that she liked her room on Level Three. Moving Kane and Ariana in the middle of the day would be too difficult. Best they stay in place until it was time to leave.

She laid her hand on the doorknob, dismissing the crone before the old woman had a chance to peek inside to discover that Sophie did not have the decadent chambers to herself. Some of the women on Level Three could be trusted; others could not. Liane knew who would keep their mouths shut and who would not, but Sophie could not tell friend from foe in this place.

When the crone was gone, Sophie slipped inside the chamber and closed the door quickly. Kane stood before the window, soaking up the sun much as she had earlier in the day. The sight of him made her smile. He wore the blue tunic of a master-in-training, which was likely the only clothing available to him.

Sophie admired Kane for a moment; she had not realized how nice his legs were, until this moment. She walked to the bassinet to look down on Ariana, but before she reached it Kane turned to face her, his expression grim.

"Liane took her," he said softly. "Emperor Sebestyen has Ariana."

19

SEBESTYEN DID NOT ENTERTAIN OFTEN, BUT THE TRYFYN-
ian ambassador's visit called for a special dinner in the rarely
used dining hall on Level One. The dining hall was a short
distance from the emperor's personal kitchen, and it had been
as lavishly furnished as the rest of this Level. The long table
looked almost desolate, occupied by the four men when it
could easily seat five times that number.

Long, tapered candles provided most of the light in the
room, softening the red and blue and silver of the decor. The
Tryfynian ambassador was a bit confused by the lack of windows in the room, since of course he could not know about the
prophesy that had prompted Sebestyen's order to brick in all
the windows. He did not ask why the room was so dim, and
since the candles provided sufficient light and the fans kept
the room cool, he was certainly not inconvenienced.

Liane was a bit fascinated by the ambassador. Esmun Hern
looked more like one of Sebestyen's young soldiers than any

of the pompous old ambassadors she'd met in the past. He had black hair caught in a long thick braid, and blue eyes that were darker and livelier than Sebestyen's. He was obviously a man who spent many hours outdoors. His skin was tanned, and his body was bulky as if he were a working man rather than a diplomat.

Dinner tonight was a small affair: Sebestyen; Hern; the Minister of Agriculture, Cardel Yedden, who was concerned about the rustling that took place near the Columbyana-Tryfyn border; and Father Merryl, current head of the priests who occupied Level Two.

Liane was there at Sebestyen's request, not to sit at the table but to serve. She didn't wear her usual crimson robe, but the blue that signified Level Three. That too was at Sebestyen's order. Was he trying to make sure she knew her place? Perhaps this was to be her new position here. Servant. Maid. When she was finished here, perhaps he'd hand over his laundry to be cleaned.

She'd rather be dead.

Father Merryl, who had never cared for Liane, kept casting smug smiles her way. Of course he was pleased to see her put into her proper place for once. The old man had been at Sebestyen's side since the beginning, and he didn't want anyone but himself to sway the emperor's thoughts and deeds. It was a sign of how far she'd come in her years here that the priest disliked her so much. Maybe he had even feared her influence, at one time.

There was no need to fear a serving girl.

Her proximity gave her a chance to listen to the conversation. Sebestyen was playing it safe, for the moment, showing Hern that he was carefully considering an alliance with the clan he represented. Hern was forceful and lively, and he desperately missed the weapons that had been confiscated upon his arrival. Now and then his right hand drifted down to his thigh, where a knife normally rested.

Hern struck Liane as a man who kept his weapons close at all times. Perhaps he even slept with them. She sometimes did.

He shared one bit of startling information over dinner. The late Minister of Finance had indeed been conspiring with factions of the clan to unseat the Emperor of Columbyana. That faction had been dealt with in the same way the minister had, and Hern assured Sebestyen that his leaders wanted an alliance, not a war.

Dinner was lavish and impressive, and the wine that was served after the meal was Sebestyen's best. Throughout it all he did not look at Liane, not once. So why was she so certain he was very well aware of her presence?

Hern watched her, too, but his gazes were openly appreciative. He even winked at her, once. Sebestyen had not been looking directly at the Tryfynian ambassador at the time, but his face had hardened as if he knew and did not approve.

Yedden and Father Merryl carried much of the conversation, which was one of the reasons they had been chosen for this meal. They always seemed to have some subject to discuss, something which would keep the others entertained but was not inflammatory in any way. Sebestyen had little patience for idle chitchat. He preferred to watch and listen.

So did Hern, apparently. He listened, he responded when necessary, but he did not participate vigorously in the discussion.

Liane served food and she poured wine, but when she was not busy at the table she remained to the side, with her back against the wall and her mouth shut. Servants, after all, did not indulge in conversation with heads of state.

It was late in the evening when Sebestyen rose; a signal that the meal and the conversation were over. The others rose sharply, and for the first time Sebestyen looked directly at Liane.

"Our guest has been traveling for many days. I'm sure he'd appreciate female companionship this evening."

She felt her face blanch. Was he offering her? Or asking her to choose another woman for Hern? She could not be sure.

"What kind of woman does Ambassador Hern prefer in his bed?" she asked without emotion.

Hern turned to her, his eyes sparkling with mischief. "I prefer a fair-haired woman." His eyes raked over her hair, which as usual was down tonight. "And I do prefer a *woman*. I have no patience for inexperienced girls who don't know how to . . . participate fully."

"I assure you, all the women on Level Three know how to participate fully," she said tersely.

Sebestyen almost smiled.

"Then I will allow you to choose for me," Hern replied.

Liane nodded, then turned on her heel to leave the room.

She could go to Hern herself. He had intimated as much, not so much with his words as with his eyes and the shift of his body. Would he be a clumsy lover or a talented one? Would he poke her quick or make love to her all night? He had the look of an all-nighter.

She took the stairs down to Level Three, not the lift. Servants did not use the lift, and besides, she had energy to spare tonight.

On Level Three she made her decision, which was no decision at all. She sent Elya to Level Four and the Ambassador's chambers, then went to her room to prepare for bed.

She didn't think she'd sleep a wink tonight.

Just as she'd slipped into her nightgown—a plain and almost coarse white shift tonight—someone knocked on her door.

She answered the door and found Sebestyen standing there, dressed not in his crimson robe and surrounded by guards, but clothed as a sentinel. His hair was pulled back away from his face, and the emerald green uniform fit him perfectly. At quick glance, no one would know it was him.

She stood there, stunned, until he asked, "May I come in?"

* * *

SOPHIE CURLED UP AGAINST KANE, TRYING TO STEAL HIS warmth even though the night was not at all chilly. She missed her baby. Out of necessity, she had once again taken the herbs to dry her milk. Someone else was feeding Ariana tonight; some wet nurse who did not love her, who did not *need* her.

Three times today, she'd requested an audience with Emperor Sebestyen. All requests had been refused. She would see him tomorrow, she was told, when they were married. The emperor did not have time for her tonight. When she asked about Ariana, she was told that her child would be present at the ceremony.

Kane wanted to take the palace by force, but a force of two wasn't nearly strong enough to take Sebestyen and all his men. She would have to do this on her own, in her own way.

Tonight she did not cry. She held her pain and anger and grief deep inside. It became a part of her. It made her strong.

It made her dangerous.

LIANE PULLED THE DRAPES OVER THE NIGHT SKY WHEN SHE noted that Sebestyen looked at the window with a touch of fear. When that was done, he sat on the side of her bed.

"What did you think of him?"

"Hern?"

"Of course Hern," he said sharply. He fidgeted slightly, unaccustomed to the trousers he wore.

"He seems sincere enough," she said, taking a seat at her vanity.

"Honest about his intentions?"

"I think so."

"So perhaps I should not have him killed right away?"

Liane swallowed hard. Sebestyen could have sent for her, if

he wanted to have this discussion. There was no need for him to disguise himself and sneak into her room. He looked very different, sitting on the side of her bed. She liked his hair pulled away from his face. It did make the features look sharper, but still, it suited him. And the uniform didn't drape around him the way his robes did, but made it clear that he had a fine, fit body.

It all reminded her that if he hadn't been born emperor, he'd be a very different man.

But he *had* been born emperor, so there was no use pondering what he might've been like otherwise. It was as much a waste as wondering what her life would be like if she hadn't been captured and brought here as a slave.

"I would not kill him just yet," she said calmly. "He might be a fine ally."

"I thought as much," he replied.

For a few minutes, neither of them said a word. Sebestyen didn't stand to leave, and Liane remained motionless in her chair.

"Should I undress?" she asked, wondering still why he was here; why he stayed.

"No. That's not necessary."

She did not have time for games, not even from this man. "Why are you here?"

"I want you there tomorrow."

"Tomorrow night?" she asked. Did he want her to go to him after he'd finished with his bride? It wouldn't be the first wedding night she'd spent in his bed.

"No. I want you there for the wedding. Wear the crimson. It's your right."

Her heart leapt a little. "I have earned it."

"Yes, you have," he agreed.

The invitation had been made, and still he didn't leave. He studied her room, taking in her personal things and testing the softness of the bed.

"I need an heir, Liane," he said softly. He didn't look at her as he made this observation. "A legitimate heir to take over for me when I die. I don't have any choice."

"If you've come to me for sympathy because your life isn't filled with choices, I'm afraid this is a wasted trip. I certainly haven't made many choices for myself in the past sixteen years."

He tilted his head slowly and looked at her. "Is that what you want? Choices?"

"Maybe."

"Then make one," he said. "One wish, one choice."

He caught her off guard, and she was speechless for a moment. And then she spat out her response. "Don't marry her."

His eyebrows lifted slightly, "That isn't your choice, but mine. Choose again."

This time she didn't have to think nearly as long. "Let me go," she whispered.

He didn't give her a quick yes or no, but his hooded eyes lowered slightly. "Is that what you want? Freedom?"

"Yes."

He stood quickly, and once again he had the demeanor of emperor. "Fine. As soon as you kill Sulyen, you'll be free to go."

Liane stood quickly. "If you don't mean it, don't tease me this way. Don't offer me something you're not prepared to give."

"I'm not teasing you, Liane." Sebestyen reached out and touched a length of her hair. "You've served this palace long enough and well enough. If freedom is what you want you shall have it. I only ask that you consider the request carefully over the next few weeks, until Sulyen returns. Where will you live? What will you do?"

"I won't change my mind."

"Neither will I."

With that he left her, slipping out the door to return to

Level One and his chambers. How had he gotten past the sentinels at his door? Liane was well acquainted with the secret passageways that connected many of the Levels, but she knew nothing of a secret entrance to the emperor's chambers. If Sebestyen could slip out without anyone else knowing . . . how many nights had he done just that?

He'd been gone twenty minutes before she realized that the whole time he'd been in her room, her knife had rested not two feet away from her hand.

SOPHIE STOOD AT THE WINDOW AND WATCHED THE SUN come up. It seemed to her that the sunlight didn't only warm her skin, it soaked through it. She absorbed the heat; she savored it. When the sun was well over the horizon, she offered her hands palms outward. There was power in the sun. That's why she had always been drawn to its warmth. It was the source of her energy.

Life. The sun. Fruitfulness. Love. They all wove together to make her what she was; what she had become.

She had once tried to scare Kane away with the news that she was a witch. What would he think of her now that she had accepted her power and it had grown so strong? Many men would run from such power in a woman; she knew that, even though she had little experience with men.

Kane woke and left the bed. She heard the squeak of the mattress and the pad of his bare feet against the floor. He joined her at the window, wrapping his arms around her and holding on tight. His skin against hers was so warm, and like the sun he gave her strength.

"I want you to go," he whispered. "I'll collect Ariana and be directly behind you, I promise, but you have to leave here first."

"No," she answered in a surprisingly serene voice. "We have Liane to consider and—"

"Liane chooses not to leave with us. She can handle herself here; she's been doing just that for a long time."

"I won't put her in danger."

"I won't let you marry Sebestyen," he said in a husky and very determined voice.

She turned in his arms and lifted a hand to touch his cheek. He needed a shave, and the scar was white against his cheek. But he was so beautiful. "I'm not going to marry anyone but you, Kane Varden. When the time comes."

"Soon," he said. "The minute we get out of this place."

She smiled at him. "Soon, then."

She was not the same woman who had asked him to be her first lover; he was not the same sad soldier she'd found beneath the linara tree. But they belonged together now, in a way they could not have then.

"I, Sophie Fyne, take you Kane Varden for my husband. Now and forever, through life and beyond death, we are joined."

He furrowed his brow. "I want a priest."

"That time will come," she said. "But today I need the strength of knowing that you're my husband. Our vows are as much before God here as they will be with a priest to say the words for us."

He smiled a little. "I've never been to a real wedding."

"Never?"

He shook his head.

"I've only been to one. Isadora's. I think as long as we speak from the heart the vows are binding."

He kissed her on the forehead. "I, Kane Varden, take you Sophie Fyne as my wife. I will protect you and our children with my life. I will love you until the day I die, no matter when that day comes, and I will love you beyond that day." His eyes hardened. "I will not share you, not even with an emperor."

"Then I now pronounce us husband and wife."

He kissed her properly, not on the forehead this time, and

when the kiss quickly became involved and passionate he lifted her off her feet and carried her toward the bed. Her body thrummed and sang, it reached for Kane's in a way she had never imagined.

Love, like the sun, filled her with power.

LIANE WAS PRESENT IN THE GRAND BALLROOM BECAUSE Sebestyen had ordered her to be here. She would have preferred to sit in the small room on Level Five, where the wet nurse cared for Ariana. But last night, when he'd come to her room, Sebestyen had insisted. She'd never seen him get married before.

She was not alone, of course, though she certainly did not mingle with the other guests. In the past sixteen years she'd slept with a number of the ministers present, and more than a few of the priests. They either didn't look her way at all, or they cast suspicious glances at her. Some of the ministers had their wives with them. And of course, none of the priests wanted the others to know that they'd indulged in the pleasures of Level Three—even though all but a handful of them had done just that.

Esmun Hern looked well rested and quite happy this afternoon. He'd requested another visit from Elya just after breakfast, and she'd been more than happy enough to go to him. He was dressed, as he had been last night, in a kind of uniform that designated his clan. He wore brown trousers and a loose brown shirt, but across his chest was draped a sash of gold and red. He looked quite dashing, especially standing amongst stuffy priests and aging ministers.

Like everyone else but the sentinels who guarded the doorway, Hern was unarmed. Like last night, he occasionally reached for his thigh, where a knife usually rested.

Liane caught Sebestyen looking at her, now and then. He seemed not at all like the man who had visited her last night, but was once again the ruler she had come to despise. Did it amuse him to have her watch the nuptials? Is that why he'd ordered her to be here? She hated him more than ever, at this moment. He had promised to consider not killing Sophie and Ariana; he had actually promised her freedom. In return all she'd had to do was promise to assassinate her only true friend in the world.

No, Maddox had ceased to be her friend when she'd gone to Sebestyen with news of his betrayal. Heaven above, keeping bad news from Sebestyen was such a small, insignificant betrayal. If he executed every man who'd ever kept a secret from him, there wouldn't be a handful of men in this room.

She tried to think of what her life would be like away from the palace, if Sebestyen actually honored his promise. Was she supposed to marry a farmer or a merchant and settle down in a nice little cottage somewhere? She had often dreamed of such a life, but now that it was at her fingertips she realized how dull such a life would be. Should she ply her trade elsewhere? Whore or executioner. Love or death, for the money she'd need to survive.

By promising Liane her freedom, Sebestyen had managed to show her that she would never be free of him or this place. Maybe in death, but not before. Not a moment before.

Under normal circumstances, the family of Sebestyen's brides escorted the bride to her groom. Today the plan was for two crones of Level Three and a retinue of concubines to lead Sophie to Sebestyen. That time was coming, in just a few minutes. Music played, soft strains of a mandola filling the ballroom. There was a tension in the air, mingling with the music. The guests socialized, but they steered clear of the crimson carpet that had been laid from the closed door to the dais. The bride and her unconventional party would walk along that carpet soon, and Liane would watch as Sebestyen made Sophie his empress.

Kane could not accept what had to be, but in time he'd realize that none of them had a choice in the matter. He needed to find calm and acceptance, and perhaps in a few weeks or months they could devise a plan to get them all out of the palace.

None of the guests dared to mention the last empress, but she was on their minds. Their emperor was going through women at an alarming rate.

The doors to the ballroom opened, not slowly, but with a vengeance, and Sophie barged in. Her escort, the crones and the girls from Level Three, scurried to keep up with her. She did not cower or cast so much as a single glance to the side; her attention was fully focused on Sebestyen. The guests backed away slightly.

"Where is my daughter?" she asked as she marched toward her groom.

Sebestyen smiled. "You will see her after the ceremony," he promised.

"No, I was told she would be here, and I will see her *now*."

Sebestyen no longer smiled; no one else in the ballroom so much as breathed.

Sophie stood in the middle of the room, surrounded by the emperor's men and their wives, flanked by priests and sentinels. Behind her, the other ladies of Level Three waited expectantly.

The silver bridal gown Sophie wore began to glow, the silver turned to gold.

"I am not going to marry you," Sophie said calmly. "I have only come here to collect my daughter."

Wedding guests backed away from her, afraid to be caught in the crossfire they knew must be coming.

"Having second thoughts?" Sebestyen asked. He still seemed more amused than annoyed, even though he no longer smiled.

"No," Sophie said. "You used my love for my child and my best friend against me in order to make me agree to this wedding. What kind of a man does such a thing?" She turned around, and again the wedding guests backed away from her, so that she stood completely alone, encircled by men and women in regal dress and concubines in their finest and most acceptable gowns. Sophie Fyne was gleaming gold surrounded by bright colors.

"It makes no sense at all that you'd want me as your wife," she said, as if she truly did not understand. "You could have any woman in the country as your bride, and yet you have kidnapped my baby in order to force me to marry you. I love someone else. This morning, I took him as my husband." She looked at Sebestyen, who was no longer amused. His hands clenched and unclenched.

Did he dare to speak his mind in front of all these people? Would he threaten Ariana aloud in order to force Sophie to agree to the wedding? No, it was too late for that.

"You're making a very serious mistake," he said softly.

"I am not," Sophie said without trepidation. "I do not love you, I do not even know you. And even if I did, I could never live here." She looked around the room. It was overly warm and all the light came from candles and light rods set in the walls. "I need the sun to survive. I need light and love and happiness. You have none of these things. What kind of a man lives in this godless, airless, sunless place?"

Sophie lifted her face and closed her eyes. It seemed she grew taller . . . no, not taller, but her feet now hovered several inches off the ground. She floated above the crimson carpet, her gown glowing more and more golden. The glow was so bright, some of the wedding guests shaded and even closed their eyes.

Liane did not. Neither did Sebestyen.

Without warning an explosion shook the room. A large

portion of the ceiling flew up and out, the old skylight that had been bricked in years ago was reopened, and for the first time in seventeen years sunlight streamed into Level One.

And directly onto Sebestyen's face.

20

SEBESTYEN JUMPED BACK, BUT NOT QUICKLY ENOUGH. FOR A moment, just a moment, the sun shone upon him from his head to the hem of his robe. The prophesy he feared was not common knowledge amongst the people, but here, in this palace, they knew. His ministers and priests—and his concubine and assassin—knew what this moment meant.

Sophie did not know, but surely she could see the terror on the emperor's face. "I'm sorry," she said, taking a step forward. "I had planned only to fill this room with love so that I could make you understand why I can't be your empress, but . . . you shouldn't have taken my baby. I haven't yet learned to control anger."

Many men and women streamed from the room, knocking one another aside in order to make a quick escape. Fine, upstanding ladies raced to make their exit; normally fearless ministers ran from the ballroom elbowing one another. Liane didn't know if they were afraid of Sebestyen or Sophie. Or both.

There were a few who did not run. Liane. Hern. A couple

of priests who were more intrigued than afraid. The women
from Level Three remained, minus the crones who had been
so eager to escape, and so did a handful of sentinels who were
truly faithful to their emperor but were powerless to undo
what had been done.

Father Merryl, who had been scheduled to perform the ceremony this afternoon, stood on the dais behind Sebestyen. He
looked years older than he had last night, and while he had not
run he was definitely edging to the side, gaze firmly attached
to Sophie.

"Someone bring her the baby," Sebestyen ordered in a
hoarse voice.

Liane nodded to a sentinel, and the young man gladly left
the ballroom. She took a step toward Sebestyen, but then
caught herself. If ever a man was undeserving of comfort . . .

He sat on the dais, out of the sunlight that streamed from
above. "What are you?" he asked, his stare fixed on Sophie.

"I'm a witch," Sophie said, as calmly as if she were telling
the emperor that she came from the Southern Province or that
her hair was blond.

Sebestyen laughed. "A witch."

Father Merryl did not laugh. He left the dais with all the
speed he could muster and walked quickly toward the doorway. Some of the wedding guests remained in the hallway,
hoping to see what would happen next without coming too
close to the action. Others had fled Level One entirely.

The wedding dress that had been glowing gold gradually
returned to silver, and Sophie took a few tentative steps toward the dais where Sebestyen sat. "Why are you afraid of
the sun?"

"Prophesy," he said almost casually. "When I became emperor, a wizard divined that the sun touching my face would
be the end for me. The end of everything. And you brought it
here."

"No, my lord," Sophie said gently, but with a sure strength. "You brought it here yourself when you took my child."

She stood in sunlight. Did she know she was safer there than at any other place in this palace? The sentinels were terrified of her and her power, and Sebestyen was still afraid of the sunlight. Liane could see that even from this distance.

Sophie was the only person in the room who was *not* afraid. "If you need an empress you should search for a woman who will love you. A woman who will be your friend and your companion and your lover."

"Love is for peasants," Sebestyen said gruffly.

Sophie smiled. "Then I'm very glad I'm a peasant, my lord."

Moments later, the young sentinel who had been sent to fetch Ariana rushed into the room, the baby caught snugly in his arms. Sophie greedily took her daughter and held her close. The expression on her face was priceless. It was sunshine and hope and love. Everything Liane had dismissed as unimportant years ago.

"You think you've won," Sebestyen said from his prison of shadows. "But you haven't. This isn't over."

"You're wrong," Sophie said. "This is over, at least as far as I'm concerned. Whether or not it's over for you is up to you." She stood in sunlight, her baby in one arm, and she lifted her free hand in an obvious gesture of peace. She invited Sebestyen to join her and Ariana in the sun.

He shook his head and remained in shadows.

Kane burst into the room, armed to the teeth and wearing a sentinel's uniform that had surely been stolen. The uniform was the perfect way to blend in as they made their escape.

Kane unwisely placed himself between Sophie and Sebestyen, as if he could protect her. Liane wondered how long it would be before her brother realized that his woman didn't need protection.

"Let's go," he said softly.

Sebestyen stood. "No one is going anywhere." He approached the sunlight warily. Did he realize, as Liane did, that the damage had been done? He no longer needed to hide. He squinted; the light hurt his eyes. But he could see well enough to lift his hand and order the sentinels to surround the family that stood in the middle of the room.

They did.

Kane lifted his sword, threatening Sebestyen, and Liane took a quick step forward. Then she stopped. It had always been her plan to kill Sebestyen, but if Kane carried out that plan for her . . .

Sophie was not at all alarmed by the threat of violence. She remained calm as she placed her hand over Kane's and gently moved the tip of the sword aside. "There's no reason for anyone to get hurt today." She closed her eyes and smiled, and for a moment it seemed that the sunlight didn't shine down upon her, but from within her.

"What are you doing?" Kane asked.

"Thinking about our wedding and what came after."

"Oh." For a split second, the sword Kane held wavered once again in Sebestyen's direction. And then it dropped.

One by one, the sentinels backed away from Sophie. They appeared to be distracted, confused. The concubines who had been gradually moving away from the scene in the ballroom began to shift slowly inward. Liane's eyes were drawn to Sebestyen, and his to hers.

"Everybody out," Sebestyen ordered. Hern and the few remaining ministers left first. The Tryfynian ambassador grabbed Elya as he passed, and she smiled widely as they walked into the hallway arm in arm.

The soldiers left the ballroom last, and instead of preceding or following the women from Level Three in some semblance of military order, they mingled and touched and smiled at one another, green uniforms and pretty gowns swirling together almost making Liane dizzy. She turned her eyes to Sebestyen again. Watching him did not make her dizzy, but it did remind her of the good nights. The nights when she hadn't hated him. The nights when she'd wanted him more than anything else in this world.

Sounds of laughter drifted through the open door. Men and women, laughing and talking in hushed voices, congregated just outside the ballroom as if a witch had not just blown a hole in the roof of the palace.

"It's time to go," Sophie said, taking Kane's hand in hers. She turned to Liane and nodded once. "Come along," she said. "You're coming with us."

The four of them walked out of the room. Together. Liane thought she heard Sebestyen say her name, very softly and only once. She did not look back, but a part of her wanted to. She wanted to return to the dais where Sebestyen cowered alone.

She did not know what Sophie had done, but the effect was startling. Sentinels and servants, sentinels and concubines, ministers and concubines—even sentinel and sentinel, in one case—kissed and fondled all throughout the long hallway. They laughed and reached for one another without restraint. Hern and Elya groped at one another with abandon. Good heavens, they weren't even going to bother to go behind closed doors. Hern raised Elya's skirt and lifted her off her feet, and she wrapped her legs around him, smiling as she grabbed his long, black braid.

A glimmer caught her eyes, and Liane glanced down. A sentinel had removed his weapons and left them lying on the floor. A sword; a knife. They weren't the only ones. The men removed their weapons when they interfered with their lovemaking, discarding them in search of better things. A knife lay right there at her feet, the door to the ballroom stood open, and Sebestyen was unguarded.

Liane stopped, and the others stopped with her.

"What are you doing?" Kane asked.

Liane shook her head. Her time for choice had come and gone a long time ago. Freedom was not for her, and it never would be. "I'm staying here."

"No, you're not," Kane protested.

She reached out and touched her brother's face. "I'm so glad to see you, so happy to know that you have a family to care for you and love you. But I belong here now. I've belonged here for a long time." Where could a woman who knew only sex and death go outside of this palace? Nowhere. This was her home, this was where she'd live and die.

Sophie threw her arm around Liane and hugged tight. A tingle rushed through her body, from the top of her head to her toes, as if she were warm and cold at the same time.

"Take care, sister," Sophie whispered.

Liane hugged Sophie tightly, holding on too long. She'd never had a sister, and it was hard to let this one go. The embrace went on and on, and Liane didn't want to end it. She was safe here, for this moment. She was even loved.

It was Sophie who backed away slowly. "If you change your mind about joining us, contact Juliet Fyne in Shandley, Southern Province. I'm not sure when I'll see her again, but she'll soon know where we're settled."

Liane grabbed Sophie's arm. "Go north," she said. "Find your father, and tell him . . ." She might fail, and if she did it wouldn't be safe for Maddox to return. "Tell him not to come back here. Ever. It isn't safe. You'll find him somewhere near the Northern Palace."

Sophie didn't ask for explanations. She nodded, and Kane urged her on. They ran toward the stairway, amidst sentinels and women who ignored everyone and everything around them. Hern and Elya weren't the only couple engaging in something other than a kiss and a laugh.

They all seemed so happy. So content. Liane didn't know

what Sophie had done to them, but she suspected it wouldn't last.

When Kane and his family were gone, Liane reached down and snagged a knife from the floor.

THEY WERE AFRAID TO USE THE LIFT, SO THEY RAN DOWN the stairwell. Kane carried a sword and a knife and led the way; Sophie was right behind him, carrying Ariana.

"I don't understand what just happened."

"It's rather complicated," Sophie answered innocently.

His woman, his wife, was many things. Innocent was not one of them. They hurried down one section of the stairway and found a minister and his wife making love on the landing. The couple was not even aware that they were no longer alone.

"You were able to influence them all," he said after they'd passed the couple.

"Yes."

"How?" He grabbed her arm on the next landing, and she stopped.

Sophie sighed. "I am a witch, Kane. A true and powerful witch. Yes, I influenced them all. I pushed aside my anger and my fear, and I thought about the way my body feels when you touch me. I shared that feeling with those who were close enough to be touched by it. Not love, exactly, but . . ."

He thought of the scene they'd left behind on Level One. "Lust."

"Passion is a prettier word," she said. "Don't ask me to explain how I did it, and don't ask me what else I can do because I don't have answers to those questions. Does that scare you?"

"Yes," he said honestly.

"Still want to look for a priest when we get out of here?"

He grinned at her. "Oh, yes."

"Then why are we standing here?"

She took his hand, and they ran down the stairs. His wife, his baby. His family.

LIANE FOUND SEBESTYEN SITTING ON THE DAIS, HEAD down, dark hair falling forward and hiding his expression from her. She closed the door on the activities taking place in the hallway. How long would whatever spell Sophie had cast last before one or more of the sentinels realized what had happened? All she needed was a few minutes.

She kept the knife hidden, tucked into the folds of her crimson robe as she walked toward Sebestyen. He heard her coming and slowly lifted his head. She'd expected to see anger on his face, perhaps desolation, but he was maddeningly calm. "I knew it would be you."

"Did you?"

"It's always you. When everyone else runs from me, when everyone else hides, you're here."

She stopped in the stream of sunlight that shone onto the ballroom floor. The sunshine was warm, but her heart was cold. It had to remain cold, in order to finish what had to be done.

"I am always here because I belong to you. I'm a slave, Sebestyen. A possession. You can make my position here sound prettier than that when the mood strikes you, but in truth that's all I am. That's all I ever was."

"No. You're much more than a slave, and you have been for a very long time." He stood slowly, unfolding and standing tall. "I need you here, Liane. I can't do this without you. If you still want your freedom, I'll give it to you. But I don't want you to go. Stay."

Liane took a step forward, a trace of hesitancy in her step. Sebestyen was trying to sway her because he knew what she intended. Maybe he'd seen the knife, even though she tried to conceal it from him. She couldn't let a few words sway her. Not now.

Her feet stuttered. That didn't make sense. If he knew she had a knife, he could stop her. He was stronger than she was, and while she might be able to cut him before the struggle was through, getting in a killing blow would be difficult, if not impossible. So why was he so relaxed?

"I knew this would happen, one day," he said softly, his eyes turning up toward the hole in the roof. "I've been waiting for such a long time, it's almost a relief to have it done."

Liane's grip on the knife tightened as she neared Sebestyen. All she had to do was walk to the dais, act as if she intended to put her arms around him, and thrust the knife into his heart. It was what she'd wanted for so long, to see him dead. She likely wouldn't make it out of the palace alive, but what difference would it make? *He'd* be dead. It was what she wanted more than anything. That's why her mouth was dry and her fingers trembled. It was anticipation, not reluctance or fear. If she remembered better times as she walked toward the emperor, it was thanks to Sophie's spell.

No, others were affected by the spell, not her.

When she was close to Sebestyen he lifted one hand and offered it to her. That hand was strong, and pale, and familiar. Too familiar. She took it, with the hand that did not grip a knife. He didn't seem to notice that one hand was lost in the folds of her robe. His gaze was riveted to her face, and it remained just so—focused entirely on her. He pulled her close; she lifted the knife and pointed the tip at his side.

Sebestyen rested his head on her shoulder. "I don't think I could survive this without you. You have always given me strength. Have I ever told you that?"

"No." Just one strong push, and this would be over.

"It's the truth. I lean on you more than I dare to let anyone know."

"You don't lean on anyone," Liane said.

Sebestyen's answer was to thread his fingers through her hair and hold on tight. He pressed his body to hers and dipped down to lay his mouth on her neck. "I am not supposed to love you," he whispered, his breath warm, his words so soft she could barely hear them.

Liane's mouth went dry, her hand and the knife trembled.

Sebestyen lifted his head, took her chin in his hand, and kissed her on the mouth. He kissed her long and hard and with desperation. And heaven help her, she kissed him back.

He had never kissed her mouth before, not once, and she found the touch of his lips on hers more moving and sensual and *important* than she'd expected. It connected them in a way sex and intrigue never had. It bonded them to one another more solidly than the joining of bodies.

The words he'd whispered echoed in her ears. Had she imagined them?

He took his mouth from hers and said the words again. Louder this time, more distinct. "I love you. I've loved you for such a long time I can't remember when I didn't love you. I tried not to, I even ordered you to do things that would make you unworthy. I ordered you to kill, I forced you to pleasure other men, I made you tend to me like a slave. But it didn't make any difference. It never made any difference." His eyes were hooded but clear. "Two nights ago, when you said you'd take another man into your bed, I sent a sentinel to watch your door. He had orders to kill any man who visited you that night. Last night, I went to your room to see for myself that you were alone. The Tryfynian ambassador admired you too openly. He looked at you as if he wanted you. If I had found him in your room last night, I would have eviscerated him. If I had found you in his chamber, I would've taken his head."

"That would have meant war."

"I don't care." The blue of his eyes was bluer than before, deeper.

"It's not as if you haven't given me to other men in the past."

"I suffered for it," he whispered.

"Not as much as I did."

She'd worked for so long for this moment. She had the knife in her hand, and Sebestyen was right here. One thrust, and he'd be dead. Or dying.

Something odd and powerful washed over her, and her grip on the knife weakened; her fingers trembled. Was this what she'd really wanted all along? Not Sebestyen's death, but his love.

"I love you, too," she said. The knife dropped to the dais with a clatter they both ignored. "Heaven help me, I do."

He walked her into the sunlight. The damage had been done, after all, so there was no more reason to hide. The sun had touched his face. If the wizard Thayne had been right, Sebestyen's downfall was at hand. But not at this moment.

He undressed her; she undressed him. She had never seen him in sunlight, and the way the shadows fell across his body were beautiful. He was beautiful, and like it or not she did love him. He laid her down on a bed of crimson robes and with sunlight pouring over their naked bodies he made love to her. It had never been this way before, tender and slow and even tentative, as if they had never touched before. She knew his body as well as she knew her own, and she had never even imagined that he could love her this way.

She wrapped her legs around him while he stroked her, lifted her hips to take him deeper. She closed her eyes against the rays of the sun that beat down upon her face. There had been no dance, no foreplay, no teasing before their joining. And yet this was more powerful than any other mating she had ever known. She was on fire, not only with her body but with her spirit and her heart.

"I love you," he said again as he pushed deep inside her. "I love you so much."

They came together, their bodies shuddered and reached for release. Sebestyen moaned; Liane gasped. And when they were sated they continued to lie entangled in the sunlight that streamed into the once-dark ballroom. Liane raked her fingers through Sebestyen's hair. He had never been one for lying together afterward, but perhaps today . . .

He lifted up slowly and stared down at her. "Tell me you will never leave me."

She whispered, "I will never leave you."

"Tell me again that you love me."

There was no hesitation in her voice or in her heart when she said, "I love you, Sebestyen."

They sat up together, and on the pile of discarded robes, Sebestyen held her close. "If Thayne was right, everything will soon fall apart around me."

Liane's hand touched his face. "Whatever comes along, we'll fight it together."

Perhaps the wizard had seen her killing Sebestyen, but their love had changed that moment and that fate. Love was certainly stronger than hate. Was it stronger than destiny? That was a thought that had never passed through her mind until this moment. She had never even believed in love, not until she'd seen Kane's love for Sophie, and hers for him. And now this . . .

They rolled out of the sunlight and onto the cool stone floor. The light hurt Sebestyen's eyes, even more than it hurt hers. It would take some getting used to, after all these years. He grabbed the robes and spread them across the stone floor, then gently rolled her onto that bed and reclined beside her.

He lifted the strands of her hair and let them fall slowly. "I did wonder, through the years, how the prophesy would come true. I always knew it would, one way or another, but I never suspected that a slip of a girl could bring the sun into the palace again."

Sebestyen rolled onto his back and placed his hands behind

his head. "A witch," he said softly. "I suppose she would have made a poor empress."

Liane placed her hand on his chest, over his heart. He was sweating, and afraid, and he loved her. "You do not need her," she whispered.

"I need only you," he said with a grin.

Her heart hitched. He should not be smiling; she should not be filled with love; she should not want him again, here on this floor with words of love whispered in her ear.

It could not be the spell that made her feel this way. She and Sebestyen were stronger than the common sentinels and concubines; they would not be affected by anything so ordinary as a spell that inspired uncontrollable lust.

Besides, what she and Sebestyen had wasn't lust. It was love.

Liane laid her hand on Sebestyen's chest. She leaned across his body and kissed his throat, the underside of his jaw, and then his mouth. Heavens, she loved his mouth! Why had they never kissed before? Why had she not grabbed his face in her hands and shown him how marvelous this could be?

He was already growing hard again, so she stroked him while she kissed. She kissed and stroked until he was like steel and her insides quaked for him. She rolled atop him, straddled him, and took him into her body in one swift, slick motion.

He loved her; she loved him. What could possibly go wrong?

21

GALVYN WAS RELIEVED WHEN THE DOOR TO HIS CELL opened and the woman walked in. Her name was Liane, he remembered from that first night, and he was so happy to see her. She hadn't been particularly friendly on that night, but her face was a welcome change from the guards who hit him and mocked his pleas for release. He'd been in this place for a week or more! He'd lost track of time, but he knew it had been at least that long.

"Thank the heavens. Is Sophie here? Is the marriage to take place soon?"

The woman cocked her head and studied him as if he were an insect. A moment later, the emperor himself stepped up behind her. He laid a possessive hand on Liane's shoulder.

"This is the man who brought a witch into my palace," Emperor Sebestyen said casually.

Galvyn swallowed hard. So, they knew. They'd likely kick him out on his ear now. There would be no marriage, no position in the palace, no reward. No Sophie in his bed.

"Sophie? Are you talking about my Sophie? I . . . I didn't have any idea she was a witch," he said, his voice shaking.

"He's lying," Liane said.

"I know," the emperor replied.

They were so calm, so unconcerned about the news, perhaps they saw this small lie as an annoyance. Nothing more. He'd be banished to Shandley forever, he supposed, never to be anything more than a merchant. After a few days in this cell, Shandley seemed like paradise.

Even though the regal couple did not seem truly annoyed, perhaps it would be best to make amends for the tiny lie he'd told. "If you are interested in harnessing the Fyne power for yourself, you should know that Sophie has two sisters," Galvyn said brightly. "They're both much more powerful than she is. Juilet sometimes sees the future."

The emperor lifted his eyebrows slightly. "I thought you said you were not aware that Sophie Fyne was a witch."

"I . . . I . . ."

Liane walked toward him, reaching into her pocket for something. The keys to his chains, perhaps. A few days ago the guards had come into the cell and chained him to the wall, because they said he made too much noise. He'd only been trying to convince them to let him go. They always refused, but Liane would release him, he knew it.

"I'll never forget this," he said fervently. "Never."

"No, I don't imagine you will."

She took a vial from the pocket of her robe and before he knew what was happening she shoved it into his right nostril. With the push of a plunger, something tingly and spicy went up his nose. Immediately, the drug entered his bloodstream. He swayed, and his mouth went dry, and every muscle in his body shuddered. Oh, it was so warm in here, but warm in a pleasant way. He fixed his eyes to Liane's breasts. She was a lovely woman. Luscious, in fact. He got hard, which was amazing since they'd stopped feeding him days ago and he hadn't so much as thought of a woman since the sentinels had thrown him in here.

He closed his eyes and listened to the demands of his body. Visions such as he had never known danced through him. Sophie. Liane . . . all the women on Level Five. And, oh, Level Three! He had never been there, but he had heard such tales . . .

A new and unusual strength fluttered through him. How dare they try to hold him here? He could take on all the guards in this place, now that he'd found his new strength.

Liane unfastened his chains and his arms fell free. Maybe they were taking him back to Level Five. He would not be so noble, this time. That one servant with the red hair . . .

A rough hand grabbed his arm and he opened his eyes to see that a soldier was dragging him from the cell. Galvyn tried to fight with his newfound strength, but apparently the guard possessed an unusual strength of his own. The very strong man hauled Galvyn down the hall not toward the stairway that would lead to the lift, but away from it. Liane and the emperor followed.

Two sentinels unlocked and opened a heavy door in the floor. It swung back with a loud creak and Galvyn peered below. All was dark, and there were such terrible noises . . . and the smell . . .

With a push from behind, he fell into the pit. For the first split second, he was not worried. After all, he could fly. When he realized that he could *not* fly, he screamed. The high-pitched scream was cut off when he landed on the dirt floor with a thud. It hurt! Surely he'd broken something in the fall. All thoughts of the pretty servants of Level Five fled his confused mind.

"I fell!" he shouted toward the opening above. Liane and the emperor and one of the guards—the very strong one—peered down at him. "Help me!"

He heard sounds in the darkness that surrounded him. The

scrape of a foot on the ground; a loud, harsh breath. A titter of laughter. "I don't like it here," he said softly.

Liane shouted. "Take good care of him, gentlemen. He's the emperor's cousin."

And then the door was closed, and the light from above was extinguished. Instead of feeling such a fine rush of sensation, as he had just moments earlier, Galvyn experienced a depth of fear such as he had never known. His eyes began to adjust to the dark, and he saw figures in the near distance. Figures of men. The figures moved closer, until one bony hand reached out to grab Galvyn's arm.

"The emperor's cousin, you say?"

WITH AUTUMN CAME COOLER WEATHER THAT SUITED THE travelers. They did not travel on busy roads, but stuck to narrow trails and even made their own trails, now and then. It was best to keep Sophie away from populated areas, at least until she was sure she had this power of hers under control.

Kane and Sophie rode north, as Liane had instructed, but so far they had found no sign of Maddox Sulyen. Of course, they were still days from the Northern Palace.

Kane carried his daughter in a sling across his chest, while his wife rode beside them on her own horse. Her tummy was already a bit round, though it was impossible to tell when she was clothed. He loved cupping that roundness with his hand when they stopped for a meal or a rest or for the night. He had missed watching Sophie grow with Ariana; he wouldn't miss it with this child.

Sophie said this child would be another girl. For the past three hundred years, there had only been girl babies born to the Fyne women. Kane didn't mind. He could very well imagine leading his life surrounded by beautiful women. Beautiful witches. Sophie had also told him his daughters would be witches.

It was a frightening thought, but with Sophie as a mother, they'd do fine. And she assured him they wouldn't come into their powers until adulthood. At least he wouldn't have to worry about chasing after misbehaving daughters who could turn him into a toad!

To hear Sophie tell it, he might not live to see his daughters grow into their powers. His twenty-ninth birthday had passed not long after they'd left Arthes. According to Sophie, they now had less than a year to find a way to end the Fyne curse. He should be terrified at the prospect of falling victim to a curse, but he wasn't. Together they would find a way to end it. Surely there had never been a Fyne as powerful as Sophie to take on the task of ending it once and for all.

"Why are you smiling?" Sophie asked.

"Am I?"

"Most definitely."

"I'm just . . . thinking."

"Of tonight?"

"And all the nights to come."

Sophie's grin was as wide as his own.

Soon they would find the imperial army and Maddox Sulyen. They'd introduce Sophie to her father and deliver Liane's warning. And after that?

The fire of anger and desired revenge no longer burned in his heart, but he was still a rebel. He wanted to see Sebestyen unseated and out of that palace. In truth, he wanted to see the emperor dead.

He had to wonder what Arik would think of taking on a witch as advisor.

LIANE BRAVED A VISIT TO LEVEL SEVEN. SHE HAD BEEN SO sick this past week, and Sebestyen was getting annoyed with her.

He had not told her again that he loved her, but things had

certainly changed. There had been no more talk of a new empress to replace Rikka. Sebestyen knew he had no choice, but was in no rush to find a wife and produce an heir, an attitude that infuriated Father Merryl and a few of the other priests. They detested Liane more than ever, now that she was a true part of Sebestyen's life.

Liane was always at the emperor's side; she had even spent many a night in his bed. All night, until the sun rose, she'd slept beside him.

The sun now rose into his room, and he was not afraid of it. He still feared treachery from within and was very cautious, but he did not hide from the sun. They had not left the palace, not yet, but they had shared a few meals on his balcony. It was nice; it was almost normal.

Sebestyen talked to her; he listened to her. He did not even intimate that she might lie with another man. She was his, in a way she had never expected to be.

No, he did not say the words again, but he did love her. In his own way.

He did not always listen to her, of course. Against her advice, he'd insisted on sending a squadron of men after the Fyne sisters. He'd sanctioned the man who'd delivered Sophie, a deputy sheriff named Bors, to lead the soldiers.

Galvyn said Sophie was the least powerful of the sisters, and Sebestyen had decided that it was his duty to harness the power of the Fyne women for himself. To Liane's way of thinking that was asking for trouble, but Sebestyen saw the potential benefit in having such mighty witches at his disposal. Once they were delivered to the palace, they'd either be chained in Level Twelve or put to work on Level Seven. It was entirely possible Sebestyen would not even care to see them for himself, and would make use of an intermediary to maintain a safe distance.

Liane hoped she did not come face-to-face with the witches. If she did she'd be reminded that they were Sophie's sisters, and if that happened she'd most likely feel obligated to help them escape. She couldn't possibly risk her new position in the palace, not even for Kane's family.

Gadhra greeted her with a grin. "Are you sick, too?" the old woman asked.

"Yes." The odors from the witch's kitchen made Liane's stomach roil. She placed a hand over her nose and mouth to mask the stench. It helped, but not much.

The old woman already had a medicine prepared, and she carried the small brown bottle to Liane and pressed it into her hand. "Take this. One spoonful now, another before bed."

Liane eyed the potion suspiciously. "How did you know what I'd need?" On more than one occasion, the witch had insisted that seeing the future was not her gift. There were the dreams, though . . .

"More than half the girls on Level Three suffer with the same ailment," the hag explained.

If it was a contagious disease and she passed it to Sebestyen, he'd be furious with her. He was never sick, and she knew very well that he'd be a terrible patient if he ever came down with something that made him feel poorly.

"What if the emperor catches what I have?"

The witch laughed, short and harsh and brittle. "The boy won't catch what you suffer from."

"How can you be sure?"

Gadhra's withered hand shot out and she placed her palm over Liane's stomach. "Do you not know what's happened?"

"Is it . . . bad?" Liane asked. She had not imagined that the ailment might be serious. She simply suffered from a queasy stomach and a tendency to lose her breakfast.

"Bad, good, that all depends." The witch's grin widened. "Take care of yourself, Liane. The next emperor of Columbyana is growing inside you."

Confused by scent, shapeshifter Ryn once made the mistake of abducting the wrong Fyne sister, but when he gets his hands on Juliet he knows there has been no mistake. She's the one, and he's waited for her for a long time. She's his mate, his wife, the female who will share his bed, give him Anwyn sons, and make his cold house a home.

Juliet Fyne can see what the future holds for some, but she rarely gets even a fleeting glimpse of her own. Disturbing dreams and indecipherable flashes of knowing hint at something momentous and frightening in her days to come, but she doesn't know what that something might be or when it might arrive. Juliet has vowed to live her life unwed and unmated. She's seen the Fyne curse at work and has no desire to have her heart broken by loving and losing a man.

There's more than the Fyne curse to keep Juliet from giving herself to a man. The vivid dreams of love and pleasure that come to her often feel like more than dreams and always end with claws and pain and blood.

Since the publication of her first book in 1994, **Linda Winstead Jones** has published more than forty novels and novellas. She's a three-time finalist for the Romance Writers of America's RITA Award and a winner of the 2004 RITA Award for Best Paranormal Romance. She's also a two-time winner of the Colorado Romance Writers Award of Excellence. A compulsive taker of classes, she has studied Asian cooking, belly dancing, cake decorating, yoga, real estate, candy making, and creative writing. She was a full-time wife and mother for several years, and spent a few months here and there as a Realtor and candy maker. Linda and her husband owned a picture frame shop for several years before she left retail to pursue writing full-time. An active member of the Romance Writers of America, she lives in northern Alabama with her husband of more than thirty years. Visit her website at www.lindawinsteadjones.com.

Three sisters are about to change
destiny, and bring a terrible
family curse to an end.

Don't miss the rest of the
Sisters of the Sun
trilogy by
Linda Winstead Jones

April 2005:
Read Juliet's story in
The Moon Witch

December 2005:
Read Isadra's story in
The Star Witch

BERKLEY SENSATION
COMING IN JANUARY 2005

Crimson Moon
by Rebecca York
Needing a fresh start, a young werewolf changes his
identity and meets a woman of many secrets—who he
must protect or they'll never have a chance to explore
the passion boiling up between them.

0-425-19995-9

Derik's Bane
by MaryJanice Davidson
The first novel in the new Wyndham Werwolf Tales
from the author of *Undead and Unwed*.

0-425-19997-5

The Wicked Lover
by Julia Ross
Robert Sinclair never expected to catch an intruder in
his bedroom—let alone one that's a woman dressed as
a man. She says she needs his cravat for a wager, but
Robert suspects there's more to this lady-in-disguise.

0-425-19996-7

Stay with Me
by Beverly Long
Sarah Jane Tremont is walking on the beach in L.A.
when she is suddenly transported to Wyoming, 1888.
Now she's been taken in by a rugged cowboy with a
wounded heart that she's destined to heal.

0-425-20062-0